TIME FOR LOVE

McCarthys of Gansett Island, Book 9

Marie Force

Marie Force
Copyright 2013 by Marie Force
Published by HTJB, Inc.
Cover by Kristina Brinton
Interior Layout by Ashley Joswick

ISBN:
978-0615843841

All characters in this book are fiction and figments of the author's imagination.

marieforce.com

AUTHOR'S NOTE

Welcome back to Gansett Island and to a story I've been looking forward to writing for quite some time now. We first met Dr. David Lawrence in Book 2, *Fool for Love,* after he'd cheated on island golden girl Janey McCarthy. I wondered if it would ever be possible to redeem David's character to the point that readers would want to see him get his happily ever after. Over time, David has grown on me—and on readers—and he's proven there's more to him than the one-time lapse in judgment that ended his long relationship with Janey. He's even been positively heroic on more than one occasion.

But giving David his happy ending required a very special heroine, so I waited until the right one came along. Daisy Babson, who has known her own share of heartache—most recently in a tumultuous relationship that ended violently—turned out to be *the one* for David, as you will see in *Time for Love.*

Bringing David and Daisy together was a lot of fun, and I hope you'll be cheering for them the way I was when writing their story. When you're done reading, join the *Time for Love* Reader Group at *www.facebook.com/groups/TimeforLove9/.* Since spoilers are permitted (and encouraged) there, we ask that you wait to finish the book before you join the group.

While writing Book 9, I finally conceded that I can't continue to give you a new story for every past couple and also do right by the couple featured in the current book. So I'll be picking and choosing among past favorites for new stories as we go forward, while keeping you updated on all the other Gansett Island regulars. However, I expect Mac and Maddie will continue to appear in every book as I never seem to run out of stories for them!

Next up will be the long-awaited story for Jenny Wilks, the lighthouse keeper who lost her fiancé on 9/11. Readers are fascinated with Jenny, and I have quite a story in mind for her that I'm looking forward to writing. Make sure you're on the mailing list at *http://marieforce.com* for announcements about Book 10, *Meant for Love.*

After that, I hope to sneak in *Gansett After Dark*, which will showcase Laura and Owen's wedding along with some "after dark" time for each of the couples from the previous books. It'll be a great opportunity to catch up on what everyone is up to and to see them living out their happily ever afters. I've got plenty of other stories, tricks and surprises up my sleeve, so buy your ferry tickets and head on over to the island, where the fun is just beginning!

Very special thanks to Sarah Spate Morrison, Family Nurse Practitioner, for answering many questions for me, as well as my behind-the scenes team Julie Cupp, Holly Sullivan, Nikki Colquhoun, Kristina Brinton and Ashley Joswick; copy editor Linda Ingmanson; and beta readers Ronlyn Howe, Kara Conrad and Anne Woodall. You all help me so much with every book, and I couldn't do what I do without you.

And to you, my faithful readers, thank you as always for making all my dreams come true! You're simply the best!

xoxo

Marie

CHAPTER 1

Daisy scurried about the spacious living room, picking up toys, folding blankets, plumping pillows and generally doing anything she could to stay busy. It had taken forever to get her friend Maddie's three-year-old son Thomas into bed. He'd been excited to have Daisy babysit for him and his sister Hailey, and Daisy was praying she'd heard the last of both kids as she prepared for her special guest.

Thinking of him made her stomach flutter with nerves. Why in the world had she invited him to come over to keep her company after the kids went to bed? Why in the world was she running around Mac and Maddie's house, straightening up as if it were her own home? As if she'd ever live anywhere this nice.

Maddie sure had tumbled into a pot of gold when she met and married Mac McCarthy. Not that Daisy begrudged her friend's happiness. Quite the opposite, in fact. Maddie was one of the best friends Daisy had ever had, and no one deserved to be happy more than Maddie did.

It's just that sometimes Daisy wondered if she'd ever find the kind of happiness Maddie had with her devoted husband. Daisy's most recent relationship with Truck Henry had turned into a disaster when he got violent with her—more than once. That was over now, and for good this time.

She'd learned her lesson about giving second chances to people who didn't deserve them. Too bad she'd had to suffer badly bruised ribs and a host of other injuries before she wised up. She'd rather not think about those unhappy memories when her new friend David Lawrence was coming over to hang out with her.

Why had she invited him?

It had been a weak moment the night before. He'd taken her out for a lovely dinner at Stephanie's Bistro and had asked what she was doing the next night, which was how she'd ended up inviting him to her babysitting gig.

Now she felt like a foolish teenager waiting for the captain of the football team to show up. No doubt he had far better things to do than hang out with her on one of his rare nights off. He'd probably felt obligated to accept her invitation, and the whole thing would be painfully awkward.

When it came right down to it, they had absolutely nothing in common. She was a hard-working—if perpetually poor—housekeeper at the McCarthy's hotel, and he was the island's only doctor. She'd come from a family that invented the term dysfunctional, whereas he'd been raised with his sisters on the island and gone to a top college and medical school in Boston.

She'd dated one loser after another while he'd been engaged to Mac's sister, Janey McCarthy Cantrell. Janey was married now to Joe Cantrell and expecting their first child at the end of the summer.

Daisy had never heard what went wrong between David and Janey, but their long relationship had ended suddenly two summers ago. She could've asked Maddie and almost had a few times, but she'd been unable to bring herself to actually ask.

In the meantime, David had been so nice about coming by to check on her injuries and so gentle with her as she recovered. They'd fallen into an unlikely friendship that continued when she stopped by the clinic a couple of times to share the influx of food her friends had brought her. David worked so hard that he often missed meals, and it had seemed only fitting to share with him when he'd been so good to her.

It was foolish, she knew, to let her heart get all pitter-pattery over a guy who was just being nice to her because that was his job. It was doubly foolish, she also knew, to nurture the world-class crush that had come from his many kindnesses. Thus, it was triply foolish to be hoping that something might come of the time they'd been spending together.

Romance, Daisy thought, *is so fraught with peril.* At least it always had been for her. She simply chose the wrong men. The habit dated back to high school when she'd yearned for a boy who turned out to be a cheating pig. Next came a lovely guy who became a mean drunk and then another with a gambling addiction she'd failed to recognize until he'd wiped out her meager savings account.

Then came Truck and his meth addiction and meaty fists.

Daisy shuddered thinking of the awful night when Truck most likely would've raped and killed her if the island's police chief, Blaine Taylor, hadn't broken down her door and stopped him from finishing the job.

A knock on the sliding glass door made her startle. Had she really wasted all that precious time thinking about things that couldn't be changed? And now David was here and she probably looked like a wreck after wrangling babies all night. She combed her fingers through her long, blonde hair, hoping to restore order as she walked over to the door to unlock it.

"Hey," he said as he came in smelling of fresh air and a hint of cologne that made her want to snuggle in close to him. He wore a navy blue button-down Gansett Island shirt with khaki shorts.

Daisy had never seen him dressed so casually. "Hey."

"Are they asleep?"

"I think so. I'm told it's a minute-to-minute thing."

He smiled, revealing a flash of straight, white teeth that made her want to sigh with pleasure. She had a thing for a great smile, and David Lawrence's smile was one of the best she'd ever encountered. Coupled with thick, dark hair and serious brown eyes, that smile was downright potent. Even the slight bump in his otherwise perfect nose was appealing.

"Is that..." He brushed at something on her shoulder, making her nerve endings tingle. "Spit-up?"

"Oh crap," Daisy said, mortified. Heat singed her cheeks and made her scalp itch. "I forgot that Hailey nailed me at bedtime. I'll just run up and borrow something of Maddie's. She won't mind."

"Don't bother." He took her hand and led her to the kitchen, where he wet a paper towel and went to work on the spot on her shoulder.

Daisy had never been more acutely aware of her own intake of oxygen than she was in that moment with his face about six inches from hers as he worked with single-minded purpose to clean the spot off her thin top. While focusing on the shine of his dark hair, she concentrated on drawing in enough air to remain conscious without gulping in the deep breaths she desperately needed.

"There," he said after an interminable few minutes. As he backed away from her, his fingers brushed against her neck, and damn if she didn't gasp. "Sorry."

"Oh no, don't be sorry. I...um..."

"What's wrong, Daisy?" He studied her in that deep, dark, serious way he did so well.

"Nothing," she said in a cheerful tone that sounded forced, even to her. "Want a beer or some wine or something?"

"I'd rather know why you seem so uncomfortable. I thought we had a nice time last night. I was looking forward to seeing you tonight, but if this isn't a good time, I can go."

"No, I don't want you to go." Daisy covered her face with her hands. "I'm making a total mess of things."

"Tell me what's wrong." He covered her hands with his and gave a very gentle tug that revealed her eyes.

"I'm nervous, and that makes me feel stupid."

"Why are you nervous?"

"Because you're here. Because I invited you, and I wasn't sure if you really wanted to come or you just said you would because I asked you to and you didn't really want to—"

And then he was kissing her, and Daisy's brain cells positively fried the second his lips landed on hers.

He was a really good kisser, as if that was any big surprise. His lips were firm but soft and moved over hers in a light caress that was neither too much nor too little. It was just right, and quite simply one of the best kisses she'd ever received. Just as she began to relax and kiss him back, he withdrew.

"Sorry," he said, his forehead leaning against hers. "I didn't mean to do that."

"I'm glad you did that."

"You are?"

She smiled, because really, how could she not? He was so cute. "Maybe you'll do it again sometime?"

"We might be able to arrange that."

Daisy discovered she was no longer nervous about having him there. Now she was nervous for a whole other reason, a much better reason. "Do you want to watch a movie?"

He took a step back from her. "Sure."

"Maddie left some on the coffee table if you want to see if any of them interest you. Popcorn?"

"I won't say no to that."

"How about a beer?"

"Will you have one, too?"

"I'm going to stick with Coke."

"Then I will, too."

While she made the popcorn in an oil popper that Maddie had once told her dated back to her high school years but still worked perfectly, he went into the living room to check out the movies. Reliving the kiss, Daisy was acutely aware of him in the next room.

What did it mean? What was he thinking? Was he looking for a summer fling or something more lasting? What was she looking for? Nothing serious. That was for sure. After what had happened with Truck, she'd been prepared to swear off all men permanently. But then David kept showing up, chipping away at her defenses one visit at a time.

"These are all chick flicks," he said.

"In case you haven't noticed, I am a chick."

"Oh, I've definitely noticed."

Daisy nearly swallowed her tongue.

"Have you seen *Love and Other Drugs?*" he asked, as if he hadn't just totally rocked her with that comment. "Looks kind of good. A girl with Parkinson's falls in love with a drug rep."

"Leave it to the doctor to pick a medical movie."

"Um, I believe it's a chick-flick romance that happens to include a disease. There's got to be something in it for me."

"Who is in it?"

"Jake Gyllenhaal and Anne Hathaway."

"I should probably mention at the outset that I have a huge crush on Jake Gyllenhaal. I'd hate for you to be threatened by my ogling."

"I believe I'm man enough to handle your crush."

As she carried the bowl of popcorn and two Cokes into the living room, she tried to remember the last time she'd enjoyed a conversation with a man as much as she enjoyed every conversation with him. He never talked down to her or made her feel like she wasn't as smart as him, even though she was nowhere near as smart as him.

After she put the bowl and sodas on the coffee table, he handed her the movie and she popped it into the DVD player. She sat on the sofa, careful to leave at least a foot between them, and reached for the popcorn bowl.

David opened both sodas and put them on coasters.

As she dipped into the bowl, his hand brushed against hers. Daisy pulled hers back and then felt like an idiot. So his hand had touched hers. Why did she have to react like a teenage girl on a first date?

The movie's opening credits had just begun when Daisy heard a noise at the top of the stairs. She handed the bowl to David, got up to go investigate and found Thomas sitting behind the baby gate, his blanket and teddy bear with him.

"What're you doing up, honey?"

"I want Mommy."

"Mommy and Daddy are out with their friends, but they'll be home soon."

"Who were you talking to?" Thomas looked around her to see who was visiting.

"You know Dr. David, right?"

"He gave me a shot," Thomas said, his feathery brows knitting into an adorable scowl. "It hurted."

"Come here, sweetie." Daisy extended her arms, lifted him over the gate with the blanket and bear and carried him downstairs. "We have a visitor," she said to David.

"Hi there, Thomas," David said.

Thomas burrowed his face into her neck.

"I believe Thomas is annoyed with you. Something about a shot?"

"Ah, yes. Sorry about that, pal. Just trying to keep you healthy."

"It hurted," Daisy said, earning a smile from David.

"Do you know what else is really important to staying healthy?" David asked.

Thomas turned toward David.

"What's that?" Daisy asked.

"Sleep. We need lots and lots of sleep, especially when we're three years old and our bodies are using so much energy to grow."

"I growed," Thomas said. "Mommy measured me on the wall."

"If you want to keep growing and someday be big and strong like Daddy," Daisy said, "you have to go to sleep." She drew the blanket up to his shoulders and rubbed his back. He popped his thumb into his mouth and cuddled up to his bear.

As Daisy brushed her lips over Thomas's hair, her own hair slid over her face.

Before she could tend to it, David had it secured behind her ear. The brush of his fingertips against her cheek and ear gave her goose bumps. She ventured a glance at him and saw that he was watching her with sexy eyes attuned to her every move.

Oh my.

CHAPTER 2

When Daisy carried Thomas back upstairs, David followed to open the gate for her. She tucked him into bed and drew the covers up and over his shoulders before leaving him with a kiss to his forehead. He was such a cute little guy—all blond hair and big, blue eyes and a sweet, sunny disposition.

Maddie had him alone after the boy's father left the island without knowing she was pregnant. After they were married, Mac adopted Thomas and gave him the McCarthy name. He was a very lucky boy, Daisy thought as she left his room, leaving the door open so she could hear him if he woke up again.

David waited for her in the hallway.

"I'm going to check on Hailey while I'm up here," Daisy whispered.

"Mind if I take a peek? I'm extra partial to her after helping to deliver her during the big storm."

"Sure, come on."

With the hallway light illuminating the nursery, they tiptoed into Hailey's room. She slept with her bum in the air and her lips pursed.

Daisy adjusted her blanket and shared a smile with David before they left the baby to sleep.

"You were good with him," David said on the way downstairs.

"He's adorable. I got to hold him the day he was born and fell madly in love. I've been like an extra aunt to him his whole life."

"He's lucky to have so many people who love him."

"Now he's got the McCarthys, too. They're quite a family."

"Yeah, they sure are."

Did she detect a hint of sarcasm in his voice? It made her curious to know more about what'd happened between him and Janey, but she didn't have the guts to come right out and ask him.

"I heard how you saved Hailey's life the night she was born. Maddie and Mac are so grateful to you."

He shrugged off the praise. "I did what I was trained to do."

"Still, if you hadn't been here... I don't even want to think about what might've happened."

"I was glad I was here and able to help. She's a beautiful little girl."

"That she is."

They returned to their spots on the sofa, and Daisy reached for the popcorn bowl and the remote control to start the movie. "Let's try this again, shall we?"

Was it her imagination or did he sit closer to her this time? His leg brushed against hers. Nope, not her imagination. Thank goodness she had the popcorn to focus on as the movie about an aggressive salesman began. Not even five minutes in and he was having sex with a coworker in the stockroom at work.

Daisy felt her entire body flame with embarrassment. Next to her, David sat perfectly still. She wondered if he was equally mortified. She breathed a sigh of relief as the encounter in the stockroom ended with Jake's character being fired. Within a few minutes, he'd moved into a job as a pharmaceutical salesman.

Looking to dispel some of the tension, Daisy tried to think of something witty she could say about the movie. "He's kind of a tool, huh?"

"You could say that."

She offered him the popcorn, and he took a handful. "You still want to watch the movie?" she asked.

"I'm invested now. Gotta see if the tool gets his comeuppance."

Daisy smiled at him and tried to relax, but it was hard with her world-class crush sitting so close to her and sexy Jake shadowing a doctor as he treated a young woman with Parkinson's. Daisy's hormones were on overload.

"Yikes," David said. "Twenty-six with Parkinson's. What a drag."

"Is that unusually young?"

"Very."

They went silent as Anne Hathaway's character bared her breast to the doctor and asked about a mark that turned out to be a spider bite while Jake looked on, obviously ogling the naked breast.

"Total tool," Daisy declared. "If this was my house, I'd throw popcorn at the TV."

"Too bad they don't have a dog," David said. "He could clean it up."

"Thomas wants one, but Maddie is holding out until Hailey is a bit older. Can't say I blame her."

"You and Maddie are really close, huh?"

Daisy was relieved to be talking about something other than the bare breast on the screen. "Yeah, she's been a great friend to me. I miss her at the hotel, but I'm so glad she got the dream come true. No one deserves it more. Now how did he go from inappropriate ogling to having coffee with her?"

"It's Hollywood," David said dryly. "Things happen at the speed of film."

"Oh!" Daisy cried as the scene changed and the celluloid couple tore each other's clothes off to go at it standing up in Anne's apartment.

David shook with silent laughter next to her as Daisy watched, transfixed by the intensely erotic scene that ended with the characters on the floor panting from exertion.

"I need a cigarette," Daisy said, making him laugh harder. "Is it totally rude for me to be staring at his naked bum while you're sitting one inch from me?"

"Only if it's rude for me to be taking a good healthy look at her bare breasts."

"You probably see plenty of breasts every day at 'work.'" She used her fingers to make air quotes.

"For your information, it's very stressful to look at strange breasts at work."

"You're so full of it." She grabbed a sofa pillow and smacked him with it.

He grabbed the pillow and her hand, giving a gentle tug that sent the popcorn bowl flying off her lap. "Whoops," he said, but he didn't let go. Rather, he brought her closer, so close their noses were nearly touching and Daisy didn't dare to even breathe. All thoughts of Jake Gyllenhaal's naked rear end fled from her mind under David's intense gaze.

And then the unmistakable sounds of sex from the TV sent David and Daisy dissolving into laughter. As far as she was concerned, David was every bit as handsome as Jake, but when he laughed, *whoa.* Crazy sexy. She'd never seen him laugh as hard as he had tonight, and the urge to kiss him consumed her. It was the only thought in her entire brain. She moved toward him as he moved toward her in a moment of perfect harmony that would forever go down as one of the sweetest of her life.

There was nothing sweet about the kiss, however. The only word to describe it was hot. Seriously hot. It went from start to go in like two seconds flat as his tongue darted into her mouth. As fast as it happened, though, it was over. He drew back from her, breathing hard, his eyes wide. "I'm sorry. I didn't mean to—"

With her hand on the back of his head, she dragged him back into the kiss, taking the lead this time.

His arms came around her as the kiss transported her far away from anything she'd known before. She could barely remember to breathe as his tongue brushed against hers. Through the thin fabric of her top, her nipples pebbled and tightened when they rubbed against his shirt.

She twisted in his embrace, trying to get closer as the kiss became desperate.

He shifted them so she was under him, his body big and heavy on top of her. A twinge of panic registered at the outer fringes of her awareness, reminding her of what had happened the last time a man had pinned her down beneath him. She turned her face, breaking the kiss and drawing in greedy deep breaths. "I... I..." She pushed at his chest.

He immediately understood and sat up, releasing her so abruptly she nearly cried out from the loss.

"God, Daisy. I'm so sorry. I got carried away." He looked positively stricken, which made her ache. He'd been nothing but kind and decent and patient with her—everything Truck had never been.

"No, it's my fault." Her hands were shaking and her heart was beating so fast she worried she might pass out or something equally embarrassing. "I didn't mean to freak out. I'm so sorry."

"Don't be sorry. I shouldn't have pushed you like that."

"You didn't," she said, on the verge of tears. "You were wonderful the way you always are, and I didn't want to stop. It was just that feeling of being smothered…"

"I get it, and I'm sorry I didn't think of how you might react to that. It's only been a couple of weeks." His hand cupped her face, his thumb caressing her cheek so gently her eyes closed against the rush of emotion. "You're so sweet, Daisy. I've been dying to kiss you for days. Weeks." His voice was gruff and sexy, and her crush was on the verge of blazing completely out of control.

She opened her eyes because she wanted to see him. "Really?"

Nodding, he continued to stroke her face with just the soft movement of his thumb. "I was so afraid to touch you. I didn't want to do the wrong thing."

"You didn't. It wasn't you. It was me."

"You've been through a traumatic ordeal. It's going to take some time to be comfortable in a situation like that again."

"I was comfortable. I was so comfortable. But then…"

"You didn't like having me on top of you."

She shook her head as a tear slid down her cheek. "I don't want to scare you off. I like you so much. I look forward to our time together…" She stopped herself when she realized she might be giving too much away.

"You haven't scared me off, and I like you, too, and the time we've spent together. I look forward to it all day while I'm working."

"So do I. Every day I wonder if I'm going to see you, and I get all giddy at the thought of being with you."

He brushed the tear from her cheek and touched his thumb to her bottom lip, rubbing it back and forth.

Daisy put her tongue in its path, touching the tip to the pad of his thumb.

His eyes narrowed with barely restrained desire that made her wonder what might've happened if she hadn't panicked.

"Can we..."

"What?"

She forced herself to look at him. "Can we try again? Please?"

"I don't want to scare you."

"You won't as long as you don't do that on-top thing again."

His hand dropped from her face as he leaned his head against the back of the sofa. "Do whatever you feel like doing. You're the boss."

Daisy rolled her bottom lip between her teeth as she contemplated the sexy buffet laid out before her. She released two buttons on his shirt and slid her hand inside to rest just below his collarbone.

He drew in a breath, and his heart beat fast beneath her hand.

His reaction fueled her courage as she leaned in to place a string of kisses along his jaw. Late-day whiskers poked at her lips, stinging and abrading them. She glanced down and saw his hands gripping his thighs and was encouraged to know he wasn't unaffected by her clumsy attempts at seduction or whatever this was.

She worked her way to his lips, teasing him with light touches of lip to lip before she moved down to his neck. The pulse of his heartbeat throbbed under her lips, beating in time to the throb between her legs. It had been such a very long time since she'd experienced true desire.

"Daisy," he said, sounding tortured. "I want to touch you. Is that okay?"

"Yes, please."

"Come closer." He held out his arms to her, and Daisy straddled his lap, feeling the press of his arousal between her legs as he drew her in closer to him. "Is this okay?"

She nodded, moved by his concern.

He massaged her back in small circles that made her want to weep from the undeniable pleasure.

"Feels good," she whispered.

With his hand on the back of her head, he drew it down to his shoulder, encouraging her without words to relax against him.

She sank into his embrace, which would've been totally innocent were it not for the brush of her nipples against his chest or the insistent throb between her legs as she squirmed for a tighter connection with his erection.

He gasped, and his hands tightened on her back.

"Sorry, did I hurt you?"

"No," he said with a tight chuckle. "Not at all."

Realizing he was aroused filled her with a kind of feminine power that was all new to her. It also filled her with a sense of mischief as she rocked against him again, drawing another hiss from him.

"You little minx," he whispered. "You know you're making me crazy, right?"

"I am?" It was fun to be playful with a man, to know she was completely safe in his arms, to know he wanted her as much as she wanted him, even if the timing of such desires wasn't ideal.

He continued the massage in slow, sensual circles down her back. When he reached the waistband of her jeans, she thought he might work his way back up, but he kept going down, cupping her bottom and squeezing. "Okay?" he asked, endlessly considerate.

"So okay." She couldn't seem to get close enough to him as the throb between her legs intensified. "David…"

"What, honey? Tell me what you need."

She'd never been very good at telling men what she needed, and now was no exception. "I don't know." Moaning, she rested her forehead on his shoulder. "I don't know."

"Move against me." With his hands on her hips, he urged her to move against the hard column of his erection.

"Does it feel good for you, too?" she asked, trying not to pant like a brazen hussy, which was exactly how she felt at the moment. But she was too aroused to care.

"So good. Could I touch you?"

"Yes, yes. Please."

He found the hem of her top and dipped his fingers underneath, drawing a gasp from her when he made contact with her back. Leaving a trail of sensation, he worked his way up, releasing the clasp on her bra as he went. "Still okay?"

"Mmm." With her head on his shoulder, she breathed in the clean, fresh scent of him as his hands moved over her ribs, his thumbs teasing the underside of her breasts. She was on the verge of begging, but the words froze on her tongue when he filled his hands with her breasts. "*Oh.*"

"Still good?"

"So good. Don't stop."

"Kiss me."

Daisy raised her head and brought her lips down on his right as his fingers found her nipples, rolling and squeezing ever so gently. The combination triggered a powerful orgasm. Luckily, his lips muffled the sound or she might've woken the kids.

Completely undone by the experience, she collapsed against him, her breasts still pressed against his warm hands.

"Feel better?" he whispered, making her smile.

"So much better," she said through panting breaths. "As soon as my head stops spinning, I'd be happy to return the favor."

"No need."

She found the strength to raise her head and meet his gaze. "I know I don't have to. What if I want to?"

The pounding of heavy footsteps on the stairs to Maddie's deck had Daisy scrambling off his lap and attempting to right her clothes and hair before they were caught fooling around on her friend's sofa.

David drew a pillow over his lap, making her giggle.

His face flushed with embarrassment. "Glad you find it so funny. I feel like I'm fifteen."

By the time Mac and Maddie came through the door, Daisy and David were sitting on the sofa, the picture of innocence as Jake and Anne went at it on TV.

"Home already?" Daisy asked them as she took note of Maddie's glassy eyes. "And together?" As far as she knew, they'd been out separately with their friends.

Mac zeroed right on David sitting next to her, but didn't say anything.

"They crashed us *again*," Maddie said, her words slurring ever so slightly. "They *always* crash our girls' night."

"It's a good thing we did." Mac held his wife against him, which Daisy suspected was critical to her remaining upright. "*Someone* had a tad bit too much champagne."

"I had just *enough* champagne," Maddie said with a goofy smile. "It's put me in a *really* good mood."

"Hush," Mac said. "Let me get her to bed, and then I'll give you a ride home, Daisy."

"I'd be happy to take her," David said.

Mac looked at David for such a long time that Daisy wondered what he was thinking. "Are you sure you don't mind?"

"Not at all. I'm going that way anyway."

"Okay by you, Daisy?" Mac asked.

"Of course."

"How were my babies?" Maddie asked, hiccupping softly.

"They were great. Thomas wasn't too keen on sleeping for a while, but I think he's out now."

"Thank you for staying with them. I owe you."

Daisy waved a hand in protest. "No, you don't. Go to bed. We'll see ourselves out." As Mac ushered his wife upstairs, Daisy stood on wobbly legs and was grateful for the hand David placed on her elbow until she steadied herself.

"I just need one minute," she said. "Be right back." She went into the downstairs bathroom to fasten her bra and freshen up. Standing before the mirror, she was startled by the flushed, satisfied look to on face. She rested her hands on her cheeks, as if that might remove some of the color that had settled there. It didn't work.

Resigned to her face giving away her heightened emotions, she returned to the family room. David had cleaned up the popcorn mess and was washing the bowl.

"You didn't have to do that."

"One of us had to do it. Why not me?"

"Thank you." Daisy dried the bowl and put it away, cleaned the popcorn maker and wiped up the kitchen.

David held her denim jacket for her and turned off the TV, chuckling at yet another sex scene in the movie. "They must've been exhausted after filming," he said, making Daisy laugh as he opened the sliding door to the deck and gestured for her to go out ahead of him.

A motion-sensitive light came on as she went down the stairs ahead of him. He held the door to his silver sedan for her, and she sank into the buttery-soft leather with a sigh of pleasure. Everything about this evening had been a pleasure. Other than the one moment of panic, she'd gotten through her first post-attempted-rape encounter fairly well, all things considered.

She tried really hard not to think about that awful night with Truck when she'd nearly been killed in the midst of his meth-fueled rage. He'd held her down and tried to force himself on her. He'd been too stoned to finish what he'd started, but he'd left her bruised and sore and traumatized from the effort.

From the driver's side, David reached over to take her hand. "What're you thinking about?"

"Unpleasant memories and how they came back to haunt me tonight."

"Only for a second, and we worked through it, right?"

"Right." As her throat tightened with emotion, she squeezed his hand in gratitude. "Thanks for putting up with me."

"It's certainly no hardship. I like being with you."

She turned to look at his strong profile, illuminated by the streetlights as they left Mac and Maddie's driveway and headed for town. All too soon, he pulled up to the curb outside her house.

"Do you want to come in for a little while?" she asked, feeling uncertain about what would happen now that they'd kissed, among other very nice things.

"I'd love nothing more than to spend more time with you tonight, but I'm afraid of things going too far too fast." He reached over to do that thing he did with her hair and her ear. "You're not ready for too far too fast. And…"

"And what?" Daisy asked.

His smile faded. "There're things about me you should know before this goes any further."

"What kind of things?"

"The kind that might dull that shine in your eyes when you look at me."

"Do my eyes shine when they look at you?"

As he nodded, an aura of sadness clung to him. "You won't look at me like that anymore when I tell you what you need to know about me."

Daisy thought about that for a moment. "I'd like to hear anything you want to tell me, but no matter what it is, I'll never forget the extraordinary kindness and compassion you've shown me since one of the worst nights of my life. I'll never forget the conversations we've had or your understanding tonight when I fell apart a little bit. So whatever it is, you should know I won't forget any of that."

"You're very kind, Daisy, and you're probably far too good for me."

"That's not true."

"I haven't always been an honorable person. I've made mistakes that have hurt people."

Operating on instinct at this point, she reached out to him, cupping his face and turning him to look at her. "How can you say you're not good enough for me? You're a doctor, for goodness sake."

"All those years of school didn't necessarily make me a good person."

"Did you learn from these mistakes you made?"

"Yeah," he said, releasing a bitter laugh. "You could say I definitely learned my lesson."

"And these things you did that hurt people, would you do them again?"

"Never."

"Then it sounds like whatever it is you're so ashamed of happened for a reason. It happened so you'd learn what kind of man you want to be—and what kind you don't want to be."

Twirling a lock of her hair around his finger, he said, "How did you get so wise?"

"A lot of hard knocks of my own, literally and figuratively."

"I don't want to be another of your hard knocks."

"Then don't be."

"We need to talk about this stuff. You need to know what you're getting into."

"Can we talk about it sometime soon? Tonight has been so lovely. It doesn't feel like a night for deep confessions."

He smiled as he leaned in to kiss her. "It was lovely. Thanks for inviting me."

"Thanks for keeping me company."

"I'm going to be off-island tomorrow into Tuesday. Could I call you while I'm gone?"

Daisy hated the dismay she experienced at knowing she wouldn't see him for a couple of days. "I'd love that."

He pulled out his phone and programmed the number she gave him. "I put it in my favorites. See?"

"I feel very honored." And oddly enough, she did. While still grappling with a bit of anxiety over what he felt he needed to tell her, Daisy refused to allow anything to ruin what had been a rather perfect evening.

"Come on, I'll walk you to the door."

As they walked up the stairs to her front door, she was glad she'd forgotten to turn on the porch light when she left. She didn't need her nosy neighbors checking out who was bringing her home.

Daisy used her key in the new door Mac had installed after Truck kicked hers in. It was sturdy and made her feel safe, even when she knew there was nothing to be afraid of. Standing in the doorway, she was hit with a sudden bout of shyness as she wondered if David would kiss her again. She sure hoped so.

"I'll call you," he said.

"I'll look forward to it."

When he started to turn away, her hopes were dashed until he turned right back and put his arms around her. He bent his head and came toward her slowly, probably giving her time to say no. But that wasn't the word she longed to say. *Yes* was far more like it.

What started as a soft, sweet kiss soon took a turn toward something much deeper and more carnal. By the time he pulled back from her, Daisy had her arms tight around him. His hands were on her bottom, holding her snug against his arousal. She wanted to purr from the pleasure of his embrace.

"I should go," he whispered against her lips.

"I should let you."

She felt rather than saw his smile as he withdrew from her with a sigh that sounded regretful.

"Save Tuesday night for me?"

"It's all yours."

He took her hand and brought it to his lips. "See you then."

She went inside and watched as he got into his car and waved when he drove off into the night. The door closed with a solid thunk, and she turned the dead bolt Mac had also installed for her. Leaning against the door, she brushed her fingertips over lips that still tingled from David's passionate kisses.

How, she wondered, would she live until Tuesday? The thought was followed by another, this one much darker. What did he have to tell her and would it change how she felt about him?

Maddie sat on the edge of the bed and tried to remain upright while Mac helped to remove her top.

"So, David and Daisy, huh?"

"Apparently. He's been really nice to her since that business with Truck."

"Does she know about his track record?" he asked with a bitter edge to his voice. Mac would never forgive David for cheating on his sister, but he'd also never forget that David had saved Hailey, who would've died at birth without him. Maddie knew his feelings toward David were somewhat complicated, to say the least.

"I don't know. We haven't talked about it."

"Maybe you should warn her."

"Maybe I will." With his belly right in front of her, what else was she supposed to do but dip her hands under his shirt and take a feel of her favorite washboard abs?

"What're you up to, Madeline?" he asked with a hint of amusement in his voice.

"Champagne makes me horny. I had no idea!"

Chuckling, he said, "You're not going to remember any of this in the morning."

"I will, too!" She cupped him through his jeans. "How could I ever forget this?" Under her hand, he throbbed to life. "Mmm, look at that. You're *so* easy, Mac McCarthy."

"Maddie..."

"*Mac...* I wanna get naked. Let's go. Hurry up."

"You need to sleep it off."

"I will sleep it off, *after* you do me. Now, get busy."

He stared at her, seeming astounded at the blunt talk that was wildly out of character for her. Apparently, the blunt talk was having the necessary effect on him as he hardened under her hand.

"You're not getting busy."

Apparently resigned to his fate, he pulled his shirt over his head, revealing the most excellent chest and belly that had captivated her from the first time she'd ever seen him shirtless. Her husband was a fine, fine looking man, and she loved him fiercely. "Hurry." She tugged at the button to his jeans, her hands not working as well as they usually did.

"Whoa," he said, grabbing her hand. "Careful with the zipper, babe."

"You do it, then. Just hurry up!"

"You're bossy when you're drunk."

"You're bossy all the time, so now it's my turn." She wiggled out of her jeans and panties, pulled off her bra and tossed it across the room. It didn't even occur to her anymore to worry about baring her obnoxiously large breasts to her husband. He loved every inch of her and never missed a chance to tell her so.

She pushed back onto the bed, raising her arms above her head and letting her legs fall open. There was a lot to be said for liquid courage, she thought, as she watched her husband's eyes darken with lust. She loved that she could do that to him. "You're not hurrying," she purred.

"I'm trying to figure out who you are and what you've done with my shy, demure wife."

"Are you complaining?"

He came down on top of her, settling into the V of her legs. "Not even kinda."

"Good," she said, smiling as she dragged him into a kiss designed to show him how badly she wanted him.

"I need to stock up on champagne," he said, making her snort rather inelegantly with laughter.

"The champagne is only part of it."

"What's the other part?" he asked, looking down at her with love and desire.

"You." She reached up to comb her fingers through his dark hair. "I look at you, and I want you. You walked into the restaurant tonight, and my heart skipped a happy beat because there you were. My guy, coming to find me because he can't stand to spend even one night out without me."

"Maddie…"

"I like to pretend I'm mad when you crash girls' night, but I'm never mad. I'm always thrilled to see you, because there's never a time I wouldn't rather be with you than with anyone else."

"You humble me, Madeline." His words were a low rumble against her ear as he slid into her, hard and hot and exquisitely perfect. Always so perfect.

In the back of her mind, something nagged at her, but she was too caught up in him to stop to think about what it might be. She was forgetting something. Whatever it was, she'd worry about it later. Right now, she had far more pressing concerns as his control snapped, and he took her on a hard, fast thrill ride.

She gripped his ass to keep him deep inside her as she crested the first peak, crying out even though she knew she should be quiet with the kids sleeping.

"Shhh," he whispered, his lips curved with amusement as he continued to thrust into her.

"*So good,*" she said as her eyes fluttered closed. She let her hands fall to the mattress and loved that he reached for them, gripping them tightly as he took her up and over again before finding his own release.

As he lay panting above her, still clutching her hands, Maddie opened her eyes and let out a squawk when she found Thomas standing by the bed, teddy bear in hand, staring at her with big eyes brimming with tears.

"Why is Daddy hurting you, Mommy?"

"Oh, Christ," Mac muttered against her neck as he released her hands.

Maddie's champagne buzz fizzled as mortification set in. She didn't dare move out of fear of showing him even more and making it worse, as if it could get any worse. "Daddy isn't hurting me, honey. He's hugging me." She put her arms around Mac. "See?"

"But you were crying. I heard you."

Mac's body shook with silent laughter.

Maddie pinched his rear, and he surged deeper into her. Fabulous. "Go back to bed, and Mommy will be there in just a minute to tuck you in."

"Not until Daddy gets off of you."

"I love Mommy," Mac finally said. "I'd never hurt her. You know that."

"Go ahead, Thomas," Maddie said sternly. "I'll be right there."

When the little boy finally turned away and padded off to his room, his parents dissolved into laughter.

"Oh my God!" Maddie said, pushing at her husband. "Get off me! I have to go make sure he's not scarred for life!"

"I told you to be quiet."

"It's your fault!"

He withdrew from her and rolled over. "How in the world is this my fault? I was trying to put you to bed, and you went all vixen on me."

Maddie got up on rubbery legs and went to the closet to find a robe. "You made me scream."

"Right. Okay. I *made* you scream."

"You did!"

He rolled his eyes at her, clearly not buying her logic. "Want me to come with you?"

"No, I've got this."

"It bums me out that he thinks I was hurting you."

She went to him and bent to kiss him, patting his face. "I'll take care of it." Steeling herself for an awkward conversation with her son, Maddie went into his room to find him sitting up in bed and clutching his poor bear. "What're you doing awake?" Maddie asked as she sat on the bed.

"I heard you crying."

"I wasn't crying, honey. I was laughing. Daddy was being silly."

"It sounded like you were crying."

"I promise I wasn't, and Daddy wasn't hurting me. We were just playing."

"Why were you playing without your clothes?"

Maddie wanted to expire on the spot. "Um, we were snuggling. Sometimes mommies and daddies snuggle without their clothes."

He wrinkled his little nose in disgust. "That's yucky."

"Yes, I suppose it is," she said, suppressing the need to giggle madly. "We'll snuggle with our pajamas on from now on." She raised the covers. "Time to go back to sleep." Tucking the covers up to his chin, she bent to kiss his forehead. "Honey, you know Daddy would never, ever hurt me, right?"

As he nodded, his big eyes were solemn.

"I don't want you to worry about that. Daddy loves me so much. He loves me and you and Hailey. He'd never hurt any of us. I promise."

"He's a good daddy."

"He's the best daddy." She kissed him again. "Have sweet dreams."

He turned over and popped his thumb into his mouth—always a good sign that he was on his way to sleep.

Relieved to have survived the crisis, she got up and felt a surge of moisture between her legs. That's when she knew what she'd forgotten earlier. She managed to maintain her composure long enough to check on Hailey and return to the bedroom where Mac waited for her under the covers.

"Everything okay?"

"We forgot to use a condom."

His face sagged with shock and dismay. "Oh. Shit. I never even thought of it."

"You were the sober one! You should've thought of it!"

"So this is my fault, too?"

"Yes!"

Grinning and shaking his head, he held out his hand to her. "Come to bed."

"In a minute." She went to use the bathroom and brush her teeth. All the while, her heart beat an out-of-control rhythm as the possibility of another pregnancy left her flat-out terrified. With her hands on the countertop, she let her head drop as the implications settled into a hard knot in her belly.

Mac came up behind her and wrapped his arms around her, his face warm against her back. "I'm sorry, honey. You got me so worked up, I never gave it a thought."

"I knew you'd find a way to make it my fault," she teased.

He urged her to turn to face him. "Just because we slipped up once doesn't mean you'll get pregnant."

"It's been two weeks since my period," she said, watching his face carefully as the information registered with him.

"Still, that doesn't mean it'll happen."

"I hope not. I'm not ready to be pregnant again."

"I'm not ready for you to be pregnant again either. I may never recover from the last time."

That drew a small smile from her. "What're the odds of something like that happening again?" she asked of their daughter's wild home delivery during Tropical Storm Hailey.

"I have no desire to find out anytime soon." He hugged her and pressed a kiss to the top of her head. "No matter what happens, we're in it together, you and me. All the way."

His words went a long way toward defusing the panic that had gripped her since she realized they'd forgotten protection. But the panic would gnaw at her until she knew for sure that she wasn't pregnant. It was going to be a very long ten days.

CHAPTER 3

Daisy was up early the next morning to get ready for work. Since Mrs. McCarthy had put her in charge of the housekeeping department on a trial basis earlier in the month, she was trying to get there early every day so she was ready when the others arrived. She only had the job at all because Maddie had put in a good word for Daisy with her mother-in-law, but Daisy was determined to do the best job she could and earn the position permanently.

Emerging from the house, she was dejected to realize it was raining. Normally, she walked the mile and a half to work every day and enjoyed the exercise and the scenery along the way. But with the rain coming down hard, she went back for her umbrella and headed to the ferry landing to hail a cab.

Ned Saunders waved her over to his cab, running around the front to open the passenger door for her.

"Thank you so much, Ned," Daisy said as she got in and shook off her umbrella before Ned closed the door.

"Not a good day fer walkin' about, doll," Ned said as he fired up the old station wagon and took off toward North Harbor without even asking Daisy where she was going.

Such was life in a small town. Everyone knew your business, which wasn't always a good thing. However, since the awful night with Truck, the island community had been extra nice to her. She hadn't heard a word of derogatory gossip about her, though that didn't mean there hadn't been any.

"How ya been feelin'?"

"Much better. Thank you again to you and Francine for the casserole and the brownies. That was very nice of you both."

"I gotta give my gal credit for that. I was just the delivery boy."

Daisy smiled at him. He was so damned cute and crazy in love with Maddie's mother. They gave romance losers like her hope that there might be someone out there for everyone. "Just the same, it was nice of you, and I appreciated it."

"Our pleasure, honey. Glad to see ya up and around and back ta work. I hope yer not lettin' Linda push ya around at the hotel. She runs a tight ship, but she's a lot more bark than bite."

Daisy had learned as much since she'd been promoted. "She's been very nice to me, especially since I had to call in sick for a whole week right after I got the new job. And she brought me dinner, too."

"That sounds like the Linda I know and love."

He was quiet for a moment but glanced over at her twice.

"What is it that you're dying to say to me, Ned?"

"Tisn't my place to interfere."

Daisy smiled at him, well aware of his sweet yet meddling propensities. "And yet…"

"I'm concerned 'bout yer new friend, Dr. David."

"What about him?" Daisy asked, not wanting to hear anything about David that would change her opinion of him.

"His track record ain't the best. I'd hate to see ya git hurt again, 'specially after what happened recently."

"That's very nice of you, Ned, and I know there are things in his past he's not proud of. In fact, he's going to tell me about it himself the next time I see him. If it's all the same, I think I'd like to hear it from him."

"Fair 'nough. So long as ya know there's somethin' ya need to hear. And fer what it's worth, it's good he wants ta tell ya 'bout it. Says somethin' 'bout him."

"I agree."

"Sorry to be nosing in where my nose don't belong."

"You were looking out for me, and that's very sweet of you."

"Aww, shucks, t'ain't nothing I wouldn't do fer my own girls."

Daisy thought it was doubly sweet that he thought of Maddie and her sister Tiffany as his girls, especially since their own father had been a total deadbeat until recently. Anxious to change the subject as they approached the last intersection before the hotel, Daisy tried to think of something else to talk to him about. And then she knew what she wanted to ask him.

"How does Maddie seem since her dad came back around? She told me he set up college funds for the kids."

"Yep. Too little too late, if ya ask me, but ain't no one askin' me."

"It's something, anyway, but I do see what you mean. I can't help but wonder if he did that to guilt them into spending time with him."

"'Twas my thought as well."

"Hmm, well, we'll have to keep an eye on her and make sure he can't hurt her again."

"On that we agree." He brought the car to a stop at the bottom of the grassy hill that led to the hotel. "If it's still rainin' this afternoon, I'll be back to getcha at four."

"You don't have to do that."

"I want ta do it, so don't give me no sass."

Daisy laughed and shook her head at him as she reached for her wallet.

His hand covered hers. "Keep yer money, doll. Tain't no good here."

Charmed by him, Daisy leaned over to kiss his cheek. "You're the best. Thank you."

Daisy scrambled up the hill under the umbrella, thinking about her chat with Ned and more concerned now about whatever it was that David had to tell her.

She tried to push those worries aside as she got busy preparing the schedule for the next week and organizing the supply order that was due by noon so the delivery could make the Friday ferry.

At nine-thirty, she met with "her" team of housekeepers, which still made her feel like an imposter. What was she doing overseeing Sylvia, Betty, Sarah and Maude, who, along with Maddie, had taught her everything she knew about hotel housekeeping? When their old boss Ethel retired, Maddie had been promoted. After Hailey was born, she'd decided to stay home with her kids and had recommended Daisy for the job, which Daisy still couldn't believe.

She'd cried like a baby when Maddie first told her that she'd encouraged Mrs. McCarthy to put her in charge. And she'd totally understood when Mrs. McCarthy asked for a summer-long probationary period so they could make sure it was a good fit for both of them before they made it permanent. Daisy had never had a job with benefits or paid vacation or the kind of salary she was earning. Even with the increased salary, however, the cost of living on the island was rising all the time, and she was constantly short on cash.

However, she had health insurance for the first time since she left home ten years ago at eighteen, and she was going to do this job brilliantly even if it killed her. Some days she wondered if it would actually kill her, because she was working as hard as she ever had, even if the labor wasn't as physical as it used to be. As the manager, she still ran up and down three flights of stairs all day long and was wiped out at the end of every shift—more so since she'd been injured.

She didn't want Mrs. McCarthy to think she couldn't handle the job, so she'd been pushing herself since she'd come back to work. As she returned to her office at noon, her entire body ached, and she was anxious to take a painkiller to get through the afternoon. Two pills would be ideal, but the second one would put her to sleep. One pill would take the edge off the pain radiating from her ribs.

Daisy popped the pill and chased it with a drink of water.

Maddie came to the door, looking a little bleary-eyed, which was to be expected after her big night out.

"Hungover?" Daisy asked with a cheeky grin for her friend.

"Maybe a little."

"I'm surprised you can move today," Daisy said, inviting her into the office.

Maddie slid into the visitor chair and took a closer look at Daisy. "Are you okay? You're pale."

"Little bit of pain, so I just took a pill. It'll be better soon."

"I hope you're not pushing yourself too hard, Daisy. You were seriously injured, and you only took a week off."

"I'm fine. I promise. I love the job, and I want to be here."

"I'm glad you're enjoying it."

"I hired two new girls for the summer. They'll be here next weekend. My first hires. Fingers crossed."

"Look forward to meeting them."

"I can't thank you enough for giving me this opportunity. You have no idea what it means to me."

"Yes, I do. It wasn't that long ago that I was living on a shoestring. I understand how new opportunities can change a life. And you don't have to keep thanking me, Daisy. I recommended the person who I thought would be best for the job."

"It feels weird sometimes, being the boss of Betty, Sarah, Maude and the others. They've been here forever."

"And they don't want to be the boss. I had the same concerns, but Linda told me they didn't want the job. They were nothing but supportive of me when I was in charge."

"They've been great to me, too. They kept me in food while I was recovering."

"It's a nice group, and they'll take good care of you."

"Keep the assurances coming. I need as many as I can get."

"You won't believe what happened last night after you left."

"What?"

"Thomas caught us… you know…"

"No way." Daisy laughed at the tortured look on Maddie's face. "What did he say? What did *you* say?"

"It was awful. He wanted to know why Daddy was hurting me."

Daisy laughed so hard tears ran down her cheeks.

Maddie balled up a tissue from the box on Daisy's desk and threw it at her. "It's not funny!"

"Yes, it is." Daisy wiped her face with the tissue. "You must've been *dying*."

"I still am. He doesn't understand why mommies and daddies like to snuggle without their clothes."

That set Daisy off all over again.

Even Linda McCarthy's appearance at the door couldn't stop the laughter.

"What's so funny?" Linda asked, bending to kiss her daughter-in-law's cheek.

"I can't tell you," Maddie said. "It's too embarrassing."

"Can I tell her?" Daisy asked, wiping her face again.

Maddie put her hands over her ears. "If you must."

"Thomas caught them…" Daisy rolled her hand, encouraging Linda to fill in the blanks.

"Daisy's right. That is funny."

"Glad you think so," Maddie grumbled.

"Tell her the part about mommies and daddies snuggling without their clothes," Daisy said, losing it all over again.

Linda joined in the laughter, clearly enjoying Maddie's dismay.

"Mac caught us once when he was about Thomas's age," Linda said. "We were on the sofa getting busy, and then there he was. I let out an ungodly scream that scared the heck out of him and my husband."

"He didn't mention it last night, so I don't think he remembers."

"Let's not remind him," Linda said.

Maddie grimaced, which made Daisy laugh some more. "I'd like to forget the whole thing happened, so quit laughing."

Daisy dabbed at her tears with the tissue. "Can't help it."

"I'm never drinking champagne again," Maddie said.

"Can we get that in writing?" Linda squeezed Maddie's shoulder affectionately. "I've got to run to a hair appointment in town. See you girls later."

"Thanks for the laughs," Daisy said to Maddie when they were alone.

"Happy to entertain you with my mortification, but that's not the reason I stopped by."

"What's up?"

"I wanted to talk to you about David."

"What about him?"

"Even in my tipsy state, I couldn't help but notice we might've interrupted something when we came home last night."

"Maybe."

"I just hope you're being careful where he's concerned. There're things about him that you should know—"

Daisy held her hands up to stop her friend from going any further. "I've already heard that."

"What do you know?"

"That there're things he needs to tell me."

"And how do you know that?"

"Because *he* told me, and I want to hear it from him."

"You know that Mac and I are thankful every day for what he did for us when Hailey was born."

"Yes, and I know there're things in his past he's not proud of. We're going to talk about that when he gets back on Tuesday."

"Where is he?"

"He had to go to Boston for a couple of days."

"What's he doing there?"

"He didn't say, and I didn't ask. Listen, Maddie, I appreciate you looking out for me. I really do, and I know I've given you and all my friends ample reason to worry about me. But I'm okay. And I'm enjoying whatever this is with David."

"I want you to be careful. You've been through so much, and I'd hate to see you hurt again."

Daisy got up and went around the desk to hug her friend. "You're sweet for being worried about me, but I'm fine and well aware that there are skeletons in his closet that he needs to tell me about."

Maddie, who had stood up to hug Daisy, patted her back. "Make sure he tells you soon. It's something you're going to want to know."

The warning made Daisy's stomach drop with anxiety. She didn't want to hear anything about David that would change the way she was beginning to feel about him. But she refused to ignore potential trouble signs. She'd done that too many times in the past, most recently with Truck, and nearly got herself killed. Never again.

Maddie left to hit the grocery store while Mac was home with the kids, and Daisy went back to work, the warnings from Maddie and Ned weighed on her mind.

David's return couldn't get here soon enough for her.

Janey sat on the exam table, wrapped in a paper robe that barely stretched around her hugely extended belly. Hoping to relax before her appointment, she flipped through a fashion magazine without noticing much of anything. Her focus had been shot to hell as her pregnancy progressed. At times she felt like she was sacrificing all her own brain cells to the baby.

Joe paced from one end of the small exam room to the other. "How much longer do you think she'll be?" He glanced at his watch. "I'm on the four o'clock boat."

"I know, babe. That's why I made the appointment for two. You've got plenty of time, so stop stressing me out."

"Sorry." He landed in a chair but tapped his fingers relentlessly on the countertop next to the sink.

Janey looked at him, then at his fingers.

"Sorry," he muttered as he folded his arms. He lasted four whole minutes before he was up and pacing again.

Janey gave up on the magazine and tried to find a comfortable position on the table. Her back was killing her, as always, and sitting without something to rest against made it worse.

"What's wrong?" he asked, zeroing in on her. "Does something hurt?"

"My back. As usual."

"You should've said something." He came over to sit behind her, putting his arms around her so she could lean into his chest.

The relief was immediate and intense. "Much better, and it keeps you from pacing, too."

"Sorry, baby. I feel like my nerves are stretched so tight they're about to snap, and I'm not even the one having the baby."

"Joe—"

"I'm scared every time I leave the island for even a couple of hours that you're going to need me, and I'm not going to be here. I should have Seamus take me off the schedule—"

"Joe! Stop! Listen to me. I've got eight weeks to go. Everything is fine. You heard what Victoria said at the last appointment—most first babies are late anyway. We'll move to the house on the mainland in four weeks as we planned, and we'll be right where we need to be when the baby comes. You have to calm down. You're making me nuts."

She hated that they would miss her cousin Laura's wedding to Owen Lawry in early August. However, there was no way she'd convince Joe to stay on the island past the end of July with the baby due on August 15, especially considering his phobias about train wreck deliveries. Because he'd been so wound up, she hadn't even bothered to suggest they come out to the island for the day of the wedding and return to the mainland right after.

His forehead landed on her shoulder, his breath warm against her back. "I'm sorry. I don't mean to make you nuts. It's just that I can't stop thinking about the night Hailey was born and how many things could've gone wrong. And if David hadn't been there—"

She covered the hand he'd placed on her belly with hers. "He was there.

Hailey was fine. I'll be fine and so will our baby. Stop anticipating doom. You're reminding me too much of Mac right now."

"But he was right, and if Maddie had listened to him—"

Janey squished his lips together to shut him up. "*Enough.*"

A knock on the door preceded Victoria into the room. "So sorry to keep you waiting. We're straight-out crazy busy today, and David is on the mainland, and... and you don't care where David is."

Janey smiled at the chagrined expression on Victoria's face when she remembered she was speaking to David's ex-fiancée. "Not to worry, Vic. Ancient history." As she said the words, she clamped down harder on Joe's hand to keep him from chiming in on the subject of David. He'd chilled out somewhat since David saved their baby niece's life, but he'd never be one of Joe's favorite people.

"Anyway," Victoria said, consulting Janey's chart. "Here we are at thirty-two weeks. We'll keep seeing you every other week until thirty-six, when we go to every week."

"That's when we'll be moving to the mainland," Joe reminded her. "We're having the baby at Women and Infants in Providence."

"That's right," Victoria said. "I see that noted on your chart. You've been to the childbirth preparation classes there?"

"We did the one-day class last week," Janey said. "It's a beautiful facility."

"It sure is." She pulled on gloves. "Let's take a look and see how things are going."

Janey didn't think she'd ever get used to putting her feet in the stirrups while her husband was in the room, but Maddie had told her to prepare for many more indignities before it was over. She startled from the cold lube on Victoria's fingers and held back the urge to pee from the pressure of the internal exam.

Victoria was always very thorough and today was no exception. "I'm not feeling the baby's head descending, so I'd like to take a quick ultrasound while I've got you."

"Is that unusual?" Joe asked, immediately tense.

"Not entirely, but we like to see the baby starting to move into birth position at this point. He or she might be a little behind schedule, but I'd like to take a look just to be sure." She removed Janey's feet from the stirrups and put the table extender back in place. "Be right back."

"What does that mean?" Joe asked the second she closed the door.

"You're chilling out, remember?"

He grunted out a reply, but his face was a study in tension.

"Let's talk about something besides the baby."

"Like what?"

"I talked to your mother this morning. She's going crazy cleaning and cooking and getting ready for Seamus's mother to get here. I offered to help her, but she won't let me do a thing."

"You're damned right you're not doing a thing."

"Joseph… You and I are going to have our first major marital blowout if you don't *calm the hell down*."

"I am calm! This is me being calm!"

She narrowed her eyes and gave him her best pissed-off look as Victoria wheeled in the ultrasound machine, arranged a sheet over her lap and raised her gown to expose her belly. "Try to breathe normally and stay very still."

It took a few minutes of positioning the wand before the baby's image appeared on the screen.

Joe gasped and squeezed Janey's hand. "Oh, there he is! Wow, look at that."

The wonder she heard in his tone almost made up for the crazy way he'd been behaving the last few weeks. "I thought you'd decided he was a she."

"He, she, I don't care either way."

"Just as I suspected," Victoria said, studying the screen. "The baby is in breech position, which isn't dangerous or anything, but he—or she—is going to have to turn around before delivery, or we're looking at a C-section." She pointed to the screen. "See the feet, there?"

"Uh-huh." Fascinated by the crystal-clear view of her baby's toes, Janey wasn't seeing much of anything else.

"They should be up here by now. Everything else looks really good, though. You're sure you don't want to know what you're having?"

"We're sure," Janey said, answering for both of them before Joe could change his mind.

Victoria wiped the gel off Janey's belly and helped her to sit up. "We'll keep an eye on it and make some delivery decisions when you get closer to thirty-six weeks. In the meantime, I'd like to see you next week for another check of your blood pressure. It was a tiny bit elevated today, so we'll need to monitor that, too. You're not working anymore, are you?"

"No, my last day was Friday. Joe wanted me to relax for a few weeks before the baby gets here, and I've been so tired he didn't have to twist my arm." Doc and the staff at the vet clinic had thrown a shower for her and invited many of their patients, which Janey had loved.

"Good. Take it easy, stay off your feet, no stress. Relax. That's your job now, Mom. Dad, your job is to make sure she does nothing too strenuous and keeps the stress to a minimum. Here's your chance to earn some major points."

"Hear that?" Janey said to her husband. "Keep the stress to a minimum."

He scowled at her. "I heard it."

"Hang in there, Janey." Victoria patted Janey's arm. "You're in the home stretch."

Stretch seemed to be the key word, and she wondered at times how much more her skin could expand without bursting open. How her mother had ever done this five times was beyond her. This baby would be lucky to get a sibling, let alone four of them.

As Joe helped her into her tent of a sundress, Janey acknowledged to herself what she hadn't shared with anyone else, even Joe. She hated being pregnant. She hated feeling fat and bloated and swollen and achy all over. She hated not being able to work or have sex comfortably or even hug her husband without the big old belly getting in the way. The baby couldn't get here soon enough for her.

When she was dressed, Joe lifted her right off the exam table, like she didn't weigh an absolute ton, and deposited her gently onto her feet, giving her a minute to gain her bearings. Her balance, like everything else, was out of whack.

"Are you okay?"

"I think so."

"Do you want to sit for a minute?"

"No, let's go so you can get to work."

Janey waddled through the clinic, thankful there was no chance of running into her ex-fiancé when she looked like a beached whale. Not that she cared what he thought of her, but still. A big reason why they'd planned the delivery for the mainland was because neither of them wanted David involved, not that they'd ever spoken of that subject. It was understood.

By the time Joe drove up to the house they'd recently bought near Mac and Maddie's, Janey's eyelids were drooping. The appointment had sapped most of her energy, and she was going to need a nap. Soon.

Joe escorted her inside and waited patiently as she greeted her menagerie of pets and used the bathroom. He tucked her into bed and sat on the edge of the mattress to look down at her. "I'm sorry I'm being such a jackass over all of this baby business. The thought of you in pain or in danger or anything other than perfectly healthy makes me crazy."

"I'm perfectly healthy, and I'm going to stay that way."

"Promise?"

She smiled at his boyishly handsome face and the adorable pucker of his lips. "I promise," she said, crooking her finger at him to bring him down for a kiss.

"Don't worry about dinner," he said. "I'll grab something when I get back. Any requests?"

"Whatever you want."

He kissed her again. "Sweet dreams. Love you."

"Love you, too. Be careful out there."

"Of course I will. I've got my beautiful wife waiting for me at home."

Janey snorted with laughter. "She's *sooo* beautiful. Like an elephant is beautiful."

He leaned over her, his blue eyes intense and heated. "You are as beautiful as you've ever been, and I've never loved you more. In fact, if you're a very good girl and get some sleep while I'm gone, I'll show you how much I love you when I get home." A waggle of his brows indicated his intentions. They'd become very creative when it came to lovemaking, and he'd shown how imaginative he could be.

"Mmm. I'll be very, *very* good."

Smiling, he kissed her one more time and left her to rest. As she drifted off to sleep with no work or school or dinner or anything else to think about, she decided maybe there was something to be said for being pregnant after all.

Sarah Lawry called Daisy as she was leaving work and asked if she had dinner plans. Since Daisy had nothing at all on the agenda for the evening, she accepted Sarah's invitation with pleasure. Sarah had been a huge support to her since the incident with Truck. Sadly, Sarah had lived for years in a violent relationship with her soon-to-be ex-husband and would testify against him in court this summer. She could relate all too well to what Daisy had been through.

Knowing the court date was weighing heavily on Sarah, Daisy relished the opportunity to give something back to the woman who'd been so good to her.

After the long day cooped up in the hotel, Daisy enjoyed the walk into town in the bright sunshine. The rain earlier in the day had left behind a sweet scent, and the late-day heat had dried the puddles.

On the way home, she popped into Ryan's Pharmacy to pick up her allergy prescription, which wasn't ready quite yet. Since she now had insurance, she was able to afford the good stuff, rather than the over-the-counter allergy meds she'd relied on for years.

"So sorry for the delay," Grace Ryan, the island's pharmacist, said. She was working alone behind the counter in the back of the store, which they had all to themselves. "We've been crazy busy. I swear the entire island decided today was refill day."

"Whoops. Sorry to add to the load."

"Not a problem. Is the hotel getting busy?"

"Starting to. We're fully booked this weekend, so here we go."

"I officially survived my first winter on Gansett," Grace said. "I'm very proud of that."

"As you should be. Winter on Gansett isn't for sissies."

"That's what Evan says, too."

"How's his studio doing?"

"Really well. They're booked through the end of July and getting more calls every day."

"I think it's so cool we have a recording studio right here on the island."

"I think it's so cool that he's found something he loves to do that also keeps him right here with me," Grace said with a wink and a smile that made Daisy laugh.

"Can't say I blame you for being happy about that. Glad it's working out for you guys." Daisy couldn't help but notice the gorgeous ring on Grace's finger. "Any wedding plans yet?"

"Not quite yet. We're thinking about going somewhere warm this winter and getting everyone to go with us."

"That sounds like so much fun."

"And how are you doing? Feeling better?"

Grace's empathetic question didn't bear a trace of pity, which Daisy appreciated. "Feeling stronger every day and more determined to move forward with my life. Everyone has been so supportive and helpful."

"I love that about living here. You feel like you're surrounded by a big family, even though you're not related to most of them."

"Yes, that's it exactly. I came for one summer at the hotel and here I am, still here six years later for that very reason. There's something special about the people on this island."

"I completely agree." Standing before her computer, Grace said, "I'm seeing that you have an unfilled script for pain meds. Do you need that?"

"No, I can't take narcotics. They make me loopy. I'm getting by with the over-the-counter stuff."

"I'm glad that's working for you." Grace rang up the prescription and handed it over to Daisy. "You should come to one of our girls' nights. They're always a lot of fun."

"I've heard Maddie talk about your adventures. I'd love to come sometime."

"Great. I'll make sure she lets you know about the next one. It usually turns into date night when the guys crash, but it's still fun."

"Sounds like it. Thanks for the meds and the chat. Good to see you."

"You, too. Take care, Daisy."

CHAPTER 4

As Daisy was walking home, David called. When she saw his name on the caller ID, she was so excited she fumbled with her cell phone and nearly dropped it. "Hello?"

"Hi, there." Those two words in that distinctive deep voice brought back all the feelings he'd stirred in her the night before. "Daisy? Are you there?"

"Yes, I'm sorry. I'm here. How are you?"

"Good, just tired after a long day. How was your day?"

"Not bad. I'm on my way home now and going to dinner with Sarah Lawry. Oh! I have to tell you the funniest thing." She relayed Maddie's story about Thomas catching his parents in the act, laughing again as she told him, as if she was hearing it for the first time.

"Oh, man. That's got to be so weird."

"Just a bit."

"I like to hear you laugh. It sounds good on you."

He made her knees go weak and her head spin when he talked to her in that intimate tone. "Does it?"

"Uh-huh."

"I haven't had a lot to laugh about in the last few weeks, so it felt good to let loose with Maddie earlier. Although, I did most of the laughing. She was dying."

"I can't even think about what that must be like. The poor kid."

"The poor parents!"

"True," he said, chuckling. "Kind of a mood killer."

"To say the least. However, I got the feeling that the crescendo was what got Thomas's attention, so…"

His quiet laughter warmed her.

"I wish you weren't all the way over in Boston tonight," she said and then immediately winced when she realized the statement was somewhat revealing.

"Believe me, I wish I wasn't either."

"What're you doing there, anyway?"

"I had a couple of appointments. I should be back by late tomorrow afternoon. We're still on for tomorrow night?"

"Sure are," she said, trying not to let it bother her that he hadn't elaborated on his appointments. Work appointments? Personal? She'd love to know but would never ask.

"Good. I'll get reservations at Domenic's."

"That sounds nice. What's the occasion?"

"A night out with you."

"You're very sweet."

His voice sounded pained when he said, "We really need to talk, Daisy."

"I know."

"I just… I hope…"

"What? What are you hoping?"

"I want to be honest with you, but I don't want you to hate me after."

"I could never hate you."

"You say that now…"

"Let's postpone this conversation until tomorrow. I don't want you to worry about anything. Remember what I told you last night about how kind you've been to me since everything happened with Truck, and how I won't ever forget it?"

"I seem to recall something along those lines."

"You've got a lot of points accumulated," she said as she stepped into her house. Even though she was apprehensive after Ned and Maddie had tried to warn her, she didn't want anything to ruin the lovely memory of evening they'd shared. "Whatever you have to tell me, we'll talk about it and figure out what it means. That's all we can do, right?"

"I suppose so."

"I have stuff, too, you know."

"I bet none of your stuff is all that bad."

"You might be surprised," she said.

"I look forward to being surprised by you."

Daisy's smile stretched across her face as she curled up on the sofa with the phone cradled against her shoulder.

"You're going to think I'm feeding you a line," he said, "but I miss you. I wish you were here with me."

It was all she could do not to sigh—audibly—into the phone. "I miss you, too. I've gotten used to seeing you every day around this time. Feels kinda weird to know you're not on the island."

"Feels weird to me, too. At some point during the last few months, Gansett has become home to me again."

"What boat are you on tomorrow?"

"Aiming for the five, so I'll be there by six-thirty, okay?"

"I'll be ready."

"See you then."

Daisy wanted to sit and rehash every second of their conversation, but Sarah would be by soon to pick her up, and she needed a shower after the long day at the hotel. By the time Sarah arrived, Daisy had relived the entire phone call at least a hundred times and was wondering how she would survive until tomorrow night when she could finally talk to him about whatever was weighing on him.

Sarah was driving the battered, twenty-year-old blue Ford she'd recently bought for herself—the first she'd ever purchased on her own. She was so darned proud of that car, and Daisy was proud of her, for surviving her violent marriage and for making a new life for herself on the island.

Blaine Taylor had introduced Daisy to Sarah, thinking the two women might be able to help each other due to their common experience with domestic violence. They had since formed sort of a mother-daughter relationship, or at least that was how it seemed to Daisy. It had been so long since Daisy had seen her own mother that she was enjoying her new friendship with Sarah, a mother of seven.

When she saw Sarah's car pull up to the curb, Daisy grabbed a sweater and dashed out the door.

Sarah leaned over to unlock the passenger door for Daisy and greeted her with a hug when she got in. Daisy had been astounded to hear that Sarah was fifty-eight, because she seemed much younger than that.

"You look so pretty," Sarah said.

Sarah always had something nice to say, which Daisy appreciated. "So do you. Love is clearly agreeing with you."

Laughing, Sarah blushed as she pulled away from the curb. "I don't know if it's love, but it sure is fun."

Sarah had been dating Charlie Grandchamp for a while now, and her eyes lit up whenever she spoke of him.

"I'm glad you're having fun."

"How about you? Still hanging out with Dr. David?"

"Still hanging out," Daisy said, and making out, she thought but didn't say.

"And having fun?"

"Lots of fun. It's nice to be with someone I don't have to be afraid of—at least not physically." He was becoming a bigger threat to the well-being of her heart with every passing day.

"I know what you mean." Sarah drove to Marco's pizza place because neither of them ever had much in the way of extra money, so they kept their "dates" on the cheap. "Although, I wonder sometimes how long Charlie is going to put up with me."

"Why do you say that?"

"Every time he touches me, I flinch. Every time he makes a sudden move, I flinch. Every time he tries to kiss me, I turn away. I can tell he's starting to get frustrated with me, and I can't say I blame him."

"You still haven't told him about Mark?"

Sarah shook her head. "I hate to think about him, let alone talk about him with someone like Charlie, who has been so nice and so patient."

"Maybe if he knew what you've been through, he'd understand why you react the way you do to him."

"I'm sure he has his theories about why I'm so jumpy."

"How do you plan to get around telling him where you're going when you leave for the trial?"

"Owen asked me that, too." Sarah had been living with her eldest son and his fiancée, Laura McCarthy, at the Sand & Surf Hotel since the fall. "He thinks I ought to tell Charlie the truth about what's going on, but I'd rather wait until it's over and behind me for good before I tell him. After all he's been through himself, why would he want to be burdened with my baggage?"

"Has he talked to you about being in prison?"

"Yes," she said softly as she found a parking space and killed the engine. "He told me how he saved Stephanie from her abusive mother and landed in prison for his trouble."

"It couldn't have been easy for him to share that with you—or anyone."

"I'm sure it wasn't. I could tell he was embarrassed about having been in prison, even if he was falsely accused of being the abuser."

Daisy reached for Sarah's hand. "You should tell him your story, Sarah. If he cares about you, and I think he does, he'd want to support you during the trial."

"I don't know if I want him to. I'd be so ashamed for him to hear about what I put up with for so long, not to mention what I let that monster do to my children."

"It wasn't like you 'let' him do anything. I don't think Charlie is the type to pass judgment. He's already shown you he's nothing like Mark, hasn't he?"

"He's *nothing* like Mark," Sarah said with a harsh laugh. "Thankfully, most men aren't like Mark."

They got out of the car and walked inside, pleased to find their usual table in the back corner of the crowded restaurant available. When they were settled with sodas and had ordered a pizza and house salad to share, Sarah propped her chin on her upturned hand and studied Daisy. "So tell me everything about the handsome doctor."

Daisy thought of his laughter the night before and what it did to his gorgeous face. "He is handsome."

"That he is. He was very good to me when I arrived here in pieces, and I won't soon forget his kindness."

"He's been extremely awesome to me, too. Perhaps his specialty ought to be damsels in distress."

Sarah laughed and raised her glass. "Sounds good to me."

"There's something else though, something he needs to tell me. Something bad, or so it seems. A few people have tried to tell me, but I want to hear it from him, you know?"

Sarah nodded. "That seems only fair."

"I'm afraid that he's going to tell me something so awful I won't want to see him anymore."

"If it's that awful, it'll be just as well he tells you now before it goes any further. If you ask me, it says something about him that he wants to tell you himself, when he knows it wouldn't take much digging around here for you to get the dirt on your own."

"I had two different people try to tell me today."

"Hmm, so then it was big enough that people know about it, whatever it is."

"I think it has something to do with his breakup with Janey McCarthy, which has my brain spinning in a number of unsavory directions."

"Don't forget it's possible for people to make really serious mistakes that they regret tremendously and to learn from those mistakes and never make them again."

"I know. Do you think Mark might be capable of learning from his mistakes?"

"Absolutely not. Mark is a violent, controlling monster who will never change. I don't think there's any comparison between his brand of evil and whatever sins David Lawrence may have committed, but you'll have to be the judge of that. Something tells me that a man who is capable of the sort of kindness and compassion he has shown both of us is someone worth spending time with."

"That's what my gut is telling me, but my gut has been wrong before. More than once."

"I bet your gut has gathered some wisdom over the years and is more trustworthy than it used to be." She covered Daisy's hand on the table with her own. "The bottom line is you have to decide if you can live with whatever he tells you. If you can't, there's no shame in walking away, if that's what's best for you."

Daisy knew Sarah was absolutely right, but the thought of walking away from David filled her with an aching sadness.

Piece by piece, Carolina Cantrell removed the china from the hutch in her dining room, cleaning and dusting each item before adding it to the growing pile on the dining room table. How so much grit and grime managed to get inside a closed cabinet was beyond her. It had been somewhat appalling to realize how dirty her house had gotten while she'd been busy carrying on a wild affair with an Irishman young enough to be her son.

The Irishman in question came banging into the house, home from work after a long day captaining the ferries. Even though Joe and Janey were back on the island for the summer, Seamus continued to run the Gansett Island Ferry Company that Carolina and her son Joe had inherited from her parents. With the baby due in August, Joe wanted to work as little as possible this summer so he could spend as much time with his wife as he could.

That left Seamus working from dawn until dusk seven days a week as the tourists began to descend on the island in droves.

"What in the name of hell are you doing?" he asked, surveying the mess in the dining room.

"I'm cleaning. What does it look like I'm doing?"

"It looks to me like you've lost your bleeding mind, love. Why are you cleaning your mum's china?"

"Because it's filthy, and what if *your* mum decides she wants a spot of tea and takes one of these cups out of the cabinet and discovers that not only am I too old to ever bear her grandchildren, but I'm also a horrible housekeeper? What if that happens?"

"Caro, love." His green eyes danced with amusement that irritated her as he placed his hands on her shoulders and kissed her forehead. "You've seriously gone around the bend."

"Why? Because I want my house to be clean when your mother gets here?"

"The house *is* clean. It's so clean my nose is burning from the smell of bleach and ammonia. If you keep this up, we'll need respirators to continue living here."

She reached for another plate to dust. "Look at this dirt! It's not clean enough."

He took the plate from her and put it on the table. "It is more than clean enough."

"It isn't. You're not a woman. You can't possibly understand this." She reached around him for the plate he'd taken from her. It hadn't been dusted yet. "I'm running out of time, so if you'd please get out of my way, I need to finish this."

"I'm not getting out of your way, and this *is* finished. I can't bear to see you doing this to yourself all because my mum is coming to visit. I never would've let you talk me into inviting her if I thought you were going to go crazy cleaning and cooking."

"I'm not going *crazy*." Carolina was starting to get mad with him. "I'm doing what needs to be done."

"You're going crazy."

"No, I'm not!"

"Yes, you are! And it's going to stop right now."

"You can't tell me—" Before she could begin to gauge his intentions, he had her tossed over his shoulder and was moving through the house as she beat on his back. "Put me down! Damn it, Seamus! This is not funny!"

The crack of his hand on her backside made her see red. Did he seriously just *spank* her? Oh, he was so going to pay for that! As soon as she was standing upright again, she was going to punch his lights out. With standing upright in mind, she began to fight against his tight hold, which only got tighter. And then he spanked her other cheek. "Settle down before I drop you."

"Are you serious? You want me to *settle down?*" If he was going to play dirty, she could, too. Since she was in perfect position, she shoved her hand into his khaki shorts and pulled hard on his underwear.

He grunted out a laugh that turned to a groan when she used her other hand and pulled even harder. "If you hurt my boys, I won't be much good to ya, love."

"If you don't put me down *right now*, your boys are never going to see my girls again."

"Now don't make idle threats. Your girls *love* my boys."

"Not anymore they don't."

"I bet the boys can change the girls' mind right quick."

"Not happening. Will you please put me down? All the blood is rushing to my head, and I'm going to throw up on you."

"Since you were very nice and said please, I'll put you down."

As quickly as he'd scooped her up, he put her down and held her arms until she got her balance. The second her head stopped spinning, she punched him in the belly as hard as she could. Her fist bounced off his rock-hard abs, and she howled in pain.

"Now, love," he said in the condescending tone that had made her want to punch him in the first place, "that wasn't very smart." He took her hand and kissed her stinging knuckles.

"You make me so damned mad. Who do you think you are—"

He kissed her hard and fast, giving no quarter until the starch left her spine. "I'm the man who loves you and who refuses to watch you do this to yourself."

"You don't *understand*." All at once, she noticed he'd carried her to the woods at the far end of her property. "What are we doing here?"

With his hands on her shoulders, he turned her to face a campsite, complete with a tent and a stack of wood encircled by stones. "This is what we're doing here."

"We're camping? Why?"

"I had to get you out of that house and away from your cleaning products. Desperate times call for desperate measures."

"But your mother is coming *tomorrow!* I have so much left to do!"

"If it's not done, it's not getting done. For the next fourteen nights, we'll have a guest underfoot. Tonight," he said, sliding his arms around her, "is all ours."

She pushed on his chest, trying in vain to break free of his tight hold. "I don't have time for this! You don't get it—"

Once again, his lips came down hard on hers, possessing her the way only he could with sensual strokes of his tongue that made her forget all about why she was so annoyed with him.

Then she remembered that he'd spanked her—twice—and she pushed harder on his chest. "You're not getting off that easily."

He nuzzled her neck. "I'll get you off, too, love. Don't worry."

"*Seamus!* You're not funny!"

"Yes, I am, and you're all done cleaning and cooking and preparing. Whatever will be will be. She's just a person like you and me."

"She's your *mother*."

"I'm painfully aware of that, and if you'll recall, I told you it was a bad idea to invite her here, because I was afraid of this very thing."

"What very thing?"

"That you'd turn into someone I don't even recognize getting ready for her."

"So you don't love me anymore? Good, then we can call off this whole thing and—"

He kissed her again, backing her up to the tent and pushing her through the flaps without missing a beat with his lips or tongue. Somehow she ended up on her back, lying on a cushy air mattress that easily absorbed the weight of both of them as he came down on top of her, still kissing her.

"Don't ever, ever, *ever* say I don't love you anymore," he said, punctuating the words with more kisses. "Ever, *ever.*"

"You spanked me."

"And I quite liked it. Let's see if you liked it, too." He reached under her skirt, pushed her panties aside and pressed his fingers into her dampness. "Mmm, looks like you weren't as put out as you pretended to be."

"I was too put out, and if you do that again, I'll never put out again." As she spoke, she let her legs fall open, encouraging his gentle caress.

He slid his other hand under her to cup her buttock. "I may have to take my chances, because I rather liked spanking you."

"*Seamus!* You can't just do this stuff and think you're going to get away with it."

"Seems to me," he said, pressing his fingers into her and finding the spot deep inside that made her go wild every time, "I've already gotten away with it."

She pulled his hair—hard—and the bastard only laughed as he drove her to a quick, powerful orgasm.

"I love you more than life itself, Carolina. That's what my mum is going to see when she gets here. She's not going to notice the dust or all the so-called imperfections. She's only going to see the love."

Carolina's brain was scrambled from the orgasm and the press of his fingers between her legs. "You don't think she'll notice that I'm old enough to be your mother?"

"Nah. She's going to take one look at you and know exactly why I love you."

"Sure, she is."

"Am I going to have to spank you again, love?"

"You might have to, because I'm not at all convinced that everything is going to be just fine and dandy the way you are."

He squeezed her cheek with his big, work-calloused hand. "If I see you acting all nutty while she's here, I'll bring you out here and spank your bottom until it's pink and rosy, and then I'll fu—"

"*Seamus!*"

He shook with silent laughter. "You've been warned, love."

Janey and Joe took advantage of his full day off to invite her parents to lunch for a conversation they'd been putting off for quite some time. She'd yet to speak directly to either of them about her plans to take a year off from veterinary school to devote to motherhood. It had been weighing on her, so Joe had encouraged her to invite them over to clear the air.

Her parents had been so excited to see her pursuing her long-delayed dream of attending veterinary school and had even insisted on footing the bill for tuition. Janey felt like a wimp for avoiding the subject with them in the weeks since she'd decided to take a year off to spend at home on Gansett with the baby.

The idea of trekking back to Ohio for another year of school a week after giving birth had depressed her to the point that others began to notice. When Joe finally urged her to share what was on her mind, she'd confessed to being tormented over the thought of trying to balance school and motherhood. All she wanted, she told her husband, was to spend this time with him and their child, surrounded by their family and friends on the island.

As always, Joe had been amazing about the entire thing and had suggested they take a year off from Ohio State. He'd gone to extraordinary lengths to make it possible for her to attend vet school, even going so far as to hire Seamus to run the Gansett Island Ferry Company in his absence. Janey hadn't wanted his efforts to be wasted, but she also didn't want to spend long days away from her baby and even longer nights studying.

Joe came out to the sun porch, looking hot in a light blue polo shirt and plaid shorts that she'd had to talk him into wearing after she bought them for him. He looked so sexy that Janey licked her lips as she took a good long look at him.

"What? Do I have something on my face or something?"

She shook her head. "I like to look at you. Since when is that a crime?"

"Since you can't deliver on those heated looks as often as you used to."

Janey feigned offense. "I've been delivering just fine despite the ungainliness." She'd never been so hot for sex as she had since she'd been pregnant. Fortunately, her adorable husband was always happy to comply.

"Don't get me going when your parents are due any minute."

"All I did was look at you."

"Hello, that's all it takes." He sat next to her on the chaise and reached for her hand. "You okay about this?"

"I'll feel better once we talk to them about it. I've felt like such a baby for avoiding them on this subject, even though I'm sure they've heard the news from one of my big-mouthed brothers or their significant others."

"Maybe not," Joe said. "The boys know that vet school is a sensitive subject between you and your parents. They might've kept their mouths shut for once."

"Wouldn't that be a miracle?"

"Truly." With his free hand, he caressed her face and then kissed her. "This is *our* life, honey. We're in charge. I know you love your parents. Hell, I love them, too. But don't feel bad about your decision, no matter what they might have to say about it."

"I'll try not to. Thank you again for understanding."

"I love you. I want you to be happy. No matter what it takes. And your folks will be thrilled that you and the baby will be here this year."

At times like this, Janey was secretly grateful to David for cheating on her. If she'd married him, their marriage wouldn't be anything like the one she had with Joe. She had no doubt whatsoever that Joe was the man she was meant to be with. "And you, too."

He rested a hand on her swollen belly. "I'm a distant third to you two."

"You're first with me," she said, curling her hand around his neck and bringing him in for another kiss.

"For two more months anyway."

"Forever."

"Don't make promises you can't keep, honey. I fully expect you to fall madly in love with this little person when he or she arrives."

"I will, but I'll still be madly in love with my baby's daddy, too."

He closed his eyes and rested his forehead against hers. "I never get tired of hearing you say that. I'm so glad you called me the night everything happened with David. I'm grateful every day of my life for that phone call."

The doorbell rang, and he let out a deep, ragged sigh before he released her to get up.

"Joe?"

"What, hon?"

"I'm grateful every single day that you answered the phone that night."

Giving her a warm smile, he went to answer the door with the dogs hot on his heels.

"Where's my baby girl?"

Her dad's booming voice made Janey smile. "Back here, Dad."

Big Mac came strolling onto the sun porch, wearing a faded McCarthy's Gansett Island Marina T-shirt with shorts, deck shoes and his trademark Ray Bans nestled in his gray hair. He already had a dark tan from the hours he spent on the docks every day. "There she is," he said, bending to kiss Janey. "How's my grandbaby today?"

"Busy. Want to feel?"

"Um, no, I don't think so."

"Oh, come on." Janey placed his hand over her rolling belly. "Don't be silly."

"I'm still trying to get my head around the fact that you're pregnant in the first place," he said with a scowl for Joe.

"Don't look at me," Joe said, hands up in defense.

"Who should I look at?"

"Daddy, knock it off." The baby gave a good swift kick that made her dad smile.

"Well, would ya look at that? He's a kicker."

"He might be a she."

"Either is fine with me, as long as everyone is healthy."

"Here I am," Linda said as she came in. "Hope it's okay that I let myself in."

"Of course it is, Mom."

"Lin, come get a feel of this," Big Mac said, drawing his wife into their little circle to feel the baby doing its daily gymnastics.

"Wow," Linda said. "I can't wait to meet him or her."

"Neither can we," Janey said.

"How about some lunch?" Joe said.

"I won't say no to that," Big Mac said. "I'm starving."

"Did Stephanie only let you have three donuts this morning?" Linda asked her husband.

"She cut me off at four," he said with a pout that made his wife and daughter laugh.

"Good thing Grant is marrying her," Janey said. "We need to keep her in the family to manage his cholesterol."

"Absolutely," Linda agreed.

Joe delivered a tray of sandwiches he'd made earlier and took drink orders as Janey sent him a grateful smile.

"You're really feeling all right?" Linda asked as they enjoyed the sandwiches.

"For the most part. My blood pressure was up a tiny bit, so Victoria wants me to take it as easy as possible."

"You're not on bed rest, are you?"

"Not officially. We're keeping an eye on it, so don't worry. Catch me up on everything that's going on. I feel so out of the loop."

"Let's see," Linda said. "Grant is almost done with the screenplay, Evan is recording at the studio for the first time this week, and Adam is officially moving into your old house with Abby."

"Oh, good," Janey said. "I'm so glad they're making a go of it. I love them together."

"I do, too, now that Grant knows about it and doesn't seem to mind."

"Why would he care when he's crazy in love with Stephanie?" Big Mac asked.

"People are funny about their exes," Linda said. "Even when they're happy with someone else. I'm thankful there was no trouble between them when Adam fell for Abby, and I'm thrilled to have everyone back at home again."

"I owe Abby and just about everyone else in my life a phone call," Janey said. "Did Seamus's mother get here yet?"

"She's due in later today," Linda said.

"I'd love to be a fly on the wall over there tonight," Janey said.

"Not me," Joe said to laughter from the others.

"Can't say I blame you there, son," Big Mac said.

Joe glanced at Janey and nodded for her to get on with what she wanted to talk to her parents about.

"So there was a reason I wanted to see you guys today," Janey said tentatively.

"I knew it!" Linda said. "There is something wrong with the baby, and you didn't want to tell us."

"Honestly, Mother, there's nothing wrong! You're worse than my husband!"

"I'm in the room," Joe said.

Janey gave him a sweet smile. "I want to talk to you about school."

"What about it?" Big Mac asked, his brows narrowing. He was always touchy on the subject of veterinary school, because no one wanted to see her become a vet more than he did. His question indicated that her brothers had, in fact, kept her news to themselves.

"I've decided to take this next year off from school," Janey said, her stomach twisting with nerves as she said the words.

"Oh, thank goodness!" Linda said.

"Excuse me?" Janey asked, shocked by her mother's reaction.

"We've been just beside ourselves at the thought of the two of you and the baby so far from home, especially during the first year of the baby's life," Linda said.

Janey looked at Joe, who seemed as surprised as she was. "You have? Why didn't you say something?"

"What could we say, honey?" Big Mac asked. "You're off pursuing a dream we've wanted for you for so long. We'd never stand in the way of that, the way David did all those years ago."

Her parents had never gotten over David discouraging her from going to veterinary school while he attended medical school so they wouldn't be overly burdened with debt afterward. Her dad had been particularly incensed about it, so to hear him say now that he was thrilled she was staying home was surprising.

"I've thought a lot about that," Janey said, choosing her words carefully. "David wasn't entirely to blame. If I'd wanted it badly enough, I would've moved mountains to make it happen. It's true he discouraged me, but I was easily discouraged."

"Still," Big Mac said. "It wasn't his finest hour."

"Let's not talk about him," Linda said. "I have another question."

"Which is?"

"Do you think you'll go back to school in a year?"

With the eyes of the three most important people in her life on her, Janey found that she couldn't lie—not to herself and certainly not to them. "I don't think so."

"What?" Joe said. "You said one year, and then you'd finish."

Dismayed by his reaction, Janey said, "I know. I did say that, and I felt that way at the time, but the more I think about it, the more I want this." She gestured to the airy sun porch and the house. "I want to be here, with my family. I want my baby to grow up with his or her cousins and grandparents and all the people who love him or her nearby, not a thousand miles away." Janey's throat tightened with emotion. "You all have sacrificed so much to help me make my dream come true, but my dream has changed. Dad, I'll never forget the way you insisted on paying my tuition, even though you certainly didn't have to."

"Aww, shucks, honey, I was happy to do that."

"And Joe, you moved heaven and earth to make it possible for me to go and to come with me. I know you probably don't understand—"

He got up and moved to sit with her on the chaise, putting his arm around her. "I do understand. How could I not? No matter where we go in the world, this is our home. It's where we belong."

Janey rested her head on his chest. "All I keep thinking about is that we've got two years invested there, not to mention the tuition money."

"Don't give that another thought," Big Mac said. "Things change. I get it."

Janey released a deep sigh as an overpowering sense of relief swept through her, making her teary eyed. "Damned hormones," she said, brushing away the tears. "I want to be with my baby. I can't do everything. I'm only just now realizing that."

"Welcome to motherhood," Linda said. "The sacrifices never end, but they're the best sacrifices you'll ever make. Nothing matters more than your children."

"It's your fault, you know," Janey said with a watery smile. "You set such a high standard that I'll never be able to live up to it."

"Oh shush. You're going to be a wonderful mother."

"Thank you."

"Do you feel better?" Joe asked.

"Much."

"You know you still have the right to change your mind when you're not pregnant and hormonal."

"Good to know, but I don't think I'll change my mind. Now I have to find a way to tell Doc that he's going to have to turn his practice over to someone else."

"He'll understand, honey." Big Mac cleared his throat loudly and dramatically. "*So*, I happen to have a bit of gossip you all *might* be interested in."

"Is that right?" Linda said acerbically. "Do you need an engraved invitation to share?"

"No, I do not."

"Guys have no clue how to gossip properly," Linda said to her daughter.

"I think Daddy might be the exception to that rule," Janey said, making the others laugh.

"Thank you, Princess," Big Mac said. "I might've talked to Uncle Frank this morning, and he might've asked if it's okay if he comes back for the weekend, and he might've also asked if Betsy is still staying with us."

"Mac!" Linda said. "That's huge! Why didn't you say something?"

"I am saying something."

"How's Betsy doing?" Joe asked of the woman who'd been staying with them for a couple of weeks now. Her son Steve had been killed in the boating accident that had nearly claimed the lives of Mac, Evan and Grant and left Grant's friend Dan Torrington badly injured.

"She seems a little better every day," Linda said.

"It's nice of you guys to have her at the house," Janey said.

"We love having her around," Linda said. "She's no trouble at all and so thankful for the change of scenery. Lord knows we've got plenty of empty bedrooms these days."

"So Uncle Frank and Betsy, huh?" Janey said, intrigued by the possibilities.

"Wouldn't that be something?" Big Mac said. "I've been hoping he'd find someone new since Joann died all those years ago, but he's never even had a serious relationship that I know of."

"I don't know about you guys," Janey said, "but I suddenly can't wait for this weekend."

CHAPTER 5

Daisy couldn't recall a day that went by as slowly as Tuesday did. Every time she glanced at the clock, it seemed only a few minutes had passed. Even though she was busy at the hotel, the day still dragged on endlessly. While she couldn't wait to see David later, she was anxious about the conversation they planned to have.

Worries about what he might say and how she would feel about it weighed on her as she walked home from the hotel. It stayed with her in the shower and as she dried her hair. Standing before her closet pondering her limited options, she could think of little else but how this night might unfold.

She so wanted him to be different from the men she'd known before. There was something about him that appealed to her on the most basic level. It went beyond his dark good looks. She sensed the same kind of loneliness in him that she'd known herself.

During the evenings they'd spent together, she'd found out what it might be like to have a normal relationship for once, one in which she didn't have to constantly be on guard against emotional or physical abuse. She'd made bad choices in the past. They were her choices, and she owned them, but she didn't want to make bad choices anymore. She'd promised herself after the mess with Truck that she'd be more wise and discerning about who she spent time with in the future.

David had seemed like a wise choice, and she hoped she hadn't been wrong about that.

In the far back corner of her closet, she found a dress she'd forgotten she had. It was basic black with a cowl neckline, a cinched waist and a skirt that came to just above the knee. She'd had it forever but hadn't worn it in ages—mostly because she hadn't had an occasion where it might be appropriate.

Feeling uncertain, she hung it on the outside of her closet and took a picture with her phone that she sent to Maddie.

Is this too much for dinner at Domenic's?

While she waited to hear back from Maddie, Daisy took the dress into the kitchen to iron it on the counter.

Not at all, Maddie replied. *It's perfect.*

I'm nervous. We're going to talk before dinner, and I'm afraid of what he'll say.

It would matter to me that he's telling you himself and not letting you hear it through the grapevine.

I know… Still. I like him. A lot.

Hear him out and then decide how you feel. You don't have to decide anything right away.

That's true. Thanks for the consult.

Any time. Hope you have a good time!

Thanks! I'll report in tomorrow morning.

I'll be waiting. And Daisy…it's okay to be a little afraid of falling for someone new after what you've been through. Just don't be too afraid to take a chance.

I'll try… Thanks. Xoxo

The pep talk from Maddie helped, and Daisy tried to stay focused on all the positives of her relationship with David as she got dressed and found some earrings and a bracelet to wear with the dress. She pulled on black, high-heeled sandals and then checked the ensemble in the mirror with a critical eye.

"I guess you'll do," she said as she looked over her shoulder at the back of the dress. She'd lost weight she couldn't afford to lose since the attack and was more waifish than ever thanks to Truck's punch to her jaw that had made it difficult to eat for weeks.

Remembering that awful night, Daisy told herself that whatever David had to say it couldn't possibly be worse than what she'd already been through—and survived. Not just with Truck, but with a string of men who liked to be in control of the women in their lives and hadn't hesitated to exert some muscle to bend her to their will.

No matter what David might've done in the past, he would never harm her physically. That much she already knew for sure. No, with him she had to be far more vigilant about her emotional well-being than her physical safety. It hadn't taken long for him to become an important part of her daily life. The connection she felt with him wasn't one she'd experienced before, and that was enough, on its own, to strike a chord of fear in her.

"You're going to be strong, listen to what he has to say, and make the best decision for you," she told her reflection.

Satisfied with her self-lecture, she went downstairs and realized it wasn't even six o'clock. She had more than half an hour to kill before David would arrive, so she sat down to flip through a magazine and enjoy a glass of lemonade while she waited.

A few minutes later, a disturbance outside her door had her rushing over to peek out the window to see if David had arrived early. At the thought of seeing him, her heart beat faster with excitement and adrenaline. She was surprised to find an older woman sitting in one of the rockers on her porch.

"What the heck?" Mindful of safety, especially lately, she opened the door slowly to get a better look.

The woman's hair was standing on end as if it hadn't been brushed in days. She wore a sweatshirt with flannel pajama pants, and her feet were bare and caked with dirt. Something was very wrong here, Daisy thought as she stepped outside the door. "May I help you?" she asked softly, trying not to startle the woman.

"No."

"Are you lost?"

"I don't know."

Daisy glanced down at the woman's feet, which were cut and bruised, and wondered how far she had walked before landing on the porch.

"I'm Daisy. What's your name?"

"Marion." She had blue eyes that looked past Daisy vacantly. Between that and the cuts on her feet, Daisy was concerned that the woman was in some sort of danger.

"Is there someone I could call for you, Marion?"

"My husband is coming for me. His name is George Martinez. He'll be here soon."

"Could I offer you a drink while you wait?"

"Some water would be nice."

"I'll be right back with it." Inside, she debated about what she should do and finally decided to call Blaine Taylor. After Truck attacked her, Blaine had programmed his cell phone number into Daisy's phone in case she ever needed help.

"Hi, Daisy," Blaine said when he answered. "Everything okay?"

"Hi, there. Yes, I'm fine, but an older woman named Marion is sitting on my porch."

"Marion Martinez?"

Through the curtain, Daisy made sure that Marion didn't leave. "Yes, that's her. She seems a bit disoriented, and her feet are cut. It looks like she might've walked quite a distance on bare feet."

"Thank goodness you found her. Her sons are going crazy looking for her. Would you mind sitting with her until I can get over there?"

"Not at all. She said her husband George was coming to pick her up."

"George Martinez has been dead for ten years."

"Oh," Daisy said, saddened for Marion.

"I'll be right there."

Daisy ended the call and took a glass of ice water outside to Marion, who accepted it gratefully.

"You look very pretty," Marion said.

"Do you think so? I have a date tonight."

Marion's smile was so sweet and innocent. "I hope he's a nice boy."

"I think he is."

"I have two boys—Alex and Paul. You should meet them. They're very handsome, but they might be a little young for you. Alex is in tenth grade and Paul is a senior this year. The kids call them A.M. and P.M.," Marion added with a smile. "George and I are very proud of them."

In her mid- to late-sixties by Daisy's guess, Marion seemed too old to have children that young. "I'm sure you must be."

"What's your young man's name?"

"David."

"I have a brother named David. That's a nice name."

"I think so, too."

"Are you going to marry your David?"

Daisy laughed nervously. "We're not talking about marriage yet."

"My George and I knew right away that we'd get married. After the first time we went out, I told my mother he would be my husband."

"That's very sweet. You're lucky that you knew right away."

"We were lucky." She looked directly at Daisy for the first time. "I think you know right away if a person is the one for you. At least I did. I can't imagine what's keeping my George. He's always right on time."

Daisy patted Marion's hand, her heart breaking for Marion's loss. "I'm sure he'll be here soon."

"It's very kind of you to keep me company. What did you say your name is?"

"I'm Daisy."

"A very pretty name."

Daisy thought it a silly name that worked well for a child but not so great for an adult. But her mother was a whimsical sort who didn't think things through far enough to contemplate an adult named Daisy trying to get people to take her seriously.

Her thoughts were interrupted when Blaine pulled up to the curb in his police-issued SUV. Tall, handsome and intense, Blaine was another of Daisy's heroes after Truck's attack. His timely arrival had saved her life, and she'd always be grateful to him.

Marion eyed him suspiciously. "Who's that?"

"Hi there, Mrs. Martinez. I'm Blaine Taylor. Remember me?"

"I don't know you." To Daisy, she said, "I don't know him."

Daisy took her hand. "He's the chief of police, and he's here to help you."

"I don't need his help. My George is coming to pick me up."

"I spoke with Paul and Alex," Blaine said, his sharp eyes taking in her disheveled appearance and injured feet. "They asked me to give you a ride to the clinic to have your feet looked at."

"My feet are fine."

"They're bleeding, honey," Daisy said softly.

Seeming surprised to hear her feet were cut, Marion looked down at them. "How did that happen? Where are my shoes? Did someone tell George to bring my shoes?"

"We'll let him know," Blaine said. "The boys are going to meet us at the clinic. You don't want to keep them waiting, do you?"

Marion glanced nervously at Daisy. "Should I go with him?"

"I really think you should. Your sons are worried about you, and they're waiting for you."

Marion clamped down on Daisy's hand. "Will you come with me? Please?"

Daisy looked at Blaine, who nodded. She tried not to think about the fact that David was due anytime. "Of course. Let me get my purse, and I'll be right back, okay?"

Marion didn't seem to want to let go of Daisy's hand, but she finally loosened her grip.

Daisy went inside, grabbed her purse and a sweater as well as a pair of flip-flops for Marion to wear to the clinic. She started a text to David and found a message from him.

Getting off the boat but got called into the clinic to see a patient. Will be a little late, but I'll be there.

She replied, *I'll meet you at the clinic.*

Back on the porch, Marion was looking down at the porch, studiously ignoring Blaine.

"Ready, Marion?" Daisy asked.

"Ready for what?"

Daisy's heart broke for the poor woman. "We're going to go with Chief Taylor to meet your sons, Alex and Paul."

"But George is coming. We can't go until George gets here."

Blaine bent to rest his hands on his knees. "Paul is waiting for you, and he's really upset because he couldn't find you. We don't want to keep him waiting, do we?"

It took some more cajoling, but they finally were able to convince Marion to accept the borrowed sandals from Daisy and shuffle down the sidewalk to the backseat of Blaine's SUV. Daisy climbed in next to her and assisted Marion with the seat belt.

On the short drive to the clinic, Marion asked at least twenty times where George was and how he'd find her now that she'd left the house.

"Paul and Alex will help him find you," Daisy said each time. She met Blaine's grateful gaze in the rearview mirror and shared a sad smile with him.

When they pulled up to the emergency entrance to the clinic, two dark-haired young men ran up to the car. They had brown eyes and skin so tanned it might've been August rather than June, and both were in their thirties by Daisy's guess.

"Mom! You scared us! Where did you go?"

"Now, Paul, I just went for a walk. There's nothing to get worked up about."

Alex hung back, tension coming off him in palpable waves.

David appeared at the door to the SUV. His eyes met hers, surprise registering in his expression. He wore a white polo that offset his light tan, with khaki pants. His hair fell across his brow, making Daisy want to brush it back for him.

"Hi, Marion," he said. "How are you?"

"Who are you?"

"I'm Doctor Lawrence. Remember when I came to see you at your home?"

Of course he'd been to see her at home, Daisy thought, because that's the kind of doctor he was. She was so damned happy to see him.

"I don't know you."

"It's okay, Mom," Paul said. "Dr. David needs to look at your feet, and then we can go home for dinner."

"Will Daddy be there when we get home?" she asked, a hopeful glimmer in her eye.

"No, Mom," Alex said. "Dad died. Remember?"

Marion's face crumpled, and she let out an anguished wail. "Why would you say such an awful thing? He's not dead! He's at work! He works hard for all of us. Do you think it's easy running your own business? Until you've tried it, you have no right to speak poorly of him."

Alex turned and walked toward the clinic door, hands in pockets, shoulders hunched.

Daisy's heart broke for the entire family.

"He wasn't speaking poorly of him," Paul said in defense of his brother. "The sooner we let Dr. David check you out, the sooner we can get home."

"Yes, because Daddy is there waiting for me." To Daisy, she said, "My George is waiting for me."

"I know," Daisy said.

"This is my friend, Daisy," she said, sounding amazingly lucid again. "My son Paul."

"Nice to meet you," Paul said. "Thank you for helping Mom."

"I was happy to do it. She's very nice."

Marion beamed at her as David and Paul helped her out of the SUV and into the wheelchair David had brought outside. "Daisy! Where's Daisy?"

"I'm here, Marion."

"I want you to stay with me."

Daisy took the older woman's outstretched hand. "I'd be happy to."

"Have you met my sons? Aren't they handsome? Do you have a boyfriend?"

Daisy met David's gaze and saw amusement mixed with sadness in his expression. He mouthed the word yes to her, which made her heart flutter.

"Yes, I do," Daisy said with a small, private smile for David as he wheeled Marion inside to an exam room.

"That's too bad. I hope he's a nice boy."

She looked at David again. "He's a very nice boy."

"Paul, don't you think Daisy is pretty?"

"Very pretty, Mom," he said, sounding as embarrassed as Daisy felt.

"If things don't work out with your boyfriend, I'll fix you up with my Paul. He's very handsome."

"Mom…"

"What? You are handsome. Isn't he handsome, Daisy?"

"Yes, he is, Marion," Daisy said, trying not to laugh at the absurdity of it all.

Paul grimaced and said, "Sorry" under his breath.

"Alex is handsome, too, but he can be grumpy sometimes."

"Mom… Stop."

"What? Isn't it the truth?"

Fortunately, Victoria, the nurse practitioner who'd been so nice to Daisy after the attack, came into the exam room and offered to help Marion undress.

"Why do I have to take my clothes off? I'm not taking my clothes off!"

"I need to examine you to make sure you aren't injured anywhere else," David said gently. "It'll only take a few minutes."

"It's okay, Marion," Victoria said. "We'll help you."

"I'll wait outside," Daisy said.

"Me, too," Paul added.

Over Marion's protests, they left the exam room and went to the waiting area, where Alex was pacing. Both brothers wore dirty clothes and sturdy boots. Daisy wondered what they did for work.

"How is she?" Alex asked.

Paul combed his fingers through his hair repeatedly. "Confused, annoyed. The usual."

"We have to do something," Alex said. "We can't go on this way."

"I know." To Daisy, Paul said, "How did you end up with her?"

"I found her on my porch, sitting in one of my rockers."

"Where do you live?"

"In town," Daisy said. "On Harbor Road."

"How in the hell did she get all the way over there?" Alex asked.

"Judging by the condition of her bare feet," Daisy said, "she walked."

"God," Alex said with a sigh. "She could've been hit by a car or a million other things." He shook his head and blew out a deep breath. "I can't do this anymore. I just can't do it." His voice broke on the last word, and he rushed out the door to the parking lot.

Paul dropped into a chair, exhaustion clinging to him.

Daisy didn't know what she should do while she waited for David. She knew he probably wouldn't be opposed to her waiting in his office, but she couldn't bring herself to leave Paul sitting there alone and dejected, so she took a seat across from him. "I'm sorry you're going through such a rough time."

"Thanks. It's unlike anything I've ever dealt with, that's for sure. My brother and I, we're trying to run the business and take care of her... It's... It's a lot."

"What do you do for work?"

"We own a landscaping company. Martinez Lawn and Garden."

"Oh sure. I see your trucks around. You guys take care of the McCarthys' hotel. I work there."

He nodded in agreement. "Up until a year ago, my mom was running everything. Hard to believe, right? She's declined so rapidly." Looking directly at her, he said, "I'm sorry you got dragged into this. Looks like you were going somewhere."

"I was going to dinner with David Lawrence, so we'll go later after we know your mom is okay."

"I don't know what we would've done without him. He's been so amazing to Mom and a huge help to us."

"He's very good at what he does."

"Yes."

"If there's anything I can do to help you and your brother, I hope you'll call me. If you need someone to sit with her, I'd be happy to help. I could give you my number."

"That's very nice of you. Thank you."

They exchanged numbers, programming them directly into cell phones.

Alex came back in, seeming more in control of his emotions. "Sorry to storm out like that."

Paul waved his hand. "No worries."

"Any word?"

"Not yet."

"What're we going to do, Paul?"

"I don't know."

Daisy suddenly felt like she was intruding on an intensely private moment between the brothers. "I'll wait for David in his office. Please call me if I can help with your mom."

"We will," Paul said. "Thanks again for all you did for her."

"I enjoyed being with her." She left them and went through the double doors that led to the offices, hoping David wouldn't mind if she waited for him there. Mindful of his privacy and that of his patients, she steered clear of his desk and sat on the small sofa, drawing her legs up under her.

Spending time with Marion made Daisy wonder about her own mother for the first time in years. She'd been out of touch with her family for a long time now, long enough that she rarely thought of them anymore. However, she would never forget the way her parents had turned their back on her because she'd wanted to marry a man they didn't approve of. She'd been eighteen and in love for the first time in her life.

Thinking about that awful spring, now ten years ago, brought back feelings and memories she'd just as soon not relive. So she decided to think instead about David and the way his eyes had taken in the dress she'd worn for him and how he'd encouraged her to tell Marion she had a boyfriend.

When was the last time she'd had a "boyfriend"? With that question putting a smile on her face, Daisy tipped her head back against the sofa and closed her eyes.

David found her there an hour later, a smile clinging to her sweet lips. His first glimpse of her in the clingy black dress had wowed him after two days of thinking about her. He didn't know if he should wake her or let her sleep. She was still getting over serious injuries and was working far too hard for his liking while she recovered.

"Whatcha staring at?" Victoria asked from behind him.

David turned to her. "Nothing."

She looked around his shoulder and gave him a knowing smile. "Oh, I see. Your special friend is waiting for you."

David stepped out of the office and closed the door. "Thanks for your help with Marion."

"She's going downhill fast."

David sighed as he nodded. "Alex and Paul are in a tough spot, living on an island without a residential facility for her, and tied to the place because of their business. They're going to need to make some tough decisions soon. They don't want to put her in a facility on the mainland and then never get to see her because they're here and she's there."

"Sometimes island life sucks."

"Yes, it does. Anything else happen while I was gone?"

Victoria brought him up to speed on the status of several patients. "I should also mention that Janey Cantrell had her thirty-two-week visit, and her BP was slightly elevated. I'm going to bring her back weekly going forward to keep an eye on it."

David hated the twinge of concern that struck him in the vicinity of his heart when he heard that news. Janey wasn't his concern any longer, and he needed to remember that. "Good plan."

"Even though you asked me to keep you out of that one as much as I can, you need to be aware. Just in case."

"I know. Thanks for the update."

"So what's up with your special friend?"

"Nothing. She came in with Marion."

"She's all dressed up."

"So?"

"So where ya taking her?"

"None of your business."

"So you *are* taking her somewhere." She nudged him with her elbow. "Come on. Be a pal. I'm living vicariously through you these days."

"You need to get out more."

"Ain't that the truth? So you're not going to give me *anything*?"

"Nope. Go away. Come back tomorrow."

"Yeah, yeah, yeah. See you then."

After Victoria walked down the long hallway and through the double doors, David went into his office and closed the door. He sat next to Daisy, watching her sleep for a minute before he took a big chance and leaned in to kiss her awake.

Her eyes opened slowly and brightened at the sight of him. "Hey. How's Marion?"

"Fine, other than her feet, which will be sore for a few days."

"That's a relief."

"I saw Blaine when he was leaving, and he said you were really great with her. Thanks for that."

"She's a sweet lady. Her confusion and disorientation are so sad."

He nodded in agreement but didn't want to talk about Marion anymore. He wanted to talk about her, about them. For days now, he'd been rehearsing what he would say to her the next time they were together, but now that the moment was upon him, words escaped him.

She saved him by sliding her fingers lightly over his face. "I missed you."

He turned his face into her hand, kissing her palm. "I missed you, too."

"Kinda funny, huh?"

"What is?"

"That I missed you so much when I've only known you for a few weeks."

"It's not funny. It's sweet. It's nice to be missed."

Their eyes met, and he couldn't look away. The inner calm and serenity he always experienced in her presence soothed him as it usually did. But underneath that now was a hum of awareness and desire that had him leaning in for another kiss, this one more lingering.

"Did I mention how beautiful you look?"

"I don't think you did," she said with a smile that lit up her eyes.

He liked it when she smiled. He liked that he'd given her reason to, until he remembered all the things he needed to tell her, which made him ache with regret over his past mistakes. "We need to talk."

"So talk. Tell me what you think I need to know, and we'll figure it out."

He ached even more at the thought of never again seeing the special glimmer in her eyes that she seemed to save for him. But continuing to put it off wouldn't change anything, so he took a deep breath and forced himself to meet her earnest gaze. "You know I was with Janey McCarthy for a long time. Thirteen years."

She nodded.

"We were engaged for the last two years we were together while I was finishing my residency in Boston." He looked away from her and out the window behind the sofa, focusing on the bushes that grew along the side of the building. He'd give everything he had, everything he'd ever have, not to have to say these next words. But knowing so much was riding on Daisy's reaction to hearing them, he made himself look at her as he said them. "I cheated on her."

She blinked once and then again. Otherwise her expression never changed. "Oh."

"I made a very bad mistake during a particularly stressful time in my life that I've regretted every day since." Over the hammering of his heart and the dryness in his mouth, he forced himself to continue. "The worst part… She… Janey… She came to Boston to surprise me on our anniversary and… and she saw me. In our bed with someone else."

Daisy closed her eyes and exhaled.

"I'll understand completely if, after hearing this, you decide that spending time with me isn't something you want to do." As he said the words, he wished with every fiber of his being that he was a better man, one who was worthy of her.

She kept her eyes closed and the fingers of her right hand pressed to her lips. He wondered if she was trying not to cry.

"Daisy?"

She opened eyes that were swimming with tears.

The tears slayed and shamed him.

She blinked them back and managed to contain them. "You said it was a particularly stressful time. Was that because of the residency?"

"Not entirely. I'd been feeling pretty crappy for a couple of months. I had a sore throat that wouldn't quit and fatigue unlike anything I'd ever experienced. But I was a resident. We were all tired, so I blew it off for months. When I finally couldn't ignore it anymore, I went to the doctor and was diagnosed with non-Hodgkins lymphoma. Do you know what that is?"

"Cancer?" she asked, her voice little more than a whisper.

He nodded. "It was the most shocking thing I'd ever heard. Here I was in my late twenties, healthy as a horse—or so I thought—and the doctor is telling me I have cancer. The news sent me straight off the cliff, to say the least."

"What did Janey say?"

"I didn't tell her."

"You didn't tell your fiancée that you had *cancer*?"

"Janey and I had been living apart for a really long time by then. After everything blew up, we were able to see with hindsight that our relationship had been over for a while, but neither of us had acknowledged it."

"Is that why you cheated on her?"

"God, no. I never would've hurt her like that intentionally. No matter what, I still loved her. All I can say in my own defense is that I wasn't at my best during the weeks that followed the diagnosis. I just kept thinking over and over and over again that I'd spent all these years in school and for what? I was going to die before I was thirty, and I hadn't even lived yet. I did stupid, stupid things. I got drunk, I blew off work, I didn't tell Janey about the diagnosis, which I absolutely should have, and I slept with one of my chemo nurses—in the bed Janey helped me buy for my apartment. I screwed up everything. By the time I emerged from the fog of shock, my engagement was over, my residency was in serious jeopardy and my nose was broken."

"How did that happen?"

"After Janey caught me with the nurse, I guess she went running to Joe because he was on the mainland when everyone else was here. I didn't know she'd come to Boston or that she'd seen me with someone else. I never even knew she was in the apartment that night." The thought of what she'd witnessed still had the power to sicken him even after all this time. "I tried to call her for days, and she didn't answer. I couldn't figure out what was going on. When I finally came here to track her down, everyone else already knew what'd happened. I got off the ferry and made the mistake of saying hello to Joe. He punched me in the face." David ran a finger over the bump in the bridge of his nose. "Busted my nose."

"I can't believe he just hit you like that!"

"It was the least of what I had coming, Daisy. Please don't turn this around on him. He was looking out for her, which I'd had my chance to do and blew it big-time. I don't blame him. It took me a long, long time to be able to say those words. I made everything worse by blaming everyone but myself for the mess my life had become for many months after it happened."

"The lymphoma... You had chemo?"

"Yes, and I'm in remission. That's why I was in Boston this week. I get checked every six months. Everything's fine." He stretched out his arm to display the bruises in the crook of his elbow from the endless rounds of blood work he'd been subjected to the last couple of days.

Daisy ran her fingers gently over the bruises on his arm. "That's a relief."

"Very much so."

"You didn't tell me why you went to Boston."

"I didn't want you to worry."

"I would've liked to have known."

"All of this, between us, it's so new. I wasn't sure we were ready for the lymphoma conversation."

"That's fair enough, I suppose."

"I've given you a lot to think about. I'll understand if it's too much for you and you decide you'd rather not see me anymore."

She didn't say anything for the longest time, during which David had no idea what she was thinking. "My father cheated on my mother when I was in high school," she finally said, sounding like she was a million miles away rather than right next to him on the small sofa. "It was absolutely devastating to our entire family, especially because he cheated with my friend's mother."

"Shit." David shook his head, furious with himself all over again for the mistakes he'd made and the people he'd hurt. Janey, in particular, who'd done absolutely nothing to deserve what she got from him. He rubbed his hand over the whiskers on his jaw, feeling powerless to rewrite the past.

"I want you to know I appreciate that you told me yourself when it would've been easier to let me hear it through the grapevine—and believe me, the grapevine tried to tell me."

"I'm sure there were plenty of people trying to warn you away from me," he said bitterly, even though he knew he deserved nothing less.

"I wouldn't let them warn me away from you, and I won't let you warn me away either."

"You won't?" David asked, floored.

She shook her head. "What you told me is upsetting. I won't deny that. I can't even think about how it must've been for Janey."

"I don't like to think about that either. I'm deeply ashamed of that. More than you can ever believe."

"What if…"

"What, Daisy? Just say it. Whatever you want to ask. It's fine."

"What if something difficult or stressful happens again? Is that how you're going to deal with it?"

"I can't promise you that I'll always do exactly the right thing, but I can promise I'd never be unfaithful to a partner again. It was an awful thing to do to her. I was extremely disrespectful of all the years we'd spent together, and I hurt her so badly. That's the part I most regret."

"It matters to me, greatly, that you're ashamed and regretful and contrite about it. My father was never any of those things. He was belligerent about his right to be happy, to hell with who got hurt in the process. He never once apologized to my mother or any of us for what he did. And then he had the nerve to turn his back on me when I chose to be with someone he didn't approve of. Ironic, huh?"

"I'd say so."

She looked at him with those big, doe-like eyes that had touched him from the first time Truck Henry's fists landed her in the clinic. "We all have things in our past we're not proud of, David. Even me." Her lashes fell over her cheeks as she seemed to summon the fortitude to say what was on her mind. "I was married, briefly, when I was eighteen. That was the first in a string of bad choices I made where men are concerned."

"Tell me," he said. "I want to know you, Daisy."

Although this was the last thing in the world she wanted to talk about—ever—he'd shared his past with her, so how could she do less than the same? "His name was Curt, and he was everything I wasn't—brave and fearless and brazen. A typical bad boy, right down to the motorcycle with no muffler, the piercings, the tattoos, the torn leather and the long greasy hair. I lost my mind, among other things, over him my senior year of high school. My parents were divorced by then, but they came together in their mutual hatred of him."

"Sounds like it got pretty rough for you."

"It was horrible. The more they hated him, the more I dug in. Looking back at it now, I'm not sure if I married him because of him or because of them and wanting to defy them."

"How did you end up married?"

"I refused to stop seeing him, so they kicked me out of the house where I grew up and told me I was on my own. I went to his place, if you could call a stall in his grandmother's garage a 'place.' We stayed there until his grandmother decided she'd had enough of us, too, and then we hit the road on his bike. We were dead broke, but somehow we managed to survive for an entire summer by picking up odd jobs here and there. It was ridiculous when I think about it now. One night we got drunk with some guys we worked with, and they got the big idea that we ought to get married. I was so bombed that I have no memory of the so-called ceremony, but he had the marriage license to prove it was done."

David noticed that her hands had begun to tremble, so he took hold of them.

"When I woke up the next morning, I couldn't remember anything, but I was really sore… Between my legs. And the guys, they were acting very strangely. Looking at me differently… I don't know for sure, but I think he let them take turns with me."

Shock reverberated through him. "Jesus, Daisy," he whispered.

She took a deep, trembling breath. "It didn't take long to realize I'd married the kind of guy who'd let other men take turns with his wife. To say the marriage went from bad to worse, quickly, is putting it mildly."

"Did you go home to your parents?"

She shook her head. "They wouldn't have me. They said I'd 'made my bed' and I was on my own."

"How old were you then?"

"Twenty—and pregnant."

"God. The baby…"

"I lost it at nineteen weeks. It took me a long time to recover physically and emotionally from that. I kicked around for a while living on the charity of friends until I got a job at a hotel in Boston, and finally got a place with some girls from work a year after I left him."

He put his arms around her and tucked her head in under his chin. "I'm so sorry you went through such an awful thing."

Her hand on his belly had his full attention, and he had to remind himself her nearness was about comfort, not sex.

"How did you end up out here?"

"I answered an ad in the paper. I was tired of working in the city and commuting. It sounded like paradise out here, and it is, for the most part. The off-season is difficult for those of us who are seasonal workers."

"I thought you were year-round at the hotel now."

"It's probationary for the summer. If I don't get the job full-time, I may have to move back to the mainland so I can work in the winter. My rent is going up, and I don't think I can afford it, unless I get the new job, and even then it'll be tough."

"You'll get the job."

"Thanks for the vote of confidence."

David tightened his hold on her and let his lips slide over the silky softness of her fragrant hair, filled with relief that she knew his secrets and hadn't run screaming from him. He wouldn't have blamed her if she had.

"What time is our reservation at Domenic's?" she asked.

"It was thirty minutes ago."

"What time is it?"

"Almost eight."

"How did it get so late?"

David's stomach growled, loudly, making them laugh.

"Sounds like someone needs to eat."

"Want to go see if they held our table for us?"

"I'd love to."

As they stood, he kept a hold on her hand and brought it to his lips. "Thank you."

"For what?"

"For not running away from me when I shared the worst of myself with you and for trusting me with your story."

She rested her hands on his shoulders and looked up at him. "I want to be able to trust you, David. That's going to matter to me."

"You can trust me. I swear you can. I hate myself for what I did to Janey. I never want to hurt someone like that again." He slipped his arms around her waist. "Especially you, when you've already had enough heartache for one lifetime."

"I won't disagree with you there." She went up on tiptoes to kiss him, her lips soft and sweet against his.

Desire streaked through his system like an out-of-control wildfire. He drew back from her so she wouldn't feel the evidence of how badly he wanted her before she was ready to know.

"Do you mind if we stop at my place before we go to dinner? I was planning to get changed before I picked you up."

"Not at all. I'd love to see where you live."

"It's nothing special," he said as he ushered her out of the office.

"Yes, it is. You live there."

David had no idea how he'd managed to get so lucky to find this lovely woman with the heart of gold, but now that he had, he was becoming more determined all the time to keep her in his life.

CHAPTER 6

Carolina stood next to Seamus at the ferry landing as the last boat of the day from the mainland cleared the breakwater and entered South Harbor. The sun was just beginning to set over the dunes, firing the water with vivid red, orange and yellow reflections and casting a glow over the town. At least the island was at its most lovely for Mrs. O'Grady's arrival, Carolina thought, touching her hair to make sure everything was where it belonged.

"Stop fidgeting, love. You look beautiful."

"I look old."

He put his arm around her, drew her in close and spoke directly into her ear. "I'm starting a new list of grievances I need to address with my hand to your bum the next time I have the chance."

Carolina shivered from the heat of his breath against her ear and the promise she heard in his tone. She was still recovering from the shock of how decadent their night in the tent had been.

"You do not look *old*. You, my love, look sexy and delicious and ripe and—"

She pressed her hand against his mouth. "Stop it. Right now."

Naturally, he sent his tongue to do his dirty work for him. "You stop it."

"You."

His eyes danced with mischief and amusement. "No, *you*." He stopped her from replying by kissing her senseless right there on the ferry landing where anyone could see them, including his mother, who was somewhere on the boat that was about to dock.

Oh my God! He drives me nuts! Never, in her wildest imagination, could Carolina have pictured a relationship quite like this one. Her quiet, satisfying—if somewhat lonely—life before him seemed like a hundred years ago when it had actually been less than a year. At times, she craved her former uncomplicated life. But would she want to go back to life before Seamus?

No, she thought, resigned to her fate with the big, burly, outrageous Irishman who made her heart beat fast and loved her with such abandon she could no longer picture life without him. She'd had absolutely no clue that a love like this even existed. Sure, she'd seen it portrayed in movies and in romance novels, but experiencing it firsthand had been an eye-opening journey.

At times she still felt guilty when she had to acknowledge that her marriage to Pete Cantrell had been nothing like her relationship with Seamus. While she'd loved Pete with her whole heart and soul and mourned deeply when she lost him so young, the quiet, respectful love they'd shared was very different from the fiery, all-consuming passion she had with Seamus.

"Why the deep sigh?" Seamus asked, tuned into her as always.

"No reason."

"I hate that you're so wound up over this visit, Caro. I wish I'd never let you talk me into it."

He sounded so uncharacteristically defeated that Carolina decided it was well beyond time to let it all go. She loved this man. She wanted a life with him, and if his mother didn't approve, well then, so be it.

"I'm sorry I've been such a wreck." She looked up at him, swayed as always by the intense way he gazed at her, telling her with every look and touch and smile that she was his entire world. "I love you. I love us. I want this, and if she doesn't approve, well then, I guess she doesn't approve."

Resting his hand on his heart, he shook his head as if he hadn't heard her correctly. "Don't tease me, love. If you don't mean it—"

"I mean it." She kissed him. "I love you. No matter how crazy I get, please don't ever doubt that."

He took a series of deep, dramatic breaths. "I might be hyperventilating."

Carolina elbowed him in the ribs. "Knock it off."

Laughing, Seamus kept an arm tight around her shoulders as they watched the boat turn around to back into port. "Look who's at the helm," Seamus said.

"I didn't know Joe was on this boat."

"I didn't either. He must've swapped with someone."

As they watched Joe competently align the huge ferry with the pier and back it smoothly into port, Carolina was filled with pride. "He's so darned good at that."

"He sure is. I remember the first time I did it here. Damn near crapped myself with that tight turnaround in the smallest harbor I've ever seen. But Joe stood right next to me and talked me through it. He showed me all the Gansett Island tricks in that one lesson."

"I remember so well the first time my father taught him. They came home that night, and my dad was bursting with excitement. 'The boy's a natural,' he said."

"I wish I could've met your folks."

"I do, too. My dad would've liked you."

"Would he have approved of you and me?"

"Oh, God, yes. They begged me for years after Pete died to go out with someone else. They would've *loved* you and the way you boss me around."

"I do not *boss* you around."

She gave him her most withering look.

"I encourage you to expand your horizons. That doesn't count as bossing."

"Whatever you say."

The cars and trucks came first off the ferry, followed by a flood of people with suitcases, bicycles and dogs on leashes.

Because he still had his arm around her, Carolina felt Seamus stiffen.

"Holy hell. What in the name of Jesus, Mary and Joseph is he doing here?"

"Who?" Carolina followed his gaze to a compact gray-haired woman accompanied by a young man—an extremely handsome young man.

"My cousin, Shannon."

Oh perfect, Carolina thought. *A surprise guest!*

Seamus released his tight hold on her and walked toward the ramp to greet them.

Nora O'Grady's bright blue eyes lit up at the sight of her son as the evening breeze lifted a lock of her gray hair.

Seamus scooped her up and swung her around. The pure joy she saw on his face as he hugged his mother told Carolina a lot about how much he'd missed her. His extremely handsome cousin stood next to them, taking in the town with an aura of disdain. Fabulous. His hair was a darker shade of reddish brown than Seamus's and longer, Carolina observed, as Seamus hugged Shannon.

He was a bit taller than Seamus, at least five years younger, and lanky but muscular. He must have women falling at his feet, Carolina thought as the three of them came toward her with Shannon carrying a duffel bag and Seamus positively beaming as he pulled a suitcase on wheels.

Carolina had never seen him look so happy as he took her hand and squeezed it.

"Mum, Shannon, this is Carolina Cantrell, the love of my life. Carolina, my mother, Nora O'Grady, and my cousin, Shannon."

As they all shook hands, Carolina felt the heat of Nora's stare on her. How would it feel, she wondered, to meet the love of your son's life and to discover she was nearly twenty years older than him? Judging by the shock Nora was trying hard to hide, her son had failed to mention the age difference to his mother. This just got better and better.

Joe came off the boat and walked over to them. "Hey, Mom, Seamus."

Carolina smiled up at her son as he kissed her cheek. "Hi, honey. I want you to meet Seamus's mother, Nora O'Grady, and his cousin, Shannon. This is my son, Joe."

"And my fabulous boss," Seamus added.

"Oh, hey, great to meet you," Joe said as he shook their hands.

Nora's sharp gaze darted between Joe and Seamus before finally landing on Carolina. "Well," she said in a heavy Irish burr, "t'isn't this going to be an interesting visit?"

As Janey got closer to her delivery date, Maddie started bringing dinner to her and Joe at least once a week. She remembered all too well how clumsy and cumbersome she'd felt toward the end, especially with Thomas.

She'd been on her own then, panic-stricken about bringing a baby into the world without the help of the child's father. Those frightening and uncertain days seemed like a far-off time now that she was happily settled with Mac and their children, but it wasn't all that long ago.

She knocked lightly on Janey's front door, hoping she wasn't disturbing her sister-in-law.

"Come on in," Janey called.

Maddie walked into the foyer of the contemporary house Joe and Janey had bought a mile from where she and Mac lived. She absolutely loved having them close by. Janey's dogs came rushing to see who'd come to visit. "It's just me, guys," Maddie said to them as they gave her a thorough sniffing.

"I'm beached on the sun porch," Janey said.

Maddie put away the chicken, roasted potatoes, salad and brownies in the kitchen and went to find Janey stretched out on a chaise in the screened-in back porch. "What a lovely spot this is," Maddie said, taking in the mature landscaping in the big back yard and the colorful pots of flowers Janey had put on the patio outside.

"We quite love it and so do the dogs," Janey said. "Can I offer you something to drink that you'll have to get yourself?"

Maddie laughed and collapsed into a chair. "No, thanks. As long as I can sit here long enough for Mac to get the kids in bed, I'll be happy. It's been a *long* day at the ranch."

"What's going on?"

"Hailey is teething and starting to cruise around, which means she can get into Thomas's stuff, which means I have to be hypervigilant about what he's playing with so she can't get ahold of something she can choke on. And then she gets something of his, and suddenly that's the thing he most wants to play with, and he forgets all about how much he loves his baby sister. Ahh, good times."

Janey laughed. "Sounds like it. So my mom might've mentioned that you and Mac put on a bit of a show for Thomas the other night…"

"Ugh! Don't remind me. I'm still recovering from the trauma!"

"And how is he?"

"Hasn't mentioned it again, so we're hoping we can leave that special moment in the past."

"Tell me the whole thing, leaving out any disgusting details about my brother that'll scar me for life."

Maddie relayed the story in the least amount of detail possible, which made Janey howl with laughter.

"I'm going to pee my pants if I don't stop laughing," she said when she recovered her breath. "That is freaking *hilarious.*"

"Glad you think so. It was mortifying for us."

"I don't even want to think about that happening to us in a couple of years."

"The worst part is I was so gone on champagne that we got all carried away and never even thought about protection, so…"

Janey's big blue eyes went wide with surprise. "You could be pregnant?"

"God, I hope not, but we picked the worst possible time of the month to be forgetful. I can't get my head around the possibility. It's way too soon after Hailey's memorable arrival. Speaking of Hailey's memorable arrival… Have you heard about Daisy and David?"

"I heard something to that effect. What do you think of it?"

"He's been really great to her since Truck attacked her."

"Other than one particularly egregious lapse in judgment, he's always been a good guy. He wasn't the good guy for me, but that doesn't mean he won't be for someone else."

"I worry about that egregious lapse in judgment where Daisy is concerned. She's been through so much. I don't know all of it, but I sense some heavy baggage there—even before she met Truck Henry."

"I'd like to hope David has learned his lesson where infidelity is concerned. He may be the best possible guy for Daisy. He's got something to prove—to himself and others."

"I suppose. If he hurts her..."

"You have my permission to kill him."

"Thank you." Maddie hesitated, uncertain now about something else she'd planned to discuss with Janey. "So the cookout this weekend... I talked to Mac, and I told him I want to invite her. If I invite her..."

"You'd have to invite him, too."

"Right. Mac wants to know how you feel about it before we invite them. We wouldn't want to do anything to make you uncomfortable at our home."

"Honestly, I don't care at all if he's there. I loved him for a long time, but I don't love him or think about him anymore. Joe, on the other hand... He might have a problem with it."

"Have a problem with what?" Joe asked as he came in through the kitchen and went straight to his wife. He leaned over the chaise to kiss her.

"Maddie is thinking about asking Daisy Babson to come to the cookout on Sunday."

"Why would I care about that?" Joe asked, sitting on the chaise and taking Janey's hand. "Daisy's a nice person."

"Yes, she is, and she's a nice person who is dating David Lawrence."

"Ah. Hmm. Well, that might be a bit weird."

"Too weird for you?" Maddie asked.

Joe glanced at Janey. "What do you say?"

She shrugged. "I couldn't care less. He's nothing to me but an ex-boyfriend. He's certainly no threat to us."

"Then go ahead and invite them," Joe said with a sweet, private smile for his wife.

"And you'll behave?" Janey asked him, crooking an eyebrow.

Flashing a shit-eating grin, he kissed her hand. "As well as I ever do."

"I don't want any broken noses at my house," Maddie said.

"I've grown up a lot since then," Joe said.

Maddie and Janey laughed.

"Sure you have," Janey said.

"Speaking of my newfound maturity, guess what just happened at the ferry landing? Seamus's mother and cousin arrived. I was there when my mom met them, and judging from the way Mrs. O'Grady was sizing up Mom, I don't think Seamus warned her about the age difference."

"Oh yikes," Janey said. "That must've been awkward."

"She was looking at me and at Seamus and doing the math. Totally awkward. My mom looked like she was ready to kill. Just when I think I've got my head around that relationship, something happens to get me wondering again."

"Don't go there," Janey said. "It works for them. It doesn't have to work for you."

"Something tells me it's not going to be working too well for them tonight," Joe said.

"Have I been here long enough for Mac to get the kids in bed and suffer sufficiently without me?" Maddie asked.

"I think you need at least another thirty minutes and a glass of wine to ensure an adequate level of suffering," Janey said.

"That sounds really good, but I've sworn off booze after the other night."

"You've sworn off champagne. Not wine."

"Isn't champagne a form of wine?"

"Not in my house. Joseph, will you please pour Maddie a glass of wine?"

"I'd be happy to if it contributes to Mac's suffering."

"There's some dinner out there for you guys, too," Maddie said.

Janey shook her head. "You have to stop cooking for us."

"You can't make me."

"I'm not going to try very hard, don't worry." Janey rested her hands on her distended belly and winced. "I've got a kicker in there." She tried to find a more comfortable position. "Have you heard anything from Syd about the surgery?"

"It went well. She's sore, but out of the hospital. They're spending tonight and maybe tomorrow night in a hotel in Boston so they can be close to the hospital if there're any complications."

"How soon will she know if it worked?"

"Three or four months."

"I hope she gets pregnant right away."

"Me too." Maddie accepted a glass of red wine from Joe. "Thank you, sir."

"I was reading a magazine article about how most people are opting for in vitro rather than tubal-ligation reversal these days," Janey said.

"They considered that, but living out here, it's an ordeal to get to doctors for treatments. So they're trying this first. If it doesn't work, they may go that route."

"I want to snap my fingers and give her twins," Janey said.

Laughing, Maddie said, "If she gets pregnant with twins, I'll tell her it's your fault, and while we're on the subject of twins, have you heard anything about how Laura is feeling?"

"Still pretty awful. She's throwing up a lot. Owen said he's going to take her to the mainland to see a specialist if it doesn't let up soon."

"That has to be so miserable, and while she's planning the wedding, too."

"I don't think there's much wedding planning going on right now. She told me it's going to be a JP on the deck of the Surf with a buffet at Stephanie's. That's all she's capable of at the moment."

"Can't say I blame her for keeping it simple. Thank God I never had the pukes with either of mine." Maddie's cell phone rang, and she groaned. "Fair warning, if this is your brother, I'm going to be tempted to ignore it."

"You have my permission to ignore it."

"Oh, it's Tiffany. Mind if I take it?"

"Not at all," Janey said. "Tell her I said hi."

Maddie took the call from her sister. "Hey, Tiff, what's up?"

Tiffany was talking so fast Maddie couldn't hear her.

"Whoa, back up. Slow down."

Tiffany released a deep breath that hitched with what might've been sobs. "Jim found out that Blaine is moving in with me, and he's threatening to sue for full custody of Ashleigh."

"What? Are you serious? He can't do that!"

"He's doing that," Tiffany said, sniffling. "He sent a letter letting me know if we move forward with our plans, he's going after custody. He doesn't even *want* her, Maddie. Why is he doing this?"

"Because he's a son of a bitch who doesn't want you to be happy with someone else."

"I don't know what to do. What do I do?"

"Have you called Dan?" Maddie asked, referring to the island's other lawyer, Dan Torrington.

"I left him a message, but he hasn't called me back yet."

"I'll ask Mac to call Kara. He has her number. Maybe she knows where he is. I'll call you right back."

"Okay."

"Unreal," Maddie said to Joe and Janey. "Jim found out Blaine is moving in with Tiffany, and he's going after full custody of Ashleigh."

"Just when we think we've seen the full extent of that guy's douchebaggery, he goes and tops himself," Joe said, visibly disgusted.

Maddie pressed the top number on her list of favorites to call her husband. "Mac, I need you to call Kara for me. Tiffany is trying to get in touch with Dan, and he's not answering his phone."

"Is everything okay?"

Maddie filled him in on what was going on.

"Someone needs to have a conversation with that asshole," Mac said.

"Not you."

"I won't be held responsible for my actions if my path should cross his."

"Will you please call her?"

"Right now."

"Thanks. I'll be home soon." Maddie put her phone in her pocket. "I can't believe this. He divorces *her* and then pulls this crap when she moves on with someone else?"

"Typical Jim Sturgil," Janey said.

"He can't do this to her," Maddie said. "Not after all he's already put her through."

"I'm sure Blaine will be all over it," Joe assured them. "Dan will be, too."

"I want Dan Torrington to *shred* Jim," Maddie said as she got up to leave. She would call Tiffany back in the car. "That'd please me greatly."

"That would please a lot of people," Joe said. "I'll walk you out."

Maddie bent to kiss Janey. "Hang in there, kiddo. Call me if you need anything."

"I will. Thanks for dinner."

"Happy to help."

Nothing on God's green earth could get Dan Torrington to stop what he was currently doing to answer a phone that wouldn't quit ringing. And then Kara's phone started up, too, and the moment was totally blown.

"Goddamn it," he muttered, making her laugh. He released her and winced when his still-recovering ribs protested against even that small movement. They'd waited weeks to get back to where they'd been before the accident, and now that they were finally there, the outside world was intruding.

"Let's answer the calls, see what's going on, and get back to where we were," she said in that husky, sexy voice that had become the center of his world.

"Fine," he grumbled, knowing there was no point in trying to re-engage her when they were both so distracted. Try telling that to his raging boner, which had yet to receive the "game-off" message.

She got out of bed to get both their phones.

Dan propped himself up on an elbow to get the best possible view of her sweet ass as she walked out the door to the living room, where they'd left their phones on the coffee table when a heated make-out session had finally, *finally* landed them in bed.

He'd had to assure her a hundred times that he felt absolutely fine and ready to pick up where they'd left off before the sailing accident that resulted in broken ribs and a broken arm. His arm was much better. The ribs were still giving him grief, but as long as he didn't breathe too deeply, he had faith he could perform up to par. Or so he hoped…

He was about to die from wanting her. Long weeks of heated looks, tender care and devotion from her as he recovered had left him in a state of perpetual arousal. If something didn't happen soon, he was convinced he'd spontaneously combust.

"It's Tiffany," she said, handing him his phone. "And Mac left me a message to tell you to call her."

He couldn't take his eyes off the sway of her breasts, the pink nipples, the razor burn he'd left on her white skin or the patch of auburn hair at the apex of her thighs. His cock was so hard he could pound nails with it as he took his phone from her.

"She's called six times. Do I need to be worried?"

He scowled at her, insulted by the implication. "Get your sexy ass back in this bed, and don't ask stupid questions."

She rolled her eyes at him but did as she was told. That was a first.

When he had her snuggled up tight against him where she belonged, he called Tiffany back so he and Kara could get some peace to finish what they'd started.

"Oh, Dan, thank God you called."

The panic he heard in the voice of his friend and client alarmed him. "What's wrong?"

"It's Jim. He heard about Blaine moving in with me, and he's threatening to sue for full custody of Ashleigh."

"Hmm."

"What does that mean?"

"It means, he may have a case, Tiff."

"What? *Why*? We're divorced! He can't tell me who I can live with and who I can't."

"No, but because he shares joint custody with you, he can say who his daughter lives with and who she doesn't."

"You've got to be kidding me. What if I was getting married? Could he stop that, too?"

"Not as easily."

"Then that's what I'll do. I'll get married."

"Tiffany—"

"I've had enough of that dickwad telling me how to run my life. If he wants war, he's going to get it. Are you able to help me respond to the letter he sent me?"

"Absolutely. Could I call you in the morning to figure that out?"

"I guess it can wait until then."

Thank God, because he wasn't leaving this bed until the morning and neither was Kara. "I'll call you. Try to stay calm and don't worry. We'll figure it out."

"Thanks, Dan. I'm sorry to bother you. I hope I didn't get you away from anything important."

"I wasn't doing anything important," he said, squeezing Kara's breast and pressing his cock into the cleft between her cheeks.

She laughed softly, as he'd hoped she would.

"Thanks again," Tiffany said before she ended the call.

Dan turned off his phone and tossed it to the foot of the bed. "Now, where were we?"

"Nothing important, huh?"

"How did I know you'd have something to say about that?"

She turned over to face him.

"You ought to know by now that there's nothing more important than you," he said, kissing her. "Than this. Than us." As he deepened the kiss, he drew her into his embrace, their legs intertwining, her hand on his back, one of his buried in her hair, the other on her breast. In anticipation of this night with Kara, he'd recruited his friend Grant McCarthy to help him cut off the part of the cast that had covered his hand. With his palm now full of supple flesh and tight nipple, he thanked the heavens above for hacksaws.

Just that quickly, they were right back to where they'd left off before the phone interrupted them, only this time the urgency was even more acute.

Kara drew back from him, her lips swollen from kissing him. "I'm so afraid of hurting you."

He took her hand and brought it down to his erection, closing her fingers around him. "This is hurting me way more than the ribs are right now."

"Dan, come on. Be serious."

"I'm dead serious."

Her laughter filled him with the kind of joy he hadn't experienced in a very long time. Losing his brother in Afghanistan and then his fiancée days before their wedding to a tryst with his best man had hardened Dan's emotions, made him remote and closed off in relationships. Kara had penetrated that wall and worked her way so deeply into his heart that there was no room left for bitterness or regrets.

There was only her. There was only right now.

Her phone rang again, and he groaned. "I thought you shut it off."

"Ignore it," she whispered, stroking him from root to tip and then running her thumb over the slickness at the top.

"Might be a good idea to take the edge off so I last more than thirty seconds."

"You think so?"

Lying face-to-face with her on the same pillow, he gazed into her eyes. "Mmm. I've been dying for you for weeks now. My sexy nurse. Every time you walk in the room, I get hard. Every time you touch me, I need you." He slid his fingertips over her arm and felt her muscles flex as she stroked him. "Every single time."

"Thank you for not dying out there on the water. I would've hated to miss hearing you say that to me."

Dan couldn't believe it was possible to laugh when it seemed like his entire body was on fire. "Believe me, it's my supreme pleasure to have survived and come home to you. I thought about you the whole time out there. I knew I was hurt really bad, and all I wanted was to see you again. One more time."

Kara's phone rang again.

Dan blew out a deep breath that was filled with frustration. He'd dreamed about being naked in bed with her again, and now that they were finally there, the interruptions were nonstop. "Do you think you could turn that off?"

Unfortunately, she released him to deal with the phone. "I thought I had." She glanced at the phone. "It's my mom. Twice in ten minutes. That's not good."

"Go ahead and call her back," Dan said, resigned to his fate.

"No, that's okay. We're busy."

"Trust me when I tell you it'll keep."

Kara glanced down at his erection, which was painfully hard, not that he'd tell her that. "Are you sure?"

"Yeah, I'm sure." He put his arm around her and snuggled up to her. The press of her skin against his was all he needed to maintain the status quo while she called her mother.

"What's up, Mom?"

Dan was lying so close to Kara that he could hear everything her mother said.

"I thought you might like to know that your sister had her baby."

"Good for her."

Judging from Kara's dismissive tone, the sister in question must be the one who'd married Kara's ex-boyfriend.

"You don't need to be snippy, Kara. She is your sister, after all."

"Maybe on paper."

"How long are you going to do this?"

"What am I doing exactly?"

"Acting hateful toward your sister for something that happened years ago. Holding on to that bitterness isn't going to make you happy."

"I'm very happy," Kara said, her hand covering his under her breasts. "I'm beyond happy, in fact. But I still hate her for what she did to me, and I always will."

"Please don't say you hate her. And always is a very long time."

Kara had nothing to say to that.

"Do you care at all about your new nephew?"

"Sure. He hasn't done anything to me. I'm sorry he got such shitty parents, but perhaps the rest of you will see to it that he doesn't end up as shitty as they are."

"Kara…"

"I have to go, Mom. I've got better things to do than talk about them."

"His name is Connor," her mother said. "The baby is Connor."

"Congratulations on your new grandson. I'll talk to you soon." She ended the call before her mother could reply and powered down the phone. Turning to face him, she attempted a sincere smile that failed miserably. "Now, where were we?" Her hand curled around his cock.

Dan covered her hand with his, stopping her from stroking him. "Please don't act like that news didn't rock you."

"They don't matter to me anymore. I refuse to get sucked into that rabbit hole again when I've only recently found the way out."

"You don't have to pretend with me, honey." He brushed a strand of her auburn hair back from her face. "Tell me the truth. I want to know how you really feel."

"I honestly and truly don't care. Everyone is happy. What does it matter?"

"It matters that they're still hurting you, even after all this time."

"They aren't hurting me. I don't care about them."

Except she did. She cared desperately. Did she think he couldn't see the effort she was making to control her emotions?

"Don't lie to me. Don't ever lie to me." He immediately regretted his tone, which was angrier than he'd intended. But it made him damned angry that she'd been treated the way she had by the man she'd once loved and her own sister.

Apparently, his sharp words didn't matter to her, because she caressed his cheek. "I appreciate that you care so much. I really do. But they don't matter to me anymore, and they can't hurt me unless I let them. I choose not to let them."

"Knowing what they did to you is still somewhat new to me, so is it okay that I'm not over it yet?"

Her smile lit up her face and made her eyes crinkle adorably in the corners. "That's totally fine."

"The rest of your family… What do they say about the two of them together?"

"My parents have been weird about it from the beginning. They acted like it was no big deal that Kelly had taken up with my boyfriend behind my back. They had a kind of 'shit happens' attitude about it."

"Seriously?"

"You have to understand, they're all about family peace and harmony. The rift between Kelly and me has been really hard on them because they see it as a failure on their part."

"Someone needs to help them get their heads out of the sand."

"I've given up on that ever happening. When my dad gave Kelly away at the elaborate wedding they threw for her and Matt, it became very clear to me that if I stuck around Bar Harbor, I was going to have to be confronted with my sister and her new husband on a regular basis. Thus my move to Gansett Island." She leaned in and gave him a kiss. "Best thing I ever did."

"You really think so? Even after everything I've put you through?"

"I really think so." Snuggling in closer to him, she said, "While I appreciate that you care, I don't want to talk about them anymore. Not when I've waited so long to be with you again like this."

"You've been waiting, too?"

"Oh, yeah. That first night we spent together… Let's just say I've relived it a thousand or two times since then."

"Me, too. At least a thousand or maybe three thousand times."

"Thank you for forgiving me for freaking out afterward."

"I was freaking out, too, you know—and not just because you tried to lose me like a bad habit the next morning."

"You really were?"

"I've never felt like I do when I'm with you. It's totally different and way, way better than anything I've ever known."

"It is for me, too. And you're a big reason why I don't care about Matt and Kelly anymore."

Dan knew there was no greater compliment she could ever pay him than that one.

"In my best moments with Matt, it was never like it is with you."

"You stop my heart, Kara Ballard. Sometimes I think I dreamed up that day on the dock when you told me you love me. I wanted to hear those words from you so badly."

"You didn't dream it, and I want your love just as badly."

"You have it. You've had it for a long time now." Cupping her breast and running his thumb over her nipple, he captured her lips in a deep, soulful kiss that started the fire burning again, hotter than ever. The last thing on his mind at that moment were broken ribs or the arm still encased in plaster or anything other than the exquisite sensation of her soft skin against his, her legs curled around his, her tongue tangling with his.

Judging by the way he rolled them so he was on top, his injuries might never have happened.

She gazed up at him with wide eyes. "Dan! Be careful! You shouldn't be doing that."

"Kara?"

"What?" she asked, her voice full of exasperation.

"Shut up and kiss me."

She wrapped her arms around his neck and brought him down slowly.

Her concern for his well-being touched him as he lost himself in the sweetness of her lips and the sensuous strokes of her tongue.

"Condom," he said, wondering where the presence of mind had come from when every brain cell in his body seemed to be heading south to join the party.

"Where are they?"

"Bedside table."

"Don't move." She shifted carefully under him to retrieve a foil packet, rolling it on him with an efficiency that astounded him. His girl didn't mess around. "Are you okay?" she asked, looking up at him.

"I will be in a minute."

That drew a small smile from her as she took him in hand and guided him to where he most wanted to be. The relief of being joined with her after so many weeks of uncertainty was nearly as overwhelming as the clutch of her tight muscles. "Christ," he muttered. "This is going to be over before it begins."

"That's okay."

He thrust into her deeply. "Tell me again."

She arched into him, her fingers moving gently down his back, and he could tell she was afraid to hurt him even in the throes of passion. "I love you. I love you. I love you."

That was all he needed to hear. All he'd ever need to hear.

CHAPTER 7

David lived in a spacious garage apartment behind a big house on the island's west side.

"Whose house is that?" Daisy asked of the enormous contemporary that overlooked the water.

"A guy named Jared James. He's a Wall Street tycoon who's never here except for a week or two in the summer, so he wanted someone in the apartment who could keep an eye on the house, too."

"Imagine having a house like that and living in it for a week or two every year."

"I think he bought it with plans to retire here eventually, but he likes to work too much to ever retire. The guy is filthy rich, from what I hear."

"It's sad," Daisy said as David parked in front of the garage.

"What is?"

"That he's so devoted to his work that he's forgotten to live. How much money does anyone really need, you know?"

"Don't say that to Jared," David said with a wry grin as he grabbed his duffel bag from the car. He led her up the stairs to his place while trying to remember the condition he'd left it in two days ago. Hopefully, nothing was smelly or messy. "Making money is a religion to him."

"I need to get some of his brand of religion," Daisy said. "If I don't pass the probationary period and get the manager job full-time, this will be my last summer on the island. I can't do the unemployed off-season thing anymore. It's just too expensive."

"I'm sure you'll get the job. Mrs. McCarthy would be crazy not to give it to you."

"One thing she isn't is crazy, but she's not going to give it to me out of loyalty. I have to earn it. It didn't help that I had to take a week of sick leave right after she gave me the chance."

He used his key in the door and stepped inside ahead of her to turn on the lights. Thankfully, the air smelled musty rather than stinky. David opened a window to let some fresh air in and turned on a light. The apartment was better than most, with high ceilings and a huge room that served as a combined living room and kitchen. A hallway led to a bedroom and bathroom. It was small, but it was all he needed, and it had gotten him out of his mother's house, which was critical to his sanity. "The week out of work wasn't your fault, Daisy. Mrs. McCarthy knows that."

"Still… It was the last thing I needed."

"I hope you're not pushing yourself too much trying to prove something to her. You need to be taking it easy for a while longer."

"Don't worry about me, Dr. Lawrence. I'm fine."

"You're not fine—yet, but you will be soon, and I do worry."

"About all your patients, or me in particular?" she asked with a teasing smile.

Drawn in by that smile and her sweetness, he rested his hands on her shoulders. "All my patients, but some more than others." He tipped his head to kiss her and loved the soft sigh of pleasure that escaped from her lips.

It took every ounce of control he could summon to remember that she was fragile and he needed to take it slow with her. Things had gotten way, *way* out of control the other night, and he couldn't let that happen again until he was certain she was ready for it.

"Let me know if your boss needs a note from your doctor," he said with a teasing grin.

"Oh, I definitely will! Nice to have friends in high places."

With tremendous reluctance, he let his hands fall and stepped back from her. "I'll be just a second. Have a seat, feel free to snoop, whatever you want."

"I don't snoop," she said indignantly.

"Daisy, *all* women snoop. Give me a break."

"On behalf of all women, I'm offended."

"Sure you are," he said, chuckling as he left her in the living room to rush through a quick shower and shave. He donned a dress shirt and black pants, slid a belt through the loops and stepped into loafers at the same time. As he applied a small bit of cologne, he looked at himself in the mirror and summoned some calm.

He'd shared the worst of himself with her, and she was still here. Rather than feeling relieved that he'd gotten past that huge hurdle, he was more anxious than ever about not making a mistake that would drive her away. It had been a very long time since anything had been as important to him as she was becoming, but he had to keep reminding himself that she was recovering from physical and emotional trauma.

Despite her resilience and spirit, she needed tenderness far more than she needed the out-of-control desire she roused in him. There'd be a time and a place for that, he told himself, if he didn't move too fast and drive her away.

When he felt like he had found the calm he needed to proceed with caution, he left his room and returned to the living room.

Daisy was on the sofa, flipping through a photo album.

David winced when he realized what she was looking at.

She glanced up at him. "What? You said I could snoop."

He took a seat next to her. "Had to be that one, huh?" The photos of the happy years he'd spent with Janey brought back bittersweet memories.

"It was the first one on the pile. Do you still look at it a lot?"

"I haven't looked at that in ages. More than a year."

"Thirteen years is a long time to spend with someone to have it not work out in the end."

"It was a tough breakup. I won't deny that."

She glanced briefly at him before returning her attention to the photos. "Do you still miss her?"

"I miss my friend. She was my best friend for a very long time. I miss that sometimes, like when I hear something funny that I know she'd appreciate. The romantic part had been over between us for a while before we broke up. In a way, our relationship had become more of a habit than a romance, if that makes sense."

"It does. Is it okay that I asked you about her?"

"Of course it is. You can ask me anything you want to."

Her lips pursed, and it was obvious there was something else she wanted to know.

"Whatever it is, Daisy, just ask me. It's fine. I swear."

"The nurse that you slept with… Did you have feelings for her?"

David hated to think about the night he torpedoed his entire future with Janey. "God, no. That was a one-time lapse in judgment, brought on by an overabundance of stress and fear. I can make excuses until the cows come home, but that was a mistake. A very big mistake."

"Everyone makes them, you know. It's probably time you forgave yourself."

"Maybe so, but I'm not quite there yet."

Daisy closed the photo album and put it on the coffee table. "Do you have your heart set on going to Domenic's tonight?"

"I wanted to take you out for a nice dinner, but if you're not up for it, we can do it another time."

"I think I'd rather stay here and get a pizza and watch TV."

"Whatever you want is fine with me."

"I wish Mario's delivered."

"You're looking at the doctor who tended to Mario's grandson when he had the chicken pox, earning free pizza delivery for life."

"Really? That's awesome."

"One of the few perks of being the island's only doctor. What's your pleasure on the pizza?"

"Plain old cheese and maybe a salad?"

"Coming right up."

While they waited for the pizza delivery, David poured them each a glass of wine and they flipped through the TV channels looking for something to watch. Daisy vetoed the Red Sox game, and David said no to HGTV.

"*Please*? I love this show about how they completely transform a space with almost no money."

"I'll trade you one half hour of decorating for a half hour of baseball."

Daisy extended her hand. "Deal. Me first."

"I see how this is going to go," he said, grumbling as he shook her hand. He was thrilled to have her all to himself even with more than foot between them on the sofa.

When the pizza arrived, he took advantage of the opportunity to move closer to her while they ate in front of the TV. He had to admit the decorating show was much more interesting than he'd expected it to be. "Wow," he said after the big reveal, "I can't believe what they did to that place with a five-hundred-dollar budget."

"I know! That's why I love these shows. I get so many good ideas for my place." As she said the words, her mouth puckered ever so slightly.

"What're you thinking?"

"That I'll miss that place—and the island—if I have to move. I've been here long enough that it feels like home. It's too bad it's so hard to make a living here in the off-season."

"Hopefully you'll get the year-round job at the hotel and you won't have to worry about that anymore."

"Hopefully."

As another episode of the budget decorating show got set to begin, Daisy handed him the remote control. "Your turn."

"Let me do a quick score check, and then we can watch this one, too."

"You're hooked!"

"I never said that."

"You are, too. I can tell."

"I'm not admitting to anything."

"Don't worry. I'll keep your secrets."

They settled in to watch the second episode, and he caught her suppressing a yawn.

"Tired?"

"A little. It's been a long day."

"Do you want to go home?"

"Not quite yet. This has been the nicest part of my long day."

He raised an arm to encourage her to come closer to him and put it around her when she snuggled into his embrace. Brushing his lips over her soft hair, he said, "Best part of my long day, too."

"Even though I'm forcing you to watch decorating shows?"

"You're not forcing me to do anything."

"This is much better than going out."

"Definitely, but I don't want you to get overtired. We should get you home to bed."

Her hand, which was flat against his belly, moved up to his chest and kept going until her fingers were moving lightly over the whiskers on his jaw.

He was so affected by the soft brush of her fingers over his face that he could barely draw a breath. "Daisy... What're you doing?"

"Nothing."

"That's not nothing."

"Is it okay if I touch you?"

"I love when you touch me, but—"

"David?"

"Yeah?"

"Will you kiss me again like you did the other night?"

He turned to face her on the sofa, his gaze zeroing in on her full lips. "I want to more than you know, but I worry about moving too fast. I don't want to do anything to upset you like I did that night."

"You're sweet to worry, but I'm okay, and I really liked kissing you."

"Me, too. I thought about it the whole time I was in Boston."

The left side of her mouth lifted into a smile. "The *whole* time?"

Nodding, he leaned in slowly and kept his eyes open, which was how he saw the flush of her cheeks, the flutter of her lashes and the dab of her tongue on her lower lip. The movement of her tongue sent a charge of desire roaring through him, but he tried to ignore the insistent press of his cock against the fly of his pants. This was about her, about going slowly for her, about taking his time and not scaring her off.

As their lips met and her eyes closed, David kept his open so he could be certain she was with him and not reliving memories that would be better forgotten. He loved everything about kissing her, and could've so easily let the desire and the passion take over his better judgment.

He went slowly, determined not to let it get out of hand the way it had the other night. But then her tongue slid over his lower lip, setting off a chain reaction that made him groan.

Apparently encouraged by his reaction, she did it again and again until he couldn't remember his own name, let alone his vows to go slowly. Before he knew it, they were reclined on the sofa, facing each other as their tongues mated in a sensual battle.

With their bodies pressed together on the sofa, it wasn't easy for David to hold back. And then he felt her tugging at his shirt, pulling it free from his pants. Her hand on his back was nothing short of electrifying. When he'd said he loved her touch, he wasn't kidding.

Reluctantly, he eased off from the kiss, turning his focus toward her jaw and neck. She smelled so sweet, like soap and flowers. He could easily become addicted to that scent, he thought as he kissed his way to her throat and then focused on her collarbone.

Her free hand encircled his neck, keeping him from pulling back from her.

He knew he should stop before things went any further, so he dropped his forehead to her shoulder, summoning the control that had all but deserted him.

"What's wrong?" she asked.

"Nothing."

"Why did you stop?"

"Because I…"

"It's okay if you're not in the mood. I didn't mean to be so forward."

Laughing softly, he flexed his hips so she could feel the evidence of how "not in the mood" he was.

"Oh."

"Yeah. Definitely in the mood."

"Then what's wrong?" She combed her fingers through his hair, making his scalp tingle.

Every inch of him was affected by her touch. "I feel like we're moving too fast. You were hurt badly, in more ways than one, and I need to be careful with you. Yet…"

"Yet?"

"I can't get enough of you. When I kiss you, I forget all about being careful."

"I'm not fragile, David. I won't break."

"You're not fragile. You're strong and resilient, and I respect that about you more than you know. But you were seriously injured not all that long ago. It would kill me if I ever did anything to hurt you."

"It would hurt me if you treated me differently because of what happened with him."

He blew out a deep breath, uncertain of what to say to that.

"I love when you kiss me," she said. "I love when you touch me. And the last thing I'm thinking of when I'm kissing you is anything to do with him. I can barely remember my own name when you kiss me."

He smiled because he knew exactly what she meant. "I'm still afraid of moving too fast and spooking you."

"You won't."

"How do you know?"

"Because it's you, and you've been so amazing from the very beginning. I've never been in a relationship like this one."

"What makes it different?"

"I'm not afraid all the time. I'm not afraid of saying the wrong thing and making you mad or doing the wrong thing and waiting for you to explode. I feel safe with you."

"I could kill him for putting you through that."

"It was partly my fault."

"How in the world can you say that?"

"I put up with it far longer than I should have. You and Blaine both tried to warn me after it happened the first time that he was escalating, but I was convinced that he loved me and would never really hurt me. I'd be dead if Blaine hadn't gotten there when he did, so yes, I blame myself for not putting a stop to it sooner."

"I hate to hear you blaming yourself for what he did."

"I don't blame myself for the violence. I blame myself for failing to see the handwriting on the wall where he was concerned. But I learned from it, and I'll never let it happen again."

"I don't want you to ever be afraid like that again."

"Neither do I." Her palm was warm against his cheek. "I can't imagine ever being afraid when I'm with you. So don't treat me any differently than you'd treat any other woman."

"You're not any other woman, Daisy. You're special."

"I feel special when I'm with you." With her hand on the back of his head, she drew him toward her for another kiss.

He'd planned to keep it chaste, but she had other ideas, teasing him with her tongue until he had no choice but to let go of all his worries and lose himself in her sweetness. His hand traveled down her back, over the curve of her bottom to the hem of her dress. He nearly lost it when he encountered the warm, soft skin of her upper leg.

She moaned and slid her leg between both of his, encouraging him to touch her more intimately.

He wanted to so badly. It had been a very long time since he'd wanted anything as badly as he wanted her. With her body tight against his and her tongue teasing and tempting him, it was hard to remember any of the reasons why he had thought to practice restraint with her.

It occurred to him that there was plenty they could do without going too far. He slowly slid his hand up the back of her leg as her fingertips pressed into the muscles on his back. Did he dare to go a little higher? The sweet curve of her ass beckoned, almost daring him to go for it as the mewling sounds coming from her told him how much she wanted him to keep going.

His hand curved around a small but supple cheek, squeezing and kneading as the kiss intensified.

All at once, she broke the kiss and took a series of deep breaths.

"Too much?" he asked.

"Not enough," she replied, chuckling.

"Daisy," he groaned. "You're not making this easy."

"Good. Don't stop. Please, don't stop yet."

He might be capable of some measure of control, but he was certainly no saint, and he hadn't had sex in a really long time. Thus, it didn't take much encouragement on her part to continue caressing her bottom while she squirmed against his rigidly erect cock. It took very little encouragement to slip his fingers beneath the elastic of her panties and delve into the liquid heat between her legs.

"David," she said, gasping as he found the center of her desire.

"Is this okay?"

She nodded and initiated another kiss, using her lips and tongue to drive him slowly mad. And then she was pulling at his belt and tugging at the button to his pants and her warm, soft hand was wrapping around his shaft. All thoughts of going slow evaporated in a haze of desire that overtook him.

He slid his fingers into her channel, stroking her inside and out as she did the same for him. Her thumb slid through the moisture that had gathered at the tip, moving back and forth until he was on the verge of exploding in her hand.

Breaking the kiss, he pressed his face into the curve of her neck, breathing hard from the effort it took to hold back. "Daisy…"

"Hmm?"

"God… Don't stop."

"Same to you."

Even in the throes of runaway passion, she made him smile. Determined now to help her find the ultimate pleasure, he focused his attention on the tight bundle of nerves at her core, teasing and stroking and caressing until he felt her tighten and tremble as she came.

Her release triggered his, and she stayed with him all the way, her hand tight around him as he let go of the worries and gave in to the desire.

When the trembling aftershocks subsided, he eased his fingers from between her legs and drew her dress down over her bottom. "That was hot," he whispered against her lips, "but we made a bit of a mess."

"It was well worth it."

"Mmm. I completely agree." He used the tail of his dress shirt to clean up. "I should take you home."

"Not yet."

With her snuggled up to him, her hair fragrant against his face, the last thing he wanted to do was move. So he tried to relax and enjoy the sweet pleasure of holding her close. He closed his eyes, telling himself they'd leave soon. But first he wanted to hold her for a little while longer.

The moment Seamus's mother was settled in her room for the night, Carolina walked out the back door and headed down the dirt road that led to the shore. She had to get out of that house before she lost her mind. Hours of pretending that nothing was wrong had left her worn and frazzled.

She couldn't believe he'd done this to her—and to his mother. The poor woman had been shocked by how much older Carolina was than her son, which had been the first clue that Seamus had been less than honest about what he'd told his family back home in Ireland about her.

Carolina kept her head down and walked fast, guided by the light of the moon and the rage that drove her to get as far away from the house—and him—as she could get.

Pounding footsteps on the path had her spinning around as her rage intensified. "Go back to the house. I have nothing to say to you."

"I have something to say to you."

"What could you possibly say to fix this?"

"How about I'm sorry?"

"Sorry. You're sorry. That's great. I'm glad you're sorry for completely humiliating me in front of your mother, not to mention how you made her feel by blindsiding her right off the boat. You made a total mess of this, and you're *sorry?*" She tossed up her hands and turned to keep walking because she was afraid she might punch him again if she didn't get away from him. Carolina Cantrell, who'd never struck another human being in her life, driven to violence by the man she loved. Wasn't this a fine mess?

"Caro, honey, wait. Please let me explain."

"I don't want to talk to you right now."

"I know, and I totally deserve that. But can I please tell you why I did it?"

Carolina would've chosen to keep walking if it wasn't for the fact that his mother and cousin would be their guests for the next two weeks. Somehow, she had to make peace with Seamus or run the risk of alienating his family. "Fine. Tell me why you felt the need to lie to me and your mother."

"I didn't lie. Exactly."

Incredulous, she said, "What would you call it?"

"I...I told her you were older than me."

"Did you tell her how much older?"

"No."

"Then you lied."

"You don't understand."

"Make me understand, then."

"My mum, she's a lovely lady, but at times, she can be a bit... How to say this? Well, she can be judgmental. And I thought if she met you and saw how much I love you and how much you love me—or how much you loved me before you figured out I hadn't told her about the age difference... I thought maybe if she saw us together, she'd see what I see when I look at you." His hands curled around her hips. "I didn't want her to come here with preconceived notions."

"You should've told me so I'd be prepared for her reaction."

"You're absolutely right. I should have told you, and I'm so sorry I didn't. You insisted we invite her here right when everything between us had settled into a good place. Your son knows, and the sky didn't fall in. We were just getting somewhere. Finally. I didn't want her to come here and undo all that by making you feel bad about yourself or your age or anything."

"*Why didn't you tell me this?*"

"I was scared, love."

"Of what?"

"I was afraid if she knew about the age thing, she'd make it into a big deal in her mind before she even got here, and the whole thing would be a disaster. I wanted her to give you a chance."

"I was embarrassed at the ferry landing."

"I know, and I can't tell you how sorry I am to have done that to you. That's the last thing in the world I wanted."

"You had to know it would happen when she saw me."

"I'd hoped it wouldn't."

"Seamus..." She let her head fall forward onto his chest, because even when she was furious with him, she still loved him.

"I screwed up, love, and I hate that you got hurt."

"I'm not hurt so much as angry. I hated being blindsided."

"I'm so sorry. It'll never happen again. I promise."

"Don't make promises you can't keep."

In the faint glow of the moon, she could see the small smile that occupied his lips. "Forgive me, love?"

"Under one condition."

"Anything. Whatever you want."

"Shouldn't you hear it before you agree to it?"

"If it means you'll forgive me, I'll do whatever you want me to."

"I want you to tell your mother that I had nothing to do with the plan to deceive her."

"Ugh, do I have to?"

"Do you want to be forgiven?"

"More than life itself."

"Then that's what you have to do."

He moved his hands around to her back and stepped even closer to her. "I've already paid my fine. I told her it was all my dumb idea, and you had nothing to do with it. If it's any consolation to you, she's not happy with me either—and not because you're older than me. Because I didn't tell her before she came. So both the women I love best are mad at me."

"Which you richly deserve."

"Which I richly deserve. So am I forgiven?"

"You really told her I didn't know?"

"I really told her, and for what it's worth, she thinks you're lovely and can easily see why I love you so much."

"You made up that last part."

"I did not! She really said that."

"Your credibility has taken a bit of a hit tonight."

"Do you still believe I love you?" he asked.

She shrugged, knowing her indifference would drive him mad. "I'm not sure. I might need some convincing."

"Oh, love, do you know what happens when you toss a red flag in front of a bull?"

"I'm sure you'll be happy to tell me all about what happens, but you have to catch me first." Carolina pulled free of him and took off down the dirt lane she'd traversed her entire life.

He let out a bark of laughter and took off after her.

Knowing he was gaining on her, she ran faster, ducking into the brush to dodge him. She had the upper hand until her foot caught on a root and sent her flying into the darkness. "Crap," she muttered, protecting her face with her arms as she landed hard in a bush full of thorns that tore at her skin as she came down.

"Caro? Where are you, love?"

She whimpered. Everything hurt, and she was hopelessly tangled and afraid to move for fear of further injuring herself.

"Oh my goodness," Seamus said, using the flashlight app on his phone to illuminate her predicament. He pulled a knife from the leather case he wore on his belt and began hacking away at the branches.

"Watch your hands!"

"I don't care about my hands. I've got to get you out of there."

"Seamus…"

"What, love?" he asked, intent on his task.

"Hurts."

"I know, honey. I'm going as fast as I can." He cut and hacked at the branches until he had freed her limbs from the tangle. "Easy now," he said as he took her hands and helped her to stand. "Aw, honey, you're a bloody mess."

Carolina tried to walk, but her tortured skin protested.

"Don't try to move, Caro. I'll carry you. Hold on to me." He lifted her effortlessly and started back to the house. "That'll teach you to run away from me."

"I bet you put that thorn bush there to teach me a lesson."

His quiet chuckle made her smile, even though she hurt everywhere. "I never want to see you hurt like this." Back at the house, he used his foot to kick open the door and deposited her gently on a kitchen chair. "Let me get the first aid kit."

Since it hurt to breathe, Carolina remained as still as she possibly could until he returned and flipped on a light so he could better see her.

"Oh, honey, God."

Angry, bloody scratches, some of them deep, covered her arms and legs. Fortunately, her shorts and T-shirt had protected much of her body.

"We might need to call Dr. David."

"No, no doctor. We can clean it up. Hand me the gauze and some of the antibacterial ointment."

"Now, now, love, settle yourself. I'll tend to your wounds. It's my fault you have them, after all."

Carolina risked the pain of movement to touch his jaw, which was tight with tension. "It's not your fault. I was being foolish when I ran away from you. That was my fault. Not yours."

His hands trembled ever so slightly as he applied the ointment to her ravaged skin. "You never would've been out there if I hadn't driven you to seek refuge from me."

"Seamus, don't. It was a silly accident. It's not your fault."

"Well, it's not yours either."

"Why are we fighting about this?"

"Because. I don't know. Hold still." He was exceedingly gentle as he cleaned each of the cuts and scratches on her arms and legs.

The pain was tremendous, but Carolina held still and stayed quiet until he got the deepest gash on her thigh. Too bad she'd been wearing shorts instead of jeans.

"I don't know about this one, love. It might need a stitch or two."

"There are butterfly bandages in there. Let's use them and see how it is tomorrow."

Carolina bit her lip and tried to stay silent while he dabbed the ointment into the cut. Tears rolled down her face that she brushed away.

"Please don't cry," he whispered. "I can't take it."

"Sorry. That one really hurt."

"I know, love." With a strip of butterfly bandages applied to her thigh, he wiped the dirt off her legs, plucked the leaves from her hair and finished by mopping up her tears. "Now, let's get you into bed." He lifted her from the chair and transported her to the bedroom, setting her down carefully. After months of cohabitation, he knew where everything was and found her a T-shirt to sleep in. He helped her out of her clothes and into the shirt, helped her to the bathroom and then tucked her into bed.

When she was settled under the covers, he sat on the edge of the mattress, looking down at her.

"I'm sorry you got hurt. I'm sorry about this whole stupid thing. After all my preaching about how our age difference doesn't matter at all, after pushing and pushing for you to tell Joe about us, I couldn't even bring myself to tell me own mum about it." He shook his head, clearly disgusted with himself.

"Not as easy as it looks, is it?"

"No. Not at'all." He brushed the hair back from her face and looked down at her, his torment reflected in his eyes, the rigid set of his lips, the tension in his shoulders. "It doesn't mean I don't love you and want you and everything else."

"I know that, Seamus. When I was having trouble telling Joe about us, it didn't mean I loved you any less."

"And now you're all scratched and bloody because I couldn't come clean with me mum."

"I'm scratched and bloody because I foolishly thought the path was in the same exact place it was when I was twelve and tramping through those woods. Clearly some things have changed since then." Despite the pain it caused her, she raised her arm and ran a finger over his tightly set lips. "Don't beat yourself up over it. The scratches will heal. We're fine. Your mum is fine. We're all fine."

"Are we fine? Really?"

"Of course we are. Do you think I don't understand how difficult it can be to break this news to loved ones?"

"I shouldn't have let you be blindsided."

"No, you shouldn't have, and you won't do that again, right?"

"No, love. Lesson learned. I like to think I can be trained."

Carolina laughed. "That'll be the day." She curled her hand around his. "Come to bed. I can't sleep without you next to me."

"Maybe I should sleep on the sofa so I don't hurt you."

"You'll hurt me if you don't sleep with me."

He bent down to kiss her softly, tenderly. "I love you so damned much, Carolina."

"I love you just as much, even if I want to kill you most of the time."

That drew the first genuine smile from him that she'd seen in hours. "I gotta keep ya on your toes."

"That you do. *That* you do. Now come to bed so we can get some sleep."

"I'm coming, love."

CHAPTER 8

Daisy woke in the middle of the night and couldn't remember where she was until she felt David breathing under her and his arms tight around her.

They'd fallen asleep wrapped up in each other in the darkness that was offset only by the glow of the TV. She reached for the remote and turned off the power. She knew she should wake him so he could take her home, but she didn't want to be anywhere other than in his arms, tucked up against him as he slept.

So she returned her head to his chest and listened to the strong beat of his heart under her ear.

"We fell asleep, huh?" The rough, sleepy rumble of his voice made her smile. She loved the intimate feeling that went with knowing what his voice sounded like when he woke from a sound sleep. Now she wished she'd left the TV on so she could see his face, too.

"Looks that way."

"Do you want to go home?"

"Not really. The accommodations are much nicer here."

His lips skimmed her forehead and his fingers slid through her hair, making her sigh with contentment. "They could be better."

"How so?"

"There's a really nice bed in the other room."

The suggestion made her heart beat faster as the idea of being in an actual bed with him sent all her hormones into a frenzy. "That sounds good."

They disentangled from each other and stood up.

Daisy waited for David to turn on a light before she followed him to the bedroom, where he produced a T-shirt for her to sleep in. "Thanks."

"Go ahead and use the bathroom first."

"You don't have an extra toothbrush by any chance, do you?"

"I think I do." He went into the bathroom to rummage around in a cabinet.

Daisy took advantage of the opportunity to take a closer look at his bedroom, which was sparsely furnished with a dresser and a king-size bed covered by a navy-blue comforter.

"Here you go," he said when he returned, holding a toothbrush that was still in the package.

"Thanks. I'll be quick."

Daisy went into the bathroom, removed her dress and hung it on a hook behind the door. She debated whether or not to leave her bra on, but decided she'd be more comfortable sleeping without it. She tucked it behind the dress on the hook, donned the T-shirt and quickly brushed her teeth.

"All yours," she said when she stepped out of the bathroom to find that he'd turned down the bed.

He held up the covers for her. "Hop in so you don't get cold."

"Which side do you prefer?"

"Doesn't matter."

As he went into the bathroom and closed the door, Daisy felt giddy about her sleepover with the sexy doctor. There was something so special about sharing the bed that smelled like him, of sleeping next to him, of seeing his most private living space.

He came out of the bathroom wearing a T-shirt and boxer shorts and slid into bed next to her, leaving the bedside light on. "Comfortable?" he asked.

"I could be more comfortable." Daisy surprised herself with the brazen reply.

"How so?"

"If you were a little closer."

He scooted over an inch. "Better?"

"Not yet."

Another inch. "How about this?"

"Getting warmer, but not quite there yet."

He moved so he was right next to her and put his arm around her. "How's this?"

"Perfect," she said with a sigh of pleasure.

"It could be better."

"How so?" she asked, borrowing his line.

"If you turned toward me."

Daisy did as he asked. "Like this?"

"Just like that," he whispered as he kissed her.

He tasted of toothpaste and sexy man and David. His arms encircled her as he worked his leg between hers.

The rough texture of his hairy leg between her thighs was an instant turn-on as his tongue thoroughly explored her mouth. His hand dipped beneath her T-shirt, caressing her back in slow movements that made her nipples tighten in the hope that he might move to the front. But he kept his hand stubbornly anchored to her back.

Daisy decided to do some exploring of her own, slipping her fingers under his shirt to feel the rippling muscles of his belly and drawing a gasp from him when she slid her fingertips down to the waistband of his shorts. She tugged on the T-shirt. "Take this off."

He released her long enough to do as she asked, and then he was kissing her again, even more intently than before.

She ran her hands over his chest, discovering each contour and making him tremble in the process. Encouraged by his response, she scraped her thumbnail over his nipple, which caused him to startle and then curse under his breath.

Laughing, she said, "Sorry."

"No, you're not."

"I am sorry."

"I still say you're not."

"Okay, I'm not. In fact, I might even do it again."

"Please do."

"Only if you return the favor."

"Daisy," he said, groaning. "I'm trying so hard to go slow, but you're making me nuts."

"I'm sorry. I'm not usually so forward. I don't know what's gotten into me."

"Don't do that. Don't apologize for asking for what you want. I don't ever want you to feel like you can't say what you're thinking to me."

"You're bringing out a whole new side of me."

"What side is that?"

"The hot and bothered side."

"I love that side of you," he said, laughing as he kissed her.

"So what's the verdict on my shirt?"

"You sure you're okay?"

"I could be better if this pesky shirt wasn't in my way."

"In that case…" He helped her to remove it and then wrapped his arms around her, breathing deeply as her breasts pressed against his chest. "God, that feels good. You feel so good."

"So do you."

"I haven't felt this good in a really long time," he whispered.

"I don't think I've ever felt this good."

"Daisy…" He devoured her with his lips and tongue as he cupped her breast.

She cried out from the shock of his thumb and forefinger closing around her overly sensitive nipple.

"Does it hurt?" he asked, sounding alarmed.

"No, not at all. It feels incredible."

"You feel incredible. I want to touch you and kiss you everywhere."

Daisy let out a nervous laugh. "Don't let me stop you."

He kissed her and caressed her and made her crazy with his fingers on her nipples, but that was all he did.

Daisy tried to reach between them to stroke the erection that pulsated against her leg, but he stopped her.

Groaning, she hovered somewhere between frustration and arousal, wanting more but knowing he was determined to take his time. While she respected his scruples, she hoped he would lighten up before she lost her mind from wanting him.

"All in good time, honey," he whispered as he linked their fingers.

"How much time?"

"Why? Are you going somewhere?"

"I'm going slowly crazy."

"I'm right there with you."

"Then why—"

He kissed the words off her lips. "Trust me?"

"Yes, of course I do."

"I'm honored that you trust me. That means more to me than you could ever know. I really like you, Daisy, and I like what we've got going. I don't want to mess it up by moving too fast when you're still recovering. I promise that when we make love, it'll be well worth the wait."

"I just feel so…"

"What? Tell me how you feel."

"Frustrated."

His gentle laughter drew a reluctant smile from her.

"It's not funny."

"I know it isn't. I feel the same way."

"Could we maybe, you know, do what we did before?"

He dragged his hand over her thigh to press against her center. "Do you mean this?"

"Yes," she said, breathlessly. "That."

His fingers moved over her underwear, using the fabric to abrade her most sensitive area. He had her on the verge of explosive release with just a few passes. "Feel good?"

"It could feel better."

He pressed a bit harder. "How's this?"

"Still not as good as it could be."

"You're a rather demanding woman, Daisy Babson."

"You told me I should ask for what I want."

"And what is it that you want?"

"Your fingers." She felt dizzy and light-headed, which was when she realized she was barely breathing. "Under my panties."

He did as she requested, running his fingers lightly over the outer lips of her sex. "Like this?"

"*David*!"

His lips were curved into a smile when he kissed her. "Patience, my sweet."

"I'm fresh out of patience at the moment."

"The lady is sounding more and more aggravated by the second. I'd better tend to her before she exacts her revenge."

"You're a wise man, Dr. Lawrence."

He gave her exactly what she wanted, his fingers focusing on the areas that throbbed for him, sliding into her in a motion that mimicked intercourse, driving her to a powerful full-body orgasm that left her sweating and panting and throbbing under the fingers he continued to press against her.

"How was that?" he asked after a long period of contented silence.

"Pretty damned good."

"I'm relieved you didn't say it could've been better."

Laughing, she said, "It's never been better. Do I get a turn now?"

"You need sleep more than I need favors."

"Please?"

"Hmm, I've got a hot sexy woman in my bed, begging me to let her have her wicked way with me. What am I to do?"

"You really think I'm hot and sexy?"

"This isn't proof enough?" he asked, placing her hand over his erection. "You're very hot and very sexy, and I feel very lucky that you're in my bed."

"I feel lucky, too." She pushed at his shoulders until he was lying flat on his back and went up on her knees to lean over him, peppering his chest and belly with soft, openmouthed kisses that had his muscles quivering in no time. Tugging on the waistband to his boxers, she said, "Take them off."

"Daisy..."

"You're doing what you're told, remember?" Despite the brazen words, her hands trembled with nerves. Although she knew this was David and he'd never harm her in any way, the memories of another man and the constant fear of angering him were never far from her mind.

He removed the shorts and let his hands fall to the mattress, curling them into fists that Daisy fixated on. Tuning in to what had caught her attention, he flattened his hands on his belly. "I'd never, ever, ever hit you, Daisy. *Ever.*"

"I know."

"Do you? Do you really? Do you know there is nothing you could do or say that would ever make me want to hurt you that way?"

"Yes," she whispered, humbled by his intuition and tenderness. "I'm sorry. I know you never would. It's just..."

"Touch me. Kiss me. Do anything you want to. I'm all yours, and you're totally safe with me."

His gentle words brought tears to her eyes, but this wasn't the time for them. Not when he was laid out before her in all his sexy perfection. His erection stretched almost to his belly button. Before her eyes, he got harder and longer. Daisy licked her lips in anticipation and a tiny bit of fear when she thought of taking him into her body. The growing tingle of desire between her legs belied her fears as she took him in hand and ran her tongue over the very tip, which was damp with moisture.

"*Daisy*," he muttered between clenched teeth as his fingers clutched her hair.

"Mmm." Her lips vibrated against his shaft as he got even harder. Encouraged by his response, she ran her tongue down the full length of him and then back up to concentrate on the sensitive head.

"Yes, Daisy… *God*."

She added a tiny bit of suction that had his hips rising from the bed as she stroked him with her hand and tongue.

"Wait. Daisy, stop." He tugged gently on her hair, and he popped free from her mouth an instant before he came with a growl and a curse uttered under his breath. He drew in ragged breaths as his hands fell to the mattress in a helpless gesture that made her smile. "You wiped me out, baby."

He used his T-shirt to wipe his belly and tossed it aside, turning to embrace her. "You're so sexy and sweet. It's an awfully potent combination."

"So are you." She punctuated her words with a hand to his face and a soft kiss. "You make me feel hopeful again."

"That's the nicest compliment I've ever received."

"That can't possibly be true. You save people's lives!"

"Maybe so, but you, Daisy… I think you might just have the power to save *my* life."

She drew in a sharp, deep breath, astounded and touched by the revealing statement.

His arms encircled her, his lips brushed over her hair, and her breasts pressed against his chest. Safe and content in his arms, Daisy drifted off to sleep with a smile on her lips.

After a long day of appointments in the clinic, David was updating patient charts late the next afternoon when Blaine Taylor appeared at his door.

"Hey, Blaine. What's up?"

"Am I getting you at a bad time?"

"Not at all. Come on in."

"Thanks." Blaine took a seat in one of David's visitor chairs. "The receptionist said you weren't with patients so it was okay to come back."

"What's going on?"

"I heard from the assistant attorney general who's prosecuting Daisy's case."

David's stomach clenched at the reminder of the assault and attempted sexual assault case pending against Daisy's ex-boyfriend. "What about it?"

"He had a couple of questions about your statement, and he was unable to reach you, so he asked me to come over to talk to you."

"I haven't gotten to my voice mail yet. What questions does he have?"

"The rape kit came back inconclusive. Nothing to tie Truck to the attempted sexual assault."

The sexual assault count was the more serious charge and had kept Truck in jail without bond while he awaited trial. Without it, he might be released on personal recognizance, a thought David could barely stand to entertain. "Other than the fact that you caught him assaulting her and the trauma to her genital region was indicative of repeated attempts at penetration. Only because he was high as a kite did he fail to actually rape her. We all know that."

"Apparently, Truck's defense attorney, our own local hero Jim Sturgil, is claiming that those bruises could've been caused by any number of unrelated injuries. He's submitted a number of possible scenarios to the court that include…" Blaine pulled a piece of paper from his pocket. "Bicycling injuries, consensual sex, surfing accident, work-related accident, etc. He's creating reasonable doubt and questioning whether that charge will hold up in court. If you can think of anything at all that you might've overlooked, this would be the time to let me know."

David fought back a growing sense of panic. "He's out of his mind if he thinks any of those things caused her injuries. Truck Henry's penis and his rage caused them."

"You and I both know that, but without any forensic evidence that an attempted rape occurred, it's her word against his in court."

David desperately wished he'd found more forensic evidence to keep Truck locked up where he belonged. "So those charges are going to be dropped?"

"They could be. Nothing has happened yet, but Jim is fighting hard to get them thrown out."

"I've always despised that son of a bitch, but now I freaking hate him. How can he do that to Daisy?"

"You know Jim. It's all about the almighty buck with him—that and showing everyone how powerful he is." This was said with a heavy dose of bitterness. "He's actually threatening to sue Tiffany for full custody of Ashleigh if I move in with them."

"Come on… For real?"

"Yep. He dumped her after she worked two jobs to put him through law school, and now he's not going to stand idly by and watch her be happy with someone else."

"Damn, man, that sucks. Is there anything you can do?"

"I can marry her, which I'd love to do, but she said she isn't ready for that after getting divorced so recently. Now he's forcing us to consider that step before she's ready. It's a mess, and the worst part is how he's using poor Ashleigh as a pawn in all of this. Hell, I spend more time with her than he does. He's got no right to use an innocent kid that way."

"I'm sorry you're dealing with all that. If you want to talk about it, you're welcome to air it out with me. I'm no fan of his either. Never have been, but especially now that he's helping Truck to hurt Daisy all over again."

"I heard you two have been hanging out."

"Yeah. She's… She's amazingly strong and resilient after everything she's been through. I don't know what she'll do if they let Truck out of jail, though." He didn't even want to think about that possibility.

"If they let him out, it'll be with a big fat restraining order that keeps him far, far away from Daisy."

"A piece of paper won't keep her safe if he's high."

"Maybe not, but we will. We'll keep her safe."

"Yes, we will." He thought of how sweet she'd been in bed the night before and felt a rather inappropriate surge of lust that had him clearing his throat and his mind of salacious thoughts. "She's strong, but she's also fragile in some ways. Last night, we were, kissing and stuff…"

"And stuff?" Blaine asked with a knowing smirk.

"My hands, they rolled into fists, and she noticed. It wasn't because of anger."

"Of course it wasn't."

"But still… She zeroed in on those fists until I realized what I was doing. I hate that it even crossed her mind that I might hurt her the way he did."

"She knows you'd never do what he did, David. The reflex is instinct by now. It'll take some time, but she'll get past it. Until then, you have to move slowly so you don't spook her."

"I'm trying, but she's not making it easy."

Blaine tipped his head back and laughed. "Ready to move on, is she?"

"You could say that."

"You're doing the right thing taking it slow. She's been through a nightmare that would've left a lesser person curled up in the fetal position rather than starting over with someone new."

"The timing stinks. I know that, but it just sort of… happened."

"The best things in life often happen when you least expect it. At least that's been my experience."

"You mean Tiffany."

He nodded. "And Ashleigh. I love them both and would do anything for them, including wage war with her ex-husband to get him to leave us alone."

"You know," David said, "there're ways you could make his life miserable around here, all within the confines of the law, of course."

Blaine's small smile indicated he'd had similar thoughts. "Of course." He stood to leave and reached out to shake David's hand. "If you ever want to grab a beer sometime, let me know."

"I'll do that." After years of feeling like a social pariah on the island, it was nice to know he had a few new friends. "You'll keep me posted on the situation with Truck?"

"Sure. I'm on my way to talk to Daisy now, too."

"I could save you a trip and update her for you."

"As much as I'd appreciate that, I promised her I'd keep her in the loop. I don't want to disappoint her."

"I understand." Since disappointing her was the last thing he wanted to do either, David could totally relate. "Tell her I'll be there shortly." David would cut short the paperwork he'd planned to do to make sure he was there for her when she needed him.

"Will do. Take it easy."

"You, too. Good luck with the Sturgil situation. Call me if you need a partner in crime."

"You got it," Blaine said, laughing as he left with a wave.

For several minutes after Blaine left, David stared into space, his pen seesawing between his fingers as he contemplated whether or not he should go to her now or wait until after Blaine had a chance to talk to her.

Imagining her expressive face as she heard that Truck might be released from jail, David dropped the pen, grabbed his jacket and ran out of there, anxious to get to her before she heard the news.

On the way home from the hotel that afternoon, Daisy decided to take a detour into town to check out a store that she'd heard lots about but had never actually visited. After last night's encounter in David's bed, Daisy had decided it was up to her to show him that she was ready to take their relationship to the next level.

And to do that, she needed help. What kind of help she wasn't entirely sure, but from what she'd heard, Naughty & Nice was the place to find out. The bells on the door jingled cheerfully when she stepped inside a room filled with sensual decadence. There was no other word for it.

Maddie's sister Tiffany waved to her, but she was on the phone, so Daisy decided to look around on her own. In the small store, she couldn't help but overhear Tiffany's call, especially when her voice was raised.

"He *cannot* do this, Dan. We have to stop him. I won't be forced into getting married sooner than I want to because Jim is being a bully." She paused, listened. "I don't care. He can take me to court. Blaine is moving in whether Jim likes it or not. I have a hundred people on this island who will testify to the fact that I put him through law school and then got dumped when he started making money and lost interest in me." After another pause, she said, "That's fine. If he wants a fight, he's got one. Thanks, Dan. I appreciate it."

Tiffany ended the call and came over to greet Daisy with a hug. "I'm so sorry about that. My damned ex-husband is acting up again."

"Because Blaine is moving in?"

"Yes! Can you believe his gall? *He* dumps *me* and then has the nerve to protest when I fall in love with someone else and want to live with him?"

"That certainly does take nerve."

"One thing Jim has an overabundance of. Anyway, you're not here to talk about my troubles, and I'm sorry again you overheard that. Very unprofessional of me to be venting at work."

"It's just me. Don't worry, and besides, I'm no fan of his after he took Truck's case."

"I'm glad it was a friend." Tiffany stood back and took a closer look at Daisy.

"What?" Daisy asked, feeling self-conscious as she often did around Maddie's stunning younger sister. With her silky dark hair and drop-dead-gorgeous body, Tiffany was the kind of woman Daisy wanted to be—fun, fearless, sexy, confident.

"You look…different. Your cheeks are rosy and your lips are sort of swollen." She zeroed in for a closer look. "And is that *whisker burn* on your neck? Girl! Are you keeping secrets?"

Daisy raised her hand to her neck, wondering how she'd failed to notice razor burn on her own neck. "It's not really a secret."

"Who is he?"

"David Lawrence."

Tiffany's eyes got very big, and her lips pursed with what might've been concern.

"Don't worry. I already know about his litany of sins."

"How did you find out?"

"He told me."

"Did he now? Well, props to him for coming clean."

"He deeply regrets the way he hurt Janey."

"That matters."

"Yes, it does."

"So what can I help you with?"

"Well, ever since the incident with Truck, David has been very kind and very sweet to me. We started out as friends, but now we've sort of started kind of dating and making out and stuff like that."

"Mmm," Tiffany said with a knowing smile. "I *love* stuff like that."

Daisy couldn't contain the laugh that escaped her lips. Tiffany was always incorrigible. "Anyway," Daisy said, forcing herself to continue despite feeling somewhat embarrassed that she needed this kind of help. "He's been very gentle with me and is moving very, *very* slowly. Too slowly, if you know what I mean."

"Ah." A light of understanding bloomed in Tiffany's eyes. "You need a little help…moving things along. Am I right?"

"*Yes*," Daisy said, relieved that Tiffany understood the problem. "I want him to know I'm not as fragile as he thinks I am."

Tiffany bounced a fingertip on her lips. "Let me think." She eyed Daisy shrewdly. "We need to get him so hot he can't think. He can only act."

"I'm a tiny bit afraid of you right now."

Tiffany laughed and took Daisy by the hand. "Stick with me, kid. We'll have that man on his knees begging you."

While Daisy wasn't at all sure she wanted him to beg, she put her trust in Tiffany and let her lead her into a changing room.

She left the store thirty minutes later wearing a sexy new dress over positively scandalous underwear. As she walked home, the thong Tiffany had talked her into abraded her most sensitive region, forcing her to walk slowly or risk making a scene on the sidewalk.

The trip to the store had taken longer than planned, and David was due anytime. Her shopping outing had also cost more than she could comfortably afford to spend, but she'd yet to do anything to celebrate her new job, and the new clothes were a worthwhile investment toward a good cause.

She wanted so badly for David to think of her as healthy and whole rather than fragile and timid. She wanted him to see strength when he looked at her and not fear. Those days were over. The time she'd spent with him had shown her what a healthy relationship should be like, and now that she'd found him, she wanted to move forward the way any other woman would when she met a man she couldn't resist.

Thus the underwear that had her on the verge of orgasmic meltdown just from thinking about him as she walked. If they had that effect on her, she couldn't wait to find out what they did for him. She turned the corner to her street and stopped short when she saw Blaine's SUV parked at the curb. He leaned against it and talked to David, who was sitting on her top step.

Since David wasn't due for another twenty minutes, she concluded that something had happened. Daisy wanted to turn and run from whatever they'd come to tell her. But because she'd left fear behind, she forced herself to walk slowly down the sidewalk so they wouldn't know how fast her heart was beating or how tightly the anxiety gripped her.

David saw her coming and jumped up, his eyes traveling over her body in a hungry stare that indicated his approval of the new dress. He held out a hand to her, and Daisy stepped forward to take it. "What's wrong? Why are you both here?"

"Let's go inside, honey," David said. "Blaine wants to talk to you."

"Did he get out of jail?" Daisy asked, unable to move until that question was answered.

"No," Blaine said.

The flood of relief made her knees go weak. David's arm around her waist helped her to remain standing as he led her into the house.

When she and David were seated on the ragged sofa she'd found by the side of a road two summers ago and Blaine in a rocking chair she had sanded and stained after rescuing it from a yard sale, Daisy braced herself for what she was about to hear. She was grateful for David's arm around her as well as the unwavering support he'd shown her throughout the ordeal.

Slowly and gently, Blaine told her what the assistant attorney general had said about the attempted sexual assault charges that were pending against Truck. She'd feared something like this—a technicality that would get him off the hook.

"Without evidence to tie him specifically to the attempted rape," Blaine concluded, "those charges could be dropped. If that happens, the judge may approve bail while he awaits trial on the assault charges."

As she thought of Truck going free and coming back to find the woman he blamed for putting him in jail in the first place, Daisy began to tremble. And here she'd thought she was past the fear. Apparently not, if the possibility of Truck's release made her shake like a frightened doe.

"It's okay," David whispered as he tightened his hold on her. "He won't get anywhere near you. Not while I'm around."

"We'll do our very best to protect you, Daisy," Blaine assured her. "And I'll keep you posted on anything I hear pertaining to the case."

"Thank you. I appreciate you coming here to talk to me in person."

"If you need anything, anything at all, I want you to call me," Blaine said. "Day or night, I'm available. Don't hesitate. All right?"

Daisy nodded.

Blaine stood to leave.

"Tiffany is upset about Jim," Daisy said, apparently taking Blaine by surprise as every muscle in his face turned to stone. "I was with her just now. She was talking to Dan, and she sounded upset. I thought you'd like to know that she might need you."

"I definitely want to know. Thanks, Daisy. I'll let myself out."

When the door clicked closed behind Blaine, David sat back on the sofa and brought her with him so her head was on his chest. "Talk to me. Tell me how you're feeling."

"I'm scared, and I don't want to be."

"I know it's really hard, but try not to be. He's still locked up where he belongs, but if that changes, you've got a whole lot of people on this island who care about you. We won't let anything happen to you."

"I'm tired of being afraid all the time. It gets so exhausting."

"You don't have to be afraid. I'm here, Daisy. I'm right here, and I'm not going anywhere. You're not alone in this. Not anymore."

His kind words broke the dam that had been holding her emotions in check. A sob escaped her lips and tears streamed down her cheeks. She'd never had a man in her life who she could truly count on, and here he was, this amazing, sexy doctor offering to be that person for her.

"I don't want to drag you into my mess."

"I'm already there, baby, and you didn't drag me. I came willingly." He wiped the tears off her face with the gentle brush of his fingers, and then he tipped her chin up to compel her to meet his gaze. "I'm here, and I'm going to be here no matter what happens. I promise."

Daisy threw her arms around him and held on to the comfort and security he offered so willingly. Did he have any idea how much both those things meant to her? Or that she'd never felt entirely comfortable or secure with a man?

"Can we talk about this dress and how I nearly swallowed my tongue when I saw you coming down the street looking so sexy?"

That drew a watery laugh from her as she pulled back from him and dried her eyes. "I wanted to surprise you with something new."

"You surprised me all right. You surprise me all the time." He cupped her cheek and ran his thumb over her face. "You look gorgeous. Even more so than usual."

"Thank you."

"I was able to get new reservations at Domenic's, but if you don't feel like going out, I totally understand."

Determined not to let the threat of Truck's release get in the way of another lovely evening with David, Daisy took his hand. "I feel like going."

"Are you sure?"

"Very sure."

"First things first," he said, drawing her into a kiss. "I've been thinking about that all day."

"So have I, along with a few other things."

Groaning from her suggestive words, he kissed her again, longer and deeper this time, until they were both breathless and clinging to each other.

As she stared into his eyes, it became clear to her that she'd never known true desire until she knew him.

"We should go so I don't ruin all chances of ever getting another reservation at Domenic's."

"Right," she said, shaking off the stupor that accompanied the desire.

He helped her up and drew her into his embrace. "Everything's going to be okay, Daisy. We'll see to it, okay?"

She nodded and held on tight to him—and his assurances.

CHAPTER 9

Blaine left Daisy's house and went straight to Tiffany's store, anxious to hear the latest in the ongoing saga with Jim the douchebag. What he really wanted was to pay a visit to her ex-husband and teach him a thing or two about how you treat the mother of your child. But all that would accomplish was getting Blaine into trouble with the mayor that he didn't need on top of everything else he and Tiffany were dealing with.

The thing that really burned his ass was she was finally happy. They both were. He'd never been so happy, never knew this level of happy even existed. When someone threatened those he loved, Blaine's first impulse was to come out swinging. But that wouldn't help Tiffany, and his entire focus was on whatever she needed. While bashing in the pretty-boy face of her sanctimonious ex-husband might make him feel a hell of a lot better, it would probably only increase Jim's resolve to go after custody of Ashleigh—a thought that struck fear in Blaine's heart. He'd become awfully attached to Tiffany's adorable little girl and would do anything he could to keep her with them.

Outside the store, Blaine parked at the curb and went inside, the bells that had become so familiar to him announcing his arrival. And there she was, his love, his life, his woman. His entire body reacted to the sight of her as it had from the first time he laid eyes on her in her sister's room at the clinic almost two years ago now.

"Hey, baby," he said as he walked toward her, pleased by the delight he saw in her eyes. She was always so damned happy to see him. No one had ever been so glad to see him. "I saw Daisy and heard the dickhead is giving you grief again. What happened?"

"Come hug me good and hard, and then I'll tell you."

"You know I love it good and hard. Always happy to oblige."

Her dirty laugh went straight to his heart. He loved her so goddamned much that sometimes it scared the hell out of him to think about all the ways it was possible to screw up the most perfect thing in his life.

He wrapped his arms around her and breathed in the scent of strawberries that clung to her hair and skin. That scent had positively bewitched him from the very first moment he spent in her presence. "What now?"

"He's not backing down. If you move in, he's taking me back to court to get full custody of Ashleigh."

"Then I won't move in."

Her arms tightened around him, squeezing the air out of his lungs. "Yes, you will. We're not going to let him bully us. If he takes me back to court, I'll march everyone I know in there to tell the judge how he let me work two jobs to put him through law school and then dumped me as soon as the money started rolling in."

"Thank God he dumped you. Best thing to ever happen to me."

She framed his face with her hands and brought him down for a kiss. "Best thing to ever happen to me, too. He's jealous because we have each other, and he has no one. If we let him push us around now, the next fifteen years until Ashleigh turns eighteen are going to be hell on earth." Her hands fell to his chest as she took a long, perusing look at him, making his skin burn with desire.

"What?"

"I love you in your uniform." She fanned her face. "So hot."

"I love you in absolutely nothing." He nuzzled her neck and made her giggle when he hit one of her ticklish spots. "Are you done here?"

"Since I own the place, I suppose I could close up a little early. What do you have in mind, Chief?"

"Where's Ashleigh?"

"Having a sleepover with my mom, Ned and Thomas."

"A night all to ourselves?" He wanted to sing hallelujah.

"Looks that way."

"Christ, I'm already hard as a rock just thinking about a full night alone with you."

Smiling, she said, "Are you off duty as you sport this hard-as-a-rock erection?"

"As of twenty minutes ago."

Damn if she didn't cup and squeeze him until his eyes nearly rolled back in his head. "We can't let something that fine go to waste." With one, last emphatic squeeze, she released him and went to turn the Open sign to Closed and lock the door.

When she returned to him, he took her hand and led her directly to the storeroom.

"Have I ever told you this is my favorite part of your store?" he asked when he had her in the relatively private back room.

"But this is the part no one ever sees."

"Exactly," he said as he captured her mouth in a searing kiss that nearly blew the top right off his head. Cupping her ass, he lifted her and pressed her against the wall. "Have I ever told you," he asked as his lips went to work on her neck, "how insanely hot you make me?"

"I think you might've mentioned that a time or two."

He loved that she tipped her head to the side to give him better access to her neck as she pressed her heated core against his erection. "I don't know if you fully understand just how hot we're talking."

"How hot are we talking?"

"It's an inferno—an out-of-control wildfire and the surface of the sun—combined."

"That's pretty hot."

"Sometimes I think it's going to consume me, but then you're here, and you're holding me and loving me and everything is perfect. Simply perfect."

"I love you so much, Blaine. Your love gives me the strength to stand up to Jim and say *enough*, because I know that no matter what happens, you'll be there with me, and we'll deal with it together."

Touched to his soul by her words and humbled by her love, he pressed his lips to the spot under her ear, breathing in her very essence. "I love you more than life. I love Ashleigh just as much." He pulled back so he could see her face. "Marry me. Be with me forever. I'll take care of you both if only you'll let me."

Her eyes widened with surprise and filled with tears. "I don't want him to push us into something we're not ready for."

"This has absolutely nothing to do with him. It's about you and me and Ashleigh and how much we love each other. That's all."

She grasped a handful of his hair as she kissed him with strokes of her tongue that made him want to beg for more.

"Marry me," he whispered against her lips, tasting the salt of her tears.

She looked at him for a long moment that left him suspended somewhere between heaven and hell as he realized how much hinged on what she said next. "Yes. Yes, I'll marry you."

He froze, fearing his ears were playing tricks on him. "Really?"

She bit her lip and nodded. "Really."

Letting out a whoop, he spun her around until they were both dizzy. And then he propped her against the wall again and kissed her so hard his lips went numb.

"I love that you asked me here," she said when they surfaced for much-needed air.

"I asked you here this time." He'd asked her once before when they were in her bed, and she'd said she wasn't ready after just getting divorced.

"This is the only time that matters."

"Let's do it this weekend," he said, suddenly desperate to make it official before something could derail them.

"Are you crazy? We can't throw a wedding together that fast."

"Isn't your sister having a cookout?"

"Yes, but—"

"That'll be our reception." He loved the idea more with every passing second, and had no doubt that her sister and his good friend Mac would be thrilled to be a part of it. "Their yard is perfect for it. We'll get married on the beach with just our immediate families and then go to the party. Maddie will love it. She'll be all over it."

"You've lost your ever loving mind!"

"I've lost everything I've got to you and your little girl, and I've never been happier in my life. So what do you say? Can we make this happen?"

"Do you swear you're not doing this because of Jim and his threats?"

"Who? I don't recognize that name." He propped his forehead against hers. "He's nothing to me except Ashleigh's father. *You* are everything. I want you, I want us, I want Ashleigh and a bunch of other kids who look just like their mother. Well, wait, not the girls. I couldn't deal with more than one daughter who looks like you. I'd never let them out of the house."

Tiffany laughed through her tears, her arms tight around his neck.

"So this weekend? Yes? You'll talk to your sister?"

"Yes, I'll talk to her, yes, I'll marry you this weekend. Yes to everything, you crazy lunatic."

"Let's go celebrate in comfort."

"Blaine?"

"What, baby?"

"Even though you said it has nothing to do with him, thank you."

"I still say it's got nothing to do with him, but if it also helps you out of a jam, it's the very least I can do for the woman who's given me everything." He let her slide down the aroused front of him.

"Take me home."

The parking lot at Domenic's was packed, and the reception area was crowded with people waiting for tables. Great... Oh even better! Among the couples in line for a table were Janey's parents. Awesome. Their backs were to David and Daisy. *Let's hope they stayed that way.*

Daisy tucked a hand into the crook of his arm. "What's wrong?"

"Nothing." He was determined to shake off the funk he felt coming on. While he might not be the McCarthy's favorite person, he had saved their granddaughter from certain death at birth. He hoped they remembered that when they saw him and not the way he'd betrayed their daughter. And why did he even care anymore what they thought of him?

"Why are you all tense?"

"I see some people I know ahead of us in the line."

"I'd venture to guess you know most of the people on this island due to the nature of your work."

"A lot of them." Because he wanted to be different with her, because he wanted to be better, he said, "Janey's parents are up there. I'm never entirely sure what kind of reception I'll get from them. At least now you'll know why, if I get the big chill."

"It bothers you that they treat you that way."

Intrigued by her insight, he attempted a casual response. "They have every reason to treat me the way they do."

"But still it bothers you."

"I always had a lot of respect for them and their family."

"It hurts to have lost their respect."

"I lost it for good reason."

"Do you smell that?"

"Smell what? Garlic? Basil?"

"No, the flowers." She pointed to the huge arrangement of lilies that sat on a table in the reception area, which he wouldn't have noticed had she not drawn his attention to it. "They're my favorite. See the ones with the red in the center? Those are stargazer lilies. Aren't they beautiful? They put out one of my favorite scents. When they're in the house, that's all you can smell."

Listening to her, David wanted to fill her home with stargazer lilies so she'd always be surrounded by her favorite scent. And he appreciated that she'd managed to get his mind off Janey's parents being in line ahead of them.

"I can see why you like them."

She curled her hands around his arm and rested her head on his shoulder.

He loved that she had no problem making a public statement that they were together despite what she knew about him. As they waited to get to the reception desk, he tuned in to the conversation the couple in front of them was having with Mr. and Mrs. McCarthy.

David realized it was Jenny Wilks, the lighthouse keeper, and Mason Johns, the fire chief. As Daisy leaned against him, David listened in on what they were talking about while hoping the McCarthys might not notice him there behind Mason's towering form. The guy had to be easily six and a half feet tall.

"I've been meaning to call you, Mr. McCarthy," Jenny said. "I was hoping you'd know who is supposed to cut the grass out at the lighthouse. It's getting really long, and there's been no sign of anyone."

"That's odd," Big Mac said. "The Martinez family has had the town contract for years, and Ned was just saying this morning that the grass at Town Hall hasn't been cut either. I'll give them a call in the morning to get them out to the lighthouse."

"That'd be great, thanks."

Oblivious to his presence behind them, they chatted about the new grandchild they had on the way and how excited they were for Joe and Janey. And then they dropped a bomb that David hadn't seen coming. Janey had decided to forgo veterinary school for motherhood.

"Of course we're thrilled that she and Joe and the baby will be staying close by," Mrs. McCarthy said. "But we hope that maybe she'll still get to finish school at some point. That was always her dream."

The words were like a knife to David's heart, since he'd been responsible for denying her that dream when they were together. Her parents had never forgiven him for steering her away from vet school, which he now knew had been a big mistake on his part.

At the time, he'd thought it was the right thing because he didn't want them to be in debt for the rest of their lives. With hindsight, however, he could see how Janey had lost something important to her when he encouraged her to forgo that dream.

Mrs. McCarthy's cell phone rang, and she excused herself from the conversation. "Oh my goodness," she said. "Is she okay?"

David held his breath as he waited to hear what was wrong and whether it would change his plans for the evening.

"Yes, of course," Mrs. McCarthy said. "We'll be right there."

"What's the matter?" Big Mac asked.

"That was Joe. Janey fainted. She's okay, but I guess it scared the hell out of them." To her husband, she said, "I'm sorry about dinner, but I want to go check on her."

"So do I."

"I hope she's okay," Jenny said. "Please give them my regards."

"We will, honey," Mrs. McCarthy said. "Enjoy your evening."

As they rushed by Jenny and Mason, Mr. McCarthy noticed David. He stopped his wife from going past them. "David…"

"Mr. McCarthy, Mrs. McCarthy. Nice to see you."

Mr. McCarthy looked rattled, but he still took note of Daisy on David's arm. "Yes, um, you too. I wonder… I mean, I know you're not working right now, but…"

David didn't want to confess to having overheard their conversation with Jenny. "What can I do for you?"

"Damn, this is awkward, but Janey… She fainted. Is that something we need to be concerned about?"

David recalled what Victoria had said about Janey's blood pressure being slightly elevated at her last appointment. "Possibly. If it's okay with Janey, I could come by and do a quick check of her vitals to make sure everything's all right."

"Would you do that? Really?"

"Sure, no problem. Better safe than sorry, right?"

"Thank you so much. We're heading there now."

"Janey has my number if she'd like me to come by. It's up to her—and Joe."

Mr. McCarthy nodded in understanding.

"We hope she's okay," Daisy said.

"Thank you, Daisy," Mrs. McCarthy said as she dragged her husband out the door.

"Sorry about that," David said when they were gone. While they were talking to the McCarthys, Jenny and Mason had been taken to a table.

"It's no problem."

With his arm around her, he spoke close to her ear. "My job is often going to get in the way of our plans. I hope you know that I'd always rather be with you."

She smiled up at him, dazzling him with the affection she directed his way. "That's nice of you to say."

"It's a disclaimer that hopefully gets me out of lots of trouble for things such as tending to my pregnant ex-fiancée when I'm supposed to be spending the evening with you."

"I'm sure you'll think of some way to make it up to me," she said as they were shown to their table.

Her saucy and unexpected reply took David right back to the previous night they'd spent together. Suddenly, he was hungry for much more than food.

Their entrées arrived at the same moment his cell phone vibrated in his pocket. With an apologetic glance at Daisy, David retrieved the phone and saw Janey's number on the caller ID. Why, after all this time, his belly still did a flip-flop at the thought of talking to her would be something he would ponder later when Daisy wasn't sitting a foot from him. "Hi, there." He thought about going outside to take the call but didn't want Daisy to think he had anything to hide where Janey was concerned. So he stayed at the table but kept his voice down so he wouldn't annoy the other diners.

"Hi, David. I'm so sorry to bother you, but my parents and Joe are freaking out about the fainting thing. My dad told me you generously offered to come by. Personally, I don't think it's necessary, but they all do."

"Tell me how you were feeling before you fainted."

"A little nauseous, and I had a headache most of the day."

"Any swelling or puffiness in your arms or legs?"

"My ankles are swollen, and I had to take my rings off yesterday because they were making my fingers hurt."

David didn't like what he was hearing in light of what he already knew about her elevated blood pressure. "I'm going to come by to check your blood pressure and take a quick look. Is that okay?"

"I guess so. I just hate to interrupt your date."

"It's fine, Janey. That's my job. I'm happy to do it."

"Well, you're a very good sport. Thank you. You know we moved, right?"

"I heard that from someone. What's the address?"

She gave it to him, and he wrote it on a paper cocktail napkin. "I'll be there soon."

"Thanks, David."

He tucked the phone back into his pocket and tried to refocus on Daisy and his chicken marsala, but his brain was spinning over what Janey had told him. He was afraid she might be working up to preeclampsia, which could be a very serious situation for her and the baby.

"Why don't we get the food to go so you can take care of Janey?" Daisy suggested.

"No, it's fine. An extra half hour won't make a difference."

"David, it's okay to admit that you're worried about her, and you want to make sure she's all right. You cared about her for a long time, and that doesn't end just because the relationship did."

Relieved that she seemed to get his dilemma without needing him to spell it out, he took her hand and brought it to his lips, delighting in the flush that infused her cheeks. "Thank you for understanding. How about I check on Janey and then I'll go back to your house to watch a movie?"

"That sounds perfect."

"Sorry about dinner," David said as he signaled for the waiter. "I'll make it up to you."

"You don't have to."

"Yes, I do, Daisy. I'm being called away from our date to go check on my ex-fiancée, who may or may not be looking at a pregnancy complication. Most women would say at the very least that calls for some sparkly jewelry or some such thing."

Her laughter filled him with warmth and pleasure at knowing he'd managed to take her mind off her troubles, even for a little while. "Well, if you think that's what it'll take to get back into my good graces, knock yourself out, Dr. Lawrence. But the movie would've been more than enough."

"Damn me and my big mouth," he said as he signed the credit card slip.

He took her home and insisted on seeing her safely inside, even though she said it wasn't necessary. "It is necessary." He handed her both boxes of takeout. "Keep this warm for me. I'll be back as fast as I can."

She ran a finger down the middle of his chest. "I'll be waiting."

The words and gesture made his mouth go dry with lust. "Are you trying to make sure I think only of you while I'm with my ex?"

"That would be very devious of me."

His soft laughter brought a smile to her face. "Trust me when I tell you I think about you all the time."

"I think about you, too. Pretty much all the time."

"Glad we have that in common."

She went up on tiptoes to kiss him. "Take care of Janey, and don't worry about me. Do your job."

"See you soon." He left her with another quick kiss and made sure she was inside with the door locked before he returned to his car. Since David never knew when he might be called on to help someone, he kept a medical bag in his car. He had everything he needed to do a perfunctory exam. On the way to Janey's house, David tried to think about anything other than where he was going and who he was going to see. This was about his job and nothing more.

"Keep telling yourself that," he said out loud. "Maybe you'll actually believe it by the time you get there." To take his mind off his task, he made a quick call to Victoria.

"Hey, David," she said, sounding out of breath. "What's up?"

"I wanted to let you know that Janey McCarthy, er Cantrell, I mean, fainted tonight. I'm going to her house now to check on her."

"Yikes, that's awkward. You want me to do it?"

"It's okay. I ran into her parents, they told me about it, and I offered."

"That's nice of you."

"It's my job."

"It's your ex."

"Believe me, I know."

"Tell her to come in and see me in the morning. I'll make some time around nine thirty."

"Will do."

"So I met this guy. Oh my God, he's *amazing*. He's Irish. So sexy."

"How'd you meet him?"

"He came into the Beachcomber, and we totally hit it off. I think I might be in love."

"Honestly, Victoria, with some guy right off the ferry?"

"He's not just some guy. He's Seamus O'Grady's cousin, Shannon. Yum, yum, *yum*."

"Spare me the gory details."

"The details are quite gory, and they're going to get even gorier before he leaves if I have anything to say about it."

"Lalalala, gotta go."

Victoria was laughing when he disconnected the call.

At times she drove him crazy treating him like her best girlfriend, but most of the time she was a good friend and an excellent colleague. David would've lost his mind a long time ago without her help with women's health and midwifery at the clinic. He had all he could do to stay on top of the other demands.

Every light seemed to be on in Janey and Joe's big contemporary home when David pulled into the driveway. The place was nice. Really nice. But then what did he expect? As the owner of the ferry company that serviced the island, Joe was loaded, and Janey's family wasn't exactly poor either.

"Knock it off," he grumbled. "What does it matter to you what they have or where they live?" It didn't matter to him. Janey was his past, and he'd moved on. He was feeling hopeful again, even happy since he'd been seeing Daisy, and he chose to focus on that rather than the mistakes of the past as he approached a front door illuminated by a porch light.

He pushed the doorbell and waited.

Joe came to the door, looking a bit frazzled—and happy to see him, which was a first since the nose-punching incident. "David, come in. Thanks so much for coming over. We really appreciate it."

"Sure." David followed Joe through a nice living room and kitchen to a screened-in porch, where Janey was reclined on a chaise. Even hugely pregnant she was gorgeous, and the sight of her brought back a slew of memories he wouldn't have thought would be so easily resurrected after all the time they'd been apart.

"Hey," she said, seeming embarrassed as she smiled at him. "I fear this is much ado about nothing, but thanks for coming."

"No problem."

"It's not much ado about nothing, Princess," her father said as he hovered at the foot of the chaise. "You fainted. That's not nothing."

"Is it okay if I check your pulse?" David asked Janey.

Seeming as uncomfortable as he felt, she extended her arm. As he pressed his fingers against her pressure point, he thought of how many years they'd spent together, how many times he'd held that hand or woken to her face on the pillow next to his. A pervasive sense of sadness filled him over how cavalier he'd been with something so precious.

"Your heart rate is a little fast. Have you been exerting yourself at all?"

"No, not really."

"We haven't let her do much of anything," Joe said as he paced from one end of the porch to the other.

"Joe, sit down," Janey said.

"I'd rather stand up, if it's just the same to you."

"Joe."

He went to the end of the chaise and raised her feet to make room for him to sit with her. That's when David noticed how swollen her ankles were.

"How long have they been like that?"

"A couple of days," Janey said. "Just since it got really hot."

"Any headache, blurred vision, sensitivity to light or abdominal pain?"

"A few headaches here and there, but none of the rest."

David applied the blood pressure cuff and reached for his stethoscope. As he pumped up the cuff, he caught her watching him and gave her a small smile, hoping to calm her.

"It's funny," she said.

"What is?"

"Seeing you in doctor mode."

"Finally, huh?"

She smiled and stayed silent while he took her blood pressure.

Shit, he thought, 140 over 90, *definitely higher than it should be.* "Do you remember what your BP was the last time Victoria took it?"

"I think it was 130 over 70."

So it was creeping up. "When you fainted, did you hurt anything?"

"Just my elbow and my pride." She held up her arm so he could see the bluish tinge to the skin below the bone.

"It bends the way it's supposed to?"

"Yep." She extended her arm to demonstrate.

"You didn't hit your head, did you?"

"I caught her," Joe said.

"Good thing," David said. "You probably saved her from being seriously injured."

"What would cause the fainting?" Joe asked.

"Did you eat enough today?" David asked Janey.

"I was a little nauseous earlier, so I didn't have lunch," she confessed sheepishly.

"Damn it, Janey!" Joe said. "You can't skip meals right now. What if I hadn't been here to catch you when you fell?"

Nudged by his wife, Big Mac approached Joe and put a hand on his shoulder. "Let's go outside and get some air, son."

"I don't want air. I want to know why she's skipping meals when she shouldn't be."

"Joseph," Janey said sternly, "go with my dad or deal with my wrath. Your choice."

Joe scowled at her but let Big Mac lead him out of the room.

David smiled at Janey.

"Ugh, he's driving me crazy with his hovering."

"He's not wrong, you know," David said. "You really can't skip meals at this stage in your pregnancy. The baby is drawing a lot of nutrients from you, so you need to take in enough for both of you."

"I know, but I felt so gross I couldn't imagine eating anything."

"Somehow you have to get it in."

"I'll try harder."

"Let me take a closer look at this swelling." He pressed his fingers against her left ankle and counted the seconds it took for the dents left by his fingers to disappear. Three seconds on the left side and four on the right.

"What does that mean, David?" Linda McCarthy asked.

"It's a simple diagnostic test to tell whether the edema—or the fluid buildup—is something we need to be concerned about."

"Is it?" Janey asked.

"I'm going to tell you the truth, Janey. I don't love what I'm seeing here. The elevated BP, the edema, the fact that it took four seconds for my finger imprint to disappear and the nausea are all possible signs of preeclampsia or pregnancy-induced hypertension."

"Isn't that dangerous?" Linda asked.

"It can be if left untreated. We're going to need some more information before I can say for certain if it's something to worry about. Can you come into the clinic around nine thirty tomorrow? I'd like to run a urinalysis and put a monitor on the baby for a couple of hours just to be sure everything is okay."

"Sure," Janey said hesitantly. "No problem."

"Going forward, I want you on full bed rest. Do you understand what that means?"

Janey groaned and dropped her head back against the chaise. "Seriously?"

"I'm afraid so. For now, I'll allow trips to the bathroom and a quick shower every day, but that's it. Otherwise, you're in bed or on your chaise or wherever you're most comfortable. And I'd prefer for you to spend as much time as you can on your left side, which promotes circulation."

"It's summer, and I can't do *anything*?"

"What is it that you want to do?"

"Mac and Maddie are having a big cookout this weekend that I've been looking forward to for weeks."

"If Joe carries you to the car, and Mac has a lounge chair waiting for you at his house, I don't see why you couldn't go. It's all about you exerting yourself as little as possible."

"We can do it, Janey," Linda said. "Dad and I will help, and everyone else will, too. If David thinks it's what's best for you and the baby, then we'll help you do nothing."

"I do think it's for the best," David said, "or I'd never put you through it."

She closed her eyes and blew out a long, deep breath.

"What're you thinking?" Linda asked.

"That I'll go mad being stuck in bed for two months."

"We won't let you go mad, honey. We'll all be here to keep you entertained."

"I know." She glanced up at her mother. "Could you give me just a minute with David?"

Linda seemed hesitant to leave them alone together. "Oh, um, sure. I'll be right outside with Dad and Joe."

When they were alone, David said, "Why'd you do that, Janey? Your husband won't appreciate that I'm in here with you."

"You're my doctor. Why would he possibly object?"

"Maybe because I'm also your ex-fiancé?"

"That was a very long time ago."

"Not all that long."

"Long enough that we've all moved on, haven't we?"

It seemed to matter greatly to her that he agree, so he nodded.

"I want you to be happy, David."

"That's far more than I deserve from you."

"I don't like what you did, but I forgave you a long time ago. If I can forgive you, maybe it's time to forgive yourself, too. Hmm?"

"Maybe," he conceded.

"I heard you're seeing Daisy."

Startled by the blunt statement, he met her gaze. "Yeah."

"I like her. She's perfect for you."

"Is that right?" he asked, feeling mildly embarrassed to be having this discussion with Janey of all people.

"Uh-huh."

"Don't you have other things on your mind besides my love life?"

"So it's love?" Her delighted smile reminded him of many a sparring match with her in the past. She'd always been a worthy opponent.

"None of your business. Let's talk about you, your baby and your bed rest."

"I'd rather talk about your love life."

David laughed at the scowl she directed his way. "I know it's a major drag, but it's in your best interest and the baby's to stay as quiet as you possibly can. No strenuous activity, nothing that makes your heart beat fast."

"Well, that eliminates a few of my favorite things."

David tried not to let the memories of how much she'd enjoyed sex wash over him, but some things were hard to forget. "Definitely none of that."

"You're a real killjoy, Dr. Lawrence."

"So I've been told a few times. We'll see you in the clinic tomorrow. If you call when you get there, we'll meet you with some wheels to keep you off your feet."

"Oh, a wheelchair. It just gets better and better."

He zipped his bag and stood to leave. "It'll all be fine, Janey, as long as you follow doctor's orders."

"Joe's first question is going to be whether we should leave now for our house on the mainland."

"You have to do what makes you comfortable, but personally I don't think it's necessary. We can take good care of you here for the next four weeks and get you to the mainland to deliver with plenty of time."

"And I'll be able to travel?"

"We never know anything for certain, but based on what I know now, it shouldn't be a problem."

"I'll be quoting you later tonight when Joe is packing our bags."

"Good luck with that. I'll see you tomorrow."

"David?"

"Yes?"

"This is the second time you've come when I needed you. I just want you to know that your generosity doesn't go unnoticed."

David let her words wash over him, a gentle balm on the wounds he carried with him. "When I think of you, Janey—and I think of you often—I try not to focus on how we ended, but rather on the very good years we spent together. And I'll always come when you need me."

"There's going to be an invite coming your way to Mac and Maddie's cookout this weekend. I hope you'll come with Daisy."

"I'll try to make it." He turned to leave and nearly ran smack into Joe. Judging by the stormy expression on Joe's face, he'd heard what David said. That was okay. David didn't regret saying it.

"I'll see you both in the clinic tomorrow," David said, anxious to get out of there.

"Thank you for coming," Joe said, surprising David with a handshake.

"Any time." He let himself out the front door and found Janey's parents sitting on the porch swing.

"Everything okay?" Big Mac asked.

"It is for now, but she's going to need to stay off her feet for the next few weeks."

"Nothing can happen to my little girl," Big Mac said, his voice hitching on the last two words.

"That's the last thing in the world I want either."

Big Mac stood and came over to him, his height and size as imposing as it had been when David began dating Janey as a fifteen-year-old. He extended his hand to David. "Thank you for checking on her."

David shook the older man's hand. "Happy to do it." Aware of them watching him, he went down the stairs and got into his car. Driving into town, he allowed himself to wallow in the odd feelings that came with seeing Janey, even if she was married to another man and pregnant with his child.

This time, however, he didn't feel bitter so much as sad for what he'd had and lost, for what he'd failed to treasure the way he should have. As his thoughts shifted to Daisy, waiting for him in town, he was suddenly desperate to see her. When he was with her, there was no time for bitterness or regret. With her he found hope and renewal and other things he couldn't yet name.

He decided to call her to see if he was still welcome so late.

"Hey," she said when she answered his call, her voice husky and sleepy sounding.

"Hey. Just checking to see if you're still up or if you'd rather take a rain check."

"I'm still up, and I'm not issuing any rain checks tonight."

Smiling, he said, "I'll be there in a few."

CHAPTER 10

David pulled up to her house ten minutes later and parked at the curb. As he took the stairs to the porch, she opened the door and greeted him with a warm, welcoming smile. A profound sense of homecoming overtook him, wiping away every thought that didn't involve her.

"Everything okay with Janey?" she asked as he stepped inside.

He nodded and hooked an arm around her waist.

She wound her arms around his neck, her fingers sliding through hair that needed to be trimmed. "Everything all right with you?"

"It is now."

Smiling up at him, she looked sweet and young and gorgeous—and determined. What was that about? "I could heat up your leftovers. Are you hungry?"

"Not for food."

"You're in a strange mood."

"Am I?"

She nodded. "Was it hard to see Janey?"

"Not particularly." He drew her in closer to him, aligning her body with the erection that hardened to the point of pain when her breasts pressed against his chest. Bending his head, he nuzzled her neck, kissing the place where her pulse thudded against his lips. "I'm kind of tired."

"Oh," she said as she began to release him. "I'm sorry. I should've let you go home—"

He kissed her, thrusting his tongue into her welcoming mouth and loving the moan of pleasure that came from her throat as her tongue mated with his.

"You don't seem tired," she said many minutes later. "In fact," she said as she rubbed against him suggestively, "you seem very much awake."

"I was hoping you'd ask me to stay."

"You were? Wow, I totally missed that."

David laughed at her befuddled expression. "Next time I'll be more direct. I'll say something like 'Daisy, all I've thought about today is sleeping with you last night, and I really want to do it again if you'll have me.' Is that direct enough?"

"Yes, it is, and I'd love to have you stay with me tonight."

He kissed the furrow that formed between her brows. "But?"

She rolled her lip between her teeth, making her look adorable and uncertain. "I don't want to stop this time. I want…"

Outrageously aroused by the desire he saw in the eyes that looked up at him searchingly, he kissed the end of her nose and her poor, abused lip. "Tell me what you want, Daisy. Tell me."

"I want you. I want this. I want to feel like a normal woman who is crazy about a wonderful guy and wants to show him how she feels about him."

"You don't feel like a normal woman with me?" That bothered him greatly.

"Yes, I do, of course I do, but it's just… I…"

"Say it, honey. Whatever you want to say, it's fine. I promise."

"I don't want you to treat me like I'm fragile. You've moved nice and slow, and you've been great. Very understanding and gentle. But now…" She dropped her head against his chest. "This is so embarrassing."

He smiled as he kissed the top of her head. "Now what? Tell me."

Without raising her head, she said, "Now I want you to treat me like you would anyone else. I want to pretend, just for tonight, that nothing bad ever happened to me." She finally looked up at him with her heart in her eyes. "Can we do that?"

"I'd hate myself if I did anything to scare you or set you back."

"You couldn't. There's nothing about you that reminds me of him."

"The other night, at Maddie's house—"

She laid her hands on his chest, no doubt able to feel the galloping beat of his heart. "It was the first time. That's all. I'm ready for that now. Please, David. I want to move forward, and I can't do that if I walk around afraid of my own shadow all the time."

"I don't want you to be afraid. I want you to be happy."

"Being with you makes me happy." She extended her hand.

He took her hand and closed his fingers around hers.

"Come to bed with me."

Daisy locked the front door and shut off the lights while David waited for her, watching her every move. Despite her brave words and resolve to move forward, she hoped he couldn't feel the way her hand trembled when she reached for his again.

He didn't say anything as he linked his fingers with hers and let her lead him up the stairs to her bedroom, where she'd lit some candles earlier, hoping for this very outcome.

"This is very nice," he said as he took in the pile of pillows on her bed and the warm glow of the candles.

"I hope it's not too obvious," she said, regretting her forwardness now that she had him where she wanted him.

"It's not obvious. It's romantic and lovely, just like you."

Daisy dropped his hand and twisted her index fingers around each other. "I said all that downstairs because I really wanted you to stay, and I really want... Well, I told you what I want."

"Now you're nervous."

"Yes, which makes me feel foolish."

He brushed her hair back from her face and cupped her cheeks. "Don't be nervous. Let's just go to bed and not worry too much about what happens then. Can we do that?"

Relief flooded through her veins, infusing her with gratitude for the series of regrettable events that had brought this wonderful man into her life. "Yes, that's exactly what I want to do."

He patted her on the bottom. "Go use the bathroom first. I'll be right here, waiting for you."

Daisy grabbed one of the oversized T-shirts she slept in and went across the hall to the bathroom to change and brush her teeth. She also ran a comb through her hair and applied the sample of fragrant lotion Tiffany had given her to her hands and face. Studying her reflection in the mirror, she noticed the heightened color in her cheeks and the glazed look in her eyes. She blew out a deep breath and returned to find him sitting on her bed. He'd removed his shirt, revealing his lean, muscular chest.

She wanted to touch him and hold him and feel the way she did every time they were close to each other. As he brushed by her on the way to the bathroom, he dragged a hand across her belly, setting off a firestorm of reaction that made her knees weak.

After the door to the bathroom closed, she got in bed and pulled the covers up to her waist. She found a focal point across the room, a poster of Marilyn Monroe she'd bought to cover a crack in the wall. As a young girl, she'd admired Marilyn's gumption and confidence. Later she learned more about the reality behind the veneer and could relate to some of Marilyn's despair. Nothing was ever quite what it seemed.

Since that thought had the power to depress her when she didn't wish to be anything other than excited about the night to come with David, she pushed it aside and greeted him with a confident smile when he returned. She tried not to watch as he dropped his pants, but she couldn't seem to look away from the flex of muscle and sinew as he moved about.

Wearing only navy-blue boxer briefs, he slid into bed next to her.

Daisy left the light on and turned on her side to face him, scooting down to lay her head on the pillow.

He rested a hand on her shoulder, and the heat from his palm permeated the thin cotton shirt. "What're you thinking about?"

"It's nice to have you here with me like this."

"It's nice to be with you like this."

"It makes me feel special that you want to spend so much time with me when there are so many other women—" She didn't get to finish that thought, because he kissed the words off her lips.

"There's no one else I want to be with, Daisy." His hand slid from her shoulder to her wrist, encircling her arm before starting back up again, leaving a trail of goose bumps. "You know how you said I helped you get better?"

"You did. You came over every night to check on me, even though you didn't have to. It helped—a lot. I started to look forward to your visits every day."

"So did I. You helped me, too. For the first time since things fell apart with Janey, I feel hopeful again. I hadn't realized how much I'd missed that feeling until I had it again. You did that for me. So don't ever think this was a one-way street. We helped each other, and from that has come something neither of us expected."

She reached for him, drawing him into another passionate kiss, holding on to him as she had for weeks now. Apparently, he'd been doing the same thing. She liked knowing that she'd helped him, too.

His arm came around her, pulling her in closer to him without breaking the kiss. And then his hand was under her shirt, lying flat against her back and making her skin tingle from the desire for more.

She slid her leg between his, the coarse hair of his legs starting the tingling anew. Every time he touched her, she felt it everywhere.

"Are you okay?" he asked, his chest heaving as he drew back so he could see her face.

"I'm great. You?"

He laughed, and she realized how infrequently he did that and how boyishly handsome he looked when he did. "Haven't been this good in a very long time."

Empowered by his words and the emotion behind them, Daisy reached for the hem of her T-shirt and pulled it up and over her head.

His eyes got very dark as he took in the lacy black bra and panties she'd left on for him. "God," he said, kissing his way down her neck to her chest, "you're gorgeous, Daisy. Absolutely beautiful."

She'd always thought of herself as pretty at best, but when he told her she was beautiful, she believed it. Cradling his head against her chest, she let go of the worries and the fears and gave herself over to the desire that had simmered between them for weeks now. Even when she'd been bruised and battered and broken, she'd found him attractive.

But never had she imagined a scenario where he'd be all but naked in her bed or cupping her breasts in his big hands or dragging his thumbs over her tight nipples through the silky fabric of the bra. Tiffany had said that bra was guaranteed to clear a man's mind of all thoughts that didn't involve sex.

From what she could tell, the bra was having the desired effect on David, but all she could think about was getting it off. The feel of his tongue on the slope of her breast had her wrapping her arms around his head to keep him right there.

His fingers twisted the back of the bra, releasing the hooks and freeing her breasts.

Daisy nearly moaned from the relief, and then she moaned from the heat of his mouth on her nipple, tugging and sucking ravenously. She kept waiting for the fear to resurface, but all she felt was a deep, craving need for more. She touched him everywhere she could reach, dragging her hands over his back and dipping inside his briefs to cup the contours of his backside.

That drew a tortured groan from him. He pressed his hard length against her belly and moved to her other breast, giving it the same attention. "Something tells me you've been hanging out with Tiffany," he said as he smoothed his hand over the tiny triangle that covered her mound.

Daisy was so undone by the movement of his hand that she couldn't form the words to reply to his statement.

"Daisy?"

She forced herself to focus on his eyes as he looked down at her in concern. "Hmm?"

"Breathe, honey."

She sucked in a deep breath and realized she'd been holding her breath.

He dropped his head to her belly, his lips setting off a new firestorm of desire that surged between her legs.

She'd never felt such urgent need in her life, but neither had she ever been with a man who put her first the way David always had.

"Are you still okay?" he asked, concern etched into his handsome face.

Nodding, she said, "It feels so good to hold you this way."

"I love it, too. Are you sure you want to keep going?"

"Yes. If you do…"

He took her hand and pressed it to his thick erection, which surged under the heat of her hand. "Don't have any doubts about what I want—or who I want."

She stroked the full length of him, which made him gasp and moan.

"Christ, Daisy."

His jaw was clenched with tension, and seeing him struggle for control made her want him even more than she already did. She tugged at the boxer briefs and was relieved when he helped her take them off. She eyed his erection, which stretched to his navel and seemed to get bigger as she looked at him.

"If you touch me, we'll be all done," he said, sounding tense.

"Then why don't we save the touching for next time?"

"That sounds like a very good idea."

"Do you have protection? I never even thought of it."

"I thought of it, but I need my wallet."

"I'll get it." She reached for his pants on the floor and pulled his wallet from the back pocket. When she turned back to him, he was watching her every move with interest that made her feel self-conscious. She lowered her gaze and moved her arms to cover her breasts.

"Don't," he said, his voice a low growl.

"Don't what?"

"Don't be shy. You're gorgeous, and I love to look at you."

He already knew her so well and understood her better than anyone else ever had. That understanding made it easier for her to drop her guard—as well as her arms—and hand the wallet to him.

She watched closely as he applied the condom and seemed to lengthen and thicken before her very eyes. Her lips were suddenly dry as she experienced a moment of fear over whether or not she'd be able to go through with this. Then he reached out to her, bringing her into his warm embrace, and desire overtook the fear, clearing her mind of everything except him and how he made her feel.

He was front and center as he'd been for weeks now, and like he had when she was injured, he tended to her gently. "Talk to me," he whispered, his lips brushing against her neck as he caressed her back in soothing circles. "Tell me what you're thinking."

"It feels good to be held by you, to be touched by you. It feels different with you."

He moved his hand from her back to her breast and teased the nipple that tightened from his ministrations. "Why do you think that is?"

"Because you're different. This is different."

"It is for me, too."

"Sometime I want you to tell me how it's different."

"I will, but not now." He raised her leg over his hip and pressed his fingers to her core, using the triangle of material that Tiffany considered panties to arouse her.

"No," she said, panting, "definitely not now."

"Tell me what you want, Daisy. You have to tell me so I know how to make this good for you."

"It's already good. So good."

"I don't want you to be afraid of me."

"I'm not. I couldn't be."

He removed the thong, letting his fingertips slide slowly down her legs. "Yes, you could. If I do something that reminds you of something you didn't like, you could be afraid."

"I don't want to be afraid of you."

"Keep your eyes open. Look at me. Remember it's me. Remember how much we've shared and how close we've become." As he spoke, he continued to move slowly until he was above her, looking down at her with those incredibly sexy eyes. "Is this okay?"

Daisy held his gaze as she nodded and placed her hands on his shoulders, needing to hold on to him as he aligned their bodies.

He kissed her softly, tracing her bottom lip with his tongue. "Open your eyes, honey."

She hadn't realized she'd closed them.

"That's it. Look at me. Hold on to me."

Everything was fine, truly fine, until he began to enter her. The panic hit her so fast she had no time to prepare herself for the flashback of another man, a brutal man, trying to force his way inside of her. As if something heavy was sitting on her chest, she struggled for every breath and fought her way free, blinded by terror, until she was sitting on the edge of the bed, shaking violently. Oh God, had she *hit* him? No. Please, no.

"Daisy, honey, it's okay." He placed a hand tentatively on her shoulder, and she flinched.

The last thing she wanted right now was to be touched, even by him. Tears streamed down her cheeks, and her shoulders heaved from the sobs that seemed to come from her very soul.

"What can I do?" David asked from behind her.

Daisy shook her head because there was nothing anyone could do to help if her twisted mind was determined to turn the lovely David Lawrence into something evil and hurtful. "You... You don't have to stay. I'd understand if you wanted to go." Another sob broke free from her tightly clenched jaw.

"I'm not going anywhere unless you tell me you don't want me here."

"I want you here." The thickness in her throat made it difficult to speak. "I have no idea what happened. I was fine..."

"Believe it or not, I sort of expected it to happen sooner."

Shocked by what he'd said, she spun around to face him, wincing at the hint of blood on his lip where she'd clocked him in her haste to get free. She could only imagine what her face and tear-ravaged eyes must look like. Frightful... But the way he looked at her... Sweetly, tenderly, gently... And then he slayed her by reaching for her T-shirt, which was inside out, and helping her into it.

She took a deep, shuddering breath. "What do you mean?"

He reached out to wipe the tears from her cheeks, his touch a whisper against her skin. "The last man you cared for hurt you so badly. In every possible way. How could you not be afraid to do this again with someone else?"

"But I'm not afraid, or I wasn't before..."

"Would it be okay if I spoke to you as a doctor and not as a boyfriend right now?"

She bit her bottom lip and nodded.

"You were nearly raped, Daisy," he said softly, taking her hand.

Daisy held on to him for dear life.

"Not all that long ago. You're not ready yet, and that's fine. I totally understand."

"You've always been so nice to me, and I really appreciate that, but it might be better if we didn't see each other anymore. It's not fair for me to do this to you."

"What're you doing to me?"

New tears fell from her eyes at the heartbreaking thought of not seeing him anymore. "Mixed signals. Yes means no."

He smiled and shook his head, as if she'd said the silliest thing he'd ever heard. "You're not sending mixed signals. Unless..."

"Unless what?"

"Unless you don't actually like me as much as I think you do."

"I do like you! I like you so much. I probably even love you a little bit."

His sharp intake of air and the intense way he looked at her made her melt on the inside. "I probably love you a little bit, too, which is why you're not getting rid of me that easily." He reclined against the pillows and drew her into his arms. When he had her settled against him, albeit rigidly, he kissed her forehead and ran his hand over her back soothingly. "I'm not going anywhere. If it takes a month or three months or a year or two years, we'll get there. But only when you're ready. We'll do what you want when you want, and I'll wait because I have a feeling you're worth waiting for."

"It's too much to ask of anyone."

"You're not asking me for anything. I'll happily give you as much time as you need."

"David..."

"*Daisy...*" His stern tone drew a reluctant laugh from her.

"No one has ever been so nice to me."

"I'm sorry to hear that. You should be treated with respect and affection always. That's the least of what you deserve."

Her heart did a funny squeezing thing that left her breathless. "What about..."

"What about what?"

"You." She glanced down at his penis, which was now flaccid against his belly. At some point, he'd discarded the unused condom.

"What about me?"

"I feel like such a tease. We were all ready, and then I freaked out."

"It doesn't matter. I swear it doesn't."

"How can it not matter? You're a guy."

David's low chuckle rumbled through his chest. "Who is not governed entirely by the whims of his cock. I assure you the two of us will be just fine as long as you don't shut me out. I don't know if I could deal with that. I've become rather attached to you."

"You have? Really?"

"Really." His hand continued to move up and down her back, soothing and calming her, even as she continued to tremble. "Close your eyes and try to get some rest."

"I don't think I can sleep."

"Try. Close your eyes, think happy thoughts and clear your mind of all the things that make you hurt. I'll be right here. I'm not going anywhere."

Listening to his words, Daisy couldn't help but relax a bit. He was here. He wasn't going to leave because he didn't get what he wanted from her. He said he might love her a little bit. That last thought brought a hint of a smile to her lips. What might it be like if he loved her a lot?

Daisy would like to find out, because after tonight, after the way he'd cared for her after her meltdown, she could easily see herself falling completely in love with him.

Arriving home in the morning to shower and change before work, David thought about what'd happened with Daisy the night before. It had taken a long time, maybe even an hour or more, before she was finally able to relax and sleep. He'd been awake the whole time, which was how he'd known the exact second she'd given in to the exhaustion. She'd been sound asleep when he left her this morning with a note to call him when she woke up.

He couldn't help being a bit angry with himself for going along with something she wasn't ready for. In medical school, he'd gone through Post-Traumatic Stress Disorder training, and he knew the signs to watch for. He could beat himself up all day long for missing the signs in this case, except there hadn't been any. The only signals he'd received indicated she was as into what they were doing as he had been.

Things had been going so well for them, which was the real kicker in this whole situation. He was finally in a really good place.

While he'd expected the encounter with Janey to throw him out of sorts, it'd had the opposite effect. It had given him closure he'd desperately needed. They were able to be friendly with each other, and if she stayed on the island, she might need him before she had the baby. He'd be there for her if it came to that. But even if it didn't, he was more at peace with the outcome of their relationship than he'd been since it blew up in his face two years ago.

For the first time since then, he felt truly ready to move on and engage in a genuine relationship with another woman. But if last night's incident had shown him anything, it was that Daisy was still a long way from being ready for the same things he wanted. That was okay, though. He'd meant it when he told her he would wait.

He liked to think he was wise enough after all he'd been through to recognize something special when it came into his life. And Daisy was special. There was no denying that.

In the driveway, he noticed the sleek Porsche that Jared brought with him whenever he came to the island. His comings and goings were always a mystery to David, who often didn't lay eyes on his elusive landlord for months on end.

He took the stairs to his apartment, thinking about Daisy, hoping she'd be okay today and counting the hours until he could be with her again. Inside his front door, he stopped short when he saw his mother sitting on the sofa, nursing a takeout cup of coffee and flipping through the *Gansett Gazette*. How had he missed her car in the driveway? He'd been too captivated by the Porsche, apparently.

"Hey, Mom. What're you doing here?" He'd given her an extra key in case he ever got locked out, but he hadn't expected her to actually use it.

"I was concerned when I couldn't reach you."

David drew his phone from his pocket and noticed three calls from her that he'd missed when he'd been occupied the night before. "What's wrong?"

"Nothing other than I have no idea where my son has been the last few days."

"I've been busy, Mom. I have a job and a life."

"Too busy to call me once in a while?"

He wanted to remind her that he was thirty years old and didn't need to check in with her the way he used to, but ever since the lymphoma diagnosis, she'd been hovering the way she had when he was younger. Since she and his sisters had gotten him through the worst of his illness and the treatment, he supposed she had the right to hover. But breaking and entering was taking it a bit far, even for her.

"I'm sorry to have been out of touch." David went to the kitchen and moved through the motions of making coffee. "Things have been nuts."

"What happened to your lip?"

David stopped moving and tried to think of a story she would be believe. "I punched myself when I was pulling on something and my hand slipped."

Her raised brow indicated her skeptical reaction. "I heard you've been dating."

His muscles tightened with tension that he was certain she saw because she didn't miss anything. "Maybe. Some."

"Were you going to tell me you've met someone, David?"

"I don't know. Maybe. Eventually." His parents had been enraged—and ashamed—over what'd happened with Janey. He hoped to never again give them reason to be ashamed of him, but he also had a right to privacy, as did Daisy.

"Who is she?"

"I don't think you know her."

"I'd like to know her if she's important to you."

She was important to him and becoming more so with every passing day, but that didn't mean he was ready to bring her home to meet his parents. "I'll keep that in mind."

"Will you tell me her name?"

"Daisy."

"That's all I'm getting?"

Though he desperately wanted a shower and a shave and needed to get to work for nine o'clock appointments, he sat for a minute on the sofa. "Daisy Babson. She's the housekeeping manager at the McCarthy's hotel."

His mother's raised brow conveyed a world of disbelief. "She works for Janey's parents?"

"Yes."

"Well, you don't do anything simply, do you?"

"Janey and her parents have nothing to do with this."

"I heard you were called to her house last night."

"Jesus! This island is unreal! Don't people have anything to do besides mind other people's business?"

"No, not really. And it certainly shouldn't be a surprise to you that news travels fast around here."

"I was called there in a professional capacity. I went in a professional capacity. I performed professional duties. I did my job."

"What does your friend Daisy think of you running off to tend to your ex-fiancée?"

"My friend Daisy knows it's been over between Janey and me for two years now, and that as the island's only doctor, I'm obligated to care for everyone, regardless of what personal relationship I may or may not have with them."

"She's very understanding."

"If she wasn't, I wouldn't be seeing her."

His mother studied him for a long moment, during which he tried not to squirm under her scrutiny. "You never told me how it went in Boston."

"Everything was fine."

Before his eyes, she visibly sagged, and he regretted not telling her immediately that his test results had all come back negative.

"I would've told you if there was anything to worry about. You know that."

"I've done my share of worrying over you in the last couple of years."

"I know, and I'm sorry to have given you cause, but you have to believe me when I tell you I'm fine—physically and every other way, too." In fact, he hadn't been quite so fine in years.

"Was it weird to see Janey in her home, pregnant and all of that?"

"I've seen her pregnant before last night."

"You know what I mean, David."

"It wasn't as weird as you might think. I've come to see that we both ended up where we were meant to be. She's happy with Joe. They're good together. And I'm figuring things out. Slowly but surely." He had faith that he and Daisy would make a go of it—eventually—not that he wanted to share that thought with his mother. The relationship was too new, and after last night, too fragile to talk about just yet.

"You look good," she said, taking another perusing inventory of his features.

"I feel good."

"That's all I want to hear." She tossed the newspaper onto his coffee table. "You can have that. I'm done with it."

He walked her to the door. "Shall we talk about the rules for the extra key?" he asked, keeping his tone light.

"You wouldn't want me waiting outside in the heat when I could enjoy your perfectly comfortable sofa and your AC, now would you?" She went up on tiptoes to kiss his cheek. "Bring your friend Daisy over sometime. We'd love to meet her."

"Bye, Mom."

He closed the door behind her and shook his head, amused by the way she still could manage him like no one else ever had. In turn, she drove him bonkers and cracked him up, but he could never doubt her devotion. Sometimes he wished she were a little *less* devoted. In fact, he'd nearly turned down the offer to become the island's doctor because he worried about the close proximity to his doting mother.

Until today, she'd been respectful of his boundaries, but he couldn't blame her for coming to check on him after not hearing from him for days.

As he shaved, showered and got dressed for work, it occurred to him that she'd never asked him where he was coming from first thing in the morning. No doubt she'd put two and two together to get that he'd been with Daisy overnight. While he wasn't sure he was ready for her to have that information, and he definitely didn't care if she knew about Daisy, he was glad she hadn't asked.

Thinking about Daisy and what'd nearly happened between them made him hard in the shower. He considered taking care of business right then and there but decided he'd rather wait for her. The two years he'd spent rebuilding his life had been put to good use if it meant he was now ready for her and for what they might have together. If it took her a while longer to get there, so be it.

In some ways, he felt like he was emerging from a long, dark winter into a spring filled with optimism and hope. She'd done that for him with her gentle, sweet disposition, her appreciation of the little things that others took for granted, her unconditional acceptance of his failings and faults. He hoped he could do the same for her.

He wanted to make her smile the way she had last night before things had gone wrong. He wanted to make her laugh. He wanted to make her happy. Making her happy made him happy.

Reliving the erotic thrill of holding her and kissing her had him hard and trembling with the need for more. He hadn't felt this way since he'd been newly enamored with Janey McCarthy half a lifetime ago.

CHAPTER 11

On the way to the clinic, he called the island florist, ordered two-dozen stargazer lilies and asked that they be delivered to Daisy's home later in the afternoon. He'd love to send them to her at work, but that would set the whole island to buzzing, and he didn't want that for her, especially since she worked for Janey's mother. He wanted to be mindful of not doing anything to make her uncomfortable, so he tried to think of what to put on the card that wouldn't give too much away. It occurred to him that he should've figured that out before he placed the call. "Just put, 'Thanks for being you. David.'"

"Sure thing, Dr. Lawrence. We'll take care of that for you."

"Thank you." David stashed his phone in the breast pocket of his dress shirt. "Thanks for being you? Jesus, how lame is that?"

He was still berating himself for the stupid card when he walked into the clinic, where Seamus O'Grady and Carolina Cantrell waited for him. Carolina looked like she'd been in a fight with an angry cat.

"What happened?"

"My poor love fell into a thorn bush last night," Seamus said. He had his arm tight around Carolina, who seemed like she was annoyed and in pain. "She says she's fine, but she's feverish and ripped to shreds. I thought she ought to be seen."

"Let's get you into an exam room, Carolina," David said, signaling for the receptionist. "We'll get you fixed right up."

"Thanks, Doc," Carolina said. "I feel foolish for wasting your time over some cuts and scrapes."

"Let me be the judge of whether it's a waste of my time," David said with a smile. He was continually surprised by how apologetic his patients could be for taking up his time with their concerns.

"Come on, love," Seamus said, helping her to stand.

"Would you like me to get a wheelchair?" David asked.

"Absolutely not," Carolina said, even though every step seemed to cause her pain.

By the time he got Carolina's nasty scratches cleaned up, he was an hour behind on his appointments, so the morning flew by. He treated a case of tonsillitis, sent a boy with a potentially hot appendix to the mainland for immediate treatment and saw three people with flu-like symptoms that had him concerned about an outbreak on the island.

Victoria found him in his office, standing up as he downed a sandwich between patients and making frantic notes about the patients he'd already seen that day so he wouldn't forget the information he need to add to their charts. "Crazy morning, huh?" she asked.

"Most of them are."

"Janey was here. I had her on the monitor for an hour. The baby seems fine, but her BP is still a little higher than I'd like it to be. I agree with your plan for complete bed rest, even if she doesn't."

"She'll do it. She'd never endanger the baby or herself."

"I know, but it sucks to be stuck in bed all summer."

"Yep. Did you dip her urine?"

"I did, and the protein counts are up, too." She handed him the report.

"Shit," he said as he reviewed the numbers. "I was hoping this wasn't what it appears to be."

"So was I."

"We'll have to keep a very close eye on her over the next couple of weeks. She'll need to be on the mainland by thirty-six weeks."

"I figured you'd say that, so that's what I told her."

"Good. Glad we're on the same page."

She handed him two other pieces of paper. "Messages from this morning."

David scanned the two messages, his heart stopping at the sight of his oncologist's name on one of them. What the hell did he want?

"Everything okay?"

"Yeah, sure." Knowing his test results had all been fine, he put aside the worries about the oncologist for a moment to deal with a more pressing issue. "Could I ask you something?"

"Hit me."

"I sent flowers to Daisy."

"*Ohhhh*, things are getting serious!"

"I sent her flowers. I didn't propose."

"One often leads to the other."

"Since when?"

Her smile told him she was enjoying pushing his buttons. She usually did. "What do you want to ask me?"

"I think what I put on the card is kind of lame."

"What did you say?"

"Thanks for being you."

Her wince validated his concerns. "Hmm. That's not exactly an insult, but it could be better."

The choice of words made him smile. He'd been hearing that a lot lately.

"What's the occasion?"

"Occasion? There's no occasion. I sent her flowers."

"For no reason at all?"

He never should've involved her in this, but he desperately needed a woman's opinion, and she was handy. "There might've been a bit of a... development... in our relationship last night."

Her dark eyes lit up the way they did when she was on to a big scoop.

"It's not what you think," he said, hoping to shut her down before she got all crazy. "And that's all I'm saying about it."

"*Oh my God, you did it!* You bumped uglies, did the horizontal bop, the mattress mambo." She tilted her hips provocatively to make her point, not that she needed visuals to make her point.

"Victoria, I swear to God—"

She surprised the shit out of him when she squealed and leaped into his arms. Thankfully he caught her and kept his balance, or they both might've needed medical care of their own. "Finally! You're *back*! The protracted mourning period is *over*! Thank you, Jesus, and thank *you*, Daisy!"

Ready to wring her neck, he put her down and stepped back from her. "I'm going to muzzle you if you don't pipe down right now."

She clapped her hands together and continued to giggle and squeal as David sat in his desk chair, wishing he could take back the last ten minutes of his life. "We didn't 'bump uglies' as you put it, but we bumped a few other things."

"In that case, you're right. That card is lame in light of recent *developments*. You need to do better. Can you still fix it?"

"I asked them to deliver the flowers late this afternoon when she gets home from work, so I guess there's still time."

She sat in his visitor chair. "We need to give this significant thought."

"No, we don't. I'll think of something."

She gave him a horrified look. "You thought 'Thanks for being you' was good enough!"

"You may have a point." Her snort of laughter drew a smile from him. "So dazzle me. What should it say?"

"You were great last night, baby?"

"*Victoria...*"

"I love messing with you. It makes me happy."

"I live to serve you."

"How about, 'I can't wait to see you again.'"

David thought about that. "Does that send the right message?"

"Well, can you wait to see her again?"

As David scrubbed a hand over his face, the mostly sleepless night caught up with him. "God, I walked right into that, didn't I?"

Victoria bounded to her feet. "It does the job and apparently it's the truth, so call the florist."

"I will. So what's going on with the Irishman?"

"I'll tell you all about him, but first I want to do something else."

"What?" he asked, perplexed as she came around his desk.

She bent and kissed him on the cheek. "Welcome back. It's high time you forgave yourself and decided to move on with someone else."

"I wasn't aware that I hadn't forgiven myself."

"You hadn't. Until recently."

"Well, thank you for letting me know. I appreciate that insight."

"I'm serious. It hasn't been easy as your friend to watch you beating yourself up for a mistake you made two years ago while Janey and Joe and everyone else involved have moved on with their lives."

"I haven't been doing that, Vic."

Hands on her hips, she tilted her head, calling him out on his bullshit without saying a word.

"Okay, maybe I did some of that."

"A lot of it."

"If you say so."

"I do."

He fiddled with a pen on his desk. While Victoria was often an annoying pain in his ass, she was also insightful. And she was female, and he desperately needed her perspective on what'd happened last night. "So, the reason we didn't... was because she panicked at the moment, if you get my drift."

"Oh jeez, really? What did you do?"

"Tried to comfort her, but it was bad. She was crying and trembling." Just thinking about it made him ache for being the cause of such distress, even if he knew logically that he wasn't the real cause. He could thank Truck Henry for the damage he'd left in his wake.

Victoria looked at him thoughtfully. "What happened after she panicked?"

"We talked it out, and I stayed with her."

"Until she fell asleep or all night?"

"All night."

"That's good. You did the right thing staying with her."

"I only left because I had to get to work, but I'm going back after work and tomorrow night and the next night."

As he spoke, Victoria nodded. "That's what you need to do. After a while, hopefully she won't associate the act with him anymore."

He glanced at her. "What if she always associates the act with him?"

"She won't. You have to remember it's only been a few weeks. She may be healed on the outside, but on the inside she has a ways to go. But just like the bruises on the outside faded with time, so too will the bruises on the inside—especially if she knows she has all the time she needs. That's going to be really important to her."

"I told her I'm not going anywhere and that I want to be with her."

"Then that's what you do. Be patient and supportive and understanding. All of those things will help her heal."

"You won't say anything about this to anyone, will you?"

"Of course not. I may bust your chops relentlessly, but you know you can trust me. Or at least I hope you know that."

"I do, and I appreciate your advice. Anyway, about the Irishman…"

Hands over her heart, she said, "The Irishman is *divine*. Lovely, sexy, and oh the accent." She fanned herself dramatically. "The accent really does it for me."

"What is it with women swooning at the sound of an Irish accent?"

"We can't help it. The swoon is in our DNA." In an exaggerated Irish accent, she said, "We hear the lyrical sounds of Ireland, and we're putty, I tell you."

"And what happens when your Irish boyfriend goes home?"

"He said he might stay longer than the two weeks he and his aunt came for. He likes it here." Her saucy grin indicated that Seamus's cousin liked it here largely because of her.

"I'd hate to see you fall for a guy who lives on the other side of the ocean."

"I'm not falling for him," she said, as if that was the most ridiculous thing she'd ever heard. "I'm using him for sex. Really good sex."

"Ahh, I see. I'm glad you cleared that up for me."

"Any time. Gotta get back to work."

"Hey, Vic?"

"Yeah?"

"Thanks."

With her hand propped on the door frame, she said, "For what?"

"For being a good friend. I haven't had a lot of them since everything happened with Janey, so I appreciate the ones I do have."

She smiled. "I'm happy for you that you've found Daisy. I hope you're happy for yourself, too. She's really good for you."

"Yes, she is."

"Call the florist."

"Yes, ma'am."

She walked away, and he picked up the phone. After he took care of the lame message on the card, he made the call to Boston to see what his oncologist wanted with him. By the time Dr. Garrity came on the phone, David was having a full-blown panic attack.

"David. Thanks so much for returning my call."

"No problem, but I've got to tell you, I'm in a bit of a sweat over here. You said last week everything was fine…"

"And it is. Better than fine. Your remission is holding steady, and I see no need for concern."

David blew out a deep breath as his extremities trembled from the adrenaline that whipped through him. Right when he was finally getting his life back on track, the last thing he needed was the possibility of another health crisis.

"I apologize if I made you uneasy," Garrity said.

"Uneasy is a good word for it," David said with a laugh.

"I'm actually calling with some news that might be of interest to you."

"What's that?"

"We've had an opening in our department, and your name came up as a possible candidate for the position. You left a favorable impression after your rotation. That, combined with your personal experience as a patient, has us thinking you'd make for a damned fine addition to our team. Any interest?"

"I, ah, wow, you've caught me completely by surprise."

"I'm sure I have, since I just saw you last week and never said a word about this. However, one of our staff physicians has decided to relocate, so it leaves us with an opening. Have you given any thought to a career in oncology, David?"

"To be honest, I'm so busy with my general medicine practice here on the island that I barely have time to eat, let alone ponder my career."

Garrity's guffaw of laughter reminded David of why he'd chosen the jovial, upbeat doctor to see him through treatment. "I remember those days. Did I ever tell you I was a general medicine physician in a small town in Wyoming at the beginning of my career? I've never worked harder in my life."

"It's pretty demanding, especially when you add in the isolation factor out here."

"So what I'm hearing, and feel free to correct me if I'm wrong, is that you're happily settled and not looking to make a change."

"Your offer took me entirely by surprise, and I wonder if I could have a day or two to think it over."

"Absolutely, but not much longer. We need to get someone here ASAP. Our caseload is unfortunately bigger than ever."

"I understand. I'll get back to you as soon as possible. And thank you for the offer. I appreciate you thinking of me."

"You're our top choice, David. Ball's in your court. I'll talk to you soon."

David turned off his phone and sat at his desk contemplating the implications until Janice, the receptionist came to the door to tell him his one o'clock appointments had begun arriving. "I'll be right there."

A few weeks ago, Dr. Garrity's offer would've appealed greatly to him. He'd begun to tire of feeling like a martyr in his hometown and was yearning for a fresh start. He never could've imagined that his fresh start would come in the form of a lovely woman who made him feel whole again.

How could he possibly consider leaving now that they'd found each other? One thing he knew for sure was that after the disaster with Janey, he'd never again attempt a long-distance relationship. They didn't work for him, and he had no desire to ever go down that road again.

For now, had had to focus on his patients for a few hours. He could figure out the rest of his life later.

Tiffany decided to wait for Blaine to leave for work before she called Maddie to ask permission to hijack the barbecue.

Dressed in the uniform that got to her every time she saw him in it, Blaine clomped down the stairs. He was so hot, so sexy and so in love with her that at times she still wanted to pinch herself to believe he was real, that *they* were real.

His arms came around her, his big, muscular body surrounded her, and Tiffany relaxed against him. He was as real as it got, and he was hers to keep forever. The thought filled her with an unreasonable feeling of relief. Nothing had actually changed between them, and yet it felt like everything was changing—for the better, if that was possible.

"What's on your mind, baby?" he asked as he placed kisses strategically on her neck.

"Oh, this and *that*." She pushed her hips against the erection that seemed to be ever present when they were together.

The low rumble of his laugh pleased her. "You haven't had enough of *that* after last night?"

"I'll never get enough."

"And that, right there, is one of a thousand reasons why I love you so damned much."

"You'll have to tell me about the other nine hundred and ninety-nine reasons."

"I've got the rest of my life to tell you all about them and to find new ones."

Tiffany turned so she was facing him. "Are we really going to do this?"

"Hell yes, we are. When are you going to call Maddie?"

"This morning."

"Why are you doing that worried thing with your eyebrows?" He kissed the furrow between her brows. "I told you I never wanted you to do that again."

"You'll have to cut me a little slack if you expect me to be worry free and marry you in two days."

"We've got no worries, baby. It'll be great. I know it will, because you'll be there and Ashleigh will be there, and I'll be there. What else matters?"

"Can we even get a license that fast?"

"Leave that to me. The mayor owes me a couple of favors."

"If he doesn't come through for you, let me know. He owes me a couple, too."

His scowl was comical. "What the hell kind of favors does he owe you?"

"I can't tell you." She kissed the outrage off his sexy mouth. "Customer confidentiality."

"If Upton or his wife are shopping at your store, I'd rather have my eyes poked out with sharp spears than hear those details."

Tiffany burst into laughter. "Tell me how you really feel."

"I'd be happy to." He pulled her in as close to him as he could get her and laid his lips over hers. "I love you. I love Ashleigh. I can't wait to marry you in two days. And I can't wait to have forever with you." He kissed her again and gave her a swat on the rear as he released her. "Now call you sister so you can stop worrying that she's going to say no when you know damned well she'll go batshit crazy over this plan of ours."

"Yes," Tiffany said with a smile, "she will."

"That's more like it. I want to see more smiles and fewer frowns. You got me?"

"I got you." She grabbed a fistful of his shirt, not caring that she was wrinkling him. "And I'm going to keep you."

"Let me go to work, you saucy wench. I have a family to support."

"Wait."

"What?"

She flattened her palms over his chest and looked up at him. "I want you to know that even if I'm a bit anxious about having two days to plan a wedding… Who I'm marrying? Not one single doubt. I love you madly."

"Aw, baby," he said, letting his forehead rest against hers, "you know how to hit a guy where he lives. I love you, too. I want you to relax, enjoy and accept that whatever happens happens. Who the fuck cares what goes wrong? As long as we're married by sunset on Saturday, I'll have everything I've ever wanted. I'll have more than I ever dreamed possible."

She smiled up at him, determined to follow his advice and chill about the details. He was right. Who cared if the whole thing was a mess? She'd still be his wife, and that was all that mattered. "So when are you going to tell your parents that you're getting married on Saturday?" Was it her imagination or did he go a little pale?

"Um, today, I guess."

"Might be a good idea, since they may have other plans."

He blew out a deep breath. "Hopefully they'll change whatever plans they have."

"I'm sure they will. Now go to work. I'll see you later."

With one last kiss, he released her and headed for the door. "Call your sister!"

"Tell your mother!"

His chuckle followed him out the door.

The time with him had turned her nervousness to giddiness. She'd never done anything quite so spontaneous in her life—other than open a store full of sex toys, she thought with a giggle as she called Maddie.

Her sister answered on the first ring. "Hey! I was just going to call you! You'll never believe it, but David has put Janey on full bed rest for the remainder of her pregnancy. How bad does that blow?"

"So bad. Is she okay?"

"I guess so, but her BP is up a bit, protein in the urine."

"Those are signs of preeclampsia," Tiffany said, recalling the books she'd read while pregnant.

"They're trying to keep it from becoming that by prescribing the bed rest. Anyhow, what's up?"

"Um, well, I need a favor. It's kind of a big favor, and you should feel free to say no."

"Spit it out, Tiff," Maddie said, laughing. "Whatever it is, you know I'll do it for you if I can."

"I was wondering..." Tiffany's heart pounded erratically. "Would it be okay if Blaine and I took over your cookout this weekend?"

"What do you mean? You want to have everyone over there?"

"Not exactly. We were hoping your cookout might double as a wedding reception."

Maddie let out a bloodcurdling scream that had Tiffany holding the phone away from her ear.

"*OhmyGod!* I think I'm hyperventilating. *This* weekend, as in *two days from now?*"

"Apparently so."

Maddie went quiet on the other end of the line until Tiffany heard the distinctive sound of sniffling.

"Are you crying?"

"Maybe a little. This is so bloody exciting! But are you sure you're ready, honey? I mean, you just got divorced, and I know you're crazy about Blaine and vice versa—"

"It's probably way too soon, but we have a bit of an ulterior motive with Jim digging in about Blaine living with me."

"Ugh, he is such an asshole."

"Yes, he is, but we figured if we were married, he'd have much less of a case than if were living in sin, and Dan agreed. It was Blaine's idea to do it this weekend to take the wind out of Jim's sails, and because he can't live without me. Blaine, that is." Tiffany giggled nervously. The whole scheme sounded ridiculous as she relayed it to her sister.

"Oh, Tiff. That's so romantic. Of course you can take over my cookout. Have at it! This is so exciting!"

"Blaine said you'd be all for it."

"I love my new brother-in-law. He's so smart. What can I do? Anything! Oh my God! I can't wait to tell Mac. Have you told Mom?"

"I'll go over there later to see them," Tiffany said, encouraged by Maddie's excitement.

"How about Ashleigh?"

"She was at Mom's last night and Jim's tonight. We'll tell her tomorrow morning when she gets home."

"I'll come over later, and we'll plan everything. Will you be at home or the store?"

"Home. I've already realized I'll have to turn the store over to Patty if I'm going to pull off a wedding by Saturday."

"This is going to be so awesome. Wait until everyone finds out they're there for a wedding! Oh! Mac's Uncle Frank is coming, and he's a judge. He can marry you!"

"Are you sure he won't mind? He barely knows me."

"He'd love to do it. I know he would. I'll have Mac ask him, though."

"You don't think it's crazy, Maddie?"

"I think it's over-the-top crazy wonderful. You're getting a great guy who worships you and who'd do anything for you and your daughter. What else is there?"

"Nothing," Tiffany said softly. "Absolutely nothing."

Returning home from the clinic, Seamus insisted on carrying Carolina into the house, where his mother was brewing a cup of tea in the kitchen.

"There you two are. I was beginning to wonder where you'd gotten off to." She did a double take when she saw the scratches on Carolina's face. "For the love of God! Whatever happened to your face?"

"I had an encounter with a thorn bush last night. Tripped and fell."

"Oh my Lord! What can I do for you?"

"She needs to rest, Mum. She's been up most of the night, and we've just come from the doctor."

His mother followed them to the hallway that led to their bedroom. "What did he say? Are you all right?"

"I will be," Caro said, putting up a brave front for his mother. "My pride is more injured than anything else."

"That's not true, love," Seamus said as he put her down as gently as he could. When she winced from the pain, Seamus felt as if he were the injured one. It killed him to see her hurt or in pain. And to know it was his damned fault that she'd gotten hurt in the first place... Well, that was almost too much to bear. "You've got some very serious wounds, and you're under doctor's orders to take it easy until they begin to scab up."

Caro looked up at his mum. "Which is not at all what I had planned for your visit."

"Oh, pish. Don't you worry about me. I'm nothing if not resourceful. Seamus and I will take care of everything, won't we, son?"

Seamus felt torn in a thousand different directions after getting a call from Joe earlier, letting him know about Janey's bed rest. He was out of commission and off the schedule for the foreseeable future, which meant there was no way Seamus could stay home with Carolina, where he yearned to be.

Caro reached for his hand. "What's wrong?"

"I hate to say this, love, but I've got to go to work. That call I took while we were at the clinic?"

She nodded.

"It was Joe. Apparently they were in another exam room at the same time we were there, and Janey has been put on full bed rest for the remainder of her pregnancy."

"Oh no! Poor Janey. How awful for her, especially this time of year. And look at me, all banged up and of no use to her."

"You'll be back on your feet in no time, but you heard Dr. David. You need to take it easy until the worst of the wounds scab over. You don't want them to get infected."

As they talked, Nora bustled around the bedroom, folding abandoned clothes and straightening up. Seamus knew that Carolina would hate that his mother was cleaning or working on her vacation. "You don't have to do that, Mum."

Carolina sent him a grateful smile. She'd probably been about to say the same thing herself.

"Not to worry. Now off to work with you, my boy. I'll be here with your Caro to make sure she takes it nice and easy. Go on along. We'll be just fine, won't we, Caro?"

"Of course." Carolina took his hand and smiled up at him. But he saw the strain she was trying hard to hide from him.

Seamus bent to kiss her. "I'll be back as soon as I can."

"I know."

Lowering his voice to a whisper, he added, "I owe you big for this."

"Yes, you do."

He barked out a laugh and kissed her again. "Love you."

"Same. Be safe on the water."

Seamus straightened and had to summon the wherewithal to leave her. But Joe was counting on him, and letting his boss down was never something Seamus wanted to do. Joe had been very good to him and far more understanding than Seamus had expected over Seamus's relationship with his mum. Keeping the business running smoothly so Joe could focus on his pregnant wife was the least Seamus could do for him.

His mother followed him to the kitchen. "Sorry this happened right when you got here, Mum."

"You know there's nothing I'd rather do than putter around the house anyway. Caro and I will be fine."

"Where do you suppose Shannon spent the night?"

"I'm sure he found a warm bed and a warmer woman." She clucked with disapproval. "I've despaired of that one ever settling down, but then again, I once said the same about you, and look at you now."

"I know you were surprised when you met Caro, but I hope you can see what I see in her and give her a chance."

"'Tis clear to me that the two of you are mad for each other. I fully intend to give her every chance to show me she's worthy of my son."

"Mum…"

"Don't take that tone with me, Seamus Padric O'Grady. I'm still your mum, and don't you ever forget it."

"As if I ever could." Seamus kissed her cheek. "Behave today. I mean it. If you do anything to drive her away from me…"

"If you think that's my goal here, you don't know me at all. Now don't you have a boat to drive?"

"Indeed I do. I'll be back for dinner."

She crooked her finger to bring him down close enough for her to kiss his cheek. "Fair winds and following seas, my love."

"Thanks, Mum. And thanks for taking care of Caro. She's acting brave, but she's hurt real bad."

"I can see that, and I'll take very good care of her for you."

She followed him to the driveway, which reminded him of the many times she'd walked him to the car, lecturing about safety all the way, when he'd first begun driving. He hadn't thought of that in years. Standing before the company truck Joe had given him right after he started, Seamus had never felt so torn between what he needed to do and what he wanted to do. He turned to his mother.

"I'm sorry I didn't tell you about the age difference."

"So am I, and only because I think your Caro was embarrassed when she discovered I didn't know."

"Yes." Seamus ran both hands through his hair roughly. "You could say that."

"Why didn't you tell me?"

"Because I wanted you to meet her and know her and see me with her before you decided she was all wrong for me."

"You don't give me enough credit."

"Probably not."

"I'm not going to deny I'm disappointed that you're giving up your chance to be a father. I think you would've been a wonderful father, so that causes me a bit of grief for what'll never be. But I know true love when I see it, Seamus. And I see it here."

"You do, really?"

"I really do. So lose the pinched and pickled look to your face, and let's enjoy our visit, shall we?"

Laughing, Seamus hugged her. "I'd like that."

"If you catch sight of your cousin in town, send him home."

"Will do. He hasn't changed a bit since last I saw him."

Her grimace told the true story. "He's never gotten over poor Fiona. I'm not sure he ever will. So he runs around chasing everything in skirts, thinking that'll somehow soothe the ache inside him."

"It's how he survives," Seamus said simply.

"Yes, I suppose it is, but I wonder all the time how long he can keep it up."

Seamus kissed her cheek. "He'll keep it up until he finds something—or someone—who can soothe the ache. I'll see you tonight, Mum."

"I'll be here."

And that, Seamus thought as he drove away, was comforting.

CHAPTER 12

Carolina heard the low rumble of their voices but couldn't make out what was being said. Wondering if they were talking about her only made her more uncomfortable than she already was. She shifted in the bed, trying to sit up and find a better position, but with deep cuts on the front and back of both legs, there was no such thing as a good position. The pain brought tears to her eyes as she resettled her aching limbs.

"Ah, love," Nora said when she came into the room. "Now why are you moving all about? You'll reopen those cuts if you do that."

"I can't find a comfortable spot. Everything hurts, and I'm so sorry this happened as soon as you got here. I had all kinds of plans and things I wanted to show you on the island and…" The tears that rolled down her cheeks made her feel even more pathetic than she already did. She wiped them from her face. "Sorry for the pity party. That's not like me."

"Now, now. I can tell you're not the simpering sort of gal. From what I'm told, you raised a fine son more or less on your own. Seamus thinks the world of him, you know."

"Yes," Carolina said tentatively, not at all sure where this conversation was heading. "I know."

"Seamus doesn't give his respect to people who haven't earned it."

"I'm sorry he didn't tell you…the truth…about me…before you came."

Nora folded a T-shirt of Seamus's that he'd left in a heap on the floor and then sat on the corner of the mattress. "He told me about you."

"He told you half the story."

"Indeed."

"And you were shocked to realize the woman he'd fallen for is closer to your age than to his."

"A tad bit surprised."

Carolina waited for her to say something else, but she maintained her silence long enough that Carolina was tempted to squirm. If only it didn't hurt so much to move. "Are you angry?"

"No, but I won't deny I'm sad that he won't be a father."

"I am, too. In fact, I tried for months to talk him out of...this...for that very reason."

"And if I know my son, the more you tried to talk him out of it, the harder he dug in."

"You know him well."

"Aye, I do, which is why I'm also able to say that I've never seen him look at a woman the way he does you. He appears completely smitten."

Carolina wished she could control the flush of heat that stole over her cheeks at Nora's frank assessment.

"Is the feeling mutual?"

"Completely."

"Well, that brings me a measure of comfort. As a mother yourself, you'd understand how much knowing that means to me."

"I do." She ventured a glance at Nora. "I'm due to be a grandmother this summer."

"So I heard."

"He told me you lost your other sons. I'm so sorry."

"Aye, it was a terrible thing. Both times. It's true what they say that no mother should have to bury her children."

"Seamus is your only living son…"

"I know what you're thinking, but we have Shannon and other nephews. The family will carry on just fine."

"Do you know that when this started with Seamus, I thought of you."

"Of me? How so?"

"I thought about it as a mother, about how I'd feel if my son had taken up with a woman who could never give him children."

"How would you feel?"

"I'd be sad to never have grandchildren. From what I hear, they're the best thing since ice cream."

"I can attest that 'tis true, and while I wish Seamus would have that experience in his life, I have other children whereas you do not. I imagine my perspective is slightly different from yours for that reason."

Carolina hadn't considered that.

"Do you love him as much as he obviously loves you?"

"I do. I love him very much."

"No mother could ever ask for anything more than that for her children."

Seamus's mother knew about them, and while she had her reservations, she apparently had no plans to get in the way of their happiness. Nothing was now in the way of them living their lives happily together. For the first time since the roguish Irishman had stormed into her life, Carolina felt a measure of peace come over her.

Although her skin burned like the devil, and she hurt everywhere, she finally believed her relationship with Seamus might just work out after all.

Daisy woke up groggy and disoriented, worried that she'd slept through her alarm. But a quick glance at the clock told her she had an hour before she had to be at work. Her entire body ached, and her eyes felt gritty as she recalled the disaster the night with David had become after her panic attack.

Even though she had no desire to relive what'd happened, she forced herself to go back in time to last night, when everything had gone from fine to not fine in the fraction of an instant. The press of his erection against her had triggered a flashback to the night that Truck had tried to force himself on her. Luckily, he'd failed to penetrate her, but his repeated efforts had left her bruised and battered in her most sensitive area.

Daisy cringed when she recalled David examining her there after the attack. Did he think of that when he looked at her or touched her there? She scrubbed her hands over her face. God, she hoped not. As she turned on her side, she saw a note from him propped against the lamp on the bedside table.

Good morning!

I had to leave for work and wanted to let you sleep. I loved sleeping next to you last night, and I hope we can do it again tonight and tomorrow night and the night after… Call me when you wake up—if you have time. If not, I'll see you tonight.

David

He was so sweet and kind, and he'd traveled such a difficult path after the breakup with Janey. He deserved a woman who could give him everything he deserved, not one who freaked out when he tried to make love to her. As much as she enjoyed every minute she'd spent with him, she couldn't be responsible for keeping him from the chance to be happy with someone else.

Daisy dragged herself out of bed and into the shower, where the water washed away the tears that fell from her sore eyes at the thought of him with someone else.

Sarah, she thought. *I need Sarah.* She rushed through her morning routine, left her hair to air dry and headed out twenty minutes earlier than usual, making a beeline for the Sand & Surf Hotel.

Please let her be there, and please let her be available, Daisy thought as she walked briskly through town. She'd covered her eyes with oversized sunglasses so no one would see her raw-looking eyes or the dark circles under them. As she approached the Surf, she was shocked to see an ambulance out front and a crowd gathered on the deck.

Concerned for her friend, she approached the weather-beaten hotel. "What's going on?" she asked a woman who wore a Surf polo shirt.

"Laura has been so sick from the pregnancy that Owen called the rescue to take her to the clinic. He's worried she's dehydrated."

The EMTs emerged from the hotel with a very pale Laura strapped on a gurney and an almost equally pale Owen right behind them. Sarah appeared at the door holding Laura's infant son Holden, and the minute the ambulance drove off, Daisy took the stairs two at a time, anxious to get to Sarah. "Is she okay?"

"I hope so. She's so weak. Owen couldn't take it any longer and called the ambulance, even though she told him not to. I usually agree with her when they butt heads, but this time, I'm on his side."

Holden reached out his chubby hand and grabbed a handful of Daisy's hair. Before he could pull on it and hurt her, Sarah extricated the hair from his grip.

"What can I do to help?" Daisy asked.

"Not a thing. Mr. Holden and I are in charge while they're gone." She took a closer look at Daisy. "What brings you by? Aren't you usually in an all-fired rush to get to work this time of day?"

"Yes, but…" Daisy shook her head. "Never mind. You have other things to contend with today. You don't need me dumping on you."

As only the mother of seven could do, Sarah deftly secured Holden to her right hip and took hold of Daisy's arm with her left hand. "Inside. Now."

Daisy followed her into the hotel where Sarah put a "Be Right Back" sign up at the main desk and continued on to the kitchen in the back of the hotel. She put Holden in his high chair and sprinkled dry cereal on the tray. He dove into the snack with enthusiastic squeals that made Daisy smile, despite the torment that plagued her.

Sarah brewed coffee, put two steaming mugs on the counter and gestured for Daisy to take one of the stools. "Take off the glasses."

Daisy reluctantly pushed her sunglasses to the top of her head.

Sarah gasped. "Did he *hurt* you?"

"God, no. Never. It's nothing like that. This time it was me. We were, you know… Fooling around."

"And?"

"And when he tried to…have sex with me…" Daisy looked down at her coffee as the misery resurfaced all over again. How could she have done that to him? How could she have made him feel like he was anything at all like Truck? How could she have *hit* him? "I totally lost it. Everything that happened came rushing back as if it were yesterday rather than weeks ago."

"Weeks ago isn't that long, Daisy, especially when you haven't done that again since."

"I know, and I really thought I was ready. I didn't expect that to happen, or I never would've let it go so far. The sad part is, I really *wanted* to make love with him."

"This may not be what you want to hear, but abuse survivors can have flashbacks for years after the abuse finally ends. At times, I wonder if I'll ever be normal after what Mark put me through, but I'm determined to try. I refuse to let him get the better of me by denying myself the right to a happy future."

"I like that. That's how I want to be, too."

"You need some more time, Daisy. Don't rush things. Take it slow, and when it's right, you'll know it."

"But will David still be there when I get there?"

"What did he say last night when you were upset?"

"All the right things, but still… It's a lot to ask anyone to be patient with a situation like this."

"I've come to know him quite well since I've been living here, and if he's the kind of man I think he is, he means it. He cares about you. He's not going to rush off at the first sign of trouble."

"I've never known a guy like him. He's so…"

"Normal?" Sarah asked with a glint of humor in her eye.

"Yes! Exactly!"

"In the time I've spent with Charlie, I've discovered there's an awful lot to be said for normal. I've had enough drama to last me a lifetime."

"How are things with you two?"

"Good. Normal. Slow… Like you, I have my issues. I'm not a big fan of being touched. I keep hoping that'll change, and he's been amazingly patient and supportive, despite the fact that I still haven't told him the full story of what happened with Mark."

"A wise person once told me that when the time is right, you'll know it."

Smiling, Sarah lifted her coffee mug. "Touché."

"What a pair we are, huh?"

"We're survivors, Daisy. Don't ever forget that. We walked through the fire and came out on the other side better and stronger, but damaged, too. There's nothing wrong with being damaged. We didn't cause it, so there's no shame in it."

"You always make me think about things in a way I haven't before, and you're right. It's not my fault. But it's not David's fault either. He deserves someone who can give him everything he needs."

"Let him decide what he deserves. If it's too much for him, you'll know it soon enough. In the meantime, try to believe him when he tells you he's willing to wait for you."

"I'll try. Thank you for always being there for me. I can't tell you how much it means to me."

"It means just as much to me to have someone nearby who understands what I'm going through, too."

"I'd better get to work." Daisy got up and rinsed her mug in the sink, bent to give Holden a kiss on his chubby cheek and hugged Sarah on her way out of the kitchen.

"Hang in there, honey, and you know where I am if you ever need me."

"Same to you."

Sarah and Holden waved her off from the doorway of the Surf, and as Daisy walked to the hotel in North Harbor, she thought about what Sarah had said. She still wasn't completely convinced that continuing her relationship with David was the best course of action, but every time she thought about sending him away, she felt sick.

Once she arrived at the hotel, the morning went by in a blur of paperwork, mini-crises, inventory, and running. Daisy must've been to the third floor no fewer than ten times, and it was only eleven. While her ribs were burning, the activity kept her from dwelling overly much on her personal dilemma, and she welcomed that relief.

Right before noon, Maddie appeared at the door, looking bright-eyed and excited. "Are you busy?"

"Always, but never too busy for you." Daisy got up to remove the stack of towels that had landed on her visitor chair. "Come in."

"I have so much news I don't even know where to start."

"Good news, I hope?"

"The best news. I just hope you agree."

Something about the way Maddie said that set Daisy's nerves on edge. "What does that mean?"

Maddie flashed a sheepish grin. "I did something…"

"What did you do?"

"Remember when the town council decided to use the land Mrs. Chesterfield left to the town for affordable housing?"

"I vaguely remember hearing something about that. What's that got to do with me?"

"Mac and his cousin Shane have been working with an organization that builds houses for low-income individuals, and they've gotten the approval for the first house."

"That's wonderful. Everything around here is so expensive. It'll be great for regular working people to have affordable housing, too."

"We couldn't agree more. It wasn't that long ago that I was in dire straits financially, so I know how it feels to work all the time and never really get ahead. Which is why I filed an application for you to get one of the houses, and it was approved. One of the houses will be for you, Daisy."

Daisy's mind went blank. She heard the words that came out of Maddie's mouth, but they refused to register.

"Say something. I've been so nervous about telling you because I didn't want you to get the wrong idea about why I did it."

"Why did you do it?" Daisy asked, her voice barely more than a whisper. "Do you see me as a charity case or something?"

"No, God, not at all! Who knows better than I do how hard you work and how expensive it is to live here? I remember you saying a few months ago that you might not be able to stay here for another winter, and that's why I did it. That was the only reason why. And because you deserve a break after everything you've been through."

Blinded by tears, Daisy wiped them away. "I don't know what to say."

"Tell me you're not mad at me for doing this behind your back. I didn't want to get your hopes up if it didn't happen, and that's the only reason I didn't tell you."

"I'm not mad. How could I be? No one has ever done anything like this for me. I'm so grateful, Maddie. I've never had a friend like you."

"Our lives were very similar until Mac McCarthy knocked me off my bike. Don't ever forget that."

"I appreciate that you never forget it."

"How could I? I lived hand-to-mouth for years. I'll never forget where I came from or how blessed I've been."

"This is unbelievable," Daisy said as more tears rolled down her cheeks. She felt like she'd done nothing but cry for the last twelve hours, but these were tears of joy. "My very own house!"

"I'm so glad you think so, too! The other thing I wanted to tell you is that Mac and I are having a cookout tomorrow afternoon, and we'd like you to come. And bring David, too, of course."

Daisy used a tissue to mop up the flood of tears. "I'd love to come, but I don't know if he will."

"We anticipated that possibility, and we spoke with Joe and Janey about it. They both said it's fine with them if he's there."

"Oh, well... You actually asked them that?"

"We did."

"I'll check with him."

"Good. And did I mention my sister is getting married, and the cookout is going to double as a wedding reception?"

Daisy's mouth fell open in surprise. "Are you *serious*? I saw her yesterday, and she never mentioned that."

"Probably because it happened last night."

"They're getting married *tomorrow*."

"Yep."

"Is it because of Jim?"

"You know about that, huh?"

"She was on the phone with Dan when I went to the store yesterday."

Maddie's brow arched in question, and Daisy realized she'd said too much. "And what, pray tell, were you doing at Tiffany's store?"

Daisy made an effort to keep her expression vague. "I hadn't been there yet, and I wanted to check it out."

Maddie's husky laugh echoed through the small room. "You're a terrible liar, Daisy Babson. You should never, *ever* play poker. I hope you got something sinfully sexy that made Dr. David drool."

Daisy knew defeat when it was staring her in the face. "I don't know that he drooled, per se, but he definitely appreciated Tiffany's taste in lingerie."

"So things are moving right along?"

"You could say that."

"You're okay with...you know...everything?"

Maddie was so excited about the house and Tiffany's wedding that Daisy didn't have the heart to dump her problems on her friend. "I'm hoping I will be, eventually. He's very good to me."

"That's awesome, Daisy. I'm so happy for you. Hell, I'm happy for both of you. He deserves to be happy, too." She stood to leave. "I'll see you tomorrow?"

"I'll be there."

"And you'll try to talk David into coming with you?"

Daisy swallowed hard when she remembered that things with him were a bit uncertain at the moment. "I'll try."

"Tell him we'd love to see him."

"I will."

"And tell him we mean that."

Laughing, Daisy said, "I'll do that, too."

As she walked home later that afternoon, Daisy tried to wrap her head around the news about the house. It was one of the most exciting things to ever happen to her. Added to her burgeoning relationship with David, she could safely say things had never been better in her life.

That's when everything usually went wrong for her.

"No," she said. "Don't think that way. Maybe this time will be different." Up until last night—and even including what had happened then—everything about her relationship with David was different than anything she'd ever experienced with anyone else. For one thing, he was always nice to her. Always. She'd yet to see him annoyed or out of sorts or anything other than a perfect gentleman. In all the time they'd spent together, she hadn't known a single moment of unease or fear that he might take out his frustrations on her.

That feeling of safety was new to her, and it might be the one thing she liked best about him. Of course, he was awfully nice to look at, too, which didn't hurt anything. The thought made her smile as she took the stairs to her porch and used her key in the front door. Before the incident with Truck, she'd never felt the need to lock her door. Now she couldn't conceive of leaving it unlocked.

Once inside, she curled up on the sofa and tried to calm her racing mind. David had said he wanted to see her tonight, but they needed to talk about where they went from here. And the thought of that conversation had her nerves stretched nearly to their limit.

David left the clinic on time for once, locking the door to the emergency entrance at the stroke of six o'clock. They'd had a relatively slow afternoon that had given him a chance to catch up on the endless paperwork that had accumulated into small mountains on his desk.

Never far from his mind as he worked was the offer from Dr. Garrity. As he stepped into the warmth of the late afternoon sunshine, David thought about the implications of the offer and whether he was even interested in the job.

On the one hand, the oncology specialty intrigued him. It had been his favorite rotation and had given him the opportunity to make a genuine difference for patients who were in the fight of their lives. After his own battle with lymphoma, he had a better understanding of what cancer patients were going through and could bring that life experience to his work. He really liked the other doctors in Garrity's practice, too. They were all first-class physicians who would make for excellent mentors and colleagues.

For those reasons, the offer was highly attractive.

When he and Janey were together, their plan had been for him to come back to the island after medical school and take over the practice of the doctor who'd served the island since they were kids. He'd never really considered doing anything else. After they broke up, he'd floundered for a while after his treatment concluded, trying to figure out where he wanted to be.

He'd sort of fallen into the job on the island when Dr. Cal Maitland had left abruptly after his mother had a stroke in Texas. David had been home recuperating from the last of his treatments when Cal's departure created an opening for the job David had hoped to have all along. Without much consideration, he'd taken the offer from the town council and never looked back.

He'd been fumbling and stumbling through life since he'd broken up with Janey, not giving much thought to the grand plan while he tried to get through every day. Now, however, he felt like he was finally coming up for air, and it was time to take stock of where he was and what he wanted.

After these last few weeks with Daisy, it was impossible to ponder what he wanted without also thinking about her and how she fit into the big picture. He was anxious to talk it out with her but also hesitant to give her reason for doubts when everything was still so new between them.

As he drove by the police station, he noticed Blaine's SUV parked outside and made a spontaneous decision to stop and see his friend. He needed to bounce this dilemma off someone he trusted, and Blaine Taylor definitely qualified.

Inside, the officer on duty at the front desk asked Blaine if he was available for a visitor. A few minutes later, David was shown to Blaine's office at the end of a corridor off the main dispatch area. Blaine was standing up and on the phone, but he waved David in.

"It's all going to be fine, Mom," he said, rolling his eyes at David as he grinned from ear to ear. "Just think of it this way, we could've eloped. Isn't this better than that?" Blaine's smile got even bigger as he held the phone away from his ear.

David could hear Mrs. Taylor yelling from across the room.

"Gotta go, Mom. I love you. I'll see you tomorrow. Yes, I know. Bye." He dropped his cell phone on the desk. "Oh my God! Note to self, don't give Mom twenty-four hours' notice the next time I get married."

David's mouth fell open in surprise. "You're getting *married*?"

"Tomorrow."

"Get outta here. Seriously?"

"Yep and I want you there. We're tying the knot on the beach and then crashing Mac and Maddie's cookout and turning it into a reception."

"Oh, ah, I don't know about that…"

"Come on, David. I need all the friends I can get there. My mom is flipping out, and Tiffany's a nervous wreck even if she's trying hard to hide it."

"What's the rush anyway?"

"No rush. I've wanted this for a while now, but now that the douchebag ex-husband is giving her a hard time about shacking up with me, we figured why not move up our plans a bit?"

"That's awesome. Congratulations."

"Thanks," Blaine said with a satisfied smile. "I'm getting exactly what I want, even if my mother's having a shit fit. Anyway, what's up?"

"Nothing. Doesn't matter. You've got bigger fish to fry."

Blaine came around the desk and sat in one of the visitor chairs, gesturing for David to take the other. "Something brought you in here. How about you tell me what it was?"

David sat and leaned forward, elbows on knees. "I've been offered a job in Boston." He spelled out the specifics as well as the many advantages that came with the position. "It's a chance to specialize and to really make a difference."

"You don't feel like you're making a difference here?"

"No, I do. It's just that after having cancer, I think I could be really good at oncology. It was my favorite rotation during my residency. And then there's Daisy... Things have been really great with us, and she's liking her new position at the hotel, so it's not like she'd want to move to Boston or anything."

"Wow," Blaine said. "I didn't realize you two had gotten to the point where she'd factor into a decision like this."

"Neither did I until I was faced with the decision and thought first of her," David replied with a wry grin. "She's a significant factor."

"I sort of got the feeling you were liking general medicine and practicing here."

"I do. I like both those things. I like feeling needed here. I like that I can't leave the island without making sure I've got coverage from the mainland. That makes me feel important."

Blaine grinned. "You're like God around here."

"I wouldn't go that far."

"Ask someone like Mrs. Murtry whether you're right up there with God."

David had saved the older woman's life by performing a tracheotomy when she had a life-threatening allergic reaction.

"Or Chris Allston."

Chris had severed a finger while trimming his hedges. David had preserved the finger, arranged for a medical helicopter to transport the injured man to a trauma hospital on the mainland and had kept him from bleeding out while they waited for the chopper.

"What would Paul and Alex Martinez have done without you over the last year?" Blaine raised a brow. "Need me to go on? How about Daisy? How about Sarah Lawry? Do you feel like you made a difference for them?"

"Yes, of course. And I appreciate what you're trying to do. I know what I do makes a difference to the island residents. But is this what I want to do for the rest of my life?"

"I suppose only you know that for sure."

"Sometimes I get tired of living in the town where so many people know I cheated on Janey McCarthy," David said, getting to the crux of his dilemma.

"This may come as a newsflash to you, but you might be the only one still hung up on that. She's moved on—happily, from what I can see whenever I'm with her and Joe. The rest of the McCarthy family must surely appreciate what you did for Mac and Maddie when their baby was born, not to mention that you were there for their sons after the sailboat accident."

"They do."

"So hold your head up high around here, David. You've paid your penance, and for what it's worth, I think you're pretty damned good at general medicine. You've made my job easier on more than one occasion."

David got up and held out his hand to shake Blaine's. "I appreciate that and the pep talk when you've certainly got better things to do."

"No problem. So I'll see you tomorrow?"

"You know I'd really like to be there, right?"

"I hope so."

"Let me think about it."

"Fair enough."

"Congratulations," David said. "I'm happy for you and Tiffany."

"Thank you. I am, too."

David walked out of the police station with a smile on his face, anxious to get to Daisy's and hear what she had to say about the job offer.

CHAPTER 13

Since Blaine had to work until eight before he could break free for the weekend and Ashleigh was with Jim for the night, Tiffany decided to go to the home her mom shared with Ned Saunders to tell them her big news in person.

Francine and Ned were just sitting down to dinner when Tiffany walked in the back door.

"Hi, honey," Francine said, leaning into the kiss Tiffany greeted her with. "This is a nice surprise."

"Are you hungry, gal?" Ned asked as he gestured to a platter of barbecued chicken that made Tiffany's stomach growl.

"I'm supposed to eat with Blaine when he gets home."

Ned jumped up to give her a quick hug and returned with a plate and silverware. "We won't let on that you already ate if you don't want to tell him."

"I like how you think," Tiffany said to the man who'd been like a father to her since he got together with her mother. Thinking about what she needed to tell them—and what she wanted to ask of them—had her contending with a rather large lump in her throat.

She smiled gratefully at Ned when he poured her a glass of the wine he kept on hand for her. "Thank you."

"So what brings ya out and about?" Ned asked when he returned to his seat.

"I have some exciting news that I wanted to share with you in person."

"What's that?" Francine asked.

"Blaine and I are getting married."

"Oh, honey." Francine's green eyes were immediately misty. "That's wonderful news! I'm so happy for you."

"I know it's too soon after the divorce and all that, but it feels right to us."

Francine covered Tiffany's hand with her own. "That's all that matters."

"When's the big day?" Ned asked.

"Um…tomorrow?"

His eyes bugged as Francine gasped and coughed.

"*Tomorrow?*" Francine said in a high squeak.

"I know it sounds crazy, but Blaine's got a big idea to get married on the beach and then crash Maddie's cookout as a reception."

"You're serious," Francine said.

Tiffany nodded, hoping against hope that her mom would approve and support their decision.

Francine glanced at Ned, who was grinning widely. "What're you smiling about? This is the craziest thing I've ever heard!"

"I know, ain't it? But it's also the sweetest thing I ever heard. Blaine is pushin' it cuz of Jim's threats, ain't he, sweetheart?"

Not at all surprised that Ned had the whole thing figured out, Tiffany nodded. "That's one reason, but it's a much lesser reason than the fact that I'm crazy in love with him and want to be with him always. And he loves Ash as much as he loves me." Saying those words brought tears to Tiffany's eyes. "He loves us both so much. I never thought I'd have anything like this." She glanced at her mother imploringly. "I need you to understand—and approve."

"I do, honey. Of course I do. How could I not understand after what I saw you go through with Jim? For so long I wished for you to have everything you've got with Blaine. I'd never stand in the way of your happiness, even if this plan is the craziest thing I ever heard."

Tiffany laughed as new tears rolled down her cheeks. The food on her plate was untouched as she got up to hug her mother. "Thank you so much. For that and everything you've been to Maddie and me our whole lives."

"Now stop that this minute," Francine said sternly as she returned Tiffany's embrace.

"It's the truth."

The two women held on tight to each other for a long, tear-filled moment before they drew apart, laughing as they wiped their faces.

"My turn," Ned said.

Tiffany stepped into his open arms as if she'd been running to him her whole life.

He kissed her cheek. "So happy fer ya, gal. No one deserves it more."

Ned's softly spoken words generated more tears. "Thank you." He let her go, and she wiped her tears again. "Sorry to interrupt your dinner and boo-hoo all over you."

"Not a problem," Ned said. "We're always up fer happy news around here."

Tiffany turned to him. "I was wondering... If you're not busy tomorrow, if you might... If I could ask you, both of you...to give me away." For as long as she lived, Tiffany would never forget the expression on his dear face when her question registered with him.

He blinked several times, as if trying not to lose his composure, and cleared his throat. "I'd be honored, honey. Truly."

She squeezed his arm. "Thank you."

"This calls fer a celebration," Ned announced. He went to the living room and returned with a bottle of champagne. They popped the cork, ate the dinner that had cooled during their celebration and killed the bottle between the three of them, laughing and talking and making plans.

At some point, Ned must've called Blaine, because he appeared after his shift ended to pick her up so she wouldn't have to drive. When he came in the door, Tiffany leaped to her feet, threw herself into his arms and kissed him square on the mouth.

"We're getting *married! Tomorrow!*"

"So I've heard," he said, amused by her excitement. "Are you a little tipsy, babe?"

"Maybe just a little." She couldn't stop staring at the face that had become the center of her world in such a short time. It wasn't lost on her that she should probably be freaking out about how fast it all had happened, but she wasn't, because she had no doubt whatsoever that this was the right thing for her. *He* was the right one for her.

"What?"

Tiffany shook her head. "Nothing at all."

"Now what in the hell am I going to wear to my daughter's wedding *tomorrow?*" Francine's question made them all laugh.

Still held aloft by his strong arms, Tiffany lowered her head to Blaine's shoulder and relaxed against him. This time tomorrow, he'd be her husband. She couldn't wait.

Daisy woke when her phone chimed with a text from David.

Can't wait to see you. Be there in twenty minutes.

Her heart fluttered with excitement. He couldn't wait to see her. He was on his way over. Every one of those things was enough on its own to excite her, but all of them together sent her into anticipation overload. And then she remembered that they needed to talk, that she needed to give him an out if he wanted it.

That was only fair. Who knew if or even when she'd be ready to move forward with a physical relationship, and it wasn't right to keep him shackled to her if there was somewhere else he'd rather be.

A picnic, she decided. *We'll go somewhere and talk it out over dinner.* As she scurried around gathering what she needed, her heart shifted from fluttering to thudding. He'd said he couldn't wait to see her. Had anyone ever said that to her before? Not that she could recall.

A knock on the door startled her so badly she dropped the basket she had retrieved from a closet shelf. Immediately, her excitement evaporated. It was too soon for David. Acting on instinct, she reached for the baseball bat the previous tenant had left in the closet and held it by her side as she went to the front of the house and peeked through a side window to find a young man holding a huge floral arrangement.

Feeling ridiculous for overreacting, Daisy propped the bat against the wall and opened the door.

"Daisy Babson?"

"That's me."

"For you."

The overpowering scent of stargazer lilies filled her senses and had her heart fluttering all over again at the incredibly thoughtful gesture. "Thank you."

"They were supposed to be here before you got home, but we were backed up today. Sorry they're late."

He'd wanted them there when she got home. He'd gone to some trouble, not to mention the expense. Surrounded by her favorite scent and standing before the befuddled delivery boy, Daisy felt the door to her heart swing open. The emotional overload frightened her. She'd certainly never felt this way before about a man, especially one she was planning to let go if that was what he wanted.

As the delivery boy went down the stairs, David pulled up to the curb. Unreasonably thrilled to see him, Daisy waited at the door for him. He wore a crisp white dress shirt with khaki pants. The sight of him brought back a rush of erotic memories from the night before that made her skin prickle with awareness. Before things went bad, it had been very, very good.

"They just *now* got here?" he asked, visibly displeased.

"He said they got backed up."

"I wanted them here when you got home."

Daisy carefully placed the flowers on a table, turned to place her hands on his shoulders and went up on tiptoes to kiss him. "They're beautiful, and I love them."

His arm came around her waist to keep her pressed against him. "I'm glad."

"Major, *major* points for the most romantic gesture *ever*."

"Ever?" His smile lit up his face.

"*Ever.*" Daisy kissed him again, lingering this time to stroke his bottom lip with her tongue.

His groan and the tightening of his arms thrilled her. She loved knowing she affected him as much as he affected her. He drew back from her, looking slightly stunned as he gazed down at her. "These points you speak of… How do I go about redeeming them?"

"That's for me to know and you to find out."

"These weren't just any flowers. They're *stargazer lilies.*"

"And the points accumulated will reflect that you got it exactly, perfectly, just right."

"It's been a very long time since I got anything exactly, perfectly, just right."

Daisy smiled at him, pleased that he felt comfortable enough with her to admit that. "Well, you did today." Her smile faded when she remembered the conversation they needed to have.

"What?" he asked, tracing a finger over her lips.

Despite her intense desire never to speak again of what'd happened the night before, she forced herself to meet his gaze. "I wanted to talk to you about last night."

"There's nothing to talk about."

"David—"

This time he left his finger on her lips to stop her from saying anything more. "I meant every word I said last night. If it takes a month or a year or two years or whatever, it doesn't matter. I like being with you. I feel good when I'm with you. Do you know how much that means to me after feeling like shit for so long?"

"What if it takes forever?" she asked, voicing her greatest fear.

"I don't think it will, but if it does, so be it."

"You can't mean that. What guy would willingly offer to go without sex for that long?"

"I haven't had sex in two years, Daisy. I think I've proven I can live without it. Right now what matters is you and whatever you need. I'll take all my cues from you and give you whatever you want when you want it. Nothing more, I promise."

She shook her head. "I hate to be cynical when you're being so sweet, but my life has taught me that when something seems too good to be true, often it is."

"Not in this case." With his hands on her face, he compelled her to look up at him. "I feel good when I'm with you. I don't actively hate myself when I'm with you. That's a huge step forward for me, and that's all your doing. Please don't push me away because we had one difficult night. Maybe we'll have a dozen more difficult nights, but that's okay. I'm right where I want to be, and whatever happens, we'll deal with it."

Daisy wanted so badly to believe him. "I got some rather incredible news today."

"Funny, so did I. How about we talk about all this good news over dinner?"

"I put together a picnic, just in case."

His brows knitted with confusion, which was an adorable look on him. Hell, all his looks were rather adorable. "In case of what?"

"In case you decided to stick around."

"I have to stick around."

"How come?"

"Because I've got points to redeem, and how will I know what happens next if I cut and run?"

Amused and delighted to know he wasn't going to take the easy way out, she smiled at him. "And you want to know what happens next?"

"Very much so. Don't you?"

Daisy nodded and found she couldn't look away. "Very much so."

He took a step closer to her and then another. Placing his hands on her shoulders, he slid them slowly down her arms to join their hands. Then he tipped his head and kissed her.

Devastated by the sweet, gentle kiss, Daisy tightened her grip on his hands. Just as she was settling into the kiss, he pulled back. "Why did you stop?"

"I didn't want to get carried away."

"Please don't worry about doing the wrong thing. I was fine with everything until...you know..."

"Okay, I hear you." He kissed her again—quickly. "The next time I kiss you, I'll make it up to you. I promise."

"Will you promise me one other thing?"

"Sure."

"Will you promise you'll be honest if you get tired of waiting for me to get over my phobias?"

"I won't get tired of waiting."

"Still... Do you promise?"

He put his arms around her and hugged her to his chest. "I promise, but I don't expect to have to make good on that one."

Daisy held on to him for a long time, breathing in the familiar, comforting scent of his cologne. "And you'll come to Blaine and Tiffany's wedding with me even though the party involves your ex-fiancée's family?"

"And I'll go to Blaine and Tiffany's wedding with you. Gladly."

"Thank you," she said, smiling up at him. "Ready for that picnic?"

"I need to stop at home to change first."

"That's fine. We're not in any rush. Are we?"

"Not that I know of, but I'm always on call, which will get in our way sometimes."

"We'll work around it." She started to walk away, but his hand slid down her arm to capture her fingers. "What?"

"I like how you said that. We'll work around it. That makes me feel like *you're* planning to stick around for a while, too."

She went back to him and looped her arms around his neck. "Where else would I go when all I can think about is the next time I get to be with you?"

"That's all you think about?"

Daisy worried for a moment that she might've said too much. It wasn't like her to expose herself emotionally to a man. She'd learned the hard way to keep her thoughts and feelings to herself. But something about David and the closeness they'd shared for weeks now made her want to be honest with him, even if it meant risking her fragile heart. "Pretty much."

"How do you get anything else done if all you're thinking about is me?"

Smiling at his playful reply, she kissed his neck. "It's not easy." Daisy pulled away from him long enough to gather up the picnic basket and blanket. On the way to his house, they chatted about his day at the clinic and the family of ten that had checked loudly into the hotel earlier in the day.

She waited for him in the car while he ran into his house to get changed, which was how she caught a glimpse of his elusive landlord when he emerged from the big house, looking as if he'd been on a multi-day bender. Despite the scruff on his chin, the red eyes and the dark blond hair standing on end, Daisy could see that he was an exceptionally good-looking man.

David came down the stairs from his place and seemed surprised to see Jared on the deck. They exchanged a few words before David got in the car.

"Wow, he looks like hell," David said.

"What did he say?"

"Nothing much. Just hello and how's it going, but he's usually so polished and put together. It's weird to see him disheveled."

"Ask him to come with us."

David looked over at her. "To our picnic at the beach?"

"We've got plenty of food, and he looks like he could use a friend or two."

"You're serious."

"Unless you don't want to."

"I was feeling kind of bad about leaving him when there's clearly something wrong."

"Then what do you say we eat here with him and figure out what's going on. Then we can go for a walk on the beach by ourselves."

He leaned across the center console to kiss her. "I say you're an exceptionally good person, Daisy Babson, and I quite like you."

Delighted by the kiss and the compliments, Daisy smiled at him. "I quite like you, too."

They got out of the car and walked around to the back of the house, where Jared was staring off into space on the back deck, which was outfitted with gorgeous outdoor furniture that looked like it had never been used. Giant flowerpots full of colorful blooms sat at each corner of the spacious deck.

Daisy wondered if Jared had even noticed the obvious trouble someone had gone to on his behalf. Working at the hotel had taught her that rich people often failed to notice the little things that mattered so greatly to her.

"I thought you left," Jared said to David.

"This is my girlfriend, Daisy." David put his arm around her as she absorbed the simple pleasure of hearing him introduce her as his girlfriend. "You seem upset or something, and we thought you might like some company." He placed the basket on the table. "Are you hungry?"

Jared shrugged as if he had no idea how to answer that simplest of questions.

"I don't know what I was thinking when I packed so much food for two of us," Daisy said cheerfully, earning a grateful smile from David. "You'd be doing us a favor if you ate some of it."

"Um, sure, okay. Thanks." Jared gestured to the chairs. "Have a seat. Do we need silverware or anything?"

"It's all in the basket," Daisy said. "My friend Maddie gave me the whole setup for my birthday last year because she knows how much I love picnics. This is the first time I've gotten to use it." Daisy knew she was babbling, but she couldn't stand the sense of desolation that radiated from him. She recognized the desolation because she'd felt it herself. Recently, in fact.

Daisy unpacked the fried chicken, potato salad and tossed salad she had put together for her and David to share. She wasn't lying when she'd said there was plenty. Knowing how often David's work forced him to skip meals, she had made extra in case he was famished.

"This looks great, Daisy," David said, diving in with his usual zest for home cooking.

"Help yourself, Jared," Daisy said.

"Thank you."

Between bites of chicken, David uncorked the wine she'd included and poured some for each of them.

"Thank you." Daisy took a sip of her wine. The tart, dry flavor made her taste buds explode with sensation. "Do you want to talk about what's bothering you Jared? I know we just met, but sometimes a stranger can be better to unload on than a friend."

Jared put down his red plastic fork and wiped his face on the red-and-white-checkered napkin. "A couple of days ago, I asked my girlfriend to marry me," he said flatly, staring straight ahead as he spoke. "She said no."

"Wow," Daisy said in a whisper. "Did she say why?"

Jared bent his head and ran his fingers through his hair repeatedly, which he'd probably been doing for quite some time judging from the way it stood on end. "She can't do life in the fishbowl. She said she loves me, but she doesn't love my life. The media is relentless, the rumors, the gold diggers, the lavishness. It's not for her."

"I'm so sorry, man," David said. "That sucks."

"Big-time. I couldn't stay in the city after that, knowing it was over between us. I had to get out of there."

"You did the right thing coming here," Daisy said. "It'll be good to get some space and some perspective." She looked to David to help her out, because she had no idea what to say.

"Daisy's right. You love it here, and it's peaceful and quiet."

"You know what I've been thinking about since I got here?"

"What's that?" David asked.

"How I could go about getting rid of the money. Maybe if I didn't have the money anymore, I could give her the normal life she wants."

"But is that what *you* want?" Daisy asked and immediately felt like she was being overly forward with someone she'd just met.

"I want her. I want us. I've never been in love with anyone the way I am with her. I don't get why she couldn't see past all the reasons it wouldn't work and see all the ways it works perfectly. We're so damned good together."

When Jared's eyes filled with tears, Daisy looked away. She felt as if she was intruding on an intensely private moment.

"I'm sorry, guys," Jared said. "I appreciate what you're trying to do, but I'm not very good company tonight."

"That's okay," David said. "We've both been there, so we get it."

"This happened to you, too?" Jared asked.

David glanced at Daisy, seeming to seek her approval to tell Jared what he'd been through.

Under the table, she curled her hand around his. When their eyes met, she nodded and smiled.

David squeezed her hand. "I was engaged to my girlfriend of thirteen years and managed to completely screw it up a year before the wedding. I definitely understand how you're feeling right now, and it does get better. With time."

"How much time?"

"It'll hurt like hell for quite a while," David said. "And then one day you'll meet someone new, someone who makes you feel hopeful again." He looked at Daisy. "It won't be the same as it was before, but it's possible it'll be even better."

He wore the expression of a man who'd traveled a long and difficult path and had come out on the other side better for the journey. The warm, loving look he directed her way along with his words made Daisy feel about ten feet tall because she'd done that for him.

"It was really good of you guys to hang with me," Jared said. "I won't keep you from your evening."

"Jared," David said before the other man could make his escape. "Do yourself a favor and don't make any big decisions right away. Don't give all your money to charity or anything like that. You may regret it in a week or two when the fog clears."

Jared nodded and disappeared into the house.

"Poor guy," Daisy said.

"Poorest rich guy you've ever met."

"Money can't buy happiness."

"No, it can't. Thanks for the picnic and for talking to Jared."

"I like him, and I feel so sorry for him."

"He'll bounce back. He's usually bursting with confidence and bravado. I barely recognized him tonight."

"He's heartbroken," Daisy said with a sigh. "He has everything money can buy, but what good is it without the woman he loves?"

David put his arm around her and kissed the top of her head. "What do you say we stash the rest of the food at my place and go for that walk on the beach I promised you?"

"That sounds great."

They left his place a short time later, driving past the darkened house where Jared had gone back into hiding.

"Don't worry," David said. "I'll check on him tomorrow."

"Oh good."

He took her hand and held it all the way to the parking lot at Carpenter's Beach on the island's east side. Daisy wanted to tell him about the house and what Maddie had done for her, but decided to wait for their walk. They arrived at the beach where the sun had tucked in close to the land, ablaze in brilliant oranges and reds that fired the sky.

"Perfect timing," David said as they took the stairs down to the beach, which was deserted except for a group of seagulls dive-bombing the surf in search of fish. Still holding hands, they kicked off their shoes at the bottom of the stairs and walked to the water's edge, where waves rolled gently to the shore. The glow of the sun on the water and the skirmishing, squawking birds made for a delightful view.

"What a pretty night," Daisy said.

"Very much so." He put his arm around her. "Let's walk."

"I have to warn you that I'm a crazy beachcomber." She pulled a plastic shopping bag from the pocket of her shorts and held it up.

"What're we looking for?"

"I'll know when I see it, but mostly cool shells, sea glass and driftwood. I love driftwood."

"I'm on it."

They scoured the beach for the next half hour, filling the bag with a variety of treasures. Daisy appreciated his enthusiasm for her project and praised every shell he found as better than the one before, which made him laugh.

It was fun to be lighthearted and a little silly with a man. It was freeing to be able to share one of her simple pleasures with him and feel his genuine appreciation for what they were doing.

"Check this out," he said, holding up a starfish.

"Is it still alive?"

"Might be."

"Toss it back into the water. Maybe it still has a chance."

Rather than toss it, David walked it to the water's edge and placed it in the surf.

"Another life saved, Dr. Lawrence," she said with a laugh.

"I'll add it to my tally."

"How many lives have you actually saved?"

"I don't know," he said, seeming embarrassed by the question. "A few."

"I'd think you'd remember every one of them."

"I wish I did, but things move pretty fast and furious in an inner city ER, so it's impossible to keep track. That was my wildest rotation."

"Which one was your favorite?"

His smile faded a bit. "Oncology."

"How come?"

"I really liked the doctors I worked with. I learned a lot from them, and the patients were very special people, so upbeat and positive, even when faced with terrible odds. I tried to remember their example when I was going through treatment."

"How'd you do?"

"My depression had far more to do with how miserably I'd screwed up my personal life than it did with the illness. I tried to stay positive, but it was hard to be upbeat about anything after I lost Janey. I can really relate to how Jared feels right now. I hope I never feel like that again. Ever."

"I hope not either," Daisy said softly, realizing in that moment she had the power to hurt him and vice versa. She hoped they'd both learned from their past mistakes and would tread gently with each other's hearts. Leaning into him, she looped her arm around his waist and loved the feel of his arm heavy across her shoulders. "Something happened today that I really want to tell you about."

"I was just about to say the same thing."

"You first."

"Absolutely not. Ladies first. Always."

Daisy stopped walking and turned to face him. "You know the land Mrs. Chesterfield left to the town?"

"What about it?"

"The town council voted to use the land for affordable housing for people like me who work in the service industry. I found out today that Maddie put my name in for one of the houses, and I was approved." She blinked back tears. "I'm getting my very own house, David."

He scooped her up and swung her around. "That's amazing, Daisy! Congratulations."

She held on tight to him. "I'm so glad I can stay here. I was dreading having to leave after the season, but my rent is going up, and there's no way I can swing it. I can barely swing what I'm paying now, even with the raise I got when I took the manager's job."

"Now you don't have to leave."

"Now I don't have to."

He put her down but kept his arms around her when he leaned in to kiss her. "I'm so happy for you to have that worry off your shoulders."

"So am I. I've never felt so at home anywhere as I do here, and the thought of leaving was killing me."

"I'm really happy for you."

"Then why do you look so bummed?"

He dropped his arms from around her shoulders, bent to pick up a flat rock and sent it skipping over the surface of the water. "I was offered a job in Boston today."

"Oh."

"I know. Ironic right? The same day you get a chance at a secure future here."

Daisy crossed her arms and stared out at the horizon, trying to absorb it all. "What kind of job?"

"The opportunity to specialize in oncology and work with the doctors who guided me through my rotation in that department—and my own treatment."

"That was your favorite one."

"Yes, and I liked the other doctors in that practice a lot. I learned an incredible amount from them and, of course, I went right to them when I was diagnosed."

"So it's a job you want."

"If I was looking to make a big change, I suppose it would be what I want."

"Are you not happy running the clinic?"

"I love running the clinic, and being the island's only doctor. Makes me feel needed, you know?"

"I'm sure it does."

"Earlier today when I got the call about the offer, you know what my first thought was?"

"What?"

"I wonder if Daisy might like to move to Boston."

"That was your first thought."

"One of them."

"Boston. Wow. I've never thought about going back there since I left."

"I love it there. It's a great place to live."

"I liked it while I was there, but I like it here better."

"For the most part, I do, too, but I don't know… It might be time for a change."

Daisy had no idea what to say to that, and a staggering array of thoughts went through her mind as she followed him to an area between two dunes and helped him spread the blanket.

He stretched out on the blanket and held out his arm, inviting her to join him.

Settled against his chest, Daisy wanted to ask a thousand questions. Was he going to take the job? What if she didn't go with him? What did it mean for them? Why did they keep butting up against so many obstacles?

"Tell me what you're thinking."

"I'd rather know what you're thinking. Are you going to take the job?"

"If they had asked me a couple of months ago, I probably would've jumped on the opportunity. But now…"

"What about now?"

"Everything is different now, and it's not just about me."

"You can't make important career decisions based on what's happening with us."

"Why the hell not? Would you take a job somewhere else and not consider me or how I might feel about it?"

"Well, no, but that's different."

"How so?"

"You're a *doctor*, David."

"Oh, right I forgot that."

She poked him in the belly, making him startle and gasp.

Chuckling, he brushed his lips over the top of her head. "Your logic sort of stinks, you know."

"How so?"

"Your job, your life, your dreams, your goals are no less important than mine."

"I appreciate what you're trying to do, but your job is way more important than mine. Today, for example, they brought Laura McCarthy to the clinic. I bet you helped her to deal with the dehydration and the nausea."

"Maybe."

"And I heard Carolina Cantrell fell into a thorn bush. I'm sure you had something to do with treating her, too."

"Possibly. You're shockingly well informed."

"I was there when they took Laura from the hotel in the ambulance, and Mrs. McCarthy is good friends with Mrs. Cantrell, so she mentioned that at work today. Are they both okay?"

"They will be."

"I ordered more cleaning supplies, put the laundry staff on notice that they've got to be quicker in getting the linens washed this time of year and set the schedule for next week. You save lives. I supervise maids. Your job is more important."

"Maybe my job is more important to people who are sick, but yours is more important to people looking for a clean bed and a break from their daily grind."

"You should've been a lawyer. You missed your calling." She sighed and propped herself up on an elbow so she could see his face. "If you want this job in Boston, you should take it. It sounds like a great opportunity."

"It could be. Would you miss me if I went?"

"Yes, I would miss you."

"Would you consider coming with me?"

"I don't know. I really like it here. What if I left my job and my friends and everything to go there with you and it doesn't work out between us? What would I do then?"

"I'd never leave you high and dry, Daisy. No matter what happens between us."

"Still… I'd be starting all over. Again. I don't know if I could do that."

"Then we won't do it."

"You can't make a decision like this based on the whims of a woman who can't even have sex with you!"

Damn if he didn't laugh, *hard*. He laughed so hard he had tears in his eyes when he finally caught his breath.

"It's not funny."

"*You* are funny." He tweaked her nose. "You're happy here. I'm happy with you. We'll stay put. There'll be other jobs if we get sick of island life."

She stared at him, unable to fathom that he would actually make a decision of this magnitude based on what she wanted rather than what was best for his career. "David, listen to me. You're acting crazy—"

He shifted suddenly, pitching her onto his chest and into direct contact with his lips.

While she had many other things she wanted to say to him, the kiss suddenly demanded her full attention as his tongue pressed into her mouth and his hands in her hair anchored her to him. By the time he finally lightened his hold on her, she'd forgotten what she wanted to say, which she suspected was his goal.

He turned his focus to her neck, kissing his way to her throat and along her collarbone, nudging her tank top off her shoulder.

"I know what you're doing." He was making her breathless with strategically placed kisses as he held her on top of him in the waning daylight.

"What am I doing?" he asked, dragging the tip of his tongue along her collarbone.

She'd had no idea that was such a turn-on. "You're trying to distract me so I won't get to tell you it's nuts to make a career decision based on what I want."

"Why?" His hands found their way to her breasts, cupping, shaping, arousing.

"*David,*" she said with a protracted moan. She dropped her head to his chest, unable to hold it up any longer. "Will you please listen to me?"

"I've heard every word you've said."

"But you're not *listening*."

"I most certainly am too. You think I'm being ridiculous for making a career decision based on what's best for you rather than what's best for me. Do I have it about right?"

She raised her head to look at him. His eyes were alight with amusement. "Yes!"

"Okay, good. Can we go back to kissing and stuff now that we've cleared that up?"

"We haven't cleared up anything."

"You're starting to make me feel like you want to get rid of me."

"I don't. You know I don't, but you need to think about this and make the right decision."

"I did think about it, and I'm happy with the decision. Okay?"

"Is it really because of me that you're turning down the offer?"

"Um, may I decline to answer that on the basis that I want to end this conversation and get back to the other one I was enjoying far more?"

"Answer the question."

He sighed deeply and brought his hands to the top of his head, running his fingers through his hair.

As his erection pressed against her belly, she tried to move off him. Quick as lightning, he had his arms around her again, keeping her from getting away. "It's a combination of things, but mostly it's you."

Daisy shook her head. "That's a lot of pressure to put on me."

"No pressure. Think of it as me saying I like being here because you're here. Nothing more than that."

"Sure, nothing more than that."

"Can we get back to making out now?"

"Could I ask you one more thing?"

He moaned dramatically. "As long as it's not about my job."

"Did you hear Tiffany and Blaine are getting married tomorrow?"

"I did hear that. I saw him after work."

"Will you go with me?"

"Since I'm giving up a job in Boston to stay here with you, I suppose I'll have to go places with you once in a while."

She took a good long look at his face and realized that despite his playful aggravation, he looked more relaxed and at peace than he ever had before.

"Do I have something on my face?"

"You look good."

"So do you," he said with an incorrigible waggle of his brows. "Good enough to kiss, in fact."

"You always look good enough to kiss. I've thought that from the first time I met you. I meant you look relaxed."

"Wait, back up… You met me almost two years ago when you were stung by a bee and broke out in hives."

"You remember that?"

"I remember thinking how very lovely you were." As he spoke, he combed his fingers through her hair.

"Even covered in all those ugly red welts?"

"Even then."

"Why didn't you say something?"

"You'd just started seeing Truck back then. I didn't want to mess anything up for you."

"God, I wish you had."

"So do I. I'd give anything to have spared you what happened with him. Could I ask you about him?"

"What about him?"

"What did you see in him? I want to understand."

Daisy thought about that for a minute, allowing her mind to drift back in time to when she first met Truck. "He was fun and funny, and he really seemed to like me. I was lonely, and he was there." She shrugged, hating to think now about how naïve she'd been—again. "He hid his demons really well for a long time."

"I didn't mean to upset you by asking about him."

"You didn't."

"Let's talk about you and your sexy lips and the way your eyes get very big when you're surprised and very narrow when you're mad at me. Let's talk about this insanely sexy tank top that's been driving me crazy since the second I got to your house. And let's talk about where we're going to sleep tonight. Your place or mine?"

That simply, he got her mind off the past and focused firmly on the future. "Yours."

"All right, then. Should we head there now before it gets dark?"

"Mmm," she said, leaning in to kiss him. "In a minute."

With his arms wrapped firmly around her, Daisy lost herself in the kiss. She squirmed on top of him, wanting to get even closer. His tortured groan and his hands on her bottom made her crazy with longing. By the time she drew back to look down at him, the daylight had begun to wane. "Could I ask you something?"

"Anything."

"It's kind of weird."

"I can handle weird."

"I try really hard not to think of that night when I was hurt." She licked her lips and watched his eyes zero in on the movement of her tongue. "But when they brought me to the clinic, you saw what he'd done to me. And that makes me wonder if you ever think about that when you touch me there." She lifted her eyes to meet his gaze. "See? I told you it's weird."

"I don't think of that. I think of how sexy and hot you are, how wet you are for me, how much I want to make you come. But I never, ever, ever think about what I saw that night. I swear to you."

His bluntly spoken words made her heart race with desire and love. How could she not love him? He wasn't perfect. Not by a long shot. But it was becoming increasingly clear that he was perfect for her.

"Thank you for letting me ask you that."

"You can ask me anything you want, anytime you want."

Emboldened by his words and the affection in his eyes, she said, "Have you ever had sex on the beach?"

He smiled, as she'd hoped he would. "The drink or the act?"

"The act."

"The beach is one of the only places I had sex until I went to college. The first time we got to do it in a bed was quite something." When he realized what he'd said, he looked almost stricken. "And you didn't need to know that."

"I like hearing about your life."

"But you don't need to hear about my ex."

"She was a big part of your life."

"Yes, she was, but she isn't anymore. You believe me when I say that, don't you?"

Daisy bit her bottom lip and nodded.

"I love when you do that," he said, touching the tip of his index finger to her lip. "Incredibly adorable." His finger moved from her lip over her chin and down her neck, making her shiver. "What about you? Ever had sex on the beach?"

"Nope, but I think I'd like to sometime."

"We'll have to put that on our to-do list. But right now, I want to take you to my house, have a nice hot shower with you, if you'd like that, and hold you close to me all night long."

"That sounds like heaven."

"Then let's get to it."

CHAPTER 14

David was trapped in hell. The shower with Daisy had been among the most erotic encounters of his life. Watching the water slide over her curves and cling to her rose-colored nipples had made him hard enough to drive pilings. Pressing her against the wall and kissing her until his lips went numb and his oxygen-starved lungs screamed for mercy hadn't helped the situation very much, nor had the heated make-out session that had continued in his bed after the shower.

Though they didn't speak of it, both of them were spooked by what'd happened the night before, so they kept their hands and lips above the waist, which was why he was awake next to her thinking about cold showers and ice baths.

The sheet brushing against his cock was almost more than he could take, so he shifted to find a more comfortable position and moaned out loud when her soft belly pressed against his erection.

"What's wrong?" she asked in a sleepy voice.

"Nothing. Go back to sleep."

"You're restless."

"I'm sorry. I didn't mean to bother you."

"Tell me what's wrong."

"It's nothing. I'm just feeling a bit…tense. That's all." Tense was a good word for it.

"Want me to rub your shoulders?" she asked through a yawn.

"That's okay." He hoped she would go back to sleep, but rather she draped herself over his chest, and his cock got impossibly harder.

Her hand slid from his chest to his belly.

He tried to stop her, but desire had slowed his reflexes, and she had her hand curled around him before he knew what hit him. "Daisy," he said on a gasp. "If you so much as move, I'm going to come."

He said that hoping she might let go, but instead she squeezed him gently but insistently and then began to stroke him. "Ah, shit. Oh Christ. *Daisy...*" His hips surged off the bed, matching the rhythm that she set. It took very little effort on her part to finish him off. "Wow," he whispered when he could speak again. "That was...amazing."

"Don't suffer in silence. I feel bad enough about my freak-out without leaving you aching. You have to let me take care of you, too."

"You took very good care of me," he said, holding her close as the tension seeped from his body.

"Tomorrow night, after Blaine and Tiffany's wedding, I want to try again."

David waited to see if she would say anything else.

"I want to try to make love with you."

She sounded so brave and so fearful at the same time.

"Let's wait awhile. We're not in any rush."

"I know myself, David. Until I get past this hurdle, it's all I'll think about. Please?"

"Whatever you want, honey. I'll do whatever you want."

"Thank you," she said, relaxing against him.

David had said what she wanted to hear, but he hoped he wasn't making a big mistake by going along with her plan.

Tiffany woke to bright sunshine streaming in the French doors they'd left open the night before and Blaine's naked body curled around hers from behind. They only slept naked on the nights that Ashleigh stayed with her father or grandparents, and they had the house to themselves.

With his hand warm, large and possessive on her belly, Tiffany sighed with contentment and was on her way back to sleep when her eyes shot open. Holy hell! They were getting married today! She had no time to be lounging about in bed! She had to get up and shower and do something with her hair and what time was Ashleigh due home, and *oh my God!* They were getting married today!

She threw off the covers and was on her way out of bed when he dragged her back against him.

"Not so fast."

"I have so much to do!"

"It's six thirty, Tiff. You've got plenty of time."

"Spoken like a true guy who takes a shower, shakes the water out of his hair, throws on some clothes and gets married."

"For your information, I also plan to shave for the occasion." To make his point, he rubbed his whiskers on the back of her shoulder, giving her goose bumps.

"Please don't. You know how I love your stubble."

"My mother would never forgive me if I don't shave for my own wedding."

"Your wife will never forgive you if you do."

"Oh, baby, you drive a hard bargain." He flexed his hips and pressed his erection into the cleft of her bottom as his hand covered her breast.

She was so, so easy where he was concerned. All he had to do was touch her and she was ready for anything he wanted to give her. And right now was no exception, despite her staggering to-do list and a two o'clock ceremony planned at the lighthouse.

While he tweaked her nipple, she thought about how fast their plans had come together. Jenny had offered up the lighthouse for an afternoon wedding, Mac and Maddie had taken care of all the food and drinks as well as getting the word out to all their mutual friends that a special surprise was planned for the cookout.

Tiffany had even found the perfect dress in the latest shipment to the store. Tiffany had even found the perfect dress in the latest shipment to the store. It was a rich ivory with spaghetti straps and a large, bright, orangey-red flower positioned over her hip. A slit up the side of the dress ran through the middle of the flower. A tad bit unconventional, the dress was perfect for her, and she had no doubt Blaine would love it. She'd ordered bouquets of red and orange Gerbera daisies for herself as well as Ashleigh and Maddie.

The only remaining question was whether Ashleigh's white eyelet Easter dress still fit her, which they would determine when Jim brought her home later this morning. Tiffany couldn't wait to share the wedding news with her daughter, who would be thrilled. Ashleigh loved Blaine as much as Tiffany did, which was probably why Jim had made such a stink about Blaine moving in with them. He felt threatened by the other man in his daughter's life.

"What're you thinking about?" Blaine asked as he kissed his way down her back.

"If I told you, you might think I don't like what you're doing."

He took a bite of her bum, which made her squeak with surprise. "Tell me."

"I was thinking that the reason Jim is so mad about you moving in is because he's probably figured out that Ashleigh likes you better than him."

"That was never my goal."

"I know, but you're so good with her. When you're with her, you give her your undivided attention. Jim has never done that. He's always face-first in his phone or watching the game or doing anything he can to not engage with her. That's why I hate when she spends the night with him. I always worry that she's going to get hurt when he's not paying attention."

"For all his faults, he loves her, Tiff. He'd never let anything happen to her."

"I know. You're right, but still, I like it so much better when she's here with us."

"So do I, but I gotta say, I also love the sleep-naked nights. I love them a whole lot."

Tiffany laughed at his lecherous tone and pushed her bottom back against him, making him groan.

"I want to make love to my fiancée. Since it was the shortest engagement in history, we haven't had anywhere near enough engagement sex."

"Only if we do it like this. You aren't supposed to see me on our wedding day. It's bad luck, and I've had more than enough of that."

"Your luck's about to change, baby. I'll do everything I can to make sure of it."

"Have I mentioned yet today that I love you so, so much?"

"I don't think you have."

"Well, I do. And I'm so excited for today and every day to come."

"So am I. I can't wait until you're officially my wife."

"Oh my God! Blaine! What about rings?"

"I've got that covered. Don't worry."

"How in the word did you manage that with only two days?"

He reached around to caress between her legs. "Mmm, I love that you're always ready for me."

"All you have to do is look at me, and I'm ready."

"That's good to know. I plan to look at you a lot when we're married."

He made her laugh. He made her smile like a foolish teenager in love for the first time. He made her feel safe. He made her feel sexy and desired. He made her feel so many things in the course of every day that she could barely process them all. Most important of all, he made her feel like she mattered more to him than any other thing in the world. He was everything to her, and he always would be.

When he had stroked her to the edge of climax, he coaxed her onto her knees and entered her from behind. As always, the tight fit heightened her arousal and forced every thought that didn't involve him and the exquisite way he loved her from her mind.

"God, I love your sweet ass," he said gruffly as he cupped and squeezed her cheeks, "and the way you give yourself to me anytime I want you. I've got to be the luckiest guy in the whole world."

His words and his hands and the firm strokes of his hard cock combined to give her a world-class orgasm that felt like it went on forever. Just when she thought it was done, he would roll her nipples between his fingers or press on her clit or surge into her and hit that spot deep inside that triggered another wave of release.

"Blaine," she said, gasping.

"What, baby?"

"You're killing me."

"No, I'm not," he said with a laugh. "You can take it."

"I don't think I can take any more."

"Give me one more, and I'll let you go."

"You've already gotten four out of me!" Tiffany hadn't believed multiples were even possible until he'd proven otherwise.

"One more. Consider it your wedding gift to me."

"So I won't have to do this again later?"

For that comment, she received a resounding smack to the ass that fired her up all over again.

"That's my girl. I love how wet you get when I spank you." To make his point, he did it again, setting her other cheek on fire, and sure enough, Tiffany found herself on the brink of another orgasm. "Come on, baby. Let me feel you clamp down on me. Make my eyes roll back in my head."

He gave it to her hard and fast, keeping up a relentless tempo.

"You're...showing off your stamina...again," she said.

Grunting out a laugh, he went for broke, grasping her hips and hammering into her until he got exactly what he wanted from her. Only then did he let himself go, too.

They landed in a sweaty heap on the bed, breathing hard and still throbbing from the aftershocks. And damn if he wasn't still hard inside her. How did he do that?

"This is going to be the most awesome marriage in the history of awesome marriages," he said in a husky whisper while he planted kisses on her shoulder that made her shiver beneath him.

"If you don't get off me and get out of here, I'm going to look like a hag when you marry me."

"Not possible, but I'll give you your time to primp as long as you promise you won't be one minute late."

"I'll be there. Nothing could keep me from you—today or any day."

He surged and thickened inside her.

"Blaine!"

Chuckling, he withdrew from her. "I'm going. I'm going."

"Save it for the honeymoon." Tiffany buried her face in the pillow so she wouldn't be tempted to watch him move around the room in all his naked glory. Feeling languid and relaxed after the orgasmic frenzy, she stayed there while he showered and got dressed.

With a hand on either side of her, he bent over the bed and kissed the back of her neck. "The next time I see you, it's for keeps."

"I can't wait."

"Neither can I. I feel like I've been waiting my whole life for today to get here."

Tiffany took his hand and pressed a kiss to his palm. "Go before I'm tempted to drag you back into bed."

"Mmm, that's not much incentive to leave."

"Go!"

"I'm not feeling the love."

"I'll make it up to you later."

"Yes, you will," he said, dragging his hand down her back for one last ass squeeze. "Jesus, Tiff." He leaned over, his head resting on her back. "I can't believe you're really going to marry me. I feel like I'm living in some sort of dream or something."

"Me, too," she said softly, moved to tears by his words.

"I expect today to be one of the best days of my life, but before all the craziness, I want you to know that the very best day of my life was the first time I ever saw you, sitting on Maddie's bed in the clinic. I knew right then and there that you were meant for me." He kissed the middle of her back and strode briskly from the room.

Tiffany used the pillowcase to mop up her tears. She heard the door close downstairs and got up to find a robe as her first order of business was coffee. Halfway down the stairs, the sound of raised voices from the driveway drifted in through the open window and had her running for the back door. She threw open the door to find Jim attempting to stare down Blaine with Ashleigh looking between them like a frightened doe.

"Hey, Ash," Tiffany said. "Come see Mommy."

Ashleigh broke free of Jim's loose hold and bolted for her mother.

Tiffany was ready to scoop her up and hug her close. "Hi, baby."

"Daddy is mad at Blaine." Her quivering chin made Tiffany want to harm her ex-husband for picking a fight in front of their daughter.

"Will you do me a great big favor and go up to your room and unpack your bag?" Ashleigh's room was on the far side of the house, so that would get her away from any potential trouble in the driveway. "I'll be right there, and I have a very big surprise for you."

"Okay, Mommy."

Tiffany kissed her cheek and put her down. "That's my good girl."

Ashley dragged her Dora the Explorer overnight bag behind her as she went into the house.

The second the door clicked shut behind Ashleigh, Tiffany turned on Jim. "What's the problem?"

"I told you I don't want him around here," he said, glaring at Blaine, who seemed to be holding back the urge to pummel Jim, which he could easily do.

"Who I spend time with is no longer your concern. You got exactly what you wanted. You're no longer married to me. So please go about your business and stay the hell out of mine."

"Your business is my business when it affects my daughter."

"Unlike you, I have *always* put my daughter first and will continue to do so for the rest of my life. You disposed of me like a piece of trash you had no use for, so don't come around here now and think you have any say whatsoever in how I live my life."

"You're going to be very sorry if you don't do what you're told."

"Are you *for real?*" Blaine took a step closer to Jim so he could poke him in the chest. Jim stumbled backward but recovered his footing before he fell. "Did you seriously just *threaten* her in front of me? Do you have any idea how much trouble I could cause for you if I wanted to? Do you have any idea that your beautiful daughter is the *only* reason I haven't already turned your life on this island into a living hell? I have too much respect for *her* to tell everyone how much of an asshole her father is. But you better listen up when I tell you I will not hesitate to do everything within my power to ruin you if you don't leave your *ex-wife* alone. Your behavior is borderline harassment, and if it comes down to my word against yours, *no one* will believe you. So get the hell out of here, and go live the life you wanted without her. Other than your daughter, there's nothing for you here anymore."

Jim's face had turned bright red, but he wisely turned on his heel and stormed off. If only Tiffany could believe that they'd heard the last from him on the subject.

Blaine waited until he'd left the property before he turned to Tiffany. "Are you okay?"

She worked up a small smile for him. "You weren't supposed to see me before the wedding."

He came over to her and stood on the bottom step, which put him at her eye level. "I don't think you need to be superstitious. I have a feeling your luck is about to change."

She combed her fingers through his unruly hair, attempting to bring some order to it. "It already has." She kissed him. "Since our marriage has already been hexed, how about we go tell Ashleigh our news together?"

He took her hand and brought it to his lips. "I'd love that."

Daisy was having the most amazing dream. She and David were making love, and it was incredible. Nothing about it frightened her or made her want to shy away from him. If anything, she wanted to get closer. She wanted more. She wanted everything he had to give her. Though she knew she was dreaming, she watched the erotic scene unfold as if she were a bystander.

Right when things were heading toward the zenith, she woke up, throbbing between her legs and desperate to finish what they'd started.

She absolutely loved waking to the sight of David's handsome face on the pillow next to hers. If she thought he was gorgeous when freshly showered and polished, he was sinfully sexy when he was rumpled and in bad need of a shave. The whiskers on his jaw fascinated her, and she couldn't resist dragging her finger lightly over the stubble.

Emboldened by the fact that he hadn't stirred, she continued her exploration, running her finger lightly over his bottom lip.

He pounced, biting gently on her finger.

She screamed and then busted up laughing. "You scared the hell out of me."

Without opening his eyes, he smiled and continued to nibble on her finger. "Someone is awake early." His hand ventured under her T-shirt to rest on her belly, infusing her with his heat.

Daisy moved closer to him, wanting to feel his skin against hers, but was frustrated when her shirt got in the way. She could tell she surprised him when she removed it and tossed it across the room. Watching him look at her was among the sexiest things she'd ever experienced. "David…"

"What, honey?" With his arm around her now, he drew her in closer so her breasts brushed against the hair on his chest.

She'd never known how arousing chest hair could be until that moment, and the needy tingle between her legs intensified into a flashpoint of desire. "I feel so… So…"

"Tell me."

"Desperate," she said, the word sneaking out before she could filter herself. She was mortified until his hand covered her sex and she had no brainpower left with which to be anything other than incredibly turned on.

"Here?"

"Yes. I've never been like this before."

"Like what?"

"Forward, needy, asking for things. In bed."

"I love all those things. I love when you're forward. I love when you need me. And I love, love, love when you ask me for whatever you want in bed or anywhere else." He captured her earlobe between his teeth and bit down just hard enough to ensure she felt it throughout her entire body. "Tell me what you want," he said, pressing his fingers into her cleft and then backing off, over and over again.

She clung to his shoulders, holding on for dear life. "I…I want… I want you. I've never wanted anyone the way I want you."

"You have me. Hook, line and sinker. Now tell me what you want me to do."

Daisy wasn't sure what was more arousing—his fingers pressing against her most sensitive area or him trying to get her to say words she'd never before spoken to a man. "I want to come."

"How do you want me to make you come? Do you want my fingers or my tongue or my cock? You can have it any way you want it. You just have to tell me, so I can be sure you're getting what you want."

"I want your fingers."

Through her panties, he rolled her clitoris between his fingers, making her cry out from the unbearable pleasure.

"And your tongue." She couldn't believe she'd actually said those words, but now that they were out there, he moved quickly to comply, removing her panties and settling between legs that trembled in anticipation.

"Relax, honey. Open for me."

Somehow Daisy managed to move her feet farther apart, but not far enough for his liking. He used his shoulders to spread her open even more.

A heated flushed took over her body when he pressed his tongue into her folds and lapped at the flood of moisture that had gathered there.

"Oh damn, you're sweet. I knew you would be." He kept it up for what felt like an hour, teasing, licking, sucking, nuzzling, inflaming every nerve ending in her body on fire, until her skin was covered in a fine sheen of perspiration.

He knew exactly where to focus and drove her toward climax, but when he pressed his fingers into her, the combination set off a full-body release that made all others pale in comparison. It was positively incendiary.

She thought it was possible she screamed, but she wasn't entirely sure. Afterward, as he petted and coaxed her down gently, her throat felt achy. "Did I scream?"

"You sure as hell did," he said with a proud smile as he kissed his way up her belly to her breasts.

"That was incredible."

"It was incredible to watch."

Embarrassment reclaimed her. She looked away, but his finger on her chin brought her right back. "It was sexy and beautiful, just like you."

She smoothed her hand over his chest and stroked the erection that rested long and proud against his belly.

Keeping her gaze fixed on his, she kept a firm hold on his cock when she straddled him and guided him to her entrance.

His hands encircled her hips, his eyes widening with surprise. "What're you doing up there?"

She rolled her bottom lip between her teeth and lowered herself onto his rigid length. "That."

"I like that. Do you?"

Because words escaped her, she nodded.

"Do we need protection?"

"I'm safe and protected. If you are."

"I am."

She placed her hands on his chest, seeking leverage as she slowly took him into her body. All the while, he kept his gaze fixed on her face, probably watching for any sign of freak-out or meltdown. But there was none of that this time. There was only pleasure, the kind of pleasure Daisy had never experienced so acutely before, except for in her dream.

"Lift up a bit," he said, his voice sounding rough and sexy. "Now come back down. Yes, *yes*. Like that. Do it again."

Each time she raised herself up, she came down farther than the time before, until she had taken all of him. She could tell from the strained expression on his face that he was trying to hold himself in check. He was giving her exactly what she needed without her having to tell him. He was giving her full control.

"Look at me, Daisy."

She lost herself in the gorgeous eyes that looked up at her with care and concern and affection.

"Don't look away. I want you to know it's me the whole time."

"Does it feel good?" she asked.

"It feels too good."

"How can it feel too good?"

"You'll find out in about thirty seconds, if I last that long."

Daisy hadn't expected to laugh while making love, because she never had before. But that, like everything else with him, was different.

"Can we move a little bit? Maybe onto our sides?"

"I haven't done that before. How do we do it?"

"Hold on to me, and don't look away."

With his arms around her, he shifted them ever so slightly so they were still joined but facing each other. She trembled from the full-body caress of his skin against hers.

"Don't hold back, David." She put her arm around him and swiveled her hips. "I'm fine. I promise."

Her words seemed to shatter his control as he gave her what she wanted in deep strokes that had her crying out from the sheer pleasure.

"Eyes," he said, sounding as breathless as she felt. "On me."

She once again forced her eyes open and blinked him into focus, her heart skipping erratically at the sexy sight of him aroused, slightly out of control, his dark hair falling over his brow and his eyes on fire as he gave himself to her.

He covered her bottom with one big hand and brought her even closer to him. The change in position sent him deeper, which started a chain reaction of sensation moving through her body like mini-lightning strikes. His chest hair rubbed against her nipples, setting off another series of reactions that had her clinging to him as a deep stroke triggered her release.

"*Yes*," he whispered, "let go. I've got you." His arms tightened around her, but he never broke the eye contact when he joined her, surging into her repeatedly until he shuddered and collapsed next to her.

While he continued to throb inside her, Daisy held him close, breathing in his distinctive scent as his whiskers rubbed against her chest. She hooked her leg around his hip to keep him there awhile longer.

"Are you okay?"

"I'm great. You?"

"Spectacular."

"Yes, it was rather, wasn't it?"

His grunt of laughter made her smile. "Rather. But we might need to do it again so I can be sure before I give you a definite answer."

"It would be irresponsible to make such an important decision without having all the facts."

With his arms tight around her, he turned her as he laughed, and the light-hearted, joyful expression on his face stunned her. She'd never seen him look like that before.

"What?" he asked when he had her settled on top of him.

"You look really happy."

"I am really happy."

"I'm glad. I want that for you."

He tucked her hair behind her ears. "I want it for you, too."

"I'm getting there."

"We're getting there together."

Daisy rested her head on his chest and let out a deep breath that was equal parts relief and anxiety. Surely nothing this good could last. It never had before. Unwilling to let that thought ruin her afterglow, she closed her eyes and tried to quiet her racing mind by enjoying the moment.

For right now, everything was perfect.

The next time she woke, David was moving quietly around the room. He was dressed in plaid shorts and a navy polo shirt. When he saw that she was awake, he came over to sit by the edge of the bed. He brushed the hair back from her face and kissed her forehead. "I was wondering if you were ever going to wake up."

"What time is it?"

"Almost eleven."

"Wow, that hasn't happened since high school."

"You were worn out. You've been working too hard."

"Speaking of work, I should check in."

"I thought Saturday was your day off."

"It is, but…"

He bent to kiss her. "Then take the day off."

"Are you off, too?"

"I do house calls on Saturday mornings, mostly for elderly people who have trouble getting to the clinic. I'm off this afternoon, though, barring any emergencies."

Daisy linked her fingers with his. "That's really nice of you to do house calls."

He shrugged as if it was no big deal, when she was certain it was a very big deal to the people he visited. "Part of the job."

"No, it isn't. Do you charge for the visits?"

"Not usually."

"You're a nice guy, David Lawrence."

"Shhh, don't say that too loud. You'll ruin my reputation around here."

"I hope you know that by now, when people think of you, far more of them remember your kindness to them or their family members in their time of need than what happened with Janey."

"Is that right?"

"Are you blushing?"

"I don't blush."

"Um, yes, I believe you do."

"Want to come with me to check on Marion? She's the only one I'm planning to see today."

"I'd love to! Could I take a quick shower first?"

"Sure. I'm not on any particular schedule." He surprised her when he put his arms around her and rested his head on her chest. "Thanks."

Daisy ran her fingers through thick, silky strands of hair. "For what?"

"For helping me to realize there's more to me and my story than everything with Janey."

"There's so much more. Maybe it's time you let yourself see that, huh?"

"I like the way I look through your eyes."

The softly spoken statement slayed her and battered her defenses. "I should be the one thanking you."

"For what?"

"For what happened earlier. I don't think I could've done that with anyone but you."

"I sure as hell hope not. You'd better not be doing that with anyone else, or you'll see my not-so-attractive jealous side."

"You have a jealous side?" she asked, enjoying the playful banter. That was another thing she'd never had before in a relationship with a man.

"Only where you're concerned."

"What does this jealous side look like?"

"It's very ugly and green-eyed and focused on anyone who dares to look at my girl."

"Mmm, your girl," she said with a sigh. "I like the sound of that. Now how about you let me up to shower so we can go see Marion and get everything done. Maybe we'll have a little time before the party to…get to know each other better?"

His chuckle rumbled through her. "That sounds like a brilliant idea to me."

Daisy took a leisurely shower, used soap that smelled like him and let the massaging showerhead work the aches out of her muscles.

The bathroom door opened. "You gonna stay in there all day?"

"I'm thinking about it."

"Want some company?"

"I'd love some, but you're all ready to go."

The shower door opened to him in all his naked glory. "So?"

The sight of him in a whirl of steam made her legs go wobbly. She held out a hand to him.

He stepped into the shower with her and had his arms around her almost as quickly as he'd shed his clothes. "Good to know you can get naked that fast."

"It all depends on the incentive, and you make for some pretty sweet incentive." His hands and lips were everywhere, setting her on fire with the smooth glide over wet skin. "Ever done it in the shower?"

Daisy shook her head because she didn't trust herself to speak articulately just then.

"First time for everything," he said, pressing her against the tile and lifting her so her legs were wrapped around his hips. "Is this okay?"

As the hot water beat down upon them, Daisy curled her arms around his neck. "It's very okay."

He nudged at her with the tip of his erection. "How about this? Still okay?"

"Very, very okay."

With the tilt of his hips, he pressed inside her. "And this?" he asked, pressing openmouthed kisses to her neck that set her blood to racing.

"Very, very, very okay, but it could be better."

His husky, sexy laugh made her smile as he let her slide down onto his full length.

"Still good?"

"Mmm, amazing. But…"

"If you say it could be better, I'm going to spank your ass."

The words, which were rumbled against her ear, were like a live wire traveling through her body.

"I'm sorry, Daisy. I shouldn't have said that. I told you I'd never hit you, and I meant it."

"I knew you were playing, and I liked it."

David groaned and tightened his hold on her bottom. "God, Daisy, you're making me crazy."

"Be crazy," she said. "I swear I can take it." Gripping his hair, she dragged him into a combustible kiss and let him carry her away in a storm of passion. While they were pressed together against the wall of the shower, he showed her what she'd been missing with every other guy who wasn't him.

She held on tight as he drove them to an explosive finish.

He kissed her the entire time and drew back from her only when the need to breathe took over. "Wow," he whispered, dropping his head to her shoulder as he continued to push into her in small movements that triggered a second, less powerful orgasm. "That was incredible. You are incredible."

"So are you."

He raised his head to meet her gaze. "We're pretty incredible together."

Nodding, she kissed him again. An astonishing array of emotions passed through her heart in that tender moment. The predominant emotion was love, as pure and true as anything she'd felt before. She loved him.

Only when the water finally turned cold did they disentangle, laughing in their haste to escape the chilly blast.

David grabbed towels and wrapped her in one before putting the other around his waist. "From hot to cold in two seconds flat."

"At least it didn't happen a minute sooner. That might've put a damper on things."

He put his hands on her shoulders and kissed her again. "Nothing could've put a damper on that."

She put her arms around him and held on tight. "You definitely saw to it that I'll never forget my first shower sex."

"Good, then my work here is finished. For now." With one last squeeze, he let her go so they could get dressed.

Daisy, who was normally shy about being completely naked in front of a man, dropped her towel like it was no big deal to stand before him in the altogether. After this morning, it seemed perfectly natural to be naked with him.

He watched her intently, his gaze moving from her face to her breasts and then back up again. "You know, Marion is going to be home all day, and if we went there a little later, it would be okay."

Daisy slapped his hands away as he reached for her breasts. "Marion first. More of this later."

"Why?"

"We're all clean right now, and we used all the hot water."

"So?"

She picked up the clothes he'd discarded from the floor, pushed them into his arms and sent him out the door.

"You're no fun," he said through the closed door.

"Yes, I am."

"No, you're not."

"I'll prove otherwise as soon as we get back from Marion's."

"Promises, promises."

Daisy smiled as she got dressed. She smiled as she brushed her teeth, which wasn't as easy to do as one might think, and she smiled through coffee and breakfast of toast and cereal. He made her laugh, he made her think, he made her feel safe and treasured, and he made her want all the things she'd thought would never happen to her.

CHAPTER 15

Daisy's euphoric mood stayed with her on the ride to Marion's house. David held her hand the whole way, as if he couldn't bear to be close to her and not touch her. She loved that. She loved him. She wanted to tell him but wasn't sure he was ready to hear it—or that she was ready to say it. There was no rush, she told herself. They had all the time in the world.

David pulled into the Martinez Lawn & Garden complex, which was located on the island's north end. The early summer Saturday had brought out scores of people who roamed the retail area, buying plants and flowers for their gardens. Behind the retail space were rows of well-kept greenhouses, and acres of planted fields. He took a right turn behind the greenhouses and followed the dirt road for a mile or so until a sprawling ranch house appeared at the end of the road.

"This is incredible," Daisy said. "I had no idea their facility was so huge, and I can't believe she walked all that way to town."

"I know. They run a pretty big business. It's hard to believe Marion was overseeing everything only a year ago. Paul was here working with her, but Alex had an incredible job working for the National Conservatory in Washington. He gave up his life there and moved home when his mother took ill."

"She's lucky to have them."

"For sure, but it's taking an awful toll on all of them. I don't know how much longer they can go on the way they are."

"It's so sad. She's still a relatively young woman, too."

"I know. It's a tough situation, especially living as they do on an island and being tied here by the business."

"I'm sure you're a great comfort to them."

"I don't know about that. I do what I can, but it never feels like enough."

"Coming out here to see her is far more than most doctors would do."

"I feel like it's the least I can do to help out Paul and Alex. I grew up with them, and played baseball with Paul."

"You have ties here that you wouldn't have anywhere else."

"Are you trying to remind me of why I'm going to turn down the job in Boston?" he asked with a squeeze of her hand that told her he was joking.

"Just pointing out the benefits of working where you grew up."

"The fact that you're here, too, has nothing to do with it, right?"

"Nothing at all to do with it."

That got a big laugh out of him. "Sure, it doesn't." He pulled up to the house and cut the engine. They emerged from the car to find Marion sitting on the porch in a rocking chair. Her injured feet were propped on a footstool and a tall glass of ice water sat on a table. Marion's gray hair had been washed and styled since Daisy last saw her, and she looked very pretty.

Alex emerged from the house, brightening at the sight of David and Daisy. "Hey, guys. Come on up."

"We wanted to stop to see how your mom is doing," David said. "Hello, Marion. It's Doctor Lawrence. I've come to see how you're feeling, and I've brought your new friend Daisy with me."

"Hi, Marion," Daisy said.

"Daisy," Marion said, her eyes lighting up with pleasure. "Come have a seat next to me. I asked my boys today if you could come to visit, but they said they didn't want to bother you."

"They can call me anytime. I'll always be happy to come for a visit."

Marion held out a hand to Daisy. "It's so pretty here, isn't it? My George planted those roses."

Daisy took her hand and sat in the rocker next to Marion's. "They're lovely. Tell me about George."

"Oh, he is *wonderful*."

David stood with Alex and watched Daisy work her special brand of magic on Marion, who spoke of her late husband with such joyous affection, reminding David of the woman she'd once been before dementia had claimed her infectious spirit.

"Unreal," Alex muttered. "She barely seems to know us most of the time, but someone she met just once makes a big impact."

"That must be so difficult for you."

Alex walked to the far end of the big porch, away from Marion and Daisy's animated conversation. "I don't know how much longer I can do this, David. Everything is snowballing on us. This is our busiest time of year—our make-it-or-break-it season that gets us through the rest of the year. We just can't keep up. The lady who lives at the lighthouse reported us to the town council because we haven't cut the grass out there yet. The bitch of it is, she's totally right. We should've been there four times by now, but one of us has to be here with Mom. It's just…"

David put a hand on his old friend's shoulder. "It's a lot. It would be hard on anyone to run a business like yours while taking care of an ailing relative. You and Paul have done an admirable job of holding it all together."

"Why do I hear a 'but' in there?"

"You have to think about your own health and stress levels. You won't be any good to your mom or the business if one of you gets sick."

"What do you suggest we do?" Alex asked, his voice filled with despair. "We can't put her in a place on the mainland and leave her there with no one to visit her while we're out here."

"Can you afford some help?"

"Well, yeah, but she drove off the last two people we hired to stay with her during the day. She's not always nice when she's confused."

"You need to hire an expert—a medical professional who would live here and help out during the day while you and Paul are at work. You still have that guest house out back, right?"

"Yes," Alex said, his despair seeming to lift a bit as the idea took hold.

"You could fix that up and offer the person free housing to go with the job. Free housing on this island—or anywhere for that matter—would be an awesome incentive to get someone here."

"You really think we could get someone to move here?"

"I think you won't know until you try. Victoria and I would be happy to help you interview candidates."

"You say that as if there'd be more than one—if we're lucky."

"You never know. People flock here on vacation, don't they?"

Alex nodded and rubbed at the stubble on his face. The girls had gone crazy over him in high school, chasing after him relentlessly. David and his friends had teased Alex about that for years. None of them had ever caught him—at least not yet.

"Reach out to some nursing services on the mainland. I bet you'll get more interest than you think. I'll help you write the job description so you get someone qualified."

"That'd be great, David. Thank you. I'll talk it over with Paul, but I know he'll agree. Something's gotta give, you know?"

"I can't believe you guys lasted this long without more regular help."

"We never would've made it this far without your support. We talk about how awesome you've been through this. It's nice to have someone who knows us, and who knew Mom before, overseeing her care."

Alex's compliment cemented David's decision to stay in his current job, where he was definitely making a difference for this family as well as others. "Happy to help. I'd like to take a look at your mom's feet to make sure they're healing from her walkabout the other day."

"They seem much better, but you're the expert."

They glanced over to where the two women were deep in conversation, oblivious to their presence.

"So you and Daisy?" Alex's raised brow and broad grin were far more in keeping with the guy David had grown up with than the despair he'd shown earlier.

"Me and Daisy."

"I like her. She was so nice to Mom the other night."

"She's a sweetheart."

"I heard what happened to her with Truck. That guy's always been an asshole, but to beat up on someone like Daisy… Well, that's a whole other level of asshole."

"Definitely."

"She's okay, though? After all that?"

"She's getting there."

"I'm glad for you, too," Alex said, punching David's arm lightly. "Been a long time since I've seen you looking so good."

"Been a long time since I felt so good."

"It's nice to have you back among the living."

The walls he'd erected two years ago to keep everyone out tumbled down around him. "It's good to be back."

"How in the world did it get to be one thirty already?" Tiffany asked her sister.

"Time flies when you plan a wedding in two days," Maddie replied. She was drop-dead gorgeous in an orange chiffon dress that flattered her extravagant curves.

An outpouring of excitement and offers of help had come from the island community when word began to spread about their impromptu wedding. Chloe Dennis, owner of the Curl Up and Dye salon in town, was currently standing behind Tiffany, putting the finishing touches on the same elaborate updo she'd done for the frantically excited Ashleigh.

The local florist had come through with gorgeous bouquets of Gerbera daisies and summer flowers for Tiffany, Ashleigh and Maddie, as well as boutonnieres for

Blaine, Mac, Thomas and Ned. They'd even done a wrist corsage for Francine. Evan McCarthy had offered to provide music, Frank McCarthy was lined up to marry them, and Jenny had suggested the lighthouse property as the ideal location for a seaside wedding. All the pieces had fallen together remarkably well.

"What're you thinking about?" Maddie asked.

"I can't say, or I'll bawl my head off and ruin my makeup."

"No bawling," Chloe said sternly, making the sisters laugh. Today, Chloe's ever-changing hair was white-blonde and made longer by extensions.

"I just can't believe the way everything worked out for today," Tiffany said.

"When it's meant to be, it's meant to be."

"I wonder if Jim has heard any wedding rumors in town."

"So what if he has?"

"I worry about him showing up and making a scene."

"Your fiancé thought of that possibility and has officers coming to the light-house and our house to make sure there're no unwelcome visitors."

Stunned, Tiffany looked up at Maddie. "How do you know that?"

"Because he checked with us to see if we were okay with having cops at our house. Of course we're happy to do anything necessary to ensure you have a wonderful wedding day."

Tiffany grasped her sister's hand. "You're the best big sister anyone could ever hope to have, and I love you. Every day, but never more so than today."

"Aw jeez," Chloe said. "Now I'm going to bawl."

"No bawling!" Maddie and Tiffany said together.

"Time to go," Maddie said. "We can't keep your groom waiting."

"No, we can't," Tiffany said, shivering as she thought of his special brand of "punishment" and how he loved to dole it out. "I love him so much, Maddie." Her voice was reduced to a whisper when she thought of him and the journey they'd taken together. "I never expected anything like this to happen to me."

Maddie hugged her carefully. "I'm so glad it did. No one deserves it more than you do."

"What's this I hear about a weddin'?" Ned's voice echoed through the downstairs of Tiffany's house.

"We're coming!" Maddie called. To Tiffany she said, "Ready?"

"So ready. Let's go!"

"See you at the party," Chloe said. "You look stunning."

"Thank you so much for doing this on such short notice."

"I love being part of a happily ever after for such a deserving couple. Thanks for asking me."

With Ashleigh in tow, Maddie and Tiffany stepped outside, where Ned and Francine waited for them next to a vintage silver Rolls Royce with a tan interior. Ned wore a seersucker suit, and every one of his white hairs had been tamed into submission. Next to him, Francine positively glowed in a floral dress that made her look much younger than her years. Of course, love had a lot to do with their mother's youthful appearance these days.

"Where in the name of God did you get that car?" Tiffany asked him.

"Ya know that garage in the backa my house that no one's allowed to go in?"

As the sisters nodded in muted shock, Ned said, "This is why ya ain't allowed in there," he said, waggling a finger playfully at Ashleigh, who let out a belly laugh. "I don't wantcha sticky fingers on my fancy car."

Tiffany had no idea what to say to that. "But... I..."

"Close your mouth, honey," Francine said with a laugh. "I've learned it's better not to take him at face value."

"I guess so!" Maddie ushered Tiffany and Ashleigh into the car where a booster seat awaited the little girl. Ned thought of everything where the kids were concerned.

"Where did you get it?" Maddie asked.

"I bought it from Mrs. Chesterfield's estate after she died last year. I thought it might be nice to have someday, for an occasion just like this one."

"It's gorgeous," Tiffany said.

"Glad ya think so."

The drive to the lighthouse was all about laughter and excitement. Filled with anticipation for the celebration ahead, Tiffany watched the island's landscape go past on the way to the lighthouse, where Blaine would meet her. The closer they got to the light, the faster her heart seemed to beat.

"Take a deep breath or two," Maddie said, reaching across Ashleigh's seat for Tiffany's hand.

Tiffany held on to her sister, the way she had her entire life. Even when they weren't getting along, Maddie had always been there for her, and Tiffany had tried to do the same for her, especially since they'd become mothers. She never would've survived the early years with Ashleigh without Maddie to commiserate with, and she knew Maddie felt the same way. And now they were about to add Blaine to their family, and Tiffany couldn't wait.

On the long road to the lighthouse, they passed a police cruiser, where Patrolman Wyatt waited with his girlfriend, Patty, who was also Tiffany's assistant at the shop. They tossed rose petals at the car as it went by, and Ned tooted the horn in acknowledgement of their sweet gesture. It was good to know that no uninvited guests would get past Officer Wyatt, and Tiffany was again thankful that Blaine had seen to that detail.

The afternoon sun was high in the sky when they arrived at the lighthouse. Ned drove straight over the lawn that hadn't been mowed and around the lighthouse to the spot where Blaine, Mac, Thomas, Blaine's family and Judge McCarthy awaited them. Off to the side of the gathering, Evan sat on a stool with his guitar.

"Here goes," Maddie said. "Are you ready?"

Tiffany nodded and Ned got out to open the door for them. Maddie went first and then helped Ashleigh.

Ned and Francine came around the car and opened Tiffany's door. Ned extended his hand to help her out of the car.

Tiffany looked up at him as she grasped his hand and smiled when she saw tears in his eyes. She squeezed his hand and held out her arm to her mother.

Evan played "Make You Feel My Love" as the three of them followed Maddie and Ashleigh to where the men awaited them.

Fearing for her composure, Tiffany avoided Blaine's intense gaze until she was nearly to where he stood with Mac at his side and Thomas in front of Mac, watching the proceedings with big blue eyes. After much debate, Maddie had decided to leave baby Hailey at home with Linda.

As Evan continued to sing, Tiffany finally allowed herself to look at Blaine. He was tall and gorgeous in a tan summer suit with a white dress shirt open at the throat. Per her request, he'd refrained from shaving, even at the risk of his mother's wrath. She'd never seen anything she loved more than the way he looked at her as she came toward him on the arms of her parents.

He reached out to her, asking her without words to take the rest of her journey with him.

Tiffany kissed her mother and Ned and took Blaine's hand, smiling as his fingers curled around hers. And then he sealed the deal when he reached for Ashleigh with his other hand. The tears Tiffany had kept at bay all day long filled her eyes as that simple gesture told her everything she'd ever need to know about the man she was marrying.

Sensing her emotional battle, Blaine brought her hand to his lips and brushed them over her knuckles.

As Evan played the final notes, Maddie stepped forward to take Tiffany's bouquet.

"Blaine and Tiffany," Judge McCarthy said, "we're honored to be here today to witness the start of your lives together. Each of you has traveled a long and winding road to reach this destination. Henceforth, you'll take to the road together, through good times and bad, through richer and poorer, in sickness and in health. Have you both come here willingly to exchange these vows and to merge your two roads into one common path that you'll travel together?"

"We have."

"Tiffany, do you take Blaine to be your husband, to have and to hold, to love and to cherish all the days of your life?"

"I do."

"And do you, Blaine, take Tiffany to be your wife, to have and to hold, to love and to cherish all the days of your life?"

"I most definitely do."

His reply set off laughter among the guests and diffused the last of Tiffany's nerves. He most definitely did. How wonderful was that? She smiled up at him, happier in that moment than she'd ever been before, except for maybe the day Ashleigh was born. But this was even better, because now she had Ashleigh and she had Blaine, too. And she knew without a shadow of a doubt that this marriage was forever.

Mac produced rings from his suit coat pocket and handed them to Blaine.

Judge McCarthy nodded for Blaine to go ahead.

"First things first," Blaine said, sliding a diamond ring on her finger. "Our two-day engagement didn't leave much time for ring shopping. I hope this meets with your approval."

Meet with her approval? It was incredible! The diamond was big and round and glittered in the sun. Before she had time to absorb its full beauty, he was sliding another ring on her finger, this one a band of diamonds.

"With this ring," he said, "I thee wed." He kissed the back of her hand and then turned it to drop something into her palm. A ring for him. He'd truly thought of everything.

Her hands trembled as she pushed the platinum band onto his finger. "With this ring," she said, looking up at him, "I thee wed." She repeated his gesture, kissing the back of his hand.

"And," Blaine said, reaching back to Mac for another ring. "This one's for you, Ashleigh."

"I get one, too?" she asked, looking up at him and her mother, her big eyes full of wonder and delight.

"You sure do," Blaine said. "I love you, and I promise to be the very best step-dad in the whole wide world." He slid a tiny gold ring on her finger and bent to hug her as Tiffany dabbed at her eyes.

Ashleigh kissed his cheek. "I love you, too."

Blaine picked her up and held her in one arm, while reaching out to Tiffany with his other hand.

"With the power vested in me by the state of Rhode Island and Providence Plantations," Frank said, "it is my honor to declare you husband and wife. Blaine, you may kiss your bride."

He transferred Ashleigh to Maddie before he placed both hands on Tiffany's face and placed a lingering kiss on her lips. "Love you so much, baby."

"Love you more."

Smiling, he shook his head. "No way."

"Ladies and gentleman," Judge McCarthy said, "I give you Chief and Mrs. Blaine Taylor."

The small gathering clapped and cheered as they turned to face them. They received hugs and kisses and congratulations from everyone, including Blaine's mom, who wore a wide smile when she greeted her new daughter-in-law.

After they'd had a chance to say hello to everyone, Blaine extended his arm to her.

Tiffany curled her fingers around the crook of his elbow. She glanced at Maddie to make sure she had Ashleigh. Maddie held hands with Ashleigh and Mac had Thomas.

"Go," Maddie said, waving her hand. "I've got her."

"Thank you."

As Blaine led her back toward the car, Ned hurried on ahead of them to get the door.

"Oh my God," Tiffany said. "Guess what we forgot?"

"What?" Blaine asked.

"A photographer! We won't have any pictures."

He pointed. "Look, honey."

How had she missed Grace, Stephanie and Jenny, armed with cameras? "Where did you guys come from?"

"We've been here the whole time," Stephanie said. "You only had eyes for him."

"Can you blame me?" Tiffany asked. "Look at him."

Her friends laughed and took more pictures as they got into Ned's fancy car. Once he had them settled in the backseat, Ned went around to hold the passenger door for Francine.

Through the open window, they heard Mac say, "Let's party!"

As Ned pulled away from the group, he turned the radio up, and the sound of Big Band music filled the car and gave the newlyweds some privacy.

Blaine put his arm around her and leaned in for another kiss. "Hey there, Mrs. T, you're looking exceptionally gorgeous today. That dress… Wow. A-maz-ing."

"Same to you." She flattened her hand on his chest. "It was amazing and wonderful and very *us*. Thank you for all you did to make it happen so quickly. And the rings! How did you pull that off?"

"I put my sisters on the job. How'd they do?"

"Incredible."

"I told them exactly what I wanted, and they came back with something even better than I'd pictured. And they had a blast spending my money."

"It's too much."

"It's nowhere near enough."

"I feel so lucky and so blessed to have your rings on my finger."

"I feel so lucky and so blessed to have the rest of my life to love you and Ashleigh."

"Thank you for what you did for her and for making sure we weren't interrupted by any unwelcome guests."

"After his performance this morning, I was leaving nothing to chance on that front." With his finger on her chin, he said, "Nothing but happy thoughts today."

"And every day."

Blaine smiled, nodded in agreement and kissed her all the way to Maddie's house.

Ned took the long way around the island.

David and Daisy arrived to chaos at Maddie's house. People were running around with food and chairs, and out on the lawn a band was setting up under the direction of Evan McCarthy. Apparently, the bride and groom were on their way.

"What can we do to help?" Daisy asked Grant McCarthy as he went by carrying two huge bags of ice.

"Ask Maddie," he said with a good-natured grin. "She's the drill sergeant out on the deck, barking orders at everyone."

They followed him to the deck, where Maddie was, in fact, shouting orders to everyone within earshot.

"Give me something to do," Daisy said when Maddie took a break to breathe.

She thrust Hailey into Daisy's arms, said, "Baby duty, please," and took off down the stairs to where tables and chairs had been arranged on the lawn.

"Well, all righty, then," Daisy said to Hailey, who offered a gummy, spitty, two-tooth smile in response.

"Day, Day," Hailey said.

"Did she just say Daisy?" David asked, letting the baby grasp his finger in her tight grip.

"It's probably just gas."

"Sounded like Daisy to me."

Daisy snuggled the baby into the crook of her neck and patted her back, hoping she might doze off for her afternoon nap despite the flurry of activity around her.

"You're a natural," David said.

"You think so?"

He nodded. "Is it difficult to hold someone else's baby after what happened to you?"

"It used to be, but Thomas and Hailey have gotten me over it. I've known them all their lives and being around them as often as I am helped to get me past my own loss. But it's always there. I wonder what he'd be like now, what his interests would be. He'd be almost ten, which is hard to believe."

"So you knew he was a boy?"

"Yes."

He didn't ask her anything else, and for that she was grateful. Even all these years later, it was difficult to think about the baby she'd lost, even if he'd been conceived under less than ideal circumstances. He'd still been hers, the only other person who'd ever been entirely hers.

People continued to arrive. Luke and Sydney Harris, Patrolman Wyatt and his girlfriend Patty, Sarah and Charlie Grandchamp, along with Owen and Laura, who looked much better than she had the last time Daisy saw her leaving the Surf on a stretcher, and Laura's brother Shane. Laura seemed pale and drawn but happy to see her friends.

Adam McCarthy came in with his girlfriend, Abby Callahan, followed by Mason Johns, Dan Torrington and Kara Ballard.

As everyone came onto the deck, they greeted Daisy and David warmly, and she could feel him relax next to her as it became clear that no one was unhappy to see him there.

Victoria came out to the deck, hand in hand with a sinfully handsome man who Daisy didn't recognize. He had shaggy, dark reddish-brown hair, green eyes that were full of the devil and a smile that could stop female traffic. Victoria let out a squeal of pleasure when she saw David, and gave him a hug.

"This is Shannon O'Grady," Victoria said. "Shannon, this is my sort-of boss, David Lawrence. *Doctor* David Lawrence."

"Sorta boss," David said, scoffing, as he shook hands with Shannon. "Good to meet you."

"'Tis a pleasure to meet you, too, Doc. Vic speaks highly of you."

"Does she now?" David said with an inquisitive glance at Victoria. "Vic?"

Her sheepish grin was infectious. "I say nice things about you when you're not listening."

"Now that I believe," David said, laughing.

As Daisy continued to rock Hailey, she enjoyed the banter between David and Victoria, who clearly adored him. It was nice to know he had real, genuine friends who cared for him—not as much as she did, but enough to give him additional ties to the island she loved.

"Come on," Victoria said, tugging on Shannon's hand. "Let's get a drink. I'm in the mood to party."

"Excellent," Shannon said, following Victoria down the stairs to where Grant and Adam were minding the bar on the lawn.

"He's awfully cute," Daisy said. "Is it serious between them?"

"Apparently, she's just using him for sex."

"Seriously?"

"That's what she said."

"I can't believe she told you that."

"She tells me *everything*, much to my dismay."

"She loves you."

"She drives me crazy, but I couldn't function without her."

Daisy turned so David could see Hailey's face. "Still awake?"

"Just barely. Keep doing what you're doing. You've almost got her."

Joe came up the stairs and seemed momentarily surprised to see them, but then he recovered. "Hey, guys. How's it going?"

"Good," David said, shaking the hand Joe offered him. "How's Janey feeling?"

"Not bad. She's taking a nap upstairs right now so she'll be ready when the newlyweds get here. I figured I should wake her up so I can get her downstairs in time."

"Is she managing to stay off her feet?"

"Yes, but with much bitching and complaining," Joe said, grinning.

"I wouldn't expect anything less."

"Off I go to get her up."

David watched him go with a wistful expression on his face.

"Are you okay?" Daisy asked.

"Sure. I'm great."

"It's not a crime to admit that it can be difficult to know she belongs to someone else now."

"You don't want to hear me say that, because it might make you think I'm not thrilled to belong to you now. When I am. Thrilled, that is. To belong to you."

"Oh, well, that's nice to hear."

He leaned against the rail that framed the deck. "At times, it's difficult when the past comes back to smack me in the face, but I haven't had the urge to go back in time in quite a few weeks now. Rather," he said, dragging a finger lightly along her forearm, "I find myself looking forward to the future for the first time in a very long time."

She was still smiling at him when Maddie returned to claim Hailey, who was now asleep.

"I don't know how you do it," Maddie said as she took the baby from Daisy. "Every time, she gets the unsleepable baby to go to sleep."

"She doesn't look unsleepable to me," David said with a wink for Daisy.

"What can I say?" Daisy said, shaking her numb arms back to life. "It's my special gift."

A shout from inside caught their attention.

"David! *David*, come quick!" The frantic tone of Joe's cries had David running inside. "Janey won't wake up. She won't wake up!"

"Call 911," David said to Owen as he charged past him up the stairs.

Wild-eyed, Joe grabbed David's arm and pulled him into the guestroom. "She won't wake up."

Janey's blonde hair was spread on the pillow. Her face was pale and her lips nearly white.

As his own heart beat wildly, David checked for a pulse and was relieved to feel the rapid cadence of her heart under his fingers. Her pulse was faster than it should be, he thought, leaning in close to feel the whisper of her breath against his face. Then he pulled the covers off her and gasped at the pool of blood between her legs.

Instinct told him to deal with Joe, and he spun around just as Joe would've passed out from the sight of so much blood. He directed Joe to a chair and pressed his head between his knees. "Breathe."

Joe drew in deep breaths mixed with sobs. "Don't let her die, David. Please don't let her die."

"She's not going to die," David said with more confidence than he felt. "But we've got to get the baby out right away."

Joe looked up at him. "It's too soon!"

"I'll do everything I can for both of them."

"What can I do? I'll do anything."

Mason and Victoria came running into the room.

"Oh shit," Victoria said when she saw Janey and the blood.

"We need to get her to the clinic—now," David said.

"We can use my SUV," Mason said. "Let's go."

Joe rallied and stood, heading for the bed. "I've got her." He lifted his unresponsive wife off the bed and headed for the doorway.

David grabbed the comforter off the bed and stopped Mason before he could follow Joe down the stairs. "Drive as fast as you can. Every minute matters."

"Got it."

"I'm going with her," David said to Victoria as they rushed down the stairs. "Be right behind us."

"Oh God, David," Linda McCarthy cried as he ran through the living room. "Please take care of them."

"I will."

"Ride in front," David said to Joe as he crawled into the back of Mason's SUV with Janey and made use of the comforter to raise her hips to control the blood flow. Adrenaline pounded through his system as he went through the possible scenarios of what might've happened.

It seemed most likely this was a case of placental abruption, which often occurred suddenly when the placenta separated from the wall of the uterus. That would explain the heavy bleeding and unresponsiveness. If it was a full abruption, the chances of the baby surviving were almost nil, and Janey's life would be in grave danger, too.

They were ill prepared at the clinic for an emergency of this magnitude, but they'd work with what they had. David had never performed a cesarean section on his own but had assisted in plenty of them as a resident, so he knew what to do. Whether or not he could handle any complications he encountered during the procedure remained to be seen. The thought of Janey dying on his watch was unfathomable, so he couldn't let it happen. No matter what, he had to save her life. And the baby... Joe was right. It was too soon.

He knocked on the window to the front of the SUV.

Mason slid it open. "How is she?"

"Hanging in there. Can you call for a life-flight with neonatal support? And blood. We're going to need blood. She's O positive." That was one of many random things he knew about her after thirteen years with her.

"Already done, Doc."

"Good."

"Is she going to be all right, David?" Joe asked.

"I...I hope so." He couldn't imagine a scenario in which Janey wasn't all right, so he refused to go there. He'd trained for the last decade for situations just like this one. However, being on a remote island when disaster struck hadn't been part of the training, all of which had occurred in well-equipped, inner-city hospitals. In this case, he'd be relying on instinct as well as training. Janey's life and the life of her baby were in his hands, and even in the midst of crisis, the irony of that wasn't lost on him.

He owed her one. Hell, he probably owed her far more than one. He owed her his very best, and that was what she—and her baby—would get from him.

Victoria was right behind them when they pulled into the clinic parking lot. She flew out of her car and unlocked the emergency entrance. Mason was right behind her. They ran out a few seconds later with a gurney that they loaded Janey onto. They whisked her inside to prepare her for surgery.

"Joe," David said, stopping Joe from running after them. "We're going to do a C-section and take the baby. If we don't, we could lose them both. I need you to know... If I can't stop the bleeding, there's a chance I may have to perform a hysterectomy. Do you understand?"

His face white with shock and his white shirt, arms and hands stained with blood, Joe nodded.

"I'll tell you what's going on as soon as I know anything." David started toward the double doors that led to the exam rooms.

"David!"

David spun around to face the man who'd once been his rival and was now his ally in wanting to save the woman they both had loved.

"If it's a choice, save Janey." He choked on a sob. "Please save Janey."

David nodded and took off running.

CHAPTER 16

In the procedure room, Victoria performed an ultrasound. She pointed to the screen. "Partial abruption, but bleeding out fast."

"That's what I suspected," David said. "Let's move."

In a matter of seconds, they inserted a catheter, intubated her and started an IV to get anesthesia meds and fluids onboard. "How close is the chopper?" David asked Mason.

"Twenty minutes."

"That might be too long for the baby." A helpless feeling stole over him when he realized they could very well lose the baby before the chopper arrived.

"I'll see if they can do better."

Victoria swabbed iodine over Janey's distended belly. "Have you done this before?" she asked, her eyes serious and focused on the patient.

"Not by myself."

"Jesus, David."

They took time they didn't have to scrub and gown up, since the last thing Janey needed on top of everything else was a raging infection.

Mason returned to the room. "They're twelve minutes out."

"Better. Go to my office. Top drawer of the filing cabinet there's a consent-for-treatment form. Get Joe to sign it."

"It's not required in an emergency," Victoria reminded him.

"I want it," David said, without including the words *just in case.*

"I'm on it," Mason said.

Fortunately, a recent blood drive on the island had given them enough on hand to get her through the surgery. If there were no complications, they'd be okay, so he had to see to it there were no complications.

"Has it been long enough to ensure proper sedation?"

"I don't know," David said, desperately trying to remember the details of his anesthesia rotation. "But we're out of time. Let's do it. You're on the baby. I've got Janey. Ready?"

Victoria nodded, her brown eyes huge over the top of her mask.

David dragged the scalpel across Janey's lower abdomen, silently talking himself through the procedure he'd seen done dozens of times. He recited the steps in his mind the way he would have when questioned by an attending physician during residency: Cut skin, cut fascia, separate muscle, cut perito-neum, watch the bladder, cut uterus, deliver baby, clamp and cut cord, retrieve placenta, sew uterus, administer Pitocin and push fluid fast, ensure patient is stabilized, when stable, close the abdomen in reverse order of entry.

He knew all the steps. However, reciting and doing were two different things, especially when the patient on the table had owned his heart for most of his adult life.

With the incisions completed, they moved very quickly to deliver Janey's son, to cut the cord and to repair her uterus. David worked with laser focus to remove the placenta and manage the blood loss.

In addition to helping David with suctioning blood from the Janey's uterus, Mason kept a watch on her vital signs. "BP is 80 over 50."

Too goddamned low, David thought as he worked faster.

The roar of the chopper landing on the helo-pad in the parking lot gave a measure of relief that help had arrived for the baby. But Janey couldn't be transported until he got the bleeding under control.

David lost track of time as his entire world was reduced to the task at hand.

Sweat dampened his brow and his fingers and neck cramped, but he remained focused on the effort to save Janey's uterus and preserve her fertility.

"How's the baby?" he asked Mason.

"Haven't heard anything. They took him to the chopper."

"At least they've got the right equipment."

"Yeah."

"Was he breathing?"

"I don't know."

David said a silent prayer for the baby and for Janey, and kept working.

Victoria returned to the procedure room. "How is she?"

"Hanging in. The baby?"

"Same. He's a fighter. Four pounds, six ounces. They've got him tubed and warmed in the chopper. Joe is with him."

"Good. How long has it been?"

"Almost forty minutes."

To him, it felt like hours had passed.

"The doc on the chopper wants to know if you need help."

"I think I've got this, so I'd rather he stay with the baby."

"Joe and her parents are going crazy wanting to know how she is. Can I give them an update?"

"Tell him she's stable but not quite out of the woods yet."

"Be right back."

David kept working, kept stitching, kept praying.

"I think you're winning the war, Doc," Mason said. "The bleeding has definitely slowed, and her BP is coming up."

David had noticed the same thing, but it wasn't time to celebrate yet. They had a long way to go before there'd be anything to celebrate.

A subdued crowd was left at Mac and Maddie's house after Janey was whisked away. Mac had taken his parents to the clinic, and Grant, Evan and Adam had followed in Adam's car. Stephanie, Grace and Abby opted to stay at Mac and Maddie's so as not to overwhelm the clinic's small waiting room and because Tiffany was their close friend.

"I...I don't know what I'm supposed to do right now," Maddie said. "I want to be there for Janey and Joe—and Mac, but Tiffany...her wedding. She'll be here any minute, and we have to pretend everything is all right because they deserve this day."

"She wouldn't expect you to pretend everything is okay," Daisy said. "She'll understand there's been an emergency."

"Yes, yes, you're right."

"Hey," Grace said. "They're here."

Daisy stood back to watch Tiffany and Blaine come in, glowing with happiness that was dampened when they heard about what'd happened to Janey.

"You need to get over there," Tiffany said to her sister. "You need to be with Mac." To Grace, Abby and Stephanie, she said, "All of you need to be there. They're your family."

"I'll stay with the kids," Daisy said. "Go to her."

"Thanks, Daisy," Maddie said. "That'd be a huge help. Are you sure you don't mind, Tiffany?"

"Of course I don't mind. This is no time for a party."

"Now that ain't necessarily true," Ned said from where he stood inside the front door. "As much as we'd all like ta, we can't go stormin' the clinic and creatin' a scene. That t'aint what Janey or Doctor David needs. Her family is with her, and the best thing the rest of us can do is stay here and eat all this food ya got and celebrate the newlyweds. I know my girl Janey," he said, his voice faltering, "and she'd hate ta be the reason yer wedding got messed up."

"I wouldn't feel right having a party while Janey is fighting for her life," Tiffany said.

"Ned's right, honey," Blaine said. "There's nothing we can do for Janey and her baby except pray, so we may as well stay here and keep each other company until we know more."

"I suppose you're right," Tiffany said. Turning to Maddie, she added, "Go be with Mac."

Maddie hugged Tiffany. "I'm sorry to bail on you, today of all days."

"You're not bailing on me. He's your family now. He needs you more than I do."

Maddie gave her a final squeeze. "Love you, and I'm so happy for you."

"I'll want to hear the second you know anything."

"We'll call when we hear."

After Maddie and the others ran out the door, Tiffany turned to Daisy and Blaine. "I'm so worried about Janey and the baby. I can't even think about what Joe must be going through. And her parents..."

Blaine put his arm around her and kissed her forehead.

"Congratulations," Daisy said with a smile. "I heard it was a lovely ceremony."

"It was," Tiffany said, her eyes watering. "But this..."

"It's a terrible turn of events on such a happy day, but for what it's worth, I think Ned is right," Daisy said. "Janey wouldn't want it to ruin your special day."

Tiffany nodded and closed her eyes, took a moment to collect herself and then looked up at Blaine. "Let's go say hello to everyone and have something to eat. We can figure out the rest of the day as we go."

"Sounds like a good plan to me." He held out his hand to her.

Tiffany smiled at him as she curled her fingers around his.

Their happiness was palpable and made Daisy long for the day when all her questions would be answered the way theirs had been. And then she remembered the way David had bolted out of there to take care of his ex-fiancée without a word to her before he went.

Of course he was only doing his job, and would've done the same thing for anyone whose life was in immediate danger. But that it was Janey and that he'd run out without even so much as a glance in her direction made Daisy feel discarded, which in turn made her feel selfish. Janey was fighting for her life. What right did Daisy have to feel even the slightest bit jealous for the way David had reacted to Janey's crisis?

"You're being a jerk," she whispered to herself as she went upstairs to check on Hailey, who was still asleep. She wandered next door to the guestroom, where the bloody sheets were a sobering reminder of how grave the situation had been.

They don't need to come home to this, she thought as her hotel training kicked into gear. She stripped the bed and the pad that had saved the mattress from being ruined, gathered up all the soiled linens and put them in the washing machine with a healthy dose of bleach and detergent.

Staying busy helped to keep her mind off the way David had run from her to tend to Janey. It kept her mind off the fact that he'd never given her a thought as he left her behind. It kept her from wondering when she might see him again. It kept her from thinking too much about what he must be going through as he tried to save the woman he'd once loved.

Frank McCarthy sat with his son Shane, daughter Laura, her fiancé Owen, his mother Sarah and Charlie Grandchamp, in a gathering of chairs on the lawn, still trying to get his head around what'd happened to his niece.

"Have you heard anything at all from the clinic?" he asked Laura, who'd broken the news to him when he arrived after officiating at the wedding.

"Not a word." She rested a hand on her own extended belly. "It's so scary, Dad. What if..."

"Don't go there, hon," Owen said. "She's young and strong and healthy. She's going to be fine. She has to be."

Laura and her cousin had always been close, first as girls and now as adults. The thought of something happening to either of them was simply unbearable.

Tiffany and Blaine came down the stairs from the deck, their happiness dampened by the crisis facing Janey and her unborn child.

"I feel bad for them," Owen said. "Tough thing to have happen on their wedding day."

"I'm sure they'll make the best of it," Frank said. "What else can they do? Everything that can be done for Janey is being done."

As he said the words, a large white helicopter with a red cross on the side flew over the house in a roar of engine noise that had everyone looking up to watch it go by.

"Help has arrived," Frank said.

"Thank God," Laura replied. She dropped her face into her hands.

Owen ran a hand over her back, and Frank suddenly needed to get up, to move, to walk, to do something besides sit there and think about what his brother's family was currently going through.

Frank stood. "Can I get anyone a drink?"

They declined and he walked over to the bar, where the family's pilot friend, Slim Jackson, was holding court.

"What can I get you, Judge?"

"You can call me Frank, and I'll take whisky. Neat."

"Coming right up."

Frank turned away from the bar and noticed Betsy Jacobson coming down the stairs from the deck. Drink in hand, he went over to say hello to his brother's houseguest, who he'd met the last time he was on the island. Her curly dark hair was contained today in a ponytail that made her look much younger than her forty-eight years. The dark circles under her eyes had faded, and she had a bit of a tan that gave her a healthy glow.

"Hi, Frank," she said with a warm smile as she gave him a quick hug. "I heard you were back on the island."

Although surprised by her spontaneous show of affection, he happily returned her embrace. "I promised Laura I'd stay at the Surf this time, but I was hoping to see you here."

"I can't believe the situation with Janey. I'm so sorry. Mac and Linda must be beside themselves."

"I'm sure they are. I'd like to be with them, but the boys are all there, and the rest of us are resisting the temptation to overwhelm them with support."

"They know you're thinking of them."

"I just wish we'd hear something."

"I assume she's in good hands."

"The best possible hands. The doctor is her ex-fiancé. He won't let anything happen to her if he can help it."

"Oh, well... That's a lucky break."

"How've you been?"

"Better," she said as they strolled together to the edge of Mac's property, which overlooked the ocean in the distance where her son Steve had been killed in the sailboat accident. "Being here has helped, although I'm sure Mac and Linda are ready to be rid of me by now."

"They've loved having you."

"You know what they say about guests and fish, right?"

"What's that?" he asked, amused by her lighthearted smile and the sparkle it brought to her dark eyes.

"They both start to stink after three days. I positively reek by now."

Frank wasn't sure what possessed him to lean in close enough to breathe in her alluring scent. "If that's reek, I want to know where I can buy a bottle of it."

Her deep and lusty laughter sparked a feeling in him he hadn't experienced in years. Desire.

"I'm looking into getting a place out here for the summer."

"You should talk to Ned. He owns half the island and can probably square you away with something."

"Ned the cab driver?" she asked with eyes gone wide with surprise. "Big Mac's friend Ned?"

"One and the same."

"Well, I'll be damned. Didn't see that coming."

"His secret identity as the island's land baron is part of his mystique." He glanced at her. "Can you keep a secret?"

"I sure can."

"I've been talking to him about buying a place out here."

"Really?"

Frank nodded. "I'm retiring in September, and since both my kids have ended up here, I'd like to be where they are, especially with two more grandkids on the way."

"Good for you. That's really exciting."

"I'm looking forward to it. My work has been my life for too many years. It's time for a little balance, and having both my kids here made it an easy decision."

"Won't you miss the city?"

"Nah. It's got nothing on this place."

"There's something special about Gansett. I can see why you all love it so much."

"I'm going to be back and forth a lot this summer. I'd like to see you or, um, take you to dinner or something." God, it had been years since he asked a woman out, and apparently he was seriously out of practice if that clunky sentence was any indication.

"Or something?" she asked with a smile, poking gentle fun at him.

He liked it. He liked *her*. "Dinner. Let's start with dinner."

"I'd love that."

The minute David finished closing and dressing Janey's incision, the paramedics whisked her out of the room and ran for the chopper. David followed them, briefed the doctor onboard and then backed away as the helicopter took off with Joe, Janey and their newborn son onboard.

As it banked sharply and headed for a trauma center on the mainland, the surge of adrenaline he'd been running on drained from his system. He bent at the waist and propped his hands on his knees. He'd done all he could for her. It was in God's hands now as well as the doctors who would care for her in Providence.

"David." Big Mac McCarthy's hand on his back snapped David out of his contemplation, and he stood to face Janey's father.

Big Mac's eyes took in the blood that was all over David's scrubs, and swallowed hard. "Is she…"

"She should be fine. It's going to be a tough recovery, but I was able to save her uterus."

"And the baby?"

"I just don't know, Mr. McCarthy. He's only thirty-two weeks. I wish I could give you certainties, but we're going to have to wait and see."

"You gave them both a chance, and I'll never have the words to properly thank you for what you've done twice now for my family."

"I did my job. I did what I would've done for anyone on this island, but I'm happy I was here when Janey and her son needed me."

"Thank you."

David nodded.

Linda joined them and gave David a hug. "Thank you so much. No matter what happens, we'll always be grateful for what you did."

"I just hope it was enough."

"Did you reach Carolina?" Big Mac asked his wife.

"I did. She's stuck in bed with some deep wounds from her fall, so she won't be able to go to the mainland for a couple of days. I promised we'd keep her posted."

"Let's go find Slim and get to Providence."

Mr. and Mrs. McCarthy left, but their four sons waited to shake hands with David and thank him for his efforts on behalf of their sister. He saw them off and went inside, where Victoria and Mason were cleaning the procedure room.

"Thank you both for your help," he said.

"You were amazing, David," Victoria said. "Amazing. Any chance they have is thanks to you."

"It was all of us. I couldn't have done anything without you guys."

"We helped," Victoria said, "but you were the star. I'm so proud of you."

"Thanks. I um, I need to…" David walked out of the room and went into his office, closing and locking the door behind him. The emotion-packed hour caught up to him, and he wanted to be alone when the tsunami overtook him. He sat on the sofa, head in his hands, and finally let in the overwhelming fear he'd kept at bay the entire time Janey had been open on the table.

"Janey... God..." When he allowed himself to think about how easily it all could've gone very wrong, he began to tremble violently. He'd been in way, *way* over his head performing surgery under those conditions and on Janey of all people. "Janey..." He sat back, fingers buried in his hair and tried to calm his racing heart.

For the first time since Joe screamed his name at Mac and Maddie's house, David thought of Daisy and winced at the way he'd run from her side and never looked back. What was she thinking right about now? All at once, the only thing that mattered was getting to her. He stood and pulled off his bloody scrubs, changing back into the shorts and polo shirt he'd had on earlier.

Filled once again with adrenaline that zipped through his veins, he pulled opened the office door. "Victoria!"

Alarmed by his cry, she came out of the procedure room. "What's wrong?"

"I need to borrow your car."

She didn't hesitate when she said, "Let me get my keys."

David was coming out of his skin by the time she returned and handed the keys to him.

"Everything okay?"

"It will be," he said, leaving her stunned when he kissed her cheek and hauled ass out of there.

Victoria's old car started on third try, and David spun out of there as fast as he dared and drove directly to Daisy's house in case she'd gone home while he was in surgery. He didn't want to drive all the way to Mac's house if she wasn't there, and since he'd gotten separated from his phone at some point, he had no way to call her.

He pulled up to her house a few minutes later and was alarmed to find her door standing open. "What the hell?" The new door Mac had recently installed was in splinters and hung askew from the door frame. Running from the car, he went up the stairs and into the house, which had been trashed. The bouquet of lilies was scattered on the floor, the vase smashed to pieces. "Daisy!" The powerful aroma of the lilies filled his senses, and he screamed for her as he ran through the house, broken glass crunching under his feet. "Daisy!"

After establishing she wasn't there, he ran down the stairs and out to the street, where several of the neighbors had gathered to find out what all the screaming was about.

"Someone call the cops," he said as he got into the car. "Daisy's house has been vandalized."

"Where is she?" a woman asked.

"I'm going to find her."

He drove faster than he ever had on the way to Mac's, hoping and praying she was still there, that she hadn't come home and been attacked again. Had Truck Henry been released from jail? Why hadn't they been told? Maybe they had been told, he conceded, wondering where in the hell he'd left his cell phone. David had so many questions as he made the turn onto Sweet Meadow Farm Road. He brought the car to a skidding halt in Mac's driveway and took the stairs to the deck two at a time, calling for Daisy as he went.

Everything stopped as he burst into the house, probably looking like a madman. "Where's Daisy?"

She appeared at the top of the stairs, seeming baffled by his odd behavior.

Right then and there, at the sight of her beautiful face, safe and sound, David dropped off the cliff and landed in love. He ran for her, up the stairs, again two at a time, and took her into his arms. He kept going, seeking privacy for what he needed to tell her. Inside one of the bedrooms, he kicked the door shut behind him.

"What's wrong? Is it Janey? Did she, she didn't... David!"

He poured every bit of fear and love and desire he felt for her into a kiss he hoped she'd never forget. "I'm so sorry," he said after several deep kisses that calmed his nerves and steeled his determination to make this sweet, beautiful woman a permanent part of his life. "I ran out of here without talking to you or saying anything. I'm so sorry, and then I went to your house, and... Is Truck out of jail?"

"What? What did you say?"

"Did Truck get released?"

"If he did, no one told me." She drew her phone from the pocket of her shorts. "Oh my God! There's a bunch of calls from Providence and several from the Gansett Police. I put my phone on silent while Hailey was napping. How did you know?"

"Your house, honey. Someone was there. The door was kicked in, and when I couldn't find you... I thought... God, Daisy, I'm so glad you're here and you're okay. And I love you. I love you."

She tipped her head as if she hadn't heard him correctly. "You..."

"I love you. I'm in love with you. I have been for quite some time, but the second I couldn't find you, I knew for sure that I had to tell you. Because if anything ever happened to you and you didn't know that I love you..."

She put her arms around him and drew him into her warm embrace. "I'm fine. I'm right here, I'm fine and I love you, too. I heard you saved Janey and her baby. I'm so proud of you."

His entire body shuddered as he exhaled. "I left you here like you mean nothing to me, and that couldn't be further from the truth."

"You did what you had to do in an emergency. I'll always expect you to do what has to be done, no matter who the patient is."

"I feel so lucky to have found you, to have somehow gotten you to fall in love with me."

"Falling in love with you was the easy part," she said with a smile that lit up her eyes. "Convincing myself it could actually last has been the hard part."

"And how are you doing with that?"

"Better now."

"Were you mad about the way I left earlier?"

"I wasn't mad. I was..."

"A little hurt?"

"Maybe a little, but then I was immediately ashamed of myself in light of what Janey was going through—and what you were going through trying to save her."

"I'm sorry, honey. I swear I'll never do that again."

She rested a finger over his lips. "Don't make that promise. So many people are counting on you. Sometimes you'll have to put them ahead of me, but as long as you promise to find me when you're done the way you did today, we'll be okay."

As he kissed her again, a peaceful feeling came over him that was all new. Even at the best of times with Janey, he'd never felt the sense of rightness he experienced with Daisy. She calmed and soothed him. She knew the worst of him and loved him anyway.

"Let's go find Blaine and figure out what's up with your ex, and then I want to go home and sleep for a year—after I make love to you."

Her saucy smile was a huge relief to him after the news he'd brought her about the damage to her house. They'd find their way through this latest challenge and move forward from there.

Blaine met them on the stairs. "I was just coming to find you guys. I finally checked my phone for the first time in hours."

"So it's true?" Daisy asked. "Truck's been released?"

"How did you know that?"

"He's already been to her house, kicked in the door and trashed the place," David said.

"Son of a bitch," Blaine muttered, placing a call on his phone. "This is Chief Taylor. I want all units on the lookout for Truck Henry, and position a car at the Harbor Road home of Daisy Babson in case he comes looking for her there again." He ended the call and looked at his phone. "I missed ten calls from Providence while I was off getting married. I'm really sorry, you guys."

"Please don't be," Daisy said. "You have a right to a day off when you're getting married."

"We'll find him and get him back to where he belongs. Until then—"

"Until then," David said, his arm tight around her shoulders, "she'll be with me at my house."

Blaine nodded in approval. "Good plan. So how's Janey?"

"Stable and on her way to Providence."

"And the baby?"

"Same. That'll be a wait-and-see thing for a few days."

"They were really lucky you were right here when it happened," Blaine said.

"I know Janey will feel awful for putting a damper on your wedding celebration," David said.

"We feel terrible about what happened to her, but our day has still been amazing. In fact," Blaine added with a silly waggle of his brows, "I think it's about time I collected Mrs. Taylor and headed off to get the honeymoon started."

Laughing, they followed him down the stairs to find Tiffany surrounded by her friends admiring her new rings. The atmosphere in the group had lightened considerably since word got out that Janey and the baby were stable and on their way to Providence.

Despite the fact that he was exhausted and emotionally drained, everyone wanted to shake David's hand and thank him for what he'd done for Janey and the baby. Janey's Uncle Frank hugged him, as did her cousins Laura and Shane. With everyone back from the clinic, Grace, Stephanie, Jenny, Maddie and Sydney fell over themselves getting him food and a beer, which went down easy after the stressful day.

Tiffany and Blaine were corralled into dancing to "Make You Feel My Love," performed again by Evan, cutting the cake and tossing the bouquet before Maddie finally allowed them to leave. Before they went, though, Blaine found David and Daisy and promised to keep in touch with them until Truck was apprehended.

"Can we go, too?" David asked Daisy. "I'm fried."

"Sure, let me just find Maddie to tell her we're going."

In the kitchen, Maddie was wrapped up in her husband's arms.

"Oh, sorry," Daisy said. "I wanted to tell you that David and I are leaving."

Maddie pulled back from Mac, wiped her tearstained cheeks and turned to hug Daisy. "Thank you so much for watching the kids while we were at the clinic."

"It was nothing. I was happy to be able to help, and I'm glad Janey is okay."

"So are we," Mac said. "I'm putting a moratorium on babies in this family. I can't handle the stress."

"You can't, huh?" Maddie said. "You might want to rethink that, because I'm officially late, my love."

The look on Mac's face as he absorbed her announcement was nothing short of priceless.

"I need a really big drink," he muttered as he left the women laughing in the kitchen.

"Do you think you're pregnant?" Daisy asked her friend.

She shrugged. "I'm regular as clockwork, so probably. I have half a mind to kill him for knocking me up again so soon after Hailey was born, but I love him too damned much to kill him."

Daisy hugged her again. "Keep me posted."

"I will and thanks again, Daisy." Maddie lowered her voice. "Your handsome doctor seems very smitten."

"He's in love," Daisy whispered.

"Is he now?"

Daisy nodded.

"And you?"

"Crazy in love."

"Oh, I'm so happy for you! You so deserve to be happy after all that's happened."

"Apparently, it's not over yet." Daisy told Maddie about Truck being released and how they suspected him of vandalizing her home.

"You'll be with David, right? Until they find him?"

"He won't let me out of his sight. Don't worry."

"I will worry until I hear they've put Truck back where he belongs."

"They'll find him," Daisy said confidently as Maddie saw them out. "He's hard to miss, especially when he's high and enraged."

When they were in the car, David reached for her hand. "I won't let him get anywhere near you, so don't worry."

The man she loved was holding her hand, and he loved her, too. What did she have to worry about?

Janey's first conscious thought was that everything hurt. She fought her way through the confusion, trying to make sense of the pain. Her eyes were too heavy to open, and her mouth felt thick and dry, so dry. "Joe."

"Janey! Janey, talk to me. Oh God, honey. Please talk to me."

"What happened?"

"You wouldn't wake up, and you were bleeding."

At that news, she forced her eyes open and blinked him into focus. He looked like hell, and was he *crying*? "The baby." She tried to move her arms to feel the baby, but they wouldn't cooperate. They felt like lead weights had been attached to them. "Where's the baby?"

"Our son is in the neonatal ICU. I've been with him all afternoon."

"It's too early!" Her voice broke on a ragged sob. "It's too soon.

"He's beautiful, Janey. The doctors say he's going to be okay. He's going to be here awhile until his lungs develop some more, but he's going to be okay, and so are you." Tears rolled down his cheeks as he bent over her, kissing her forehead and stroking her hair. "You scared me so badly. I've never been that scared in my whole life. I was so afraid I was going to lose you."

"I don't understand what happened. We got to Mac's early. You wanted to get me settled before everyone started coming. I was tired..."

"Yes," he said, his lips soft against her face. "You took a nap, and when I went to wake you up so you could see Tiffany and Blaine come in after the wedding, you wouldn't wake up. You wouldn't wake up. Thank God David was there, and he knew what to do. He got you to the clinic and did an emergency C-section."

"Why was I bleeding?"

"David said you had what's called a partial placental abruption, which is very rare and happens suddenly."

"Did I do something wrong to make that happen?"

"No, honey. It wasn't your fault. One of the nurses told me she's seen instances of the mom and baby both dying from an abruption. We were so lucky that David was there and he knew what to do."

"David... I need to talk to him, to thank him."

"There'll be time for that when you're feeling stronger."

"Where are we now?"

"In Providence. The life flight helicopter brought us over. Your parents are on their way with Slim. I've talked to them twice since we got here, but I know they can't wait to see you."

"They must be so worried."

"We all were."

"I want to see the baby."

"You can't get up quite yet, but I took some pictures for you." He turned on his phone and took her through the series of photos he'd taken of the baby through the incubator.

"He's so small."

"But he's perfect. See his little fingers and toes? And his nose is just like yours."

"Can we have others?"

"We should be able to. The doctors here said David did an excellent job."

"We owe him so much."

"We owe him everything." He kissed her nose and her lips and the tears on her cheeks.

She tried again to move, but the pain brought tears to her eyes. "Hurts."

"What does?" he asked, alarmed.

"Everything."

"Let me get the nurse."

He returned a minute later with a nurse who adjusted Janey's pain meds and taught her how to use the morphine pump to get immediate relief.

When they were alone again, she held on tight to his hand. "Joe."

"I'm here, honey."

"After seeing the pictures, I know what I want to name him." They'd been debating names for weeks now without settling on one. "Peter Joseph, after your father and you. We'll call him P.J. What do you think?"

"I think P.J. Cantrell is the nicest name I've ever heard, second only to Janey McCarthy. Thank you so much for my son and for honoring my dad with his name and for not dying and leaving me all alone to raise him. I never could've faced the rest of my life without you."

"I'm going to be around to give you grief for a long, long time."

"Thank God for that."

Her parents came bursting into the room and stopped short at the sight of her talking to Joe.

"Oh, thank you, Jesus," Linda said, bursting into tears.

Janey couldn't remember the last time she saw her mother cry like that—or her dad who was crying just as hard. "I'm okay," she said when Joe stepped back to let them see her. "And so is the baby. His name is P.J. Peter for Joe's dad and his middle name is Joseph. What do you think?"

"That's a lovely name," Linda said.

Big Mac nodded in approval. "P.J. Cantrell. Welcome to the family, P.J."

"I wanted to name him McCarthy, but Joe and I decided we have enough Macs running loose in this family."

"Probably so," Linda agreed.

"However, I reserve the right to use that name in the future," Janey added.

"So you can have others?" Linda asked.

"That's what they told Joe, but we'll be waiting awhile. We got way more than we bargained for this time, right, Joe?"

"We sure did." His voice broke on the last word. "I...ah, I'll be right back."

"Daddy, go after him," Janey said.

Big Mac bent to kiss Janey's cheek. "You got it, Princess."

CHAPTER 17

On the verge of completely losing his composure, Joe hurried from the room and took a couple of deep breaths in the hallway. But nothing could stop the flood of tears or the overpowering relief of knowing she was okay. They were both okay. When Big Mac emerged from the room, Joe tried to mop up the tears that kept coming.

"Come here, son," Big Mac said, holding out his arms to Joe.

Like he had from the first time he met the strapping man who'd been his best friend's father, Joe gravitated to him, even if he was embarrassed to be caught crying like a baby by the man he idolized.

"Big day for any man to welcome his first child, but this… This would've been too much for anyone. You held up well. You took good care of your family, and I'm proud of you."

"Actually," Joe said, laughing through the tears, "David Lawrence took good care of my family."

Big Mac smiled. "Thank goodness he was right there when it happened. Life has a funny way of coming full circle, doesn't it?"

"It does, indeed."

"He might've done the heavy lifting, but you were strong for them, and that matters, too."

"The only thing that matters is that she's okay, and that the baby's okay. I had some rough moments today imagining life without her. I don't know what I'd do…"

"I know exactly what you mean. I had a few of those moments myself."

"How'd you like to meet your new grandson?"

Big Mac's smile lit up his tanned face. "What do you think?"

Joe glanced at the door to Janey's room.

"Her mom is with her. She's in good hands."

Joe nodded and headed down the hallway with Big Mac's arm around his shoulders, excited to introduce his son to his grandfather.

After she tucked Thomas and Ashleigh into bed, Maddie came downstairs and went into the kitchen wishing for a big glass of wine but settling for ice water on the outside chance that she might be pregnant.

What a day this had been! Tiffany and Blaine married, Janey's baby born in dramatic fashion, and her closest friends still gathered around the fire pit in the yard, ready to rehash it all.

As Maddie filled her glass, Mac came into the kitchen. "Everyone in bed?" he asked.

"Yes, finally. They were so excited about the wedding and the baby. I didn't think I'd ever get them settled down, but I promised them a trip to the beach tomorrow if they were very good and went to sleep. I think it worked."

He kissed her forehead. "Good job, Mom."

"How're you doing?"

"Okay. I guess. I wish my hands would quit shaking."

Maddie put down her glass and took hold of his hands, which were, in fact, trembling. "What can I do?"

"I could use a hug."

"I've got one for you anytime you need it."

He stepped into her outstretched arms and held on tight. "I can't deal with all this crazy shit that keeps happening to people I love. My dad falling off the dock, you delivering Hailey during that storm, the sailboat accident and now Janey... It's too damned much."

"I know."

"And now you might be pregnant again, and while I'd love to have another baby with you, I can't bear to think about all the things that could go wrong. Maybe we should move to the mainland. I could come out here to work and—"

Maddie kissed him, putting every ounce of love she felt for him into the kiss. "This is our home." She gestured to the deck and yard. "Those are our people. Let's go join them and get our minds off it all for a little while." She knew he was on overload and would rather call it a night, but he followed her down the stairs to the yard, where his brothers and all their closest friends had formed a tight circle around the fire. As usual, Evan was messing around with his guitar as everyone talked and laughed and traded insults and good-natured jabs.

"We were just taking bets on whether or not you two were fooling around while we're in your yard," Evan said. "But even you aren't that quick, Mac."

"Bite me," Mac muttered. "I have little kids. I can be quick when I need to be."

"Mac!"

Maddie's outrage sparked laughter as the circle widened to make room for them.

"Any more news from Providence?" Stephanie asked from her perch on Grant's lap.

"Just that my folks are there, Janey's awake and they have a beautiful son named Peter Joseph, who will be called P.J."

"That's such a relief," Grace said.

"Seriously." Adam put his arms around Abby and buried his face in her hair, apparently needing a moment to himself after hearing good news about his sister.

"How is she?" Grace asked.

"Sore but asking lots of questions and wants to see the baby. He's in the NICU. They said his lungs need to develop some more, so he'll be there awhile, but otherwise, he's doing great."

"Thank goodness," Sydney said.

"I love his name," Stephanie said.

"Pete was Joe's dad's name," Mac said. "He died when Joe was seven."

"It's so nice they named the baby after him," Maddie said. "I love that."

"Carolina will, too," Mac said.

"I sure hope Janey can have other kids," Laura said, her hand resting on the belly that had sprouted early in her pregnancy.

"I bet no one is talking about the next one tonight," Evan said.

"No shit," Mac replied. "I'm putting a moratorium on babies around here." This was said with a meaningful look for his wife. "No more."

Maddie stuck out her tongue at him and patted her belly, which made him scowl playfully at her.

"Dude," Owen said, "you're sitting smack in the middle of what could be the biggest potential baby boom in Gansett Island history."

Mac's groan had everyone laughing and throwing empty beer cans at him. "Knock it off! You're getting me all wet."

"You've always been all wet," Adam said, earning an obscene gesture from his oldest brother.

"We'd like to respectfully request a variance to your moratorium," Luke said, earning a warm smile from Sydney.

"I'll grant it for you," Mac said. "But the rest of you have been warned."

"Whatever," Evan said. "Always the big bossy brother."

"And don't forget it," Mac said.

"While we're all here," Sydney said, rubbing her hands together and turning her attention toward Jenny, "you have to tell us how the date with Mason went."

Jenny's deer-in-the-headlights expression was comical. "I do?"

"Oh yeah," Abby said. "Do tell."

"It was…nice. He's very nice."

The guys went crazy moaning and groaning.

"What?" Jenny asked. "He is nice!"

"No guy wants to hear that you had a 'nice' time after a date," Shane McCarthy informed her. "That's like saying a girl has a 'nice' personality."

"What is wrong with the word nice?" Jenny asked.

"Are you going to see him again?" Grant asked.

"I...uh, I mean..."

"There you have it," Grant said. "Nice is a nonstarter when it comes to dating."

"Don't listen to them," Kara said to Jenny. "There's something to be said for nice guys. I'd like to find one for myself."

"Hey!" Dan said as the others howled. "That's just rude!"

"What? Nice is hardly the word I'd used to describe you. Irritating, annoying, persistent..."

"Charming, sexy, a god in bed," Dan finished for her.

"Extremely full of yourself," Kara countered, starting a new wave of laughter.

Dan hugged her from behind and kissed her neck.

"So who's our next fix-up for Jenny?" Stephanie asked.

"Here's a big idea," Jenny said. "Let's talk about this another time."

"No time like the present," Laura said, glancing at her brother.

All eyes turned to Shane, who held up his hands defensively. "Don't look at me. I'm far too *nice* for her."

"Very funny." Jenny threw a marshmallow at him. "I want that," she said wistfully, glancing at Dan and Kara. "I want what all of you have. I want what I had with Toby."

"You'll find it, Jenny," Sydney said. "Probably when you least expect it. That's what happened to me. Just stay open to the possibilities."

"I know. You're right." Jenny paused and seemed to make an effort to shake off the unusual melancholy. "Anyway... Enough about me." She turned to Abby. "Are you guys all moved in?"

"Getting there. *He* has a lot of stuff." Abby used her thumb to point at Adam. "Where am I supposed to put *four* computers in that little house?"

"You get me, you get my computers," Adam said.

"Oh jeez." Mac sat up straight. "That just made me think of Janey and her traveling zoo. Someone needs to go over there to let them out and feed them."

"We'll do it," Adam said as he and Abby got up to leave. "I'm fully trained on the menagerie."

"I'll take the morning shift," Mac said.

"We'll all take turns until they get back," Evan said.

"We'd better go, too." Owen helped Laura to her feet. "Our days start early with Holden."

"And the puking," Laura said. "Let's not forget the puking."

"I'd love to forget the puking," Owen said with a grimace.

"I hope it lets up soon, Laura," Maddie said. "That's got to be so miserable."

"It's horrible. I can't wait to get through this trimester and hopefully start to feel better. I'm just glad I felt up to coming today after my visit to the clinic yesterday. I would've hated to miss Tiffany and Blaine's big day."

"Let us know if you need anything," Grace said. "I'm happy to help with Holden if need be."

"Thanks, Grace," Laura said. "We may take you up on that. Thank goodness Sarah is with us. I'd be lost without her."

"You'd better hope my dad doesn't steal her away from you," Stephanie said with a teasing smile.

"Bite your tongue!" Laura said.

As the party broke up, Mac and his brothers put out the fire and gathered up the last of the empty cans and cups. Mac and Maddie walked to the driveway to wave them off and then went into the house, shutting off lights as they went.

"If the mess is any indication, another successful party," Maddie said, eyeing the mountain of dishes in the sink.

Mac took her hand, shut off the kitchen light and led her to the stairs. "It'll still be there in the morning."

"I'm going to pretend the magic fairies are coming overnight to make it all go away."

"Let me know how that works out for you."

"Spoken like my number-one morning cleanup man."

"*Great.*"

They checked on the kids and found that Ashleigh had moved from the air mattress on the floor to Thomas's bed. The toddlers, who were fast asleep, had their chubby arms wrapped around each other.

"How cute are they?" Maddie whispered.

"Best friends forever."

After making sure Hailey was also asleep, they went to their room and got ready for bed.

This was the best part of Maddie's day—the time she spent alone with Mac after they'd taken care of everyone else. It was their time, and she cherished every minute she got to spend with him. He was waiting for her when she crawled into bed, exhausted from the hectic, emotional day.

As always, he welcomed her into his embrace, his strong arms wrapping her up in his love. "Everything was great today, honey. You throw an amazing party-slash-wedding."

"I could've done without the emergency C-section in the middle of it, but all that matters is they're both okay."

"And we've got a new nephew. P.J. Cantrell. Mom said he's small but so cute. I can't wait to see him."

"I bet he'll be Hailey's BFF."

"Probably."

"Mac, I want you to know I heard what you said earlier about moving to the mainland."

"I was venting. We'd never be happy there, although we would be closer to major medical facilities, which would come in handy in this family."

"True," she said, smiling as she kissed his chest.

"It makes me crazy, as husband and father and uncle and son and brother, to know that so much of what happens is out of my control." He sifted his fingers through her hair as he spoke. "I remember being here as a kid and feeling so confined, and now it's the isolation that gets to me. The thought of you or one of the kids or anyone in my family needing something and not being able to get it…" His deep sigh finished the thought for him.

"We need to have faith that whatever happens, we'll figure it out, and we'll do our best, because that's all we can do. Our kids will grow up with their cousins and so many friends and people who love them. I'd rather surround them with love than shelter them with safety."

"Say that last part again."

"I'd rather surround them with love than shelter them with safety. That part?"

"Yes, that."

"Do you agree?"

"Yeah, I do. It's a good point." He continued to play with her hair and look into her eyes. "Life was so much less complicated when I was living alone in Miami."

"Want me to get your old place back for you?" she asked with a teasing smile.

He shook his head. "You couldn't pay me to go back to that life. Not unless you were there with me. And our kids."

"We kind of like it here, and we kind of like having you here with us."

"Just kind of?"

She snuggled in closer to him, close enough that she could kiss the pout off his lips. "When we got married, I thought I had this love stuff all figured out because you'd shown me how it was supposed to be done. But I've discovered that was just the beginning of what I'd come to feel for you. I love you so much. I love our family and our friends and our house and our life here. I love everything about it, but you, you're the best part because you're mine. No matter what else happens during the day, when it's over, there's this. I live for this."

"I live for this, too, you and our kids. I love you all so much. But you… You think I showed you how the love stuff is done, but you're the one showing me. Every day. I still think about that day in town when I might've let you go by on your bike and missed the best thing to ever happen to me."

"Thank goodness you never look before you leap."

"Thank goodness is right."

"When it all gets to be too much for you, hold on to me."

"What do you think I'm doing right now?"

Her eyes closed as she released a contented sigh. "Don't let go."

"Never."

On the way back to the island on his final trip of the day, Seamus received a cell phone call from Carolina. He didn't usually have his phone on when he was at the helm, but knowing she was hurt—and home alone with his mum... He'd kept the phone close at hand all day.

"Seamus!"

The connection was a bad one, and all he could hear was her voice, some sniffling and crackling on the line before it went dead. He tried twice to call her back to no avail.

By the time he tore out of the parking lot on the way home, he was a bloody wreck, wondering what in the name of Sam Hill had gone wrong. If his mother had said something offensive to her, so help him, he was going to have it out with his mum.

He'd worked up quite a head of steam when he pulled into the driveway and came to a skidding stop. He was out of the truck and into the house so fast he nearly knocked over his mum as she bustled around the kitchen making dinner.

"You missed quite a day," she said.

"Caro... Is she okay?"

"Go see for yourself."

He bolted for the bedroom, where she was sitting up in bed, bright-eyed and smiling. Seeing her looking happy and healthy was such a relief that he stopped short in the doorway to collect himself.

"Well, come here, will you?" She held out a gauze-covered hand to him.

Not wanting to hurt her hand with the power of the emotions running through him, he went around her outstretched arm and sat gingerly on the side of the bed. "What the hell is going on?"

She rested her hand on his leg. "We're grandparents! Janey had the baby."

"Wait, what? Isn't it too soon?"

Carolina tearfully told him the story of Janey's emergency C-section and the dramatic arrival of P.J. Cantrell as she showed him the pictures Joe had sent her. "They named him after Pete," she said softly. "Isn't that wonderful?"

"Aye, it 'tis, love. A wonderful tribute indeed." He leaned forward and kissed her.

She curled her hand around his neck and held him there, looking into his eyes.

"You're the sexiest granny I've ever met," he whispered.

Laughing, she said, "Sure I am. All scratched and gouged and bloody. *Sexy.*"

"Always. Congratulations, Carolina. Your son has made you very proud today."

"So very proud. I just wish I could be there with them."

"The second you feel up to traveling, love, I'll get you there. I'll get you to your boy and his family."

"Our family. Yours and mine."

Damn if his heart didn't stop beating for a second when she said that. "Aye?"

"Aye."

He pulled back from her so he could see her better. "What're you saying, Caro?"

"You asked me to marry you some time ago, and I wasn't able to give you the answer you wanted, but now…"

"What about now?" Filled with irrational hope, he barely dared to breathe as he waited to hear what she had to say.

"I was worried about what Joe would say about us, and he seems to have come around to the idea. I was worried about what your mother would think, but we had a good talk today. She said she's sad that you'll never be a father, but when I told her you'd be a hands-on grandfather to Joe and Janey's baby… You will be, right?"

He swallowed a huge lump in his throat. "God, yes. I can't wait to meet the little guy and spoil him rotten."

"She and I agreed you'll be an excellent grandfather. What would you like him to call you?"

Clearing his throat, he said, "My sisters' kids call my father Da."

"Grammy and Da," she said, trying it on for size. "What do you think?"

Nodding, he said, "Works for me."

"It'd probably make things easier to explain to P.J. if his Grammy and Da were married, don't you think?"

"I suppose it would set the right example for the boy," he said, loving the glimmer of humor in her beautiful eyes as she led him to where he'd wanted to be all along.

"So..."

"Oh, no way. This one's *all* on you. I've asked and asked and been turned down over and over and over again. A man's fragile ego can only take so much rejection."

"All right, then." As he watched her screw up her courage to ask a question that was a sure thing, he had never loved her more. "Seamus Padric O'Grady, would you please, for the love of God and all that's holy, marry me and make an honest woman—"

He kissed her hard and long and deep.

"—out of me?"

"Yes, love. 'Twould be my honor to marry you and make an honest woman out of you, as long as it's still okay for me to sneak up on you in the middle of the day and have you on the kitchen table once in a while."

Her face flushed with color as it always did when he talked dirty to her. "We might be able to work something out where the kitchen table is concerned."

"I love you, Caro. I love you, I love Joe and Janey, and I'll love P.J. as if he were my own flesh and blood."

"I know you will. Why do you think I asked you to be his grandpa?" She held out her arms to him, and he moved slowly and carefully to rest his head against her chest.

When she wrapped her arms around him, he let out a deep sigh of contentment.

"Thanks for waiting for me to work it all out in my mind."

"You're certainly worth all the pain and agony you put me through."

She tugged hard on a handful of his hair.

"Aw, love, you don't want a bald, old grandpa chasing you around the kitchen table, now do you?"

"I just want you chasing me around the kitchen table."

"You got it. Once a day and twice on Sunday, but only if you're good."

Her laughter filled his heart to overflowing as one word cycled through his mind again and again: finally, finally, *finally*.

Ned dropped Tiffany and Blaine at her house and tooted the horn as he took off in the Rolls Royce. Arm in arm they started down the long driveway that led to the house.

"He's going to get a ticket if he drives like that on my island."

Tiffany had her high-heeled sandals looped around her fingers and her bridal bouquet—returned by Grace after she caught it—hanging from the same hand. "His new son-in-law will square it away for him."

He put his arm around her. "Is that why you married me? To keep your family out of trouble?"

She rested her head against him. "Someone's gotta do it."

"I knew it. You're only after the uniform."

"It does make me hot for you."

"Mmm, remind me to never retire."

"One hell of a day, huh?"

"One hell of a day. Thank goodness Janey and the baby are okay, and we still managed to eke out a bit of a celebration despite the drama."

"I can't believe we pulled this off with only two days' notice."

"That'll learn you to never underestimate your new husband."

"As if I ever would. I learned that lesson early on with you. Hello? Ceiling fans?"

That drew a deep rumble of laughter from him. "Speaking of ceiling fans…" The words died on his lips when they rounded the corner to the back deck and found Jim Sturgil sitting on the stairs.

With his hair standing on end and his dress shirttails pulled from his pants, he hardly resembled the pressed and polished attorney he'd become since they returned to the island.

"Jim?" Tiffany stopped walking and felt Blaine's body go tense next to her. "What're you doing here?"

"This is my house. Remember?"

"Do we really have to go over this again?"

"What do you want, Sturgil?" Blaine asked.

"I'd like to speak to my wife, if it's just the same to you."

Tiffany and Blaine exchanged glances, and she nodded, letting him know it was okay to answer Jim any way he wished to.

"Actually, she's not your wife anymore. She's mine, as of about two thirty today. So you can see you really have no business here anymore. This is her house, not yours. And she's my wife, not yours. You got everything you wanted, and now so do we. Unless you want trouble—and I mean really big trouble—you need to head home."

Jim stared up at them, the glow of the porch light highlighting the shock on his face. "You're married."

"You heard him, Jim. We're both asking you—as nicely as possible—to please leave."

He stood slowly, and Tiffany held her breath waiting to see what he would do and hoping it wouldn't be something awful.

"You didn't waste any time."

"I'm done wasting time," Tiffany said.

"Well, I suppose I deserved that."

Tiffany decided to take advantage of the weak moment. "I don't want to fight with you about Ashleigh. It's not what's best for her. It's time to stop fighting and move on, Jim. Enough is enough."

After a long, pregnant pause, he turned and walked down the driveway, hands in pockets, shoulders hunched.

"Oh hey, Sturgil," Blaine called after him. "Great job getting Truck Henry out of jail on a technicality. You'll probably be hearing from him tonight."

"What for?"

"He's already gone after Daisy Babson again. We've got him in custody. Not even twelve hours out of jail and he's locked up again. You sure can pick 'em, Counselor. You might want to give some thought to what your daughter will think of you someday when she finds out you're making a living from defending guys who beat up on women."

"Screw you. Don't talk to me about my daughter."

"Someone's gotta."

Luckily, Jim decided to give Blaine the last word. He turned and took off, probably heading to deal with his wayward client. Tiffany blew out a deep breath, relieved that he was gone.

"You're trembling, honey. I hate how he does that to you."

"Let's hope that's the last time." She forced a smile for his sake. "Now, where were we before we were rudely interrupted?"

"I believe," he said, pressing kisses strategically against her neck, "we were talking about ceiling fans."

"Ohhh, I love ceiling fans."

"So I've noticed." They went up the stairs to the back door, and when she started to go in ahead of him, he pulled her back. Lifting her into his arms, he twirled her around and made her laugh. "We've gotta do this right, baby." As her arms encircled his neck, he kissed her passionately, possessing her the way only he could, the way only he ever would.

His lips still fused to hers, he carried her over the threshold, kicked the door shut behind them and headed straight upstairs, laying her on the bed and coming down on top of her.

"*That* was quite sexy," she said when he finally broke the kiss and turned his attention to her neck.

"You think so?"

"Mmm. I think just about everything you do is sexy, including the way you talked me into a wedding two whole days ago."

"That was one of my better ideas, wasn't it?"

"Yes, it was."

"So from now on, whenever I come up with a harebrained scheme, you're going to just roll with it because I've proven I'm always right."

"Wait a minute…"

He laughed as he kissed her. His hands were everywhere, tugging at the zipper that ran down the side of her dress and then starting at the hem to push it up and over her head, leaving her only in the ivory lace teddy she'd worn under it.

"Oh, damn, Tiffany. You take my breath away. You're so beautiful. And now you're my beautiful wife, and I'm so happy."

His words sparked an urgent need in her. "Get this off," she said, pulling on his suit coat and the buttons on his dress shirt.

"Easy, honey. We've got all night. And all day tomorrow. And tomorrow night."

Ashleigh was spending the weekend with Mac and Maddie so they could have some time alone. "I'd like you to perform your husbandly duties immediately."

Taken aback by her directive, he stared at her as his grin unfolded slowly across his face. "So that's how it's going to be, huh?"

"Yep. Now get moving before I get cranky."

"We wouldn't want that to happen." He got up, lit the candles they kept on the bedside table and went to set the ceiling fan to their favorite setting—high. "Spread your legs," he said gruffly as he shed the suit coat and began slowly—too slowly, if you asked her—to unbutton his shirt.

Tiffany moved her feet apart.

With his shirt hanging open, he leaned over the bed and took her by the hips, positioning her on the bed to maximize the impact of the fan. He slid his fingers over the silk that covered her until he found the snaps between her legs and tugged them open.

The rush of the air against her sensitive flesh had the usual effect, making her squirm on the bed as he continued to slowly disrobe.

"I know what you're doing," she said through gritted teeth.

"What am I doing?"

"You're letting the fan do all the hard work for you so you can come in at the end and steal all the glory."

He laughed and wrapped his hand around his erection, stroking himself as he watched her intently. "Is that so? Seems to me like all the *hard* work is always on my shoulders."

"It's not on your shoulders, dummy. It's between your legs. Now get over here and make love to your wife."

Shaking his head at her audacity, he came down on top of her. "You wait until now, after you get a ring on my finger, to show me this side of you?"

Tiffany smiled, more in love with him than she'd ever imagined possible. "I was afraid you wouldn't want me if I let you know you're not the only one who can be bossy and demanding in bed."

"Boss me, baby. Demand anything you want. I'm your slave."

She wrapped her arms and legs around him. "Love me. Just love me."

"I do," he said as he entered her slowly, taking his time because he knew that drove her crazy. "I love you more than anything, and I always will."

"Show me."

He did as he was told, over and over and over again until they had no choice but to sleep.

David held Daisy's hand all the way to his house. "I need a shower in the worst way," he said when they walked inside.

She curled up on the sofa, tired but content after the day of dramatic twists and turns. "Take your time."

He double-checked that the door was locked before he went into the bathroom. That he cared so much about making her feel safe with him was one more reason to love him. And that he loved her... That was the most amazing thing of all.

"He loves me," she whispered into the quiet night air in which the only sound was that of the shower running in the other room. Under normal circumstances, the news that Truck was out of jail and looking for her would've been the only thought in her head. But tonight, knowing David was in the next room, knowing she was locked safely in his home, knowing he loved her as much as she loved him... There was no room in her mind for thoughts about someone who'd already gotten far more of her time and care than he'd ever deserved.

David came into the room wearing a towel around his waist, his chest still damp and his hair pushed back from his face with impatient fingers. In all the weeks she'd known him, in all the time it had taken to become close to him, she'd never seen him look so alive or so engaged or so happy. He glowed as he sat on the coffee table facing her.

"I want to say something to you, and it's going to sound absolutely insane. But I'd really like it if you could listen to the whole thing before you tell me I'm crazy, okay?"

Daisy was discovering that she loved this euphoric version of David even more than she loved the quiet, thoughtful, caring man she'd come to know. She nodded, willing in that moment to give him anything he asked of her.

"I've been walking around in a daze for two years. It's been like dragging my feet through quicksand, you know? No matter how hard I tried, I couldn't seem to find my way out of it. It wasn't even about Janey anymore. That was over such a long time ago. It was about me and about finding my way. No matter what I did, I couldn't find the way out until I found my way to you."

He reached for her hands and bent his head to kiss both sets of knuckles. "Today I realized I have a very real purpose. I'm here, on this island where I grew up, to save people who matter to me. I saved Janey's life. I probably saved her baby, too. I was meant to be here so I could do that for her today. I was meant to be here the day Chris Allston cut off his finger while trimming his bushes and when

Mrs. Murtry had an allergic reaction. I was meant to be here to help Paul and Alex through this journey with their mother and to make it possible for them to keep her at home for as long as they can. I was meant to be here the night Sarah Lawry showed up battered and broken and when Hailey McCarthy came into the world blue and unresponsive."

Deeply moved by his words and the emotion behind them, Daisy said, "You were meant to be here the night I ended up in your clinic after Truck tried to kill me."

"Yes, and I was meant to be with you just about every night since then. When I went to your house today and saw what he'd done, all I could think about was getting to you. The fog had lifted, the daze was gone, and what matters to me—*who* matters to me—became very, very clear."

She blinked back tears. "David…"

"When I told you I love you, I hope you know I meant it. I didn't say that because I'd hurt you by leaving you to take care of Janey." He propped his head on their joined hands. "I said it because when I realized you could've been hurt or worse… All that mattered was you and being with you and protecting you and making sure no one ever hurts you again."

Without thinking much about what she was doing, she moved onto his lap and wrapped her arms around him, bringing his wet head to rest against her chest.

"Don't take that house, Daisy. Move in here with me until we can buy our own place together. I want to wake up with you every morning and come home to you every night and…and I need you. I need *you*. Just you."

She couldn't believe what he was saying.

He looked up at her. "I need you to keep the fog away. I need you to show me the way."

"But that house… It's my security for the future."

"When we buy a house together, we'll put it in your name. If anything happens between us, you'll keep it."

"You can't do that! Most of the money to buy it would be yours."

"I want you to feel safe and secure. I want you to feel completely at home wherever we are. I don't care what I have to do to make that happen. I just want you with me." He looked up at her imploringly. "I love you, and I want to move forward with you by my side. Will you come with me and live with me and be with me?" His sweet words were punctuated by sweeter kisses.

She knew she ought to think before she leaped, but he'd offered her everything that was most important to her. How could she say anything other than, "Yes, I'll come with you." Placing her hand on his face, she kissed him.

Without breaking the kiss, he stood with her in his arms and walked them to the bedroom. As he laid her on the bed, his cell phone rang, making him groan with frustration. "I swear, if this is a kid with the sniffles, I won't be responsible for my actions."

Daisy laughed and released him so he could answer the phone.

"Dr. Lawrence." He watched her as he listened to the caller. "Yes, she's with me, and I'll give her the news. Thank you for letting us know." Ending the call, he placed the phone on the bedside table and crawled onto the bed next to her. "They've got Truck in custody. The police tried to call you, but when they couldn't reach you, Blaine told them to call me."

"I put my phone on vibrate when I was watching Hailey, and I never put the ringer back on." She glanced at him. "They've really got him?"

"They really do. The state police are coming over to pick him up tomorrow. His bail has been revoked twelve hours after he was released."

"Some people never learn, do they?"

"And others do. They learn what really matters in life, and they do everything in their power to protect it."

Daisy reached over to try to bring some order to his messy hair.

He turned his face, leaving a trail of hot kisses on her palm and wrist.

"Want to know when I first realized I loved you?" she asked.

"Uh-huh."

"When you sent me the lilies. You heard me when I said I loved them, and that touched me so much. I knew I was in big trouble after that."

"Want to know when I first knew?"

"It wasn't today when you thought Truck had found me?"

He shook his head. "That was the final nail in my coffin."

"You make it sound so romantic," she said, laughing.

"It was when you made it your mission to feed me. You showed me every day how much you cared, and I wanted to be around you all the time."

"Now you can be," she said, still trying to believe this was really happening.

"Now I can be." He raised himself up on one elbow. "Is this okay?" he asked as he hovered above her.

"Very okay, but it could be better."

His lips curved into a smile as he kissed her softly at first but with increasing urgency as she responded enthusiastically. As he came down on top of her, it never occurred to her to be worried or afraid or anxious, because this was David. Her David, and he loved her.

The emotional day fired their passion for each other, and Daisy couldn't seem to get close enough to him. She tugged at the towel around his hips as he helped her out of her dress and ogled the second bra and panty set she'd bought from Tiffany—this one light blue with lacy trim.

"I want to kiss you everywhere," he whispered against her ear, setting off a flurry of sensation throughout her body.

"Next time," she said, still not quite used to saying what she wanted in bed.

"Is someone in a big rush tonight?"

"Very big." She took hold of his erection and stroked him. "And getting bigger."

David sputtered with laughter that quickly turned into a groan. He caressed her breasts through the silky bra and ran his hand straight down the middle of her, pushing her panties down her legs. When he was positioned between her legs, he gazed down at her, his heart in his eyes. "Is this okay?"

"Could be better," she replied with a coy smile, raising her hips to show him what she wanted.

He bit his lip to keep from laughing as he entered her, teasing his way in by giving her small increments before backing away and starting all over.

"David! Stop!"

He froze. "Are you okay?"

"I meant stop teasing me."

"Oh, okay. You scared me for a second there."

It mattered so much to her that he cared about frightening her. "I'm absolutely fine. I've never been better, and I want you right now."

Keeping his eyes open and fixed on hers the entire time, he gave her exactly what she wanted, taking her on a wild ride that sent her flying more than once before he pushed hard into her the last time, letting go with a cry that came from his soul.

He collapsed on top of her and rested quietly for a second before he seemed to realize what he was doing and started to move off her.

"Don't go," she said, tightening her arms around him.

"Are you sure?"

"I'm very sure."

"So how was that?" She felt the smile on his lips as he kissed the slope of her breast.

"Couldn't have been better."

"Oh, we'll see about that."

Daisy shivered with delight and anticipation of all that was ahead for her and her sexy doctor.

Thanks so much for reading *Time for Love*! Make sure you're on my mailing list at *http://marieforce.com/* to receive notification when Book 10, *Meant for Love*, is available. If you enjoyed *Time for Love*, please consider leaving a review at the retailer of your choice or on Goodreads to help other readers find my books.

When you're done reading, join the *Time for Love* Reader Group at *www.facebook.com/groups/TimeforLove9/*. Since spoilers are permitted (and encouraged) there, we ask that you wait to finish the book before you join the group.

Not yet a member of the McCarthys of Gansett Island Reader Group? Come join the fun in the Tiki Bar at www.facebook.com/groups/McCarthySeries/. Get your Gansett Island T-shirts, hats, bumper stickers, beach bags and towels at www.promoplace.com/30687/stores/marieforce/. **Join us Memorial Day Weekend 2014 for a ReaderWeekend in Rhode Island**, complete with a day on Block Island, the real-life inspiration for Gansett Island. Find out more at *www.facebook.com/ groups/MarieForceReaderWeekend2014/* or at *http://marieforce.com.*

Until next time, may you have fair winds and following seas all the way to Gansett Island!

Other Contemporary Romances Available from Marie Force:

The Treading Water Series

Book 1: Treading Water

Book 2: Marking Time

Book 3: Starting Over

Book 4: Coming Home

The McCarthys of Gansett Island Series

Book 1: Maid for Love

Book 2: Fool for Love

Book 3: Ready for Love

Book 4: Falling for Love

Book 5: Hoping for Love

Book 6: Season for Love

Book 7: Longing for Love

Book 8: Waiting for Love

Book 9: Time for Love

The Green Mountain Series

Book 1: All You Need Is Love, Feb. 14, 2014

Book 2: I Want To Hold Your Hand, June 2014

Single Titles

Georgia on My Mind

True North

The Fall

Everyone Loves a Hero

Love at First Flight

Line of Scrimmage

Romantic Suspense Novels Available from Marie Force:

The Fatal Series

Book 1: Fatal Affair

Book 2: Fatal Justice

Book 3: Fatal Consequences

Book 3.5: Fatal Destiny, the Wedding Novella

Book 4: Fatal Flaw

Book 5: Fatal Deception

Book 6: Fatal Mistake

Book 7: Fatal Pursuit, March 2014

Single Title

The Wreck

About the Author

Marie Force is the *New York Times, USA Today* and *Wall Street Journal* best-selling, award-winning author of more than 25 contemporary romances, including The McCarthys of Gansett Island Series, the Fatal Series, the Treading Water Series and numerous stand-alone books. Her new series, Green Mountain Series, is coming in 2014. While her husband was in the Navy, Marie lived in Spain, Maryland and Florida, and she is now settled in her home state of Rhode Island. She is the mother of two teenagers and two feisty dogs, Brandy and Louie. Subscribe to updates from Marie about new books and other news at *http://marieforce.com/*. Follow her on Twitter *@marieforce,* and on Facebook at *www.facebook.com/MarieForceAuthor.* Join one of her many reader groups! View the list at *http://marieforce.com/connect/. Contact Marie at marie@marieforce.com.*

CPSIA information can be obtained at www.ICGtesting.com
Printed in the USA
LVOW07s1054230713

344214LV00009B/60/P